DREAMERS

ALIEN CADETS
BOOK 2

CORNELIA CLARK

Lanmon Books

 Formatted with Vellum

Joseph said, "As for you, you meant evil against me, but God meant it for good, to bring it about that many people should be kept alive, as they are today."
—Genesis 50:21

SAM GOT comfortable in the chair next to Nat, waiting for the interview to start.

The studio lights were bright and warm on his face, something he was becoming all too familiar with ever since the trial. He was now accustomed to the smell of stage makeup, hot bulbs, and coffee.

He was also used to the back-and-forth of live interviews, and the pandemonium that went on just out of sight, beyond the camera lenses.

But this interview was different. He and Nat were on the Spo space station, and he could see the blue curve of Earth in the porthole. New Zealand and the edge of Australia were drifting away from him.

The hosts for this interview were not Hollywood types either, but rather a team of Tergre aliens. They were expressive little creatures that topped out around four feet. They had long anteater noses and soft fur in varying shades of brown, cream, and sometimes green.

Compared to the insectoid Spo, they were downright adorable, and they gave off a strangely familiar scent, rather like wet grass and wet dog.

Usually microphones and cameras swung around him like Spo scavenger birds, and cords snaked across the floor in makeshift river systems, but the Tergre setup was more streamlined. They had a number of cameras, but they were small drones, hovering and moving on their own.

The two Tergre newscasters were on stools that put them at the same height as Sam. The paler one rubbed its tan fur and wiggled its anteater nose. It made noises that were the Tergre equivalent of vocal warm-ups, a kind of alien tongue-twister. The other one was a darker brown, with a green tint around its eyes. Sam wondered if the fur grew green, or they had some kind of algae or fungi growing in there like a sloth.

One of the cameras flew close to Nat's face as she cleaned her glasses, and she waved it away. "Too close, please," she said. "We don't want pictures taken up our noses."

One of the Tergre twizzled a small laugh. "And no wonder," he said.

He spoke in his language, actually, but Sam's glasses put a translation in the heads-up display. Nat and Sam both wore computerized glasses now with a display screen and a tiny camera embedded in the frames. They were connected to Akemi.

She was safely installed in the Spo space station within the biobank that housed what was left of her mind. She could communicate with the station computers, but she could also communicate through the glasses.

These Tergre love sensational journalism, so be careful, Akemi sent to Sam. *I'm watching some of their older feeds, and it's a mix of talk show TV and Gossip Girl.*

"Hm, good to know," Sam said.

With small barks and toots, the Tergre informed them that it was time to start. Two of the hovering cameras lit up while the others hung back.

"We are here with two of the newest species to the Galactic

Council, the humans!" said the dark Tergre. "Don't let their flat, hairless faces fool you, they are smarter than they look. In one of the most watched trials in the last century, the humans turned the tables on the prosecutors."

"That's right," said the pale Tergre. "With stunning evidence, riveting cross-examination, and a twist ending, you'll never guess what they're doing next. Watch and pledge to hear more."

Nat spoke under her breath. "We've been reduced to click-bait journalism."

But very successful *click-bait journalism,* Akemi sent to them both.

"Now, this young human is Sam Locklear, a Spo cadet graduate and the new *ruler of Earth and humanity!*"

"Yikes, no," Sam said, "I'm only a representative, which is very different. We're in the process of forming a newly elected group, the Human Coalition Government. They will be in charge of Earth."

"They fired you from the position already? How ungrateful!" The Tergre looked toward a camera. "Answer our live poll! Should Sam Locklear be angry: yes or *absolutely* yes?"

"Er—I'm not angry," Sam protested. "This is a good thing."

"But, Sam Locklear, will the Coalition Government honor the Rik treaty? That is what the universe wants to know. Do those scum still have a sponsor?"

"I don't know that *scum* is the best word..."

Nat snorted softly; she was not a fan of the Rik. "It's not the worst word."

The Tergre laughed. "It is not! Here we have Natsuki Fujimara, another Spo cadet graduate and *mate* of Sam Locklear."

"Nope, she's not that either," Sam said quickly.

Nat only rolled her eyes. "We don't love the Rik, but they *do* have an intergalactic fleet that they nearly used to invade and destroy us. It only seems fair that we should get it."

"True, true! But in return for sponsorship? Has humanity forgiven them for the attack seven years ago? Will the Rik *prosper* from this failed attempt at conquest?"

Nat's mouth twisted unhappily. "I think I'll let Sam field that one."

"Forgiveness isn't on the table," Sam said. "But restitution is. We've learned from human wars that sometimes turning your enemy into your ally is the best and safest path for everyone."

"They *would* have much to offer you," the pale Tergre admitted. "As much as we despise them, they have their claws in nearly every system."

"Exactly. And if they work *with* us for sponsorship, they'll have legal protection. They won't be hounded to extinction." Another camera was hovering a little below his chin, and Sam tilted his head to look down at it. "The Rik have a limited time opportunity. If they have already taken a human body, they are to relinquish themselves to us for identification. We need to record those who were lost to them. But if they do it willingly, we won't prosecute for inter-species murder."

"So it *is* forgiveness?"

"Limited amnesty, if they offer full cooperation," Sam said. "If any individual Rik *don't* turn themselves over, they'll be caught and prosecuted to the full extent of our law. And we do have the death penalty."

The Tergre twizzled happily. "Only the humans and the Merith practice the death penalty. Take our online poll: Yes or no to the barbaric death penalty!"

Nat grimaced. She didn't like that policy any more than Sam did, but she'd told him she was more than willing to make an exception for the Rik. "We are also setting up a colony on the moon to process Rik criminals," Nat explained.

"It's humane," Sam said. "And if they come willingly, there will be a path to citizenship."

"More humane than they deserve," the dark Tergre said. "We'll get a tour of it soon to show our wonderful viewers. But in the meantime, what should we do if we see a Rik who hasn't turned themselves in?"

"Tell the nearest Spo embassy," Nat said. "The Spo have a presence on almost every major planet in Council space, and they are partnering with us in this project. They will find and send the Rik to our lunar prison."

"But how will we know if they are Rik or human?" the Tergre asked.

"Let us worry about that," Sam said. "There aren't many humans around the galaxy yet, although a few have been hired by the Spo to work in the embassies and identify fakes—Rik. At this point, you can assume they are Rik. We have a phrase on Earth, 'If you see something, say something.'"

"An excellent slogan and good advice! Are you sure you shouldn't be the *ruler of Earth and humanity?*"

Nat nudged him with her shoulder. "We're sure. He's already too cocky."

"Your loyalty is overwhelming," Sam said dryly.

The Tergre hooted. "Apparently she is not the only one who thinks so. We have a surprise guest today, who also thinks Sam Locklear needs to step aside!"

Nat was just as startled at the sudden turn as he was. "What?"

But the hatch that led to the hallway suddenly cycled open. Two more hover cameras proceeded in, leading a handsome older gentleman with silver-gray hair and very white teeth. He raised his hands and waved like he was on a campaign trail.

"Hello! Thanks for having me."

Sam exhaled long and slow through his nose. He rose and offered his hand. "Welcome, Senator Fontley. It's great to see you."

"Is it, Sam?"

Both Tergre twizzled again. The pale one's nose was twitching so fast it looked like it was about to sneeze. "This is one of the new Human Coalition Government, Senator John Fontley. He has told us privately that Sam is a dangerously damaged boy who shouldn't speak for anyone. Right, Senator?"

Sam dropped his hand.

Senator Fontley shrugged and shook his head sadly, as if to say: *Well, facts are facts.* "It's not his fault, of course," the Senator said, "but does *anyone* come out of Spo hands undamaged? Would either of *you* want to be a Spo cadet?"

The Tergre honked their disapproval.

Sam sat again. "The Spo treated us well and trained us. I certainly don't condone everything they did on Earth during the rebuilding, but I'm not their victim. None of us are."

"On the contrary," the Senator said. "All of you are, and all of us will be, if we continue with this disastrous Rik treaty."

Sam sighed. Senator Fontley had been a politician even before the cataclysm and the Spo. He'd taken to the new political sphere like a duck to water and gotten elected easily. People were relieved to see someone from before, someone who reminded them of how things used to be.

And he'd taken a vehement dislike to Sam and the other cadets.

"You say the Spo can be trusted to help us," the Senator continued, "but what about the children who were taken who are *not* accounted for? Those who never returned? What happened to them?"

"There were a few tragic accidents," Sam said, "but they *are* accounted for."

"All of them? I have it on good authority that there are dozens —dozens!—that were never brought back."

"That's not accurate," Sam said.

"I shudder to think what happened to them," he said theatrically. "And although I can't imagine they survived, can you imagine if they *did*? These poor children trying to navigate an unfriendly galaxy alone and unprotected."

The Tergre agreed enthusiastically. "And everyone they meet will assume they are Rik."

Nat pressed her hand to her head. "That's ridiculous. The Spo had no reason to leave any cadet stranded."

The Senator only shook his head. "How can we know? They've certainly left *us* stranded. And that brings me to the current issue. Earth is for humans and *humans alone...*"

2

CLAIRE RAN out of her cage and slammed the door shut behind her.

Faal, the large, bird-like alien who'd bought her years ago, lay inside, trapped and injured.

She'd been planning this for months, but he'd been gone a long time. She'd knocked him to the floor with a branch from one of the trees in her enclosure.

He'd built her a 'habitat' with imported oak trees, and she'd painstakingly sawn through a large branch—leaving it hanging by bark and sapwood. She had rigged a rope to break the rest loose, and she'd wondered every day if she was going to end up hurting herself by accident. Or get punished for trying.

"How dare you?" Faal called after her, cold fury in his raptor voice. "Do you know what sector you're in? Do you know what planet you're on? You know *nothing*, human. You won't make it off the grounds."

Ignoring him, Claire gasped and ran on, speeding through the smooth underground tunnels toward one of the exits. The walls gleamed like marble, and the barks, meows, and growls of unknown creatures echoed from distant halls. The walls were interrupted here and there by arches and more barred enclosures. Artificial sunlight fell in columns across the floor as she ran.

"I came to bring you good news," Faal shouted after her. "But now you will pay for this insult."

One of his zookeepers would hear him soon, but she had a plan for that.

Claire threw the meat she had saved into the next cage she passed. The spider-like creatures in there, terrifying black and orange animals that often fought among themselves, began to shriek. Their high-pitched cries were eye-watering as they fought over the meat. She'd counted on that, as they would drown out Faal's cries—and the alarm, once it sounded.

Two enclosures down, with her reflection flickering along next to her in the polished rock, she flung some of the fertilizer that had been used in her enclosure. The monkey-like things in that cage thought it smelled like poop, which she'd discovered nearly a year ago. They began to fling their own poop back at her as she raced on her way. Their poop was oddly similar to banana peels both in color and texture. It was incredibly slick.

Claire turned at the next intersection, darting to the right. Behind her she heard one of Faal's zookeepers reach the spiders. He was cursing in Merith, wondering why they were in a frenzy. With any luck, he would not hear Faal for another few minutes.

She figured, in the best-case scenario, she had about ten minutes until Faal's security team or one of the zookeepers realized he was trapped and came to release him.

Claire sprinted down the next hall to the huge open habitat on the right. She made a cooing noise in the back of her throat. A number of peaceful, somnolent little critters were kept here in a sort of open park where Faal sometimes brought guests.

"Come here, little guy, come here," she said. She dashed over to the nest where Kit usually slept during the day, and stood on her tiptoes to look inside, but the weskit wasn't there. She could still hear the spiders shrieking; perhaps the sound had spooked him.

"Where are you?" she called softly, trying not to sound frantic. She could devote about thirty seconds to this, no more. She cooed again, shading her eyes from the simulated sunshine, and searching the vines to where they disappeared into the trees. She cooed once more, and it broke on a sob. She had to go.

Claire backed to the door. "Come on, little guy, come to me. I'll leave the door open—"

A thick weight landed on her back, and tiny clawed hands clung to her cloud of brown hair. "Yes!"

Claire was nearly there. At the end of this hall there was a gate, which she knew was an ornate airlock. When she cycled the door open, air hissed outward from the pressurized zoo and Claire dashed through almost as fast.

She'd learned from the zoo arrangement that Merith aliens and humans could breathe the same atmosphere, but she hadn't breathed this planet's natural, unfiltered atmosphere since she was brought to the zoo three years before. Hopefully she wouldn't have a bad reaction.

Behind her, she heard oaths and thumps as several of the zookeepers slid and tripped on the banana peels of the monkeys. That would slow them down a bit. It was a comedy gag that might save her life.

A wide corridor of stairs lay in front of her. The steps were about twice as high and twice as deep as human stairs would be, built for the long spindly legs of the Merith. She tried to take each step in a single stride, but every third stair or so she had to make an extra hopping jump.

At the top of the stairs was a wide courtyard with a reflecting pool that mirrored the emerald color of the noonday sky. Decorative trees surrounded the pool, like the palm trees from her hometown near Orlando but with feathery yellow flowers.

The humid atmosphere filled her throat like wet cotton balls, and the weskit coughed wetly behind her, rubbing his furry face against her shoulder.

"I know, hang in there," Claire said.

Through the courtyard and out another wide arch, Claire came to an abrupt halt at the edge of a cliff. The ocean roared at least eighty feet below her.

She reeled back, seeing the waves crashing onto a crescent of black beach far below. She knew where the saltwater tanks in the zoo were, but she hadn't realized the zoo was so far above sea level...

No time to think about it now. She ran inland.

This was the crucial moment. She'd stolen a kind of transportation pass from one of Faal's zookeepers, having finally pieced together that some of them didn't live on the estate, but came to and fro each day. They were not all terrible aliens. One of them in particular seemed to even have a bit of empathy and had made a bit of a pet out of her. He had talked to her, teaching her more of their language and letting her feed the other animals at times, which was how she had learned the layout of the zoo.

His pass meant there was transportation nearby, and that meant there was a possibility that she could escape. If it was automated, or whoever operated it didn't know she was an escaped 'animal'...

And if she had time to get there before Faal's security team came after her...

Those were some big ifs, but it was the best chance she'd had in three years.

A paved path led in the right general direction, and ran alongside a shallow stream, artfully landscaped to twist and turn as it headed toward the cliff and the ocean.

Acres of open land stretched before her. Stupid rich people and their stupid huge yards!

A square shadow passed over the road in front of her and Claire thudded to a stop, looking up into the cloudy, green sky.

A shuttle! It headed to her right, and as it swept noiselessly over her, she saw three black circles, like a target, on its side. That same symbol was on the card she'd stolen. Claire sprinted after the shuttle, heading straight across the spongy greenish grass to what she now recognized as an airfield. Her bare feet sank into the cold vegetation, but the scratchy plants didn't bother her. She hadn't worn shoes in a long time.

Behind her she heard the distant wail of the alarm.

The shuttle landed on a wide tarmac, and two Merith aliens disembarked. She froze for a moment. Even though she knew that this whole planet was populated by the Merith species, she always thought of her owner as "*the* Merith," as if he were the only one.

These two were females, which were not quite as large as the males, but just as terrible-looking to Claire. At one time she'd thought them beautiful, like falcons in human form, but now she just found their overdeveloped upper bodies and spindly legs disgusting. Their beaks always looked sharp, and their one large eye was cruel and predatory under its double eyelid.

The Merith were like Odysseus's cyclops come to life, and Claire hated them. Each of their eyes had a vertical pupil like a cat, and as wide a range of coloring as the plumes of a tropical bird. Claire had memorized the golden-red gleam of Faal's eye, and she'd come to hate the way it twitched when he tested her.

Claire pulled the zookeeper's satchel off her shoulder and gently stuffed the weskit inside. "Be good, Kit."

Claire walked as smoothly as she could toward the shuttle, as if she had every right to be there despite her threadbare sun dress, leggings, and bare feet. She had long suspected that the zoo she'd been kept in was not exactly kosher with the rest of Faal's species. She wasn't sure if it was illegal or just distasteful, but she was hoping that she might find allies on the outside.

The two Merith did not stop her. They did turn and look after her, but Claire refused to meet their one-eyed gaze again. She stepped into the shuttle with the stolen card in hand.

The interior was sterile and dim, and the floor was warm against her feet. Three more Merith sat inside, two reading from some sort of screen, and one with her single eye closed, clearly dozing. Several rows of Merith chairs remained empty.

Just another morning commute, perhaps? But was this more like a public bus or a private jet?

A waist-high wall separated the passengers from the pilot. And when she looked at the pilot, Claire suffered a shock. He was a Spo, not a Merith, and he was crouched over the steering column like an overgrown praying mantis.

Claire touched the tattoo on her face. It marked her as a cadet of the Spo aliens. They were a species she knew all too well. They were the ones who'd invaded Earth. She'd forgotten the harsh bleach-like scent they gave off, but it took her back to her first days as a cadet. Squaring her shoulders, she showed the card and bowed slightly.

"Fair shade and wet wind," she greeted in the formal Spo way. "May I ride?"

The Spo's translucent skin washed faintly purple in surprise. It looked at her card, and back at her face.

"You work for Faal?"

"Yes. I will get supplies for him today." It was a thin lie, and Claire knew it.

The zookeepers ordered most of the special fare from off-world, but they also regularly brought supplies for the indigenous animals with them.

The Spo eyed her, one eyestalk twitching down and taking in her bare feet and rough clothes. *He doesn't know,* Claire told herself. He doesn't know what a human should or should not be wearing.

The Spo reached one of his clammy hands forward and Claire's nose wrinkled at the stench of bleach. He took the card, rubbed it against a smooth patch of the bulkhead, and then gave it back to her.

"Fair wind."

Claire slumped into one of the oversized chairs in the passenger area while the pilot took the shuttle into the air. The two large Merith went back to their screen, but she could feel that they'd been watching her. They began to talk as the shuttle lifted off.

"Ugly larva, no?"

"Faal has strange tastes. Too strange."

"Safer not to say so."

They must assume she didn't understand them. She allowed herself a deep breath as they flew over a country she could best describe as Arkansas on crack. So green and hilly with twisty roads and only the occasional large estate. She could only assume the Merith preferred solitude—or at least the rich ones did. They were like birds of prey that maintained their own territory.

Their flight was interrupted by a burst of chatter from the pilot's area. It was a kind of radio or communication device, and the Merith voice coming into the shuttle was icily familiar. Faal was describing her. "The criminal is small, with two eyes, two legs, two arms, and bushy brown hair. It is to be detained at once and held under Faal's orders. Repeat..." The words played again, and Claire realized it was a recording, probably going to every shuttle on the planet.

The handful of other Merith in the shuttle stared at her with their large bright eyes.

"Come up here."

Claire looked up and saw the ugly Spo beckoning her. A larger city was quickly coming toward them on the horizon. "Just let me get out there. You'll never see me again."

One of the other Merith snorted. "No one will *ever* see you again. You've angered Faal."

The pilot snapped his clawed fingers. "Come!"

One of the Merith rose imposingly from his seat and Claire subsided for the moment, deciding the Spo was the lesser of two evils.

"Sit," the Spo said, pointing to the floor next to him.

Claire crouched but kept her feet under her while the pilot brought the shuttle down into a huge airfield crowded with crafts.

The three Merith left quickly, clearly glad that the pilot was going to deal with the fugitive.

Claire tensed her muscles to spring for the door. All the Spo could jump like Olympic athletes, and he would probably pin her to the floor with his claws in seconds, but she had to try.

The Spo shot out a hand and gripped her shoulder. "I won't harm you, Cadet."

Claire scoffed. "That'd be a first. Will you let me go?"

"Yes. But I have advice."

"Really?" The Spo were all about survival of the fittest; maybe her desperate escape attempt had gained his respect.

"You can't escape Faal on this planet." The Spo faded to orange. The color of disgust. "Faal would watch his mother melt if the color amused him."

Claire could've laughed if she wasn't so tense. "You seem to know him well."

He pointed to a colossal ship that took up nearly a quarter of the field. It was far longer than it was tall, like a toppled skyscraper, and it still towered at least three stories above all the other ships. "You chose a good day to survive. That ship is called *Final Say*, and it's been commissioned by the Diadina. You could take it. Get to Comboda or further out of Merith mainspace."

"Who is the Diadina? Would she take me on?"

The Spo looked confused. "The Diadina is... the Diadina.

The Pontifex's wife, the queen of all Merith. Do you not know the title? She abhors Faal; they have a feud. If any ship will take you away in defiance of Faal's orders, it is hers. Go to the aft entrance," he pointed out one of the many ramps attached to the spaceship, "and ask to work. Tell them about Faal."

"I will. *Thank* you."

The Spo clicked ominously. "The desert remains hot through the night," he warned. "You may thank yourself if you survive to Comboda."

He released her arm and Claire psyched herself up for another dash into danger. "Wish me luck."

"We don't believe in luck." He pointed at her tattoo. "But you have the colors of a leader. You might yet survive."

3

THE SKY WAS GROWING overcast with dark purple clouds as Claire crossed the airfield.

Ground-cars and cargo-haulers zipped around her at breakneck speeds, their lights blinking on as the storm settled in.

She choked back a hysterical laugh at the realization that Merith, with their single eye, only bothered with one headlight. Did every species copy their faces when making cars?

Burly aliens, both Merith and Spo, unloaded crates, pallets, and huge pods from the incoming ships. Claire was thankful they were too busy to look around and notice her because she heard Faal's announcement playing again over some sort of loudspeaker.

The cruiser *Final Say* loomed above her now, opaque and uncaring. The bulk of the cruiser rested on a double row of squat antigravity generators, giving it the strange appearance of a giant egg-carton.

She was nearly there when she caught a glimpse of one of Faal's zookeepers. He was not the one she liked; he was one of the hulking ones who enjoyed messing with the animals. She recognized his burnt orange uniform and the contrasting blue of his eye.

Claire dodged between two speeding ground-cars, narrowly

avoiding a crushed foot, and took off as fast as she could, no longer trying to be inconspicuous.

A few drops of rain fell and left a burning trail on her face. If the atmosphere was breathable, the water should be *basically* water... but she hoped they didn't have an acid rain cycle or something terrible like that.

Claire dashed up the last ramp. It was wide, easily big enough for four lanes of traffic, and opened into a loading bay as big as a warehouse. At least a hundred crew bustled about, preparing for departure and docking the two shuttles that fit into the larger ship.

"Get out of the way, *bruck!*" someone shouted. Claire scurried to the side to let a forklift pass. 'Bruck' was a term she'd heard at the zoo. It meant roughly, "Ugly thing I don't know the name for."

When the forklift passed, the zookeeper was right behind it. His sharp beak snapped in triumph, and his long, clawed arms came for her.

Claire yelped and slid into a gap in the thick wall of the loading bay. It was only an 18-inch crevice that must lead to the mechanism of the ramp or the airlock. She edged in sideways, narrowly avoiding the Merith's reaching hands. The crevice was too narrow for him.

"You want to get crushed in there?" he taunted. "Maybe better than what Faal will do to you. I'll take back a piece of your skull for him."

She pressed up against giant gears, finding herself between two cogs.

Honestly, if it was between this and Faal, she'd take her chances, but finally some luck came her way. A scuffle broke out.

There was some shoving, and the zookeeper cursed, "Did you not hear the bulletin? Faal seeks this thief. You shelter her at your peril."

A Merith female appeared at the mouth of the gap, silhouetted against the light. This Merith's eye was a surprisingly beautiful shade of turquoise, with a pale-yellow starburst around her slit pupil. She must have been nearly eight feet tall, which was quite tall for a female, and heavily muscled. She looked at Claire, then turned to face the zookeeper.

"Do you not know what ship you're on?" she growled at him. Many Merith were completely bald, but this one had something like dreadlocks that hung past her shoulders. Three more crew lined up with her, shoulder to shoulder.

"The Diadina will take your name to the Pontifex himself if you do not get off our ship."

The zookeeper was angry, but from his shifting, it was clear he was uneasy. "You don't want this rat on your journey. Drag her out and I'll go."

The female's gaze didn't so much as flicker in Claire's direction. "I would sooner spit in Faal's eye than anger the Diadina."

They forcibly pushed the zookeeper down the ramp and Claire silently blessed the pilot for telling her about their feud.

CLAIRE FOLLOWED a Spo crew member through ornate and empty corridors. Most of the crew seemed to be Merith, but there were a few Spo like this one.

"So, the Diadina, is she—powerful?" The Pontifex was not quite a king, as far as Claire understood, but the pilot had said the Diadina was queen.

The Spo twisted one eyestalk to look at her as he walked. "That is a strange question to ask about a Merith. They would say, "The smallest wings can ride the storm," or something of that kind."

"What would you say about her?"

He turned a corner into an even more posh hallway, lined with silky draped cloth. It hardly looked like a spaceship at all. Many of the doors were missing, replaced by heavy curtains.

Claire saw sparkles in some of the cloth and wondered if jewels were sewn into them the way they were in the hems of Faal's robes. The entire effect was more like that of a palace than a spaceship.

"I would say... She is a survivor. If she helps you, it is for her own sake. Try not to drip on her things."

Her skin still tingled unpleasantly where the strange rain had gotten to her, and Claire could do nothing about her hair. The rain made her natural hair even more untamable.

The Spo held aside a forest green cloth and gestured for her to enter one of the rooms. It smelled faintly of raw fish—like sushi—and there was a sound like ocean waves in the background.

The Diadina was alone and finishing a meal. She looked delicate for a Merith and poised as she sat before an ornately carved wooden table.

"What is this?" the Diadina said in a high, clear voice. "You know how I loathe the Rik."

Claire frowned. She didn't even know what a Rik *was,* surely they couldn't look that much like humans. "I am not a Rik; I am human."

"I still would have tossed it out," the Spo said, "but that this creature is also—eluding Faal. It was pursued to the very mouth of our ship."

The Diadina dismissed him with a flick of her domed head. She was probably beautiful, as Merith went. She had a ridge of feathers along her shoulders, draping like a cape, and a delicate, silvery-gray beak.

"Tell me at once," the Diadina demanded. "What has Faal to say to me? Why did he send you?"

"He didn't send me, I swear. I was an—an animal to him. I promise I hate him more than you possibly can."

"I doubt that." There was a delicate rope tied around her waist like a sash, and it had knots all down the length of it. "Do you not see my vendetta chain? It is all his."

"I see." Faal had the same rope, but she had only learned a little about the custom.

"And you claim to be human?" the Diadina said.

"I *am* human. I was one of the Spo cadets, but then I was— sold to Faal." Claire gestured to the tattoo on her cheek, it was the only evidence she could provide that she'd been a cadet. It was a pale swirl of curves and dots on her brown skin. Most of the tattoos were a single color, either dark on light skin or light on dark skin. Hers, however, had several shades. She'd been given the fancier ink as a leadership candidate. Lucky her.

"I've lived in his zoo for three years," Claire explained. "If you've been there, you might have seen me."

The Diadina snapped her beak. "*I* do not visit Faal of Merith II, no matter what my husband may do."

"I'm sorry. I don't know much about you, but I am a fast learner, and I will work hard."

"I can do nothing illegal," the Diadina continued. "If you are truly a thief and a criminal, I will be culpable for removing you from the planet."

"The only thing I've done is escape. I might have hurt Faal in the process, but I was defending myself."

The Diadina's face twitched slightly, as if she might appreciate that, but she didn't enlighten Claire. "I will take you on that assurance, but if I find you've deceived me, you will regret it."

She whistled softly and the Spo came back into the room. He must have been just behind the curtain.

"She can stay until Comboda, possibly Selta, if she is useful. Take her to Kitteh's quarters."

Claire's heart stuttered with relief, and she felt light-headed. Her vision wavered as she followed the Spo back out. She didn't know if it was the acid rain, or the missed meals, or the race across Faal's compound—but her strength was giving way.

Or maybe it was the accumulated relief of escaping prison on an unknown planet with an alien psychopath.

Whatever it was, as she ducked under the green cloth and back into the hall, she lost her balance and collapsed on the floor. Her last sight was the jeweled fringe of the curtain swinging back to slap her in the face.

4

CLAIRE WOKE ON A COT. Her skin felt sunburned and tight, her mouth tasted like fish, and her stomach churned unpleasantly. A muffled quietness blanketed the room, but she could hear breathing. She was definitely not alone.

The room was dim, and Claire made out the still forms of other Merith women on the fixed bunks. They seemed to be asleep, but like birds, they made no snoring noises.

Her sundress was damp, but no longer so wet; she must have slept for a while. Kit had climbed out of the bag, and was resting on her feet, warming them, while snuffling slightly.

Claire didn't want to make noise, but her stomach felt horrible. When she realized it wasn't going away, she sat up and Kit slid off onto the floor.

She grabbed the recycling bin between her bed and the next and vomited into the small container.

"It's sick," said the Merith in an upper bed. "Foul."

"Apologies," Claire choked out, spitting into the square container. Another wave of nausea hit her, and she threw up again, the last of her long-ago last meal leaving her system.

"Are you done, bruck?" said the Merith next to her. She was the crew chief who had gotten Claire this spot, the one called

Kitteh. "I've seen your kind. It was the rain that set you off. Your skin is too thin for it."

Another Merith woman spoke up, rolling over and snapping her beak. "And our skin isn't? Only the Vel are unaffected by the alkaline rain. And still we were sent to load in the storm!" She took out a bottle from under the bed and squirted her eye, which looked red and swollen.

Suddenly Claire looked back at Kitteh. "Wait. You've seen my kind? Where? How long ago?"

Kitteh lay back against her bed again. "They have been in the Council news. The Spo sponsored you into the Council, yes?"

"They were supposed to... But no one seems to recognize me, so I thought perhaps we failed."

"No, your species won their trial," Kitteh said. "Weeks ago. You didn't know?"

"Then humans are part of the Council, one of the ten?" Claire asked.

"Yes, but it isn't ten any longer," Kitteh said. "Where have you been? It is thirteen? Fourteen? There are a lot of new species these last few years. You Humans, the Melifleurs, now the Rik. There are new species in the reports almost every circuit."

"Who are the Rik? Do I look like one?"

Kitteh did the half-lidded eye thing again. "I believe you now; you must have been imprisoned in Faal's zoo, or you would never ask such stupid questions. The Rik are scum. They are body-snatchers who kill and take. They have taken many humans. They planned to take the whole planet, but that has been stopped."

Claire floundered in the sudden flow of information. "That's —insane. Are you sure? Do you know where my planet is?"

She shrugged, like she didn't care if Claire believed her. "Earth is in Spo mainspace, until the Humans carve out their chunk."

"And does this ship—visit Spo mainspace?"

"No, our circuit begins and ends at Selta." Kitteh's arm muscles rippled as she gestured to the recycle bin, but her voice wasn't unkind. "Clean that out before you sleep."

Claire found the facilities and rinsed the bin out, returning slowly to the cot she'd been given. It reminded her of the Spo barracks.

When she slept again, she dreamed. Only it wasn't so much a dream as a memory, but then, it was a memory she'd dreamed so often that sometimes Claire wondered if she still remembered the details or created them.

The dream started in the Spo barracks, where she'd lived during her first years as a cadet. She'd woken in the middle of the night with a pounding headache and overwhelming thirst. In her dream, she climbed down from the top bunk in the dark and slipped between the rows of beds towards the communal bathroom. Jenelle's bed was already empty, and in the dream she felt the horror of it in a way she hadn't known at the time.

The other girls in the room were her cohort, her crew, and in many ways, her family after the Spo took them. But one girl in particular, Jenelle, was her friend. Against all odds, they'd known one another on Earth before they were taken, acquaintances at their large middle school in Florida. In space, that was practically a blood bond.

Claire made it to the bathroom and almost to the row of sinks, when she heard scuffling in the outer hall. The Spo had put mirrors on both the floor and walls of the bathroom, not understanding human mirror usage, and she saw her reflection below her as she walked to the hall door. The reflection held out her hands, trying to stop her, but Claire couldn't stop. She walked past the sinks and swung open the door.

The first thing that met her eyes was Jenelle, struggling with one of the Spo. It wasn't their direct mentor, but another Spo who oversaw the program.

Jenelle was a pretty blond girl. Sometimes Claire saw Jenelle in the dream, but sometimes Claire's own face was superimposed over it.

The Spo held her right arm with one clammy hand, twisting it up behind her back, and in the other hand, he held a tranq gun. There was a cloth in Jenelle's mouth, preventing her from shouting.

Claire froze, taking in the scene that she clearly wasn't meant to see.

The Spo flinched n surprise, and Jenelle took her opportunity. She struggled and kicked backward, trying to claw his face with her left hand. She managed to get the rag out of her mouth, but the Spo was much stronger than her. He planted his four legs and wrapped his arm around her torso, capturing both her arms, and lifting her completely off the floor.

"If you scream, I'll kill her," the Spo said to Claire. "Go back to bed, right now, and forget this."

A small, horrible part of her wanted to obey. A worse part of her still wished she had. "I can't—what are you doing?"

Jenelle's eyes were huge, the whites reflecting like milk in the pale light of the hallway. "Take—take her," she gasped. "She's the one they'll want."

Claire recoiled.

"Claire's the best of us," Jenelle went on. "Look at her stupid tattoo. Don't you want—the best?"

Claire had replayed this so many times in her head. She forgave Jenelle for it. Her friend had been terrified. Desperate. Alone. She couldn't have been thinking straight.

But she was sure articulate for someone so afraid.

When the Spo hesitated, Jenelle pressed the point. "You have a buyer, don't you? I overheard you before. But won't your buyer want the very best human, if they're determined to own one?"

Claire looked at her friend in shock. "O-Our mentor. We need to get help." She finally raised her voice calling for any of the Spo she trusted. "Jason...! Greg! Anyone!"

It had all happened so fast. Claire never found out whether she would have found the courage to fight or not.

The Spo fired the tranq gun at Jenelle's leg and tossed her limp form over his shoulder. He fired at Claire point blank in the stomach.

Sometimes the dream stopped there, sometimes it kept going.

Claire awoke in a trouncer cage waiting in a loading bay. The bay was well-lit, and the smell told her the Spo was still there. Sure enough, he waited nearby with an alien—Faal. It was the first time she'd seen him, with his sharp beak and single gold-red eye.

Jenelle lay in the next cage, eyes open and glassy. Her lips were blue, and her chest wasn't moving. Claire flinched away, refusing to take in any more details.

"What did you *do*?" she demanded.

"Jenelle had breathing difficulties," the Spo said coldly. "She had a poor reaction to the tranquilizer."

"You murdered her. She was my—friend."

"Was she, despite everything?" Faal asked. "How interesting. You were right," he told the Spo, "this one is worth more."

The Spo used a pole to push her cage toward the edge of the bay and toward the lifting platform that would load it onto a shuttle. "She would have had to go anyway. She knew about the sale."

"But what are you—why?" Claire gasped for breath. "Why either of us? We'll be *missed*."

"No, you won't. Cadets die. Sometimes even two at a time, though that will be harder to explain. Still, it can be done."

The last thing she saw as the platform lifted her up and into a cramped shuttle was Jenelle's blonde hair on the floor of the cage.

Sometimes the dream stopped here, but sometimes it kept going...

"Bruck, wake yourself, wake!"

Claire opened her eyes and lashed out at the Merith leaning over her. She scratched at the large, vulnerable, blue eye, determined to do damage or—

Kitteh caught her wrist in a massive fist and blocked her other arm with a forearm strike. Claire jerked free and rolled off the cot. She ducked beneath it, to put something between her and... and...

Claire closed her eyes. It wasn't Faal, and she shouldn't have attacked. She had probably yelled in her sleep and woken her. Claire rose from her crouch, her heart still pounding. The other Merith women in the room were staring at them.

"I'm so sorry," Claire said.

"You are violent in your sleep," Kitteh said. "Are you spacesick?"

"No," Claire said, scraping her sweaty hair away from her neck. "I'm just... a little broken." Faal liked to say that, and he was probably right.

Kitteh nodded. "Perhaps you ought to learn to fight. Going for my eye was good, but it's predictable to a Merith. Going under the bed was very bad. Your movement is limited, and you cannot run. Perhaps if you fight while you're awake, your mind will rest when you sleep."

Claire crawled back under her thin blanket while the other Merith went back to their beds.

Claire didn't exactly blame herself for Jenelle's death. Yes, Claire wished she had screamed sooner. She wished she'd run in the first moment. But ultimately Jenelle's death was not her fault.

She didn't blame Jenelle for what she'd said, either...but it was an unclosed wound. Maybe Jenelle had offered Claire up with some other plan in mind. Maybe she'd thought if she delayed the Spo, they'd have a chance. Maybe she'd just panicked.

Or maybe she *had* meant to trade Claire for herself, in a sort of horrible mental break like in 1984. Maybe she would've regretted it and she and Claire could have reconciled.

Or maybe she had started to resent that Claire was more suited to cadet life than she was. Maybe Jenelle had really hated her all along...

Whatever her thinking, she was gone, and there was never any closure.

Claire had decided one thing to be true. Aliens brought out the worst in humans.

Sometimes Claire wondered what would have happened if Faal had taken the both of them. Maybe Jenelle would have escaped with her. Maybe they would have escaped sooner.

"We're free, Jenelle." Claire whispered into the darkness. "We escaped. Maybe we can forgive each other now."

5

CLAIRE WAS tired after another long day of serving on *Final Say*. It was a lot like the cruise ships that left from Florida and went down to the Bahamas or Central America. The Diadina had chartered the ship, with her own security and arrangements, but there were hundreds of other passengers of all species.

Like a Disney cruise, which Claire had once taken with her family when she was eight, there were servers everywhere. They cleaned everything in sight, and did mounds of laundry. Claire supposed laundry was a universal constant.

They also prepared mountains of food, which was no small task with so many aliens with different food requirements. There were the half-raw meats and diced fruits of the Spo; the vegetarian and grain dishes of the Tergre; and the strange soil preparations that the slug-like Crosspointers ate, among others. Claire had never boiled mud before, but it smelled a lot like a hot, humid day in Miami.

Beyond the cooking and cleaning, the staff did any other strange thing that was asked of them.

Sometimes Claire's jobs were normal, like washing fine Merith ceramics by hand. Sometimes they were a little stranger, like sewing a different color of gems into the cloth of the Diadina's least favorite scarf. Then there was the downright weird. The Diadina had accidentally mixed two kinds of sand on her sand table, and Claire spent a long afternoon sorting different colored grains. She gathered that the sand table was an art installation.

Sometimes the Diadina talked to her when Claire was nearby. She complained about Faal and praised her husband, the Pontifex. She exclaimed over gifts from her guests, who visited her suite as if it was a throne room. She exclaimed just as much over their children, when they accompanied their parents. She seemed to genuinely like children, even the Spo kids, who looked like overgrown crickets with large eyes and baby voices. Claire tried not to stare, but she had never seen a baby Spo before, and that was good, because they were the stuff of nightmares.

The Diadina had also taken a liking to Kit, and she let Claire bring him into her suite. The children liked him as well, and Kit was very patient with them.

Tonight, Claire played with the last of her food while she relaxed in the mess hall. Kit had eaten too, and he lazed in her lap like a well-fed cat while she petted him. She'd found that the Tergre food was the most similar to what humans could eat, although they were largely vegetarians. Kit seemed to like the Merith food a bit more.

She had been on the ship for several weeks now and was finally feeling comfortable enough to hang out during mealtime and watch the news reports that appeared on the huge screen in the crew mess hall.

Her fingers froze as she watched the news reports tonight, however. The two furry Tergre newscasters were speaking Spo and there was a flickering line of text at the side that were Merith subtitles.

"If you missed our interview last week, we're returning to our human contacts with an update! We're orbiting Earth, the human home world, but if you're still not sold on the newest species to the

Council, you're not alone. Let's show some of the footage they've shared with us."

There was a short video of a male gymnast spinning on a pommel horse with an Olympic symbol in the corner of the screen. How on Earth had these Tergre gotten an Olympic video? They showed a rowing competition next, followed by a child's birthday party with candles on a cake. The Tergre flinched when the child smiled, and shiny braces were revealed. Then there was a heavily muscled sumo wrestler. She had no idea how they were picking these videos, but it was awful and also kind of hilarious.

"Now we have our two guests from last week, Sam Locklear and Natsuki Fujimara."

Claire leaned forward as two cadets came into view, seated next to the Tergre. She hadn't met them, but she wondered if they'd been stationed near her during their cadet years.

"Thanks for having us back," Sam said.

"You're welcome! Now, Sam, as *potential* ruler of Earth and humanity—"

"You guys have got to stop calling me that," he said, with an uncomfortable smile. "I explained our new governmental structure."

"Still, your trial has been one of the most watched in recent history, and you made quite an impression."

They cut to other footage, this from humanity's trial. It was confusing to Claire—something about a rogue Spo and a blonde assassin girl who confessed to a Rik plot... Claire was even more distracted when she saw that Faal, *her owner Faal*, had been one of the aliens presiding over the trial. Was *that* why he'd been gone for so long? She'd had her escape plan in place, then he disappeared for six months.

While she'd been slowly losing her mind, he'd been there—talking and listening to other cadets. Somehow it made her hate him even more.

"And we ran several polls last week!" the Tergre went on. "Would you like to hear the response?"

Nat smiled. "Do we have a choice?"

"Not really! The galactic consensus seems to be that humans are less off-putting than the Vel, but we wouldn't want to meet one on a dark ship corridor. Over sixty percent judged humans to be as or more aggressive than the Merith, and over seventy percent hope that you'll make the Spo loosen up a bit."

"*That* might be impossible," Nat said. "But they're not so bad once you get to know them."

Claire snorted. Maybe they weren't *all* bad, that pilot had helped her, but she was dubious about the species as a whole.

"You humans are at least full of surprises. First, you decide to sponsor the Rik, your *enemies* in the sentience trial. Now you are diving into galactic trade like you've been here for years."

"We have some issues," Sam said, "but business is something humans understand very well."

"We understand cultural exports—a major source of revenue —are beginning at once! Viewers, answer our poll: would you pay for human entertainment?"

Another Olympic video: a pole vaulter flying through the air and arching over the bar to land on his back. It was followed by a commercial for McDonalds' hamburgers. Claire's mouth watered.

"I wish you luck," the Tergre said. "Perhaps you will even be invited to join the galactic competitions hosted by our very own planet this year!" There was a short advertisement for a sports competition that was mainly populated by the adorable Tergre racing through high grass, whipping each other with some kind of flexible pole, or swimming across rushing rivers. They looked sort of like beavers when they did that.

"Speaking of performances," said the second Tergre, "the Diadina will grace the largest underground party in the galaxy with her presence. The party will be in Lower Selta, lasting for weeks, and the Diadina will stop there on her tour. She will be performing during the concert week and many expect her to—"

He broke off when the video feed suddenly shook violently. "What—what?"

Nat could be seen clutching her chair and Sam staggered to his feet only to clutch the wall as he made his way out of frame. The Tergre made frightened sounds, and the feed cut abruptly to another set of Tergre who were clearly in a different studio.

"We are getting reports that—er—there was an explosion on the Spo space station. I'm sure our team will be fine."

"Very unlike the Spo," the other said, "because they are extremely safety conscious. I'm sure we'll have communication back any moment..."

But the moments passed, and even the cheerful Tergre looked perturbed. "We will update you as soon as we have news. Now another video from the upcoming Seltan rave—"

"Those are you, yes? The humans?" One of Claire's fellow shipmates asked.

"Yes, those are—me," Claire said. "I really hope they're okay."

6

AKEMI'S BRAIN had only been installed on the alien space station for a few months, but she'd been having a blast with it.

She realized a few weeks ago that she could flash the external lights at people on Earth when they waved at her. She could also process all kinds of satellite data simultaneously, and so she made sure to wink at anyone who took the trouble to stay up late and watch her sail across the dark sky.

Occasionally Akemi still had bad days. The loss of her family and physical body sometimes weighed on her like a literal ache she couldn't rub away. But mostly she forced herself to be grateful. Only months ago, she'd been an extremely ill girl living in the preserved section of New Tokyo. Now she was cutting-edge alien technology. She'd even begun hosting the first alien fashion blog because she got to see all the visiting aliens when they came to the space station. *How* was no one commenting on the Merith love of feathers or the Crosspoint obsession with body paint? The world needed to know.

But sadly, the secret of her new existence was still so little known that no eyes were turned towards her as she streaked across the sky in serious distress.

A series of explosions had rocked the resting station and sent fire—a terrible danger in space—surging through the air systems.

The first few escape pods burst out of Akemi's skin—the skin of the space station—like ruptured boils, and smoke rolled through her halls. The smoke partially blinded her from the internal cameras, but she knew the Tergre news crew had scampered to their own shuttle and launched almost immediately.

Akemi was still hopeful she could contain the damage and fire, so there wouldn't have to be a complete evacuation... but she was defeated by a second round of explosions.

She frantically monitored water systems and airlocks, trying to isolate the fire from the people still aboard. So much of the space station had been damaged in the double set of explosions that her options were limited. Every few seconds another escape pod burst free.

Most of the station's protections were automatic, so there was little to do but watch and wait. The station's heat censors (which usually would tell her where people were located by body heat) were overloaded with fire and told her nothing. The only way to calculate how many aliens and humans were still on board was with the escape pod records. Already eighteen of twenty-two pods were away, and nearly a hundred souls accounted for.

Another pod left with nine Spo aboard.

Akemi put a hold on the last pod. Nat and Sam, the two people she cared about the most, were still on the space station. The Tergre had offered to bring them along, but they'd refused.

Akemi was linked to their new glasses, and she could see and hear through the camera embedded there. She followed their progress through the smoke-filled halls. She should've been able to hear them as well, but the sirens of the station had drowned out their voices.

When they both stumbled through a familiar hatch, Akemi suddenly realized where they were. They were almost to the engine room, where the computer that housed her brain was located. She caught a glimpse of Nat's ashy face when Sam glanced at her. Nat's mouth moved, but Akemi still couldn't hear over the whine of warping plastic and the wail of alarms.

What are you doing? Get out of here! Akemi put the words in the heads-up display on Sam and Nat's glasses where her words would transparently overlay their vision.

You can rescue me from the rubble later, she sent. *I don't need oxygen. Go! I've saved a pod for you.*

Both Sam and Nat ignored her; Nat might have said something about not leaving her behind.

Sam crouched lower still and put a hand on Nat's back to push her down as they slunk into the engine room. It wasn't quite as loud in here, but the thick smoke near the ceiling looked almost liquid in its darkness.

Half her attention was on that last escape pod that she'd over-ridden. All the others had now deployed, but there were four people on that last pod that were in danger until she released them. She felt guilty for the terror they must be feeling, but there was no way she was letting it go without Sam and Nat on board. Whoever was inside was pounding on the release button. They surely thought the pod was broken, and they were panicking. Unfortunately, there was no display panel in the basic pod, so she couldn't reassure them.

Get out of here! The space station is lost.

Nat and Sam flew to the biobank, the portion of the computer that housed the biological operating system (in other words, her brain). It had a small door, like a miniature air lock, and Sam twisted it open with a hiss of decompressed air.

There was no point in arguing any more. *I set the last escape pod to release when you enter the override code—my name. Be fast.*

Akemi could still exist without a connection to a computer. It had happened twice now, and she'd stayed aware the whole time.

However, both those times the shutdown had been done carefully, with a slow, sequential process. There was no time for that now, and Sam unceremoniously yanked the spherical part of the biobank out of its sophisticated housing.

Akemi felt a flash of nerve tingling pain. If she'd had a mouth she might have cried out. With a sizzle and a flash of light, she lost consciousness.

AKEMI SLOWLY BECAME AWARE AGAIN, but she was sluggish and confused. Ugh.

A single verse filled her head.

For this reason the good news was told
To those who are now dead.
For they were destined to die like all people
But they live forever in the spirit.

She realized with a shiver of unease that it wasn't a poem at all, it was a verse about death, that she'd read in her studies since becoming a disembodied mind. Akemi could usually distract herself with fashion and writing and data, but there was no denying that she was less than a breath away from death.

There were some who though she was already dead. And perhaps some who *wanted* her dead. The explosion had nearly done it.

"Akemi, can you hear me?" Nat's voice broke into her thoughts.

"Is she responding to you?" Sam's voice replied. "I'm not getting anything."

"—and you had the gall to hold my escape pod! I could have you court-martialed for risking the lives of everyone on this pod, and yourself, too!" An angry voice filled the tiny pod.

"Please, shut up," Sam said.

It's okay. I'm here. Akemi sent the message to their display.

"Akemi, please respond if you hear us." Nat was starting to sound frantic.

Can't you see this? I'm fine...

From the camera on Nat's glasses, Akemi could see Sam fiddling with a small, black polyhedron the size of a basketball. It had so many faces it was almost a sphere. Thin power cords ran from it to the capsule's rudimentary computer system. Sam held up the sphere to look on the bottom, running his fingers over several small ports there.

"The electronics don't look damaged." He set it down on the floor to check the connection to the wall.

For all intents and purposes, that black sphere was *her*. She'd seen it before, but being joined with a ship or space station was one thing. Seeing the tiny container holding the remains of her brain, dumped like a broken TV on the floor of the capsule...

Akemi realized what was wrong. The escape capsule was extremely simple. It could hold them in a stable orbit until it got within proximity of a Spo ship. Then the capsule computer would automatically slave itself to the ship, which would handle docking and extraction of passengers.

In other words, she was lucky she could think at all or receive anything from their glasses. She was literally a computer rebooting without enough RAM to hold her whole operating system.

She was trapped. That was unfortunate, but once a real ship picked them up, she'd be able to explain.

Nat was running her hands over the cords, probably checking for breaks. "I don't want to unplug and re-plug her more than necessary. It could cause errors, but I don't want to leave her unconnected either."

Angry voice again. "I don't appreciate you mucking around with the controls! How do I know you won't make our capsule spin into the moon?"

Sam and Nat finally looked at the man, and Akemi saw that it was

Senator Fontley. He was one of the newly elected representatives of humanity, part of the newly formed Human Coalition Government. He didn't look particularly imposing now, with his clothes thrown on and his knees black with soot from crawling through the halls. His nose was red and running and his teeth were clenched.

There were three other Spo in the capsule with them, but Akemi assumed from their complete silence that they didn't speak English. She recognized one of them as a kind of handyman on the space station, the other two she didn't know.

"We won't spin into the moon, Senator," Nat said. "The space station ejected us in a stable Earth orbit, roughly a fourth of the way between Earth and the moon."

"Yeah, if we spin into anything, it'll be the Earth," Sam added.

"What?" The senator's hand twitched, like it was just itching to slap someone.

"We won't do that either," Nat said firmly. Her voice was low and rough from the smoke. "This capsule couldn't go off course if it tried. We're trying to make contact with my sister, so if you could give us a minute—"

"I'm sorry, Miss Fujimara, but I have seen no compelling evidence that this thing even has human intelligence. The human soul is a precious and fragile thing. It can't possibly be housed in *that*." Senator Fontley shifted his feet away from the tangle of Spo limbs in the center of the round capsule. "Could you give me a *little* room, please?"

The Spo were a large race, compared to humans. The adults were easily six to ten feet tall at their full height, though their slanted spines usually kept them a little closer to human eye level. Their skin was hard and chitinous, and at the moment, the central portion of the round pod *was* rather full of jointed legs.

Sam spoke briefly to them in Spo. "I apologize for delaying the capsule. It is our responsibility to preserve this computer or else I would not have put you at risk. I'm sure our capsule will be retrieved as soon as possible."

They still looked stressed, but their color began to fade towards a more neutral yellow. "We understand," said the oldest Spo. He gestured toward Nat and the sphere. "Responsibility first."

Nat took off her glasses and examined them for damage.

Sam fiddled with the ports in the wall of the capsule. "I think I should rewire her to this port. See this here? It should have at least half again as much capacity... I should have thought of that originally."

Akemi did not want him to rewire anything. She still felt rattled from the last cold shut down, but she had no way to tell him to leave it alone.

Almost all the equipment in their new glasses was for *her* to monitor *them*. She could track their temperature, their head and eye movement, and of course, see everything they saw. But the only way she communicated with them was with the data display and she couldn't use that.

Oh, she mentally kicked herself, except for the anti-theft protocol. She could overheat the glasses so they would burn whoever tried to wear them without permission.

Sam's glasses were still on his face, so she focused on Nat, who was holding hers in her hand.

Normally Akemi's output to the glasses was as easy as talking, but now she had to focus. The capsule computer was so slow. She painfully made the connection to Nat's glasses and sent the heating command.

Nothing happened.

Nat frowned and put her glasses back on her nose.

Even in Akemi's weakened state, she felt a flare of pride at the glasses she'd chosen. They were designer frames, and they looked fantastic on Nat, highlighting her high cheekbones and perfect Japanese facial structure.

"Ow!" Nat flung her head forward and the glasses flew across the capsule. Akemi got a whirling view from that camera.

"What happened? Are you alright?" Sam bent over Nat, whose hands covered her face.

"What now?" the senator demanded. "I told you to leave it alone."

"Injury? Assistance?" asked one of the Spo.

Nat finally sat back, revealing her nose gingerly. From Sam's glasses, now very close to Nat's face, Akemi could see a bright red burn across Nat's nose, and two red spots from the nose-piece. The skin around her eyes was tight and pink, like a bad sunburn, and the whites of her eyes were bloodshot.

"Ow. It smarts, but it'll heal. I was just startled."

Akemi had never tried the anti-theft protocol, and now she'd burned her sister! She felt terrible, but Nat began to laugh with relief. "That was smart, Akemi. We will leave you be, but you owe me one."

Senator Fontley sniffed and wiped his reddened face. "You can't trust any technology from the Rik. I'm sorry for your loss, but that isn't your sister."

"The situation is more complicated than it seems," Sam said. "At least give us the benefit of the doubt, Senator."

Fontley shook his head. "I don't know why I even try with you cadets. You're both brainwashed by the Spo. Puppets."

"There's no need to be rude," Nat said. "I know you were frightened, and I'm sorry you were delayed, but we all made it off the space station. This is a valuable computer, you should be glad we salvaged it."

"Frankly, I would have been happy to see it burn."

Nat recoiled. Sam put his arm around her, glaring at the senator. "To clarify, neither you nor the Human Coalition have the authority to tell us what to do with the computer. The Spo have leased it to Nat, *personally*." Sam took a deep breath. "You've asked me not to undermine you in public, and I won't, as long as you stop pushing Nat in private."

The senator stiffened. "Is that a threat?"

Sam clenched his jaw. "If you want it to be."

7

AFTER THEIR CAPSULE WAS RETRIEVED, only a couple hours after the explosion, Nat waited patiently as she was treated for smoke inhalation and minor burns and questioned exhaustively. Eventually she was allowed to shower and change out of her uniform, which still reeked of smoke.

When she was clean, Nat put on an ill-fitting uniform and stared out the tiny port window of the cabin. The burnt husk of the space station floated below, surrounded by a cloud of debris. It looked forlorn and forsaken—lightless, empty, without a single ship docked.

I tried to save it. I don't know what happened. This shouldn't have been possible.

"It's not your fault, Akemi," Nat said.

Several other ships kept pace with the space station and trawled through the debris, looking for salvage.

Someone knocked at the door and Nat jumped. "Who is it?"

"It's just me." Sam also wore a badly fitted but clean uniform. It stopped several inches short of his ankles and wrists, and he'd left it unbuttoned around his neck. Sam's hair was growing back from when it had been shaved several months before, and it was finally starting to lie down on his head instead of standing straight up.

She and Sam had spoken in countless meetings and press conferences and negotiations, but they hadn't had much time for themselves.

On the day of the trial, she'd been whisked away to the Spo medical quarters as soon as it was over. A failed Rik procedure, a desperate fight, and oxygen deprivation had left her in terrible shape. Plus, the Spo had wanted to do quite a few diagnostics, to make sure the Rik hadn't irrevocably screwed up her brain when they tried to take her body. Her time in the infirmary stretched from hours to days and then Sam had had to go back to Earth. Then she'd remained on the space station with Akemi until their parents could be brought up...

What with one thing and another, it had been a month before they really got to see each other, and when they did meet again, there were twelve Spo, three Rik, and thirty members of the press there as well. Not exactly a private reunion.

"Hey." Sam pulled Nat into a hug. "You look like you're trying really hard not to shiver."

She leaned into him. "Good guess."

Sam's arms tightened. "I don't know if you realize how glad I am that you're alive. You already had your close call with death, you know? It wasn't supposed to happen again. Not so soon. I was afraid we'd run out of time for good."

"Me too. I *hate* fire." Several months ago she'd gotten serious burns on her legs and hands when someone attacked them with a Molotov cocktail.

"I know, but you handled it. It's over."

"It's not over," she countered grimly. "There was no way this was an accident. We're looking at terrorism or sabotage."

"Maybe."

"And Senator Fontley. I do not like that man." Nat rubbed her forehead again. "Another migraine is coming. I wish I could turn off my mind."

Nat had suffered terrible headaches every now and then, ever since the Rik tried (and failed) to re-contour her brain. She supposed that it was a small price to pay for living, but it didn't make it pleasant.

Sam massaged her temples. "Is this okay?"

"Yeah, thanks."

"We haven't really talked since... I don't know when."

"You mean, you don't want to have a personal conversation in front of the Tergre and the galaxy?"

"Viewer poll," Sam said, mimicking their voices, "Should Sam Locklear—"

"Supreme Leader of Earth, don't forget."

"—finally kiss his girlfriend?"

Nat raised her brows. "Am I your girlfriend?"

"It's up to you. The Spo stuff—trying to match us up—if that still bothers you..."

"It was a long time ago," Nat said. "The Spo aren't in control of our whole lives now."

"Then—"

"But I don't know if I can handle this right now. I'm so worried about Akemi."

"The bioexpert says there was no permanent damage."

"I know." Nat tapped her glasses. "Akemi told me that also. But she's already lost her *life*, Sam. If she loses this half-life she's been given, I don't think I can stand it." Nat pressed her forehead into his shoulder.

Hey, don't make this about me. I think you should kiss him. Be his girlfriend. Marry him!

Nat folded the glasses and put them in her pocket. "That's enough out of you."

Sam smiled. "She's on my side, isn't she?"

"Maybe."

"I love you," Sam said.

Nat froze. Somehow the words were both expected and shocking. She knew Sam loved her, and she loved him, too, but she wasn't sure it was the same. She loved him as someone who had survived something terrible with her. She respected and trusted him. And yes, he was so handsome and good, and also her best friend. But it was complicated now. She couldn't quite get the words out and everything they would mean for the future.

"I'm not saying that to pressure you. I just want you to know it's not going to change. I love you and when you're ready, I'll always be here." He kissed her forehead. "I'm really glad you're safe."

"I—I'm glad you're safe, too," Nat said, faltering. "But we need to find out what's happening."

"You always put duty first." The tattoo on his cheek tugged upward. "Just like old times."

Someone knocked at their door and Nat sighed. "Duty usually comes and finds us."

True to Sam's promise, Akemi hadn't experienced any more blackouts after their escape pod was recovered. The Spo had provided her with a perfectly serviceable mobile computer and connected it before disconnecting her from the pod.

The Spo normally used trouncer brains in their biocomputers —organic processors that lasted only a few hyperspace jumps before being discarded. The trouncers were apex predators on their home planet, and the fact that their brains burned out so quickly made her extremely nervous. She didn't want to be disposed of any time soon, so she wanted as little wear and tear on her brain as possible.

Everyone was speculating about the attack on the space

station. Akemi—once she had enough space to really get going—was reviewing all she could remember of the moments before the string of explosions ripped through her beautiful halls.

The Spo were unanimous: it had to be sabotage.

Akemi couldn't immediately rule out malfunction or accident, but she was inclined to agree. For the last few months, she *was* the space station. It had been an extension of her identity as much as her own hands and feet and ears. How could she have been so compromised and missed it? But then again, how could someone have sewn explosives into her skin, and she missed *that*?

Either way, it was a professional and personal crisis and Akemi was determined to get to the bottom of it.

If it was sabotage, someone on the space station must have been responsible, because the explosions had occurred from the interior. The space station was designed to withstand significant attacks from outside. Even if an explosion did rip through into the domicile area, that section could be immediately partitioned to prevent the spread of fire or loss of air.

That many simultaneous explosions from the interior of a Spo space station was unheard of.

It was now six hours after the explosion (T+6 hours) and the first reports of the forensic team were coming back. They were examining the ruined hulk of the space station, in which, Akemi now learned, five Spo had died. Akemi felt a sharp, sinking grief, though she had not personally known them. She had been their temporary home, and she'd failed them.

This wasn't a simple malfunction, Akemi sent to Sam. *I haven't reviewed every option yet, but I know it.*

Sam and Nat were in the captain's personal quarters now, along with Senator Fontley and several Spo officials. It wasn't a large ship, and this was the roomiest place for them to meet. Akemi could only glimpse the dimly lit room through Sam's glasses; Nat wasn't wearing hers. On the space station, she'd had over a *hundred* viewpoints at any given moment, and now she was down to one.

"We just retrieved another escape pod with eight aboard," the captain said. "But more importantly, my sergeant found the remains of a device. Here is the image." He brought up a large, gritty photograph on the viewscreen that projected onto his table. The photo showed fragments of a blue cylinder embedded in one of the blackened walls of the station. The cylinder was tapered with a slight bulge at the base. "The blast exited the top of the cylinder, leaving the rest of the casing in surprisingly good condition," he explained.

A Rik cluster bomb, Akemi said.

"On first inspection, it looks like a charge-directed, Rik cluster bomb," the captain agreed.

Sam shook his head. "The Rik have less reason to hurt us than anyone. They don't want the treaty to fail."

"They did not hurt *you,*" the captain said, flushing mottled grey with displeasure. "They killed five of *my* people and destroyed a Spo space station."

"Another species could have used Rik devices," Nat said.

The captain flushed even deeper with displeasure. "Who else would do such a thing? It is not an honorable way to start a war. If the Vel or the Merith wished to begin a conflict, they would do it in the traditional way and attack a frigate. Even the Tergre, although they prefer subterfuge, would not deem this a worthy move."

"Then perhaps there is a personal motive, or some species has changed their pattern," Sam said. "It does happen."

"Who has been on the space station more than the Rik?" the captain returned. "Other than the humans and ourselves, they are the most frequent visitors. They have had more opportunity than anyone. You may think you've won them over with your amnesty at the trial, but I expect they hold much resentment towards all of us for orchestrating their failure."

Fontley nodded. "No Rik can be trusted."

A small blonde woman appeared in the doorway. "Even me? The only thing *I'm* orchestrating is a new wardrobe. *What* are you two wearing?"

Shara's okay! I was worried about her.

"Shara," Nat nodded wearily. "We were wondering if you'd made it off the space station."

"Aw, don't be so effusive, Nat, you're embarrassing me." Shara was small and cute and deceptively deadly. She was a Rik assassin, but she'd turned against her superiors and given Sam the evidence he needed to win. Despite their history, Akemi was friends with Shara.

The captain stiffened at her arrival, but Shara obviously didn't care. She sauntered into the room and pointed at the photo. "This isn't Rik style at all."

The captain's eyestalks twitched unpleasantly. "I say it is."

Shara shook her head, making her blonde hair bounce on her shoulders. "I admit the Rik are disappointed we can't do our full-scale migration slash invasion of Earth. But what good is this mess?" She gestured to the picture. "It'd be a tragic gesture of defiance, and that is *so* not our style. We don't do drama."

Nat opened her mouth to protest, but Sam held up his hand. "As much as we might take issue with that, Shara does make a good point. The Rik are pragmatists. What does this achieve?"

It hurts our relationship with the Spo. It might destroy our treaty with the Rik.

"Who else could it be?" the captain retorted.

Akemi was already pondering that. She had logged and monitored every alien delegation that visited the space station since she arrived. These cluster bombs couldn't have been in place for very long, or they would have been found during routine maintenance.

"Akemi, give us a list of visitors for the past week," Nat requested.

Ten Tergre cultural ambassadors, including news crew

Three Council members from Merith II and Comboda.

One Crosspoint who came to negotiate the Melifleuran tree loan.

Eight Rik, who came to inspect the new prison facility on the moon. They left an hour before the explosion.

Sam protested, "I know that last one sounds bad, but the Rik agreed to our terms! The negotiation was done."

Senator Fontley frowned, as he generally did when Sam said anything. "I think you're all missing the point. This computer *thing* could have done the sabotage itself!"

What?

"Why would Akemi risk her own life?" Sam said. "Even if you don't believe she is a person, why would a computer destroy itself?"

"It could be controlled by someone else. Or it could be programmed to self-destruct. You allowed an experimental alien computer—*created* by Rik scientists—to be in control of the space station."

Akemi did not like where this was going. Senator Fontley hated all aliens (probably terrified of them), but for some reason he'd fixated on her. Granted, she was a strange thing to understand, but she was *human*. That should count for something. His suspicion hadn't seriously worried her, but with this explosion, his accusations suddenly had new weight.

"The facts are clear: this abomination was in control of the space station, and it just exploded, killing five of your people, and endangering even more."

"It wasn't her. Didn't we just say these bombs had to be implanted within the last week or two? She doesn't have *hands*."

Nat rubbed her eyes hard. "Our speculation is just that, speculation. Without proof, we can't say anything more."

"And Nat needs to rest," Sam said.

The captain waved for them to leave. "There are more capsules to retrieve, and I believe a Merith ship picked up a few as well. We shall speak again after the next shift."

Shara led them down the hall. "I just know this wasn't a Rik attack. I think it's called intuition. Humans have that, right?"

Sam grimaced. "*Humans* do."

Shara grinned back at him. "Yeah, totally. Which means I do, too."

NAT MANAGED to get some decent sleep before someone scratched at their door, the way the Spo sometimes did.

Sam slept heavily, too, sprawled on the bed next to her. His forehead was relaxed, loosening the creases that formed when he was stressed. Shara slept on a few extra cushions on the other side of the bed.

Nat answered the door quietly, hoping Sam might stay asleep.

Her mentor was just lifting his clawed hand to scratch the door again. Nat was so used to the Spo aliens that her mentor's insectoid face, glistening eyestalks, and clicking mandibles weren't the least scary. In fact, she was so relieved he had survived that she hugged him. "Greg! You're okay."

"I am." Greg patted her back gingerly. "And you?"

He saw Sam sleeping on the bed, but he couldn't see Shara, sprawled on her cushions on the far side. Greg didn't say anything, but his color of satisfaction was so clear it was almost human.

"Don't look so smug," Nat said. The door slid shut behind her as she stepped into the hall, and she stooped to pull her shoes on. "Just because Sam and I might end up together, you think you're so smart."

"I am smart," Greg said simply. "And I am genuinely glad that you and Sam are... together."

"Whatever." It was no use. Greg would consider their relationship his doing no matter what she said. Hopefully he wouldn't make a big deal out of it.

"Your children—"

Nat smacked his bony shoulder. "If you dare to say a word about even the *possibility* of our children or their genetic material, I will never, ever let you meet them. Should they ever exist. Got it?"

Greg looked slightly hurt. "Very well. It is urgent that I speak to you about Akemi, however. Is that topic off-limits as well?"

"Go ahead."

"I do not believe she was involved in the space station sabotage, but many Spo are saying that it is possible. I understand that your Senator Fontley is also of this opinion."

"Unfortunately."

"The theory is spreading rapidly. Emotions are high. I think it might be best if Akemi were not nearby for a while."

"You think they'd destroy the computer. But where can we take her? Earth? They could extradite her if she is accused."

"Further away than that."

"But we can't just leave."

"No, you're still too public. If you and Sam disappear immediately after the space station explodes in the night sky, humanity will reasonably assume you are dead."

"That'd be bad." Sam was a global celebrity these days, and Nat was close behind—but it was a dangerous kind of fame. Most people on Earth wanted the Spo gone *yesterday*, and they didn't understand why it might take a while to phase them out. Even though the Spo had already helped form a provisional government, Sam was still the face of the transition. Many, with no help from the Tergre, were convinced he was in charge. He wasn't, not by a long shot, but if he disappeared without a good reason, there would be problems.

Greg nodded, accepting that Nat understood the situation. "The Rik who are under suspicion are headed to a moon called Selta. It's in Tergre mainspace, and it is completely neutral. I propose you go to Earth and show everyone you survived. Then you and Sam can take Akemi there to investigate this explosion."

"How do you know that's where they went?"

"One of the Council members gave us the information. His ship had only just left the space station before the explosion. They noted the Rik ship departing, but they stayed to help with search and rescue."

"That was lucky timing," Nat said. "Do we believe him? Which Council member was it?"

"His name is Faal of Merith II. He's generally agreed to be the third most powerful Merith in the galaxy, and his estate is one of the twelve wonders of the Merith Confederation."

"Yikes. I remember him now. He did support us when he voted in the trial."

"Yes. If he had unsavory plans for Earth, I would expect them to involve smuggling, not sabotage. His agents have gathered species from every mapped sector of space. He even visited the interdicted Velvidian Enclave to retrieve a Crested Raptor before their star went nova. He may not be truthful, but he has never dabbled in terrorism."

"So, we take him at his word, and we follow the Rik to Selta? It is a good idea for us to go, but Akemi will be sad to leave Shara. They were close. Maybe—" Nat groaned. "Maybe we should bring Shara with us."

Greg clicked his claws dubiously. "I am not certain a Rik assassin is a good choice for this investigative team."

"I don't like her either, but she loves Akemi—as much as she can love anyone. We'll keep tabs on her, but I believe she'll be loyal. We could label her a Rik *specialist* and be vague about the details."

Greg pulled out his pad. "That is satisfactory. I'll write to our ambassador on Selta at once. He can host you. The embassy there already hired a human detective to investigate Rik imposters. Perhaps he will be an aid."

Greg paused in writing his message. "Will Senator Fontley wish to accompany you? He could argue that a Coalition representative should be present."

"Are you kidding? You'd have to pry that man out of our solar system with a putty knife. He loathes space travel and can't stand aliens."

Greg nodded. "Perhaps that is for the best." He turned to take his leave but then stopped and patted her again on the shoulder, as gently as he was capable of. "I am glad you survived, Nat. I am very fond of you."

"You, too, Greg." He was ruthless and even a killer, but in his own way, he'd been a father to her. "I'll miss you."

8

CLAIRE WATCHED the news reports slavishly after the explosion. The reports were a little hush-hush about the investigation, other than the fact that Nat and Sam were going to Selta to look into a lead.

That got Claire excited. Selta was one of the planets on the Diadina's tour. Perhaps Claire would have a chance to find them.

About a week before they would land at Selta, after scrubbing out a room that a group of Tergre children had used to play some kind of mud-ball fight, Claire was approached by another passenger.

"Excuse me. Are you a human?"

It was a Crosspoint who was asking. They were giant slugs, a translucent whitish-grey, and they glided along on their bellies. They didn't have any of the slime and mucous of Earthly slugs, but they were a little too Jabba the Hutt for her taste. Nonetheless, they seemed to be well-liked. This one's head was about even with her chin.

She had no idea how they moved so smoothly. She instinctively leaned away from its translucent bulges. "Er—yes. I'm human."

"Ahhh," he said. "The Human. The Diadina thought I might

like to have a conversation with you." He spoke the Spo language in a warm, gravelly voice. Not the way Spo was usually spoken.

"Why?" Claire asked warily. "Who are you?"

"I have the honor to be the Second Junior Representative of the Crosspoints of Empter to the Galactic Council." There was a note of quiet humor in his voice. "We are not so prestigious as the Crosspoints of Cross, so there is no need to bow."

Claire had indeed begun an awkward bow, as she'd seen some Merith do before Faal. "If you're a representative to the Galactic Council, were you part of the human sentience trial?"

"I was not a voting party, but I did observe it. Thus, my interest in humans, you see. I was most surprised when the Diadina told me she was employing one. But this is not a comfortable place for talking, is it?" He gestured to the bare, clean room. "If you please, come to my cabin when your shift is over, and we may speak at leisure."

Claire asked her crew boss, Kitteh, about the Crosspoint. "The Diadina told me not to be friendly with the other guests. But he came and found me. What should I do?"

"The Crosspoint are peaceable, you may visit if you wish." Kitteh cocked her head to one side. "What was his name?"

"Um... he didn't say. He's a junior representative from Empter."

"It should be fine. However, I would warn you that Crosspointers are...devious. They are telekinetic, in that they can move physical things, but it is said they can move minds as well. The Pontifex never allows Crosspoints in his palace, and the Diadina rarely has them as guests."

With that pleasant thought in mind, Claire went to his room.

She left the service corridor at the nearest junction (after checking a map) and stood nervously before his door. It opened before she made contact.

"Come in, Human! Come in. I've made the atmosphere cooler for your enjoyment. Is it correct?"

"It's very nice, thanks." Much of the ship was kept warm, maybe around eighty degrees.

"Ah, good. I've been doing my reading, you see, on Earth and humans."

In his suite, instead of chairs or cushions, he had shells. Large, spiral shells like—"Snails," Claire exclaimed.

"Oh yes, quite," he said, backing into one and settling in comfortably. The other shells looked empty but they were opaque, so she wasn't quite sure.

"No, no, it's just me," he said, guessing her thoughts. "These are for guests, but for you I have a chair."

Claire looked around, not seeing a chair. There was a door to the bedroom, a kitchenette, and an instrument that looked like a piano if it was chopped up and glued back together with neon glitter glue. The Crosspoint also had daubs of bright paint on himself. They seemed to really like color.

A spotted rug lay on the floor, silky and cool, and a Spo *death-glass* hung on one wall, green with mottled orange on the edges. No chair.

"Oh, I forgot," he said. A simple, straight-legged chair glided out of the bedroom and settled itself a few feet away from the shells.

It was really unnerving to see a chair hurtling across the room like that.

The first time she'd seen a Crosspoint, she and the other cadets were waiting in a huge Spo gymnasium. It had only been days since she and the other kids had been taken from Earth. They had milled around, trying to see if by some crazy miracle there was someone they knew in the crowd. Most of them spoke English, but there'd been clumps of kids speaking Mandarin, Swahili, Korean, Russian...

Claire had stumbled about with the others, looking into faces and away, hoping against hope to see a friend, and feeling terribly guilty for wishing this nightmare on a friend. That was when she'd found Jenelle. They'd hugged and clasped hands... Claire shied away from that thought.

Anyway, the Spo had brought four Crosspoint in to do their tattoos. The facial tattoos of the cadets weren't like human tattoos. Somehow they used an ink that changed the pigment at a cellular level.

The Crosspointers had put on a bit of a show. Four purple globes the size of basketballs looping and spinning through the air in a rhythmic dance. They spun faster and faster, leaving light trails like sparklers on Fourth of July.

Amid oohs and ahs, the globes suddenly fell towards the crowd. She and Jenelle instinctively ducked with everyone else, but of course the globes froze inches above them. Slowly they trailed toward the double doors where they hovered over four slugs, Crosspointers.

"Meet the Crosspoint," one of the Spo teachers had said. "Next week we will introduce you to the Merith, then the Vel, and Tergre. The Crosspoint have useful skills, and they have been our allies for generations. You must learn the capabilities and weaknesses of all the species in the Council to be effective representatives."

The Crosspointers had glided to the center of the gymnasium. "We are Crosspoint. We have no written language, no hands, no feet... yet we are ranked a Level 7 culture in the Council. Earth's bountiful blessings will do you no benefit, and indeed much harm, if you do not know how to trade effectively with other species."

The globes had begun to spin again, at first aimlessly, then slowly forming a gyroscopic pattern above the aliens' heads.

"For instance, the Spo have asked us for a favor. To mark all of you as Spo cadets, you will receive a badge of security, and identity."

The color had leached out of the spinning balls, and Claire had realized it was ink. She had felt heat on her cheek. Hot, hot, hotter—

All the kids in the room had grabbed their faces, some doubled over, some dancing around in panic.

Then it had stopped. They'd all stared at each other—at the bold tattoos they now sported on their left cheeks. On the paler teenagers, like Jenelle, the tattoo was a vivid black. On the ones with darker skin, from the very dark Africans to those merely medium brown, like Claire, the tattoo was a stark white.

Claire touched the tattoo now as she sat in the chair the Crosspoint had teleported. "So, you wanted to speak to me?"

"Indeed. I have spoken with several Rik, but not yet with a human."

"Everyone keeps saying that. Are there so many Rik? Do they really look like us?"

The Crosspoint paused and stared at her, searchingly. "You don't know the Rik relationship to Earth?"

"A little. The trial is over and somehow we ended up sponsoring the Rik, whoever they are."

"Hm. Yes. You would be interested to learn, in that case, that it was discovered that the Rik perpetrated the Large Hadron event that precipitated Earth's trial. It was a plot to discredit humanity and give the Rik a chance to move in."

Claire gasped. "The Hadron—it wasn't us? We all believed it was terrorists!"

He gave her a moment to process, but then broke in.

"Since I have the joy of meeting a human on my travels, most unexpectedly, I must repeat, I have several questions I would like to ask you."

"I'm not sure how much I can help you. I haven't been on

Earth in a while, and obviously I'm not up to date on current events."

A rope suddenly slithered out of the nearest shell and tethered Claire to her chair, firmly wrapping around her torso and around her arms and thighs.

"What are you doing?" Claire tried to wriggle free, but she'd taken a moment too long, and the rope was tight. All she managed to do was tip the chair forward, and she yelped in anticipation of face-planting on the floor.

But the chair froze. She was halfway to the ground, at a forty-five-degree angle. Slowly the chair righted itself, from two legs to four, and she felt it when the telekinetic force of the Crosspoint let go and the chair rocked back slightly.

Her position: tied to a chair, unexpectedly helpless, sent Claire into another memory.

It was in Faal's zoo, in the early days. He never trusted new acquisitions and insisted on having them securely tied up for his visits. Particularly animals with opposable thumbs.

He'd stood in front of her, politely offering two flasks. "Now that you are familiar with the effects of this drug," he shook the flask on the right, "And after I explain the side effects of this Melifleuran secretion," he shook the flask on the left, "You get to choose which to take today."

Claire had just waited, knowing he would want to expound more before he made her choose.

"You see, it is very hard to understand the evolutionary values of a given species by asking direct questions. You do not know the answers yourself, so your response could only consist of what you think I want to hear, or some interpretation of your own ignorance."

"What do you want to know?"

"Many things. I have developed a series of psychological tests that require no explanation on the subject's part, merely a choice.

The first choice is one that juxtaposes the mind and the body. The Melifleur are a tree-like species, somewhat new to the Council, and one of their only interesting cultural exports is this hallucinogenic drug. It could render you insane, but most likely will only confuse your electrical processes for a few days. In other words, it incapacitates the mind."

Claire already knew what the other one would do. They'd given it to her originally to save her life, when she had a bad reaction to a non-human food. It had made her violently sick for several days, but it had cleared her system of the poisons she'd reacted to. If she took it again, she would be sick again.

Faal continued. "The choice, as I said, is between body or mind. Sickness or madness?"

Claire didn't immediately answer. Faal rephrased his question. "What do you think *she* would have chosen?"

Faal knew how Jenelle had turned on her, and also about her death. He'd even questioned Claire about it while she was on another of his drugs that made her very drowsy and honest. He'd explained that it was an interesting insight into the human subconscious. "Her first decision to give you up was correct—it was survival and survival is sanity. But your psyche appears to value selflessness and now punishes you for the attempt *she* made. You feel guilt both for her death, and for your anger against her. I wonder if it is because she failed, or whether you would have been tormented regardless."

Since then, he'd taken to questioning her about both herself and Jenelle. Claire nodded tiredly toward the flask on the right. No matter what happened, she would not go mad. Her stomach was already protesting the decision.

Faal moved toward her with the flask and Claire shook her head. "You already tried this test. You must be slipping."

But then... this wasn't Faal in front of her. She shook her head, confused. This wasn't even a Merith alien, it was the Crosspoint who'd tied her to a chair. "You can't—make me choose anymore."

The Crosspoint stared at her calmly. "Are you ill?"

Claire closed her eyes, reasserting reality. "I'm not ill. I might be a little broken."

"And why, do you think—"

But Claire's mind was rapidly clearing. This was not the zoo. She had rights here. "I am an employee on this ship. How dare you tie me up? The Diadina will notice if I don't appear." Claire spoke as collectedly as she could. "Why are you interested in me? Do you work for Faal?"

"Now that is an interesting question," he said. "I do not work for Faal. Do you? I have heard that he has Rik employees." His voice was still calm and polite. Claire was completely confused.

"I don't work for Faal; I hate him! And I am *not* Rik, I'm human. But I already told you that."

"I do not like liars." While his voice was still soft, Claire noticed that several objects in the room shuddered slightly with his words. The Spo deathglass clinked against the wall; a few notes of the psychedelic piano clinked. "The Diadina is beginning to trust you. As I am a friend and loyal admirer of hers, I am determined to have the truth before she is taken in."

"I'm not a liar."

"You still claim to be human? No. The Spo locked the planet down for seven years. Humans are not journeying through the galaxy on cruise ships. However, I have met many Rik in human bodies, and they are everywhere."

"But—"

"And they are all liars. The mere act of taking a body is not necessarily a lie, but the pretense is, and Crosspoint do not like pretense." He slid out of the shell to get closer to Claire. "This tattoo on your cheek; it is the Spo cadet mark."

"Yes, it is. Because I was *in* the Spo training program."

"I know. Which means you are a Rik who stole a cadet's body."

"No, it doesn't mean that! And if you hate lying, how do you feel about tricking me in here, pretending to be kind, in order to interrogate me?"

The Crosspoint closed his eyes for a moment, but she sensed his full attention was still fastened on her, she could almost feel it.

Claire was angry. She ran through her mental list of betrayers: first the Spo, who'd sold her to Faal. Then Faal himself, of course. Next was the zookeeper who'd pretended to be sympathetic, but in actuality was completely devoted to Faal and reported all her first escape attempts...

"I don't like lying either," Claire said. Her voice was as cold as the Crosspoint's had been.

He opened his eyes. "Now that was interesting. I recognized several species in your thoughts and a stab of emotion as clear as lightning. You do hate lying."

The rope around her thighs loosened though the part around her chest held tight.

"You can read minds?" Claire asked.

"Not well, across species. But I've not usually felt such anger from a Rik. Perhaps that is human."

"I *am* human."

"Hmm. And sincerity. Certainly not a Rik trait in general."

"Where would you take me if I *was* a Rik?" Claire asked, thinking of a new possibility.

"They've made a prison on the terrestrial moon."

"The moon?" Claire gaped. "Then, fine! Even if you think I'm Rik, someone will realize I'm human and take me home. I'd be so close."

That wasn't the way she would choose to go home, as a captive once more, but just the idea of home was enough to give her hope. Maybe this was a chance in disguise.

"I would first take you to the nearest Spo embassy where you'd be processed. You would have an equal chance of being shipped back to the Rik planet or given to Faal if he claims jurisdiction."

He flinched backward as if she had shoved him. "You are disappointed—despairing. Yes, I see."

The rope released her, coiled itself neatly, and flew to a locker in the eating area. "I believe you. You are human, but I had to test you."

Claire stood up from the chair. "There had to be another way to find out. I've really had it with aliens who feel entitled to test me."

9

THE CROSSPOINT mainly stayed away from her, but the day before the ship would reach Selta, Claire saw him enter the common dining room. All the ship's guests had food synthesizers in their cabins, but most of them preferred to eat 'real' food, prepared by hand. For that, they came to this central dining room where they could receive food appropriate to their species and wealth.

She tried to slip out unobtrusively, but it was no good.

"I would like to speak with you again," the Crosspoint said. "I am going on from Selta, and I may not see you thereafter."

Claire nodded noncommittally. She'd pinned her next hopes on Selta. The Diadina was stopping there for several months, and Claire was hoping to find out if the cadets from Earth, Sam and Nat, were also there.

"You probably won't see me," she agreed. "I'm going to stay on Selta."

"Excellent. You will have many chances there. I've heard there are human cafés springing up already." There were three Merith with him, and the Crosspoint introduced her. "Friends, this is the human I told you of. An actual human—I have checked."

"I thought they were furry."

"No, you're thinking of the other new species, the one the Vel are sponsoring. The humans are from Earth, part of the Spo Enclave."

"I've heard they're dangerous," said another.

"All sentient species are dangerous."

"I've heard they're mad, as well."

"Perhaps, but with great sincerity," the Crosspoint said. "They feel nothing like the Rik when you challenge them."

Claire snorted. Challenge?

He noted her noise. "I won't be the last who mistakes you for a Rik. There are many Rik on Selta." He looked intently at Claire. "You hate deception, like I do. I respect that. May peace flow by your side, and truth shine on your head."

Against her will, Claire was slightly touched by this benediction... but she really hoped he was wrong about the Rik problem on Selta.

The next morning, the Diadina summoned Claire.

"What will you do now?" she asked. "I intended to turn you away sooner, but I am torn. You are a quiet thing. You repeated nothing of what I said to you—foolish, important, or otherwise. An attendant who can be trusted is hard to find."

"Wow, thank you. Are you offering me a job?"

"Yes. You would be safer with me. Faal knows you are on this ship and his agents still have instructions to search for you at every stop we have made."

"They have?"

"There was no point in telling you if you did not disembark. He has agents on Selta as well, although it is a Tergre world."

Claire felt the familiar fear rising in her stomach. "Will Faal or his men be waiting when we land?"

The Diadina suddenly looked very tired. She twitched her knotted belt, her feud belt. "Faal is *always* waiting. Sometimes I think the fight is not worth it..." she trailed off and restarted. "I've done you a favor. I intentionally changed our flight plan, to put us on the western side of Selta, further from our original berth. If you decide to leave, I suggest you plan to exit with the bulk of the crew. However, I strongly caution you to stay."

"I appreciate it, and I might take you up on it—but I'd like to try and find my own people."

THE FOLLOWING DAY, Claire waited in the loading bay with all her possessions. They were more than they had been. She had a knapsack of sorts from Kitteh, along with two uniforms that had been adapted for her. Kitteh told her to go ahead and take them with her—they wouldn't fit a Merith any longer. Kitteh had also given her a salary for the last month.

Kit rode freely on her shoulder, and he must have sensed that things were about to change, because he had a firm grip on the strap of her bag.

So at least this time she wasn't going into an unknown planet completely without resources. She had enough money to live for a week or two on Selta, clothes, and at least a chance of evading Faal.

The descent was the smoothest of glides. The ship settled into a divot in the moon's surface (one of many hollowed out for this purpose), and it lined up with one of the many tunnels that snaked to the interior. Selta had no atmosphere and was composed of two bustling cities below the surface.

The crew began to gather nearby, waiting for the doors to open and the rush to begin. Kitteh and her crew were grouped on the right. They chattered with lots of expressive blinking. The Spo crew were loosely grouped on the left, clearly self-segregated from the Merith.

When the orange lights around the bay doors began to flash, Claire's optimism rose. The atmosphere rushed in. The air was dry and cool, and Claire took a refreshing, deep breath. The coolness felt wonderful after the stale warmth of the ship, even though the smell was all wrong. There was a faint metallic tang of sulphur and rust.

Claire headed down the tunnel with the first group of crew, hiding among the tall Merith and gangly Spo.

The tunnel dumped out into a central docking cavern, and Claire stopped short, stunned. Cavern was the right word, she supposed, looking at the towering rock ceiling, but not on the scale of any Earthly cavern. Three major highways merged messily in two giant roundabouts. And that was just in the middle. It was like a multi-level airport carved underground.

Other small tunnel entrances, like the one she'd just come out of, liberally dotted the edges of the cavern on two levels. Lifts and ramps connected the higher tunnels to the 'ground' level and gave the whole thing the feeling of a beehive.

Kit mewled softly.

"It's okay," Claire told him. "I think we'll be alright."

She followed the crew into a huge elevator, and the drop left Claire's stomach lagging behind. When they reached the next level, the crew scattered, and Claire was truly alone.

Upper Selta, the city nearest that spaceport, reminded her of a mega shopping mall. It housed level upon level of stores, apartments, restaurants, and all kinds of alien recreation. She saw one place that, based on the pictures in the windows, offered to remove your eyeballs, clean them, and put them back. Another shop offered glowing body paint—probably for the Crosspoint— and yet another offered to grow scales all over your body.

The halls were spacious and lofty and so open that Claire could almost imagine she was outside.

She wasn't. Upper Selta was nearer the crust, she'd been told, but it was still completely subterranean.

She turned a corner and almost got flattened by a speeding ground-car, except that Kit nipped her ear. She stumbled back, realizing she'd just stepped into a hall that had no pedestrians, only strange-looking cars. On the floor was a yellow line. When she put her foot on it, it buzzed and vibrated her whole body, but in her distraction, she hadn't noticed. Those must be the traffic warnings.

"You were right, thanks, Kit." She scratched behind his ears, comforted by his weight. She turned back to the pedestrian tunnels that were full of flashing lights, jostling crowds, and noise. Did that shop really offer to make you taller? Aliens bumped into her as they rushed by. It seemed everyone had somewhere to go.

Claire had asked Kitteh this morning where the Spo embassy was located. She thought that's where the cadets would probably stay, while they investigated.

"The embassy is in Upper Selta," she'd said, after looking it up. "It is near to the largest of the spinner drills."

"The what?"

"It is a tourist attraction, near the center of Upper Selta. From our berth, you will need to go inward and down eight levels. I can't give you exact instructions, but if you ask about the spinner drill, you will get to the embassy."

Claire allowed the press of the crowd to lead her on, flowing through a hall that resounded to music like whale song, to a court-yard illuminated dimly green with swathes of luminescent paint splashed across every surface. The next hall was narrower, flooded with the smell of food. She smelled something spicy and familiar, like cumin, maybe, combined with the unmistakable smell of fish.

There were large platform escalators that continuously moved, taking large groups of people up or down. Claire waited in a crowd to step onto one of them and go down.

She noticed other people were taking a different route down-ward. At certain openings in the floor, there were curving coils of polished metal twined about each other like the double helix of DNA. Each strand was probably a foot thick, and the curve about five feet across. Some aliens straddled and slid down on their belly. Some went down them feet first, like a slide, and others stood on a lower coil, while holding onto an upper one while they twirled downward.

After watching for a while, Claire copied what she was seeing. She grasped an upper strand and put her feet on the strand closest to her. Her feet and hands slid easily down the low-friction metal, and she spun through the hole in the floor to the next level. A bit of friction slowed her at the next floor, although the hole continued, leading down and down. How far could she descend in one go, she wondered, and how dizzy would she be at the bottom?

Claire jumped off the slide-pole after two levels. She stumbled at her landing, but she was laughing. It was an exhilarating way to travel.

Looking carefully at the next set of shops and pondering whether she might buy lunch, Claire didn't immediately see the woman—the *human* woman—sprinting through the crowd until she was almost on top of her. A Spo was chasing her, maybe fifty paces behind.

"Stop," the Spo shouted. "You have nowhere to go."

The woman was black like Claire, but darker-skinned. Her eyes widened as Claire grabbed her wrist.

"Hey, do you need help?" Claire asked. "Maybe we can—"

But the woman only shook Claire off and kept running. Claire didn't know what was happening, but the first human she'd seen in three years was running, and she was darned if she was just going to watch it happen. The Spo was coming fast behind her, and Claire threw herself in front to trip him.

It worked, but wow, it hurt. They both went sprawling, and his hard exoskeleton meant she took the brunt of the blow.

Poor Kit trembled in fear; he had sunk his claws into the side of the bag and clung on with his head tucked down.

Claire's training with Kitteh was fresh in her mind. This Spo was stronger than her, but they had certain weak spots. Punching a Spo was pretty useless, so Claire kicked one of his double-jointed legs backward as he clambered to his feet. She blocked a blow from his foreleg and kicked another leg sideways.

He staggered on the slick floor, but then he got in a good blow that sent Claire reeling to the side of the walkway. The crowd had gotten louder because of the commotion. Claire's head spun.

The Spo reached her and grabbed her by her pack, lifting her off her feet.

He was already flushed an angry mottled brown. "You are the third in three days. We are tired of it."

"What?" She hadn't expected to win the fight, but she'd hoped to last a little longer than this. She'd succeeded in slowing him down at least. From the corner of her eye, she saw Kit peeking out, bristling at the Spo holding her aloft.

The Spo raised a small tablet and spoke into it. "*Basher*, can you hear me?"

"Yeah, go ahead." The answer sounded a lot like a human voice.

"I'm detained on nine," the Spo said, effortlessly keeping her kicking feet from reaching him. "I'm sending a location and description for you to pick up the other fake's trail."

"Got it."

"Is your partner human, by any chance?" Claire asked.

The Spo shook her once more. "It doesn't matter what he is; you are coming with me, Rik."

"No, *I'm not*." Claire squirmed as she dangled from her armpits.

Kit had avoided being dislodged despite the fight and his fear. He suddenly leapt, valiant and snarling.

"Kit, no!" Claire cried. "He's too big."

But Kit sank his teeth into the Spo's wrist joint—once, twice, three times. With a flinch and a curse, the Spo flung them both, ripping her shirt in the process, but giving her a ten foot head start.

Claire ran.

10

ONLY TWO LEVELS and a few blocks away, Basher got the location from his partner and finally caught up with the fleeing woman in the western quadrant of Upper Selta, Section 42. It was a ritzy sector, which he'd nicknamed the Hamptons.

Technically, they'd been following her trail for a week, but only in the last hour had it turned into an armed pursuit.

When Basher first approached her, she'd appeared genuinely surprised and happy to see another human in this alien warren, just as any real human might have been. Basher had sized her up at once: tall and confident, good-looking, with expressive features. She was almost certainly a Rik with a human body. They often chose young, healthy, and beautiful people like her. The new technical term was F.A.C.s—Fugitive Alien Counterfeits—but Basher just called them fakes.

He gave this one full credit for being a decent actress. Much better than some Rik he'd encountered.

"Can I buy you a drink?" Basher had asked. "I'd love to hear how you ended up out here."

"Of course. It's on me." She'd showed her teeth in a dazzling white smile. "Have you had a Seltan scratchwet drink? It's the closest thing I've found to a microbrew beer."

Basher had been impressed. That was surprisingly detailed for a fake, and she spoke with a decided British accent.

"Are you from Europe?" he'd asked. That was Test One. He couldn't legally arrest this woman until she gave him sufficient cause to doubt her identity. It was ridiculous, but Basher had a very tenuous contract with the Seltan officials. If they felt he was abusing his power, he'd be dropkicked right off this moon.

The Europe test was simple. Much of the continent had been vaporized seven years ago when the Large Hadron Collider was bombed. Sometimes fakes didn't understand the extent of the damage, or they just didn't remember the name of the continent they'd destroyed.

"I am," she said, "but I was spending my gap year in South America when the Hadron explosion occurred."

"Wow, lucky you, then. And how did you end up here?"

"I was offered a job by the Vel. Of course, I knew nothing about the Vel *then*; they looked like intergalactic space lizards, but you know what things were like. The tsunamis from the explosion and then the Spo taking over; everyone was crazy. The Vel offered to take us far away... so I went."

She'd taken their drinks from the server at the bar and carried them to a small table. The glasses were matte black, and the drink frothed just below the rim. Her hand didn't shake at all as she raised a glass.

"Cheers," she said, and they clinked glasses.

Basher pretended to sip, letting the froth touch his lips, but no more. The fakes were fond of a poison called *sasoikeo*, and he wouldn't take the chance. He'd only been hunting fakes for a couple years now, and he already knew of three agents who'd been poisoned.

Her story about the Vel was *technically* possible. He'd been informed that a few fast-acting aliens *had* come to Earth before the Spo locked it down.

"What about you?" she'd asked.

"Same sort of thing. I was a police officer, and then I did security for the Spo generals on Earth. Eventually I got offered a private security gig with the Spo out here. Our trial was amazing, wasn't it?" This was Test 2. The Rik had tried their darnedest to get humans judged as non-sentient animals, but the sentience trial went against them. It was pure luck that the Rik hadn't lost everything. The human representative, a kid named Sam Locklear, had decided the Rik might be more useful as an indentured species than a desperate enemy, and so they'd achieved a strange half status.

Basher had caught one Rik who ground his teeth and spat at the mere mention of their loss.

The woman's eyes widened innocently. "Quite amazing. And what kind of officer were you?"

"I was a homicide detective. NYPD." He put the drink to his lips again, letting foam touch his mouth. He couldn't do this for long, or it would become obvious that he wasn't drinking.

"Do you plan to go back to Earth?" he asked her. "The Spo have a deadline to pull out, and the economy is already picking up, with galactic money starting to trickle in. Do you have any family waiting for you?" Fourth test.

"No. My family lived in Surrey, but they all died."

"Sorry. Seems like another life before the Hadren event, doesn't it? No aliens, no hardship. How many slaves did your family have?"

He asked the outrageous question with a casual smile. Slavery, or indentured servitude, was not uncommon in the galaxy...

"Well..." She'd faltered for the first time and took a long drink. "Just a few. Didn't seem important at the time, did it?"

Bingo. Basher had put his hand on the pellet gun under his jacket. "You're under arrest—"

She'd grabbed his drink and splashed it in his face. Basher was on his feet before the glass hit the ground, but she was already at the door.

Good reaction time, but where would she go? Selta was a closed moon and he knew where her ship was berthed. The best she could hope was to lose him and somehow sneak back to her ship when he'd given up.

He'd contacted his partner as he ran, and thankfully his partner had taken the lead on the chase. Basher was fast, but Spo were always faster. When his partner took over, Basher had fallen back and gone to get a ground car to go directly to her ship.

He wasn't there yet when he got his partner's update. "Got it," Basher said. He redirected the small vehicle—more like a souped up golf cart than a car—to head her off.

Coming to a messy interchange, he saw several Melifleuran trees swaying violently to his right—so he headed that way. He trailed her by disturbance for quite a while before he finally caught sight of the woman vaulting over a table about fifty yards further down the boulevard. She glanced over her shoulder and saw him. Immediately she ducked into a shop selling crystals. Basher assumed there'd be a back way out of it.

Sure enough, he found a narrow alley that led to a delivery street behind this set of businesses.

She was heading in the general direction of the Chunnel, which was what he called the tunnel that led deeper into the moon to the city of Lower Selta. If she made it to the Chunnel, she would have a chance of disappearing in the lower city.

Basher leaned out of the car as he drove, hoping to catch sight of the fake. He almost missed her. He was glancing through the open back doors of shops and seeing snatches of the foot traffic beyond. Out of the corner of his eye he saw the movement above— a leg disappearing onto a roof. She'd climbed up and out of the service road.

Basher drove on further and then ditched his groundcar in an alcove. He scrambled up a ladder and peeked over, his gun close. *Perfect,* the fake was jogging past him, looking over her shoulder. He gauged the distance and leapt, tackling her to the grooved metal roof.

She jackknifed and slithered loose, jumping through a hatch into the building below.

The hatch, he was pretty sure, led into a private estate. Basher didn't pause to think. Pretty much everybody hated the body-stealing Rik. They'd probably excuse him for trespassing.

The front door was wide open, and a Merith maid was yelling into the street. Basher dashed past her and found that the fake had led him further into the Hamptons.

Luckily for him, it was lunchtime, and she was slowed by the posh crowd.

"Let me through. I can arrest her!" Basher shouted.

The fake ducked into a side tunnel, but now she was out of luck, or her internal map had misled her. It was a dead end. She threw her back against a maintenance door, and had a gun pointed at him before he could close the distance. Basher was maybe two arm lengths away. He'd almost had her. Other bystanders fled past him.

"Stop right there, pig," she said.

"At least you remember police insults correctly."

"I don't know about that. I just think you're a pig." She laughed, bitter and angry.

"At least I'm satisfied with my body, I didn't have to steal another."

"Nobody's happy with the body they're given. Certainly not Leticia. She had a lot of work done. The Rik have just perfected the art of self-improvement."

"Who's Leticia?" He edged closer.

"My donor."

Basher hated it when they told him the name. He was almost

close enough for a kick to the hand holding the gun. Most fakes didn't watch the feet.

Basher went for it. Her gun went off as he kicked, spewing an arc of fire that warmed his leg.

What she hadn't anticipated was the effect of the weapon. Since it fired an actual flame, the heat sensors of Selta responded. Basher knew them well and a quick glance up had him rolling forward to avoid the gate that slammed down to isolate this portion of the street. Selta, being a closed environment, had extremely sensitive environmental controls.

The gate almost caught him, but he rolled to his feet just past it. She was still gaping at her sudden lack of exit routes as Basher twisted her arm behind her back and shoved her against the wall.

On Selta, guns were supposed to be limited to security and police personnel, and that clearly worked about as well here as it did on Earth. Basher panted. He felt like he'd chased her across half of Selta.

He forced her down to the floor and handcuffed her wrists together.

"You—you are not allowed to attack another sentient life form..." she sputtered.

"Yeah, but you're not technically sentient," Basher said. "You should have turned yourself over when you had the chance. On Selta, you're in my jurisdiction. I don't even have to read your Miranda rights."

Technically she was still a beautiful woman, but now that he knew for sure it was a Rik inside her, Basher had no pity. The Rik had been stealing human bodies for years, before humans even knew aliens existed. If they continued to pose as humans, they were liable for prosecution for the bodies they'd taken and the people they killed. It wouldn't give this poor woman, Leticia, her life back, but the Rik who took her body would be punished.

Basher commed his partner. "Got her. Made a bit of a mess in 42."

"I did not get the other."

"That's not like you. Are you hurt?"

"I am fine, only humbled. I tailed it back toward the spaceport; I know which ship it retreated to."

"Great. Let's get this one locked up and we'll start on the next."

11

CLAIRE MANAGED to make it back to the *Final Say*. She hid herself in the loading bay without speaking to Kitteh or anyone.

A catwalk ran along the upper walls, and it was lined with small storage lockers that didn't get much use. Parts of it were in shadow, hidden behind the two small shuttles that docked there. Claire curled up in the darkest spot of the catwalk, arms around her knees, and kept watch on the ramp that led up to the ship.

She hadn't given up on finding Sam and Nat, but the confrontation with the Spo had rattled her. She'd only evaded him by sheer luck, spinning down several levels and reaching a platform escalator just in time to hide among a group of Vel and Merith. She'd retreated here to regroup and think. Maybe she should take the Diadina's offer of a job...

The purr of the large caterpillar ground-cars made the catwalk buzz comfortingly as they moved pallets down the ramp. Kit slid down the back of her shirt and curled up against her back. It was his favorite spot when she was anxious.

Some Merith came and went, as well as ground crew, and entrepreneurs looking to make a little cash with on-demand, last-minute shipping. Beggars occasionally came up the ramp, and a group of prospective passengers came through on a guided tour.

Claire's adrenaline spiked with every group that made its way up the ramp and under her twitchy feet.

Then her head whipped back to the ramp. A human voice. It was speaking Merith, but *so* differently from how an alien sounded.

There he was, a man at the top of the ramp. He walked with several Merith and a Spo, and while she couldn't quite make out his words from here, he seemed to be asking questions. Claire smiled involuntarily as she watched. Didn't he know the Spo didn't gesture that way when they spoke?

He was a young man of average height, which looked short next to the Merith, and he had thick, black hair. He looked Indian or Pakistani, maybe, and he had a certain intensity that said cop to her, although he wasn't wearing a uniform.

Claire stayed frozen as he came onto the ship, just taking in the details. The sound of his voice rose above the hum of machinery, and it was so acutely human.

But—

With horror, Claire realized he was walking aboard with *Faal.* Faal *himself.* Why were they together?

Claire had been poised to stand, her muscles clenched, but she went rigid when she saw him. Faal was angry, and he limped slightly.

As the man reached the flat landing, almost underneath her, he ran a hand through his hair just like her dad used to do. "*If* our quarry is the same person, I'll discuss jurisdiction—"

"Here! Attend me," Faal interrupted him, speaking to one of the crew. "I am here for the thief."

Her eyes darted between the two, forcing sense into the scene. Faal looked coldly serene, surrounded by his five personal bodyguards. They'd all paused beneath her, and Claire held her breath.

If any of them looked up into the shadows above, looked hard, they would see her.

Claire's jaw ached while he and Faal continued to talk until the ship's steward arrived.

"The human left the ship already." The steward bowed to Faal. "We had no intention of insulting you by harboring a criminal."

"Save your speeches. I know the Diadina changed berths purposely to confound me." Faal looked the steward over. "As a matter of personal property and theft, I demand to know where the fake has gone."

Claire sucked in a sharp breath. Faal claimed she was a fake. If this man believed the lie, he wouldn't help her.

She desperately wanted to reveal herself. This was another chance to make contact with a human. But as strongly as she wanted an ally, she dreaded exposing herself to Faal.

Kitteh came up to the group just then, and they turned away from Claire's hidden spot to speak to her.

Claire used the moment to ghost silently further down the catwalk to the narrow metal ladder. She scrambled down and ducked behind a crate, heart hammering. She saw Kitteh's eye flicker, watching her hide.

Kitteh had been kind to her, for the most part. Would she betray her now, too?

"You must allow me to search the ship," Faal said. "I have a personal grievance with this thief—"

Kitteh cut him off. "With all due respect, you will not search this ship. All personnel are hired under private contract, and I have no obligation to show you the contract or my crew."

Claire let out her breath. Kitteh stood her ground like a queen. Claire could've kissed her.

"What you *will* do is kindly leave this ship," she continued. "If you think the Diadina will allow Faal of Merith II to search a ship of her passage, you are mistaken. And I will make sure she knows, if I must."

Faal glared at her. "The Diadina has taken temporary residence on Selta. The ship no longer falls under her domain."

"Her servants are still removing her belongings. While they remain on the ship, it is technically still under her charter."

Claire smiled despite her tension. She never would have expected Kitteh to champion her like this.

The man began speaking, but his voice was quieter than Faal's and it was muffled by a burst of noise by the ramp. "... authorized by Spo... fakes and criminals."

"I don't have any fakes or criminals, Rik or otherwise. You too will exit the ship. Orgat!" Kitteh called. He was Kitteh's bruiser, a Merith male that made even Kitteh's hulking presence seem delicate. He was using a huge crow bar to open a slightly melted pod, and at Kitteh's call he came over to them, swinging it like a walking cane. Claire didn't blame the guy for stepping back.

Orgat began to swish his crowbar with more intentionality.

Faal clicked his beak sharply. "Very well. I will take this up with the Pontifex." He limped back toward the ramp, along with his guards.

The cop followed.

Claire gritted her teeth; she was losing her chance—maybe her only one. She gripped the crate's sharp edge, her fingers aching, and made up her mind.

"Wait! Hey!" she said. Her voice felt thin and weak. "*Hey! Don't go!*"

Kitteh made a sharp sound, motioning her back, but they'd heard her. The man spun around, and Faal did also. He nearly lost his balance.

Claire froze, ten feet away from the man, every nerve humming. "Please give me a chance to explain. I guess I'm surrendering. But don't—don't let Faal near me, please. It's more complicated than he made it sound."

Up close, he looked older—late twenties, maybe. His

eyebrows were up in surprise, and he took a step toward her. For a second, he almost looked reassuring, but then his eyes locked on the tattoo on her face. He clenched his teeth and strode toward her.

Claire took an instinctive step back, putting her hands up, palms forward. "I know what you've been told, but I'm not a Rik or a fake, and I'm definitely not a thief. I haven't been on Earth since—"

The man grabbed her arm and twisted her around, forcing her wrist up behind her back. Her bruises protested.

"Ouch! Wait a second. I need your help."

He grabbed her other arm and brought it back. Pain flared in her ribs from her collision with the Spo, and she felt a handcuff clip around one wrist and then the other. Her torn shirt flapped around her shoulder.

"Be quiet," he snapped at her. "I'm tired and I've run across half of Upper Selta today. I am in no mood to listen."

"But, but, I'm not—" Claire floundered with words as he pulled her towards the ramp. She'd waited so long to find another human—and now he wouldn't even look her in the eye.

The man forced her in front of him, pushing her down the ramp toward Faal.

"This is the thief I've been searching for," Faal hissed. "I will take her now." His claws began extending from his feet, digging into the rubbery surface of the ramp. "You injured me, Claire. It is an insult I will repay with interest."

Claire shied away from him and his claws.

The cop pulled her back to the middle of the ramp. "Oh no, you don't."

"I wasn't trying to run away. Faal has been chasing me—"

Faal grabbed her shoulder, jarring her painfully again. She could feel his claws barely pricking her shirt. "This thief is wanted for crimes on Merith II." He'd switched to English, which he'd mostly learned from her. "You will give her into my custody. Along with the stolen items."

"Respectfully, as I explained at length," the man said, "I need to process and log her identity before I sign her over to you. Your extradition will have to go through the Spo embassy."

"I do not appreciate the delay," Faal said, in a deadly voice.

The cop hesitated. "I apologize, but as the situation is unusual, I must insist. Also, I do not see the animal she allegedly stole from you."

Claire stiffened. She could feel Kit's stiff little body against her back; he was scared. It stupidly hadn't occurred to her that taking him from the zoo would be stealing. Kit shouldn't have been in that place either. No one should.

"The weskit is very small," Faal said. He looked at Claire carefully and then laughed harshly. "It's right there." He gestured at the lump Kit made in her shirt.

The cop jerked his head at Claire. "Get the animal out."

Claire shook her head. She couldn't do it with cuffs on anyway.

"It *is* the stolen animal," Faal insisted.

"Fine," the cop snapped. He unceremoniously stuck his hand down the back of her ripped shirt and dragged Kit out.

"You stole this?" he said, holding Kit in a tight grip, at arm's length.

"I didn't exactly *steal* him," Claire faltered. "I... freed him. But Faal is just using that as an excuse to get me back."

"Do not flatter yourself," Faal said coldly. "Your visit was already over."

To her shock, Kit let out a cheerful mew and nimbly slipped out of the man's grasp and scampered up onto his shoulder. The cop, to his credit, didn't flail about in surprise but just looked cautiously at the animal now two inches from his face. Kit stroked the cop's thick hair with one tiny hand and then tapped the man's chin politely.

"He's hungry," Claire said. "He wants you to feed him. Trusting little idiot."

His face twitched, and this time his smile broke through.

"That is the animal," Faal declared. "It is rare and extremely valuable. She will be prosecuted on Merith II for the theft." Faal tightened his hand on Claire's arm.

"Humanity's claim comes first," the man said, gripping Claire's other arm. "Murder is a greater charge than theft."

"I didn't murder anybody either," Claire said. "Don't you have to have proof?"

"I have what I need. You attacked my partner as he was in pursuit of a Rik." He jerked his chin at her ripped shirt. "You left a piece of your shirt as evidence."

Faal glowered. "I will follow up with the embassy." He swept down the ramp with his bodyguards and she breathed freely again.

The cop tried unsuccessfully to grab Kit off his shoulder, while also holding on to Claire. Every time he got a hand around Kit, the little guy would dance out of his grip and hop onto his other shoulder. The man gave up trying to dislodge Kit and instead tugged Claire with him.

"This is a political nightmare," he said. "I hope you're happy."

12

BASHER PUT a hand on the girl's—*the fake's*—head and pushed her into the back of his car. The little lemur thing on his shoulder nimbly climbed down and settled in her lap before he shut the door. He didn't have the first idea how to deal with that.

At least she was being quiet now. He was already edgy after his argument with Faal and his rundown with the other Rik woman.

This one looked so young. That was all he could think when she ran out of the shadows of the loading bay. She didn't look more than eighteen or nineteen, which meant the Rik probably took her body when she was only ten or eleven.

He slid into the front of the car and placed his hand on the plate to start it. His fingers were trembling slightly.

A quick glance in the back showed the girl looking over her shoulder. The Spo tattoo stood out against her skin, with a strange multi-colored hue.

"I suppose you think that tattoo proves you're human," Basher said. "Did you find a Crosspoint to fake one up for you?"

"No."

"Right. Yours looks decent, but we're all getting wrist tattoos now." He raised his arm and pulled back the sleeve of his shirt to show her. "Everyone leaving Earth gets one. So next time you're going to try and fake a tattoo, get this one."

She sniffed and Basher clamped his lips shut. He didn't even know why he was baiting her.

Perhaps it was just that she was so young. It was getting under his skin, and he wanted her to crack and admit that she was Rik.

Usually the Rik preferred to steal adult bodies when they switched, because the brain kept a lot of its working memory—particularly language. An adult's vocabulary and experience gave them more to work with than a child's. But sometimes they went for kids anyway.

When Basher thought about his job too hard he felt ill. She swiped her face as if she was crying, and Basher ground his teeth. "It was a mistake to get on Faal's bad side. I suppose you wanted to sell that lemur-cat thing on the black market. Bad move."

"What did you mean when you said you'd hand me over after processing? Who do you work for?"

The fear in her voice was probably real. As a Rik, she would be better off on the lunar prison colony than being extradited to Merith II for Faal to deal with.

"I'm employed by the Spo embassy," Basher explained grudgingly. "But since you committed a crime in Merith territory, Faal has jurisdiction over where you are prosecuted. Of course, you committed a much *worse* crime on Earth, when you stole that girl's body. A judge on Selta will probably determine who gets you first."

"But we'll go to the embassy?" she asked.

"Yes."

"Good. That's where I was trying to go anyway. I heard that several cadets were coming here to investigate the explosion on the space station."

"They're not here yet."

Faal of Merith II had also offered to help with the investigation, which struck Basher as strange. Faal had come to the embassy a week ago, accompanied by five heavily armed Merith. Ostensibly, his visit was "to offer assistance in the investigation into the bombing." He suggested "he might be of assistance in slicing through the Seltan bureaucracy."

Faal had presented Basher with a small scroll of animal hide tied with an emerald green ribbon. In addition to Faal's universal contact information, it had held a list of his four residences on Selta. A few more inches were devoted to a general authorization that gave Basher the right to use Faal's name as a reference should he be in need.

It had been unexpected to run into Faal today, searching for the same quarry. He'd looked furious that Basher refused to relinquish this Rik. Basher wondered if Faal's offer of help with the bombing was still on the table. Probably not.

"I understand why you think I'm lying," the girl said suddenly, as they edged into the descent tunnel, and began to drift downwards in the antigravity shaft. The huge shipping cavern was lost from view, and she finally turned around to face forward. Her voice was halting. "I hardly believe it myself, because it's such a crazy story—"

"Save it," Basher said. "Let me guess. It's been *so* long since you saw humans that your language skills are rusty. And goodness, you may just have forgotten some details about your life on Earth. Some mean alien stole you away, but you've been trying so hard to get back. Am I close?"

"Is that such a common story?"

"Yeah. You should pick another alibi. The Spo keep vigilant records of their cadets."

"Not if they fake their death."

Basher scoffed. Perhaps he should have passed this one off to Faal at once. They drifted straight down, with that sinking elevator feeling, and he watched the cars in adjacent tunnels drifting upward.

"*Is* that such a common story?" she asked again. "Do you meet many Rik claiming to be cadets."

"It's such a fake story, is what it is." He settled back into his seat as their car began to slow, queuing above the eight exit slots. "I'm not anxious to hear a new variation on an tired theme." He forced himself not to look at her again. Her wounded expression was an act.

"But there must be some way to prove I'm not a Rik." Her voice was getting stronger. "You must have some objective way to show it, or you couldn't prosecute me."

She paused, but Basher didn't reply. He steered the car toward the Spo embassy.

"Idiots," she said suddenly. "The Spo are such *idiots*. I was with them for years and they never thought to warn us about the Rik? They were all, 'We can give you the best education of the sentient worlds, blah, blah, blah.' We were supposed to be so freaking *grateful* for the opportunity. And yet they forgot to add, 'Hey, watch out for back-stabbing mentors and body-stealing Rik?'"

Basher flicked another glance at her. "Really? That's the angle you're going with, that your mentor betrayed you? Like I said, the Spo keep records."

"I hope they *do* have records! Then I can prove that one of their horrible instructors sold me to Faal. He's a collector of exotic *animals,* and he's angry that I escaped."

"Well, as you stole one of those exotic animals, I hardly blame him for being angry."

She ground her teeth as the car slowed to a stop in front of the formal entrance to the Spo embassy. An arch of white rock towered over the door, and two Spo guards squatted nearby.

Basher opened the back door and held the fake's arm as she

awkwardly got out, still handcuffed. She whimpered as she straightened, and Basher wondered how hard his partner had hit her. He had to admit, he was grudgingly impressed that she'd fought him at all.

The lemur climbed up onto her shoulder and looked around with large, unblinking eyes.

It was cute, he had to admit. It didn't really look like a lemur; the proportions of the body were wrong. It was more cat-like, but with a skinnier tail. And the eyes and hands were too big...

Basher shook his head. It was an alien animal. If he tried too hard to make it fit a terrestrial pattern he'd make himself crazy.

One of the Spo guards stepped forward to hold the girl's other arm so that Basher could get his ID token from his pocket.

The girl misunderstood and tried to jerk away. "Don't leave me with the Spo—please."

"Calm down. I just need to unlock the security door. Then I'll escort you to a cell and you'll have time to prove you're human."

Basher forced himself to look away. It would be horribly easy to believe her. Pressing his ID token to the spot on the door where it would read his electronic signature, Basher took her inside.

"The Spo only have a few containment cells," he told her. "They used to only need them occasionally, when a Spo got in criminal trouble on Selta. They'd lock him up here for extradition to their home world. But since the Rik trouble, the cells have been getting a lot more use."

"How long have you been here?"

Basher shut his mouth. He never shared information with the Rik, what was wrong with him? He silently took the first right and then led her down a flight of stairs into the processing area. To either side were one-way windows showing the first two containment rooms.

"Your things will be stored here," Basher told the girl. He

opened one of the small lockers and put her bag inside. "If you're really human, you'll get it back."

He surprised himself again. He hadn't meant to say that, and he certainly hadn't said it to anyone else.

"The lemur will have to go in a cage," he added.

"He can't stay with me?"

"No. Just put him right in here." Next to the lockers was a rack of cages and the bars were close enough together to keep the lemur inside. Alien pests were sometimes a problem on Selta, and if they couldn't be immediately identified, they had to be stored for a while. These cages were usually for that purpose, but they'd do for this animal as well.

"He'll be lonely," she said.

"He'll be fine, I'll—never mind. Just put him in the cage." He'd almost said that he would check on her pet.

"It's okay, Kit." She gently pried him off her shoulder and placed him in the cold cage.

Basher slammed the door before the lemur could jump out.

There were only four containment cells, and all were full or almost full now. The first cell only held five Rik, which was where he would put this girl. Those five were sitting cross-legged on the floor, in a line between the bunk beds.

"You'll go in here."

"Those are Rik? They aren't dangerous, are they?"

"Maybe you should have thought about that before attacking my partner. Now, go in." Basher did not want to get sucked into her charade any further.

She hesitated. "What's your name?"

He didn't answer. He wanted to shove her in the door, but he didn't want to touch her anymore if he could avoid it.

"My name is Claire Kindler." She offered her hand as if to shake his. "Maybe you can search the records and see when I was supposed to have died—"

"Get in," he repeated.

She dropped her hand, and he closed the door behind her as fast as he could.

Through the one-way glass, he watched her stand just inside the door, and he was relieved that she could not see him. He didn't want her to see that she'd shaken him.

She was watching the five Rik meditate on the floor with an uneasy expression. They didn't open their eyes or respond to her at all, and Claire was shifting her weight uncertainly from foot to foot. Finally, she moved, almost on tiptoe, to the closest bunk, and sank down on the bed.

She tucked her feet under her and rubbed her side as if in pain.

Could she really be human? The odds were very, very low, but maybe it was possible.

The Spo had taken precautions to make sure that the Rik never got a hold of any of their cadets. Each cadet class had a mentor who was personally responsible for the lives of their cadets, and if a cadet was lost—well, it would be a big deal. Most likely this girl was lying about being a cadet. Perhaps she had seen the recent videos of the trial featuring other kids her age with the Spo tattoo on their cheek. She'd tried to copy it, not knowing how distinctive it was.

And yet...

What if the girl *had* been a cadet and was sold to Faal? Basher couldn't even imagine that. Aliens still gave him nightmares on occasion, and he was a capable adult man who joined them of his own free will. How would it be to have no power, sold to some alien and completely cut off from Earth?

The girl looked up just then, staring at him, and Basher jumped.

No, he reminded himself, *she can't see me.* She was looking at her reflection in the mirror.

As he watched, her nostrils flared, and her eyes turned red. She bent her head down on her knees, and he could see the tears running down her cheeks. His hand was on the door before he got a grip on himself.

No. A Rik could cry as well as anyone, this wasn't proof of anything. Basher took his hand off the door. He needed some distance, fast.

His Spo partner was in the storage room, peering at the lemur thing. "I'm not certain where this comes from, but it is very appealing, no?"

Basher had yet to see any form of sentimentality from his partner, so this was a first. He paused to look in the cage again. "Didn't it bite you?"

"Yes, but I do not hold that against it. Survival is sanity."

"I guess," Basher said reluctantly, as the lemur stretched its hand out to him. Basher touched its six fingers gently and realized his own hand was still shaking. He quickly dropped it to his side, but he was sure his partner saw.

"Are you ready to greet the human delegation?" his partner asked. "They should be here in less than an hour. They've already arrived on Selta."

Basher hadn't been entirely honest with Claire when she asked about the cadets. They weren't here yet, but they were arriving at the embassy today. He'd have to ask them about her story.

13

CLAIRE LOOKED at her blurry reflection in the large mirror and wondered if she could have handled that differently. Was there any way she could have made that man believe her?

It had all happened so fast—fighting that Spo, seeing Faal, and then being arrested. She warily examined the small cell. The aliens—fakes, Rik, whatever they were called—sat side by side between the tightly packed bunk beds, knee to knee. They didn't move or open their eyes, and it was creepy. Hadn't they heard her come in? Was this some kind of séance?

There were four sets of bunk beds, two against each wall, and the only other furniture was a Spo toilet in an alcove—sleek and metallic and more like a pod than a bowl—in the back corner.

Claire perched on the nearest bed, trying to decide what to do when they finally talked to her. They might assume she was one of them—but would they turn on her when they realized she was human?

The five of them looked harmless enough, except for being a little too good-looking. There were three women in the group, and two of them had to be twins. They were beautiful Chinese women, late-twenties maybe, and the only discernible difference was the length of their hair. One had black silky hair to her waist and the other had it chopped off at her jaw line.

A plump, middle-aged woman sat next to them. Her blond hair was braided in a crown around her head.

Two guys sat on the end: a lanky academic-type and an athletic black guy.

As she watched, the tall, academic guy slowly lifted his head, peeked one eye open to check on the others, and then unashamedly winked at her.

The blonde woman seemed to be in charge, because she slapped her knees and in an operatic voice sang, "That is the end. The e-e-e-end."

Claire instinctively thought of the phrase her dad said about opera, "It's not over 'til the fat lady sings."

The woman rubbed her eyes and pushed herself to her feet. She wore a flowing black dress with spaghetti straps.

"Hello, newcomer," she said in a melodic voice. "Welcome to the Artists' Enclave."

"T-the what?"

"No, no. We agreed to call it the Progressive Performance Palace, remember?" said one of the twins.

"I," she said with emphasis, "agreed to no such thing."

The tall guy rolled his eyes. "Do let us have that whole argument again." He had a British accent. "Or we could find out who this is."

They turned to her and waited.

"My—my name is Claire."

"Claire. Yes, hmm. *Claaaire*," the opera woman drew the name out long, with vibrato. "A bit plain, isn't it? But I don't recognize you. What's your story? Were you one of the specialty transfers?"

"No." Claire knew this was a good opening to explain that she was not Rik, but she lost her nerve. "What about you?"

The opera lady curtsied. Actually, curtsied, with raised skirt and crossed ankles. "I'm a singer. You may remember me; I was the guest performer at the Supreme Director's last gala. I've chosen the name Diva."

Claire couldn't help but smile. She wondered if the woman even knew 'diva' was often used to describe someone full of herself or if she just thought it meant performer.

The black guy nodded to her, a short jerk of his thick neck, "I go by Athlete, for now. I haven't picked a name."

The tall guy rubbed his five-o'clock shadow and yawned again. "My name is Sage."

The long-haired twin came forward to look at Claire. "We're just called Young Twin and Old Twin. I'm not very creative."

Claire shook her head, starting to feel like she was in a surreal sort of circus. "Which one are you?"

"I'm Young Twin, of course. Old Twin is old enough to be my grandmother." The girl tilted her head, her shiny hair spilling over her shoulder. She peered into Claire's eyes. "You certainly got a pretty human. I love her eyes."

Claire stared at Young Twin's eyes as well, black and friendly, and realized how easy it would be to pretend these people were human. They were strange, and they weren't hiding what they were, but they were also utterly human. There was nothing in their appearance to disgust her.

"Crap. I've definitely fallen through the looking glass."

Sage waved his hand. "Ah, a Carroll reference. How deep does the rabbit hole go?" His scholarly, British accent almost made her smile.

"Sage is in charge of literary illusions," one of the twins said.

"Check out her tattoo," said Athlete. He'd walked to a bunk on her right, but now stepped closer, pointing to her cheek.

Young Twin came close again and reached out to touch the

tattoo. Claire forced herself to hold still while the girl stroked the tattoo with her fingertips.

"It's an excellent copy," Young Twin said. "The artistry is almost perfectly Spo, and the skin feels unchanged, as the Cross-point would perform it. It's excellent, really, except for being all wrong."

Claire closed her eyes for a second, savoring the skin-to-skin contact she'd craved.

"Didn't you know that you need the wrist tattoo to get past the Spo?" Sage asked her. "Yours looks like the cadet mark, and it was bound to get you arrested."

They all held out their left hands, palm up, to show their tattoos.

"I did the best I could with ours," Old Twin said, "but I only had cheap pigment and a low-res image to work with. Clearly it didn't get us far." She gestured to the cramped cell. "I wish I could get to whoever made yours. It's first rate. You could be human."

"I am human," Claire said slowly.

"Oh, that's very good," Diva said. "How do you get that moist look in your eye?" She turned to the twins. "I *am* human. I am *human.*"

Claire could almost see her eyes bulging as she tried to make them wet.

"No good," said Young Twin. "That's rubbish."

"You are all idiots," said Old Twin. "Clearly she's telling the truth."

Claire raised her hands defensively. "That's why I told you right away. I'm not trying to trick you or spy on you. But soon someone will figure out that I'm human and let me go. So... this is just temporary."

They looked fascinated. It was distinctly uncomfortable.

Old Twin turned away. "Yes, she's only the second wild

human we've met out here, but let's not start drooling. It doesn't make any difference to us that she's human."

"Um. It makes a big difference," Sage said.

"If she's a problem we'll smother her in her sleep," Old Twin said. "Simple."

There seemed to be a lot of eye gaze communication going on all of a sudden. Sage and Old Twin exchanged looks—perhaps they were the leaders?—and then seemed to meet the others' eyes in some sort of sequence.

Whatever was being said, it passed off without being verbalized. Diva lay back fluidly in her bed, Athlete began a set of push-ups, and Sage went to the toilet in the corner. He grabbed a square of toilet paper and blew his nose. The twins separated, one to a top bunk, the other, to the bottom bunk.

"Um. Wait," Claire said. "You're not really going to smother me in my sleep, are you? That wouldn't do you any good. I don't intend you any harm."

"Maybe we get a laugh out of killing," Old Twin said flatly.

"But—" Claire stopped. Maybe they *did* get a kick out of killing. Here they were in *human* bodies that they didn't even pretend were their own. They were all murderers, no matter how innocent they seemed.

Claustrophobic fears, both of locked spaces and hostile aliens, had been her companions for a long time. How stupid to think she'd escaped it.

"Old Twin is lying," Sage said, without heat. "We don't enjoy killing. At least, not that I know of. We haven't killed anyone." He threw his tissue in the trash bin. "Old Twin just likes to act like the monster everyone expects."

"I don't kid myself," Old Twin said from her bunk. "We *are* monsters, and we are capable of killing her."

"We won't though," Sage said to Claire. "We don't believe in killing humans."

Claire choked. "You don't *believe* in killing humans? You—you're in a human right now."

Sage grimaced. "Fair enough—but we weren't the ones who did that killing. Perhaps I should qualify: we don't believe in killing humans *anymore*."

Sage pulled a small notebook out from under his mattress and began writing in it with a pencil.

Surely she wouldn't be in here very long. Wouldn't the cop want to interrogate her, if he thought she was Rik?

The aliens were quiet, and Claire longed to lie down and sleep, but dared not. Her ribs throbbed from the blow she'd taken earlier, and she had nothing to take her mind off it except her companions.

Athlete had finished his set of push-ups and gone on to do several sets of lunges, sit-ups, and side presses. His rhythmic motion drew Claire's eyes, although she felt a little awkward watching him. She would have thought that knowing these people were aliens would make them *feel* alien, but she found herself enjoying the humanity of their presence, despite her distrust of them.

Sage was engaged with his notebook, occasionally smiling to himself.

Old Twin lay with her back to them all, and Young Twin fidgeted around on her bunk, sometimes watching Athlete, sometimes watching Claire.

"They don't give you a private bathroom, huh?" Claire asked eventually.

She laughed. "We're lucky they give us light and heat, let alone a separate loo."

"A loo?" Claire repeated. "Are you from England, too? I mean, not you, but..."

"Yes. Sage, myself, Old Twin, and Diva. Athlete is from Chicago."

"But you're not... really from there. Unless— that person is still alive in there?" It was a horrid idea, but she had no idea how their form of body stealing worked.

Sage spoke up. "No, they're completely gone. But I don't think we should talk about it with you. You'll either come to hate us more, or you'll get morbidly interested in the process. Neither is healthy, but both seem to be normal human reactions."

"That guy who brought me in, he's one of the ones who hates you?" Claire asked.

"Yes. His name is Basher. I don't blame him for the hatred, but it's not healthy for him. And it's not exactly a picnic for us, either. You don't seem to have developed that hatred however, and I can't imagine why."

"I guess I haven't had time," Claire said. "I only found out about the Rik recently. It hasn't sunk in yet."

"How is that possible? Everyone in the galaxy, beyond the borders of your closed world, knows that most of the "humans" they encounter are Rik. I'm surprised you weren't arrested long ago."

"I haven't been out and around, exactly."

"We don't want to know," Old Twin interrupted from her bunk. "We are not your friends, and you are not ours. The less said, the better."

"That was rude," Sage said.

She turned and gave him a significant glare. "She has no reason to trust us, and every reason to distrust us. As she *should*, yes?"

Sage looked troubled, and Claire almost felt sorry for him. But he nodded without looking Claire in the eye, and turned his back to her.

She must've dozed despite herself. She woke with her head pillowed uncomfortably on her raised knees, to the sound of her name whispered nearby. Her eyes were still closed, so she held the pose, pretending to be asleep.

"Claire needs to go. Don't be friendly. If she fears us, perhaps she'll do our work for us and be gone before nightfall."

"I know, I know," Sage whispered. His voice was far too near. "But she's human. She's interesting."

"Don't be interested. She shouldn't be here."

Oddly, what discomposed Claire the most was hearing them use her name. How long had it been since anyone used her name? To the zookeeper and Faal she'd been *the human,* to those on *Final Say* she'd been another anonymous bruck.

But her name wasn't the point. It sounded like Old Twin wanted to be rid of her, and she was warning Sage not to be friendly. Strange, but not surprising...

"She's awake," Diva said softly.

Claire's eyes flew open. Diva's face was barely an inch away from hers.

"I knew because your breathing changed," Diva whispered happily. There were flecks of green in her blue eyes. "I think we should keep her. Who better to teach us how to be human?"

14

BASHER ENTERED the reception hall of the embassy through a rear door. The cadets had already arrived, and they were somewhat dwarfed by the nine Spo greeting them.

The reception hall was a large room with a vaulted ceiling and something few Seltan compounds had—skylights. The skylights brought in three solitary beams of natural light, a rare luxury on Selta. The Spo had paid a small fortune to connect to the surface from their embassy. Like in ancient Mayan temples, mirrors were used to bounce light down long shafts until it reached this room. Each of the skylights was surrounded by three rings of copper suspended from the ceiling. There were nine rings altogether to represent Spo mainspace—their nine-system home territory. The rest of the room was almost bare, to draw the eyes upward to this display.

Basher moved forward to greet the guests, and they immediately shifted toward him. He knew how they felt. When you're surrounded by aliens, the sight of human movement immediately draws your eyes. He recognized the two from the trial video, but not the other girl. Perhaps she was another cadet, although she didn't have the facial tattoo.

"Welcome to Selta," he said. "I'm Bashar Kapur. It's good to meet you."

"Natsuki Fujimara—but you can call me Nat." She shook his hand with a smile. She was a beautiful girl, but she looked somewhat haggard—as if she could use a few weeks of good sleep and good food. Her glasses emphasized the size of her eyes, which made her look almost gaunt.

"And I'm Sam Locklear." The young man gave Basher a strong handshake, but like Nat, he looked stressed.

Basher was more than a little curious to meet them both. He'd watched a recording of the trial, along with all the Spo security guys, and he'd been impressed with Sam's handling of the trial. There were rumors that Sam had even manipulated the Spo emperor into a corner. That, of course, was *not* televised, but Basher would've paid good money to see it.

On the other hand, Basher thought Sam's bargain with the Rik was a terrible idea. He understood the kid's motivation, but Basher had spent a lot of time tracking these Rik down, possibly more than any other human. He knew they couldn't be trusted. Frankly, he hadn't been at all surprised to hear that the Rik were suspected of the explosion at the space station.

The blonde woman looked better rested and better dressed than either Sam or Nat, and she was grinning brightly. "Hi! I'm Shara. I understand you're helping the Spo catch Rik criminals out here. They must think highly of you."

She held the handshake a little too long and Basher slid his hand away. "Thanks. It's a pleasure to meet you."

The embassy librarian stepped forward to speak next. He was called the librarian, anyway, but as far as Basher could tell his job was usually a mix of butler and janitor. He looked happy to be part of the welcoming ceremony.

"First, allow us to present you with your own personal tokens for the duration of your stay in the Spo embassy."

He held forth three glass containers, each the size of a jewelry box. The Spo specialized in glass art, perhaps because they came from such a sandy planet. Basher had one of those boxes himself.

The Spo explained, "These are made on the southernmost continent of our home planet. The black sand there is used to create this gray glass, which is then shaped by hand to form these containers. Please accept them as a gift with our compliments."

Sam and Nat bowed appropriately at this pause, and Shara hurried to follow suit.

"If you would now open the box, you will find your ID token," the librarian continued. "These may be used to open any exterior door of the embassy, when you should wish to depart or return. It can also be used to lock the door of your personal quarters. Each token is distinctive to its owner, and when you lock your door with it, no one but security can open it."

They all bowed again. The tokens were about the size of a walnut, but cubed. Basher's own token was cheap plastic, but these shone like titanium. Apparently they got the special version.

Nat looked inside the box at the words inscribed in the lid.

"Behold, I own the door," she read.

"Yes, it is a line from one of our famous poems," the librarian explained.

Nat nodded. "I've read it. *There the warrior through the night, Devoured the enemy, even'd the score.*"

"You've studied the writing of So'omat?" the librarian asked. He flushed violet with surprise and pleasure.

"He was one of my favorites of the Spo poets," Nat said.

At that point, the librarian would have whisked Nat off to the library—the poor guy seemed ecstatic to find someone who appreciated Spo literature—but Basher intervened.

"Perhaps she could arrange to meet you at the library tomorrow. For now, they are scheduled to settle into their rooms and receive a tour."

He led them away out of the reception hall. "I under-stand we'll be investigating the possible terrorists that bombed the space station. I'm afraid I don't have any leads yet. Faal of Merith II has already offered his assistance, but I might've made an enemy of him after that." Basher's eyes drifted to the tattoo on Sam's face, and he couldn't help examining it for a moment. "Sorry for staring. I've just seen another of these."

There were hundreds of tattoo variants for the cadets, but this one was nearly identical to hers.

AKEMI LOOKED AROUND THEIR SUITE, through Sam and Nat's glasses.

Hm. Very posh.

Bashar led them down another stairway after they left their things. "If you'll come down to the containment level, I'd like to get your opinion on something."

He's hot, Akemi noted. *I mean, I know Sam's your type, but if I was ten years older (and corporeal) I'd be into this guy.*

Nat choked. "Excuse me, Bashar. What were you saying?"

He smiled, though it looked a little forced to Akemi. "I can explain down there. I usually go by Basher, by the way."

"A Spo nickname?" Nat asked.

"No, a human one, actually. I grew up in Boston and got into more than a few fist fights. At some point in junior high, Bashar became Basher."

Yeah, I like him.

The first part of the tour was dominated by Shara's endless questions and comments, but Akemi was amused to see that Basher was too distracted to notice how Shara was trying to attract his attention.

Sam went to one of the windows, looking at the Rik inside.

This group looked nearly military in their similarity. "They can't see us?"

"No, it's a one-way mirror, imported from Earth. The Spo love them."

"What are they saying?"

Basher went to the wall and flipped a switch.

"—that's no use. You should never—" The Rik looked toward the mirror and shrugged. "Never mind."

"They know when you're listening?" Sam asked.

"Yep. They all have an impressive sense of surveillance. They know when they're being recorded, too." He turned the switch off and the Rik inside flipped him off with a middle finger and a smile.

Yikes, that's disturbingly human, Akemi said.

Nat stepped back instinctively.

"They can't see you," Basher reminded her. "They know we're here, but they can't see us. I'd really like you to look at this other group."

He brought them to the next detention room, and Akemi had a shock. There was a girl in the room with a cadet tattoo on her cheek.

"A cadet?" Sam said. "Is this what you were talking about?"

"Who is she?" Nat asked.

Basher rubbed his mouth uncertainly. "She says her name is Claire Kindler and that one of the Spo sold her to Faal. She seems to think they faked her death."

Akemi began to rifle through the Spo databases in her records, looking at pictures of each of the cadets.

"Why do you think she's a Rik?" Sam asked.

Basher ticked off the list on his fingers, "She attacked my partner to help another Rik escape. She confessed to smuggling a stolen animal off Merith II. And Faal seems pretty confident she's Rik. But...you're the cadets. Is it possible she's not lying?"

Akemi found the file.

Here it is.

Claire Kindler, Spo cadet from Florida. Akemi skipped the less important data. *It says she died in training about three years after she got there.*

The image in the file was definitely a younger version of the girl in the cell. She looked healthier in the picture, plump and smiling.

Now she sat on a lower bunk, arms wrapped around her knees, watching the other Rik in turn. She wore a badly-fitted uniform that looked as if it had been cut down from a Merith outfit and was now ripped across one shoulder.

"So, what do you think?" Sam said. "Did she get sold to a Merith?"

Basher looked puzzled. "That's what I'm asking you."

"Oh, no, I wasn't talking to you." Sam tapped his glasses. "These are... smart glasses. I'm looking up her info. She was a cadet at one time, we know that much."

"Could the Rik have turned her after that?" Basher said.

"No, no chance." Shara said.

"Are you sure? Assuming the Rik managed to fake her death and get her away from the cadet facilities, what's to stop them taking her body then?" Basher argued.

Nat took a deep breath and pressed her fingers against the glass, as if she needed a physical reminder of her location. "The Rik tried to turn me, just a few months ago. It nearly killed me, but it didn't work." She adjusted her glasses. "The reason it didn't work was because the Spo inject cadets with a nanotechnology that subtly changes our memory mapping. If it has a few months to set, it protects us from the Rik process."

Basher frowned. "My partner didn't tell me that. He thought she could very well be Rik."

"He might not know about it. The Spo were keeping it a big

secret. They didn't want the Rik to know they had an inoculation. Plus, like I said, it takes months to set—I think they're trying to improve it." Nat rubbed her forehead. "I still get headaches from the Rik attempt on me. Believe me, that inoculation works."

Shara's grin had faded.

"When did this girl end up in the cadet program?" Sam asked Akemi.

Looks like...roughly a year after you and Nat. She was in the third wave of cadets.

Sam pondered. "So she left Earth about six years ago and at least a couple of those years she spent with the Spo cadets. Then we have a death certificate, although clearly she's alive. Perhaps she wasn't inoculated before the Rik stole her? But then that raises another question: how would they steal her from the training facility on the Spo planet? That's not easy."

Basher was starting to feel uneasy also. If there was the slightest chance she was human, she deserved protection. "If she was inoculated, you're telling me there's no way the Rik could get around it?"

"No," Nat said flatly. "If they'd had any experience turning a cadet, they would have succeeded with me." Sam put his arm around her.

"She *says* she's human, but Rik often stick to their story for days, so I didn't set much store by that," Basher said.

"What does Faal say?"

"I'm not a fan of his," Basher admitted, "but he hasn't given me any real reason to distrust him." Basher tried to remember the exact words of their conversation. "He said she was a thief and a fake; that she'd stolen from him and injured him. Wouldn't he be more discreet if he basically enslaved her?"

"Not necessarily," Sam said. "The Merith have a history of slavery and servitude. He may not think it matters that much even if she is human."

Basher frowned. "That's true. Well, I'll administer the blood test, then we should know for sure. It's still developmental, but the Spo have given us the go-ahead to try it out on all the fakes we catch."

"Wait. There's a blood test?" Shara demanded.

"Of course, the Spo *would* keep it a secret." Sam rolled his eyes. "So why are you conflicted about this? Just test her."

"The blood test is unproven on humans," Basher explained. "The drug cocktail, as far I understand it, indicates if someone's carried the Rik nanotech in their blood." He grimaced. "If she *is* a Rik, the residue in her blood will neutralize the drug."

Nat frowned. "So... if she's *not* a Rik, what happens?"

"It hasn't happened yet, and I'm no biologist," Basher said. "But they tell me a true human would get 'mild blood poisoning.'"

"What idiot designed it that way?" Sam asked. "Couldn't they have done it backwards so only the Rik got sick?"

"Beats me," Basher sighed. "It is kind of a witch-hunt, isn't it? Only the innocent suffer."

Shara looked a little confused.

"A witch-hunt—you know, in medieval Europe they'd throw a woman into a lake, tied up. If she sank, she was innocent. Much good it did her," Nat said.

"So, you've got to throw her in the lake?" Shara said.

I don't think blood poisoning CAN be mild, Akemi said.

Nat repeated this, and Basher frowned. "If she reacts, it should take hold sometime early tomorrow morning. I'll keep an eye on her."

8-12 hours, Akemi confirmed. Nat relayed it.

Basher gestured to Sam's glasses. "Do you have any more of these? They seem really handy."

Tell him YES! Akemi shouted at Sam and Nat. *He can have the extra ones that Senator Fontley didn't want.*

She loved Sam and Nat both, and Shara was great, but Akemi was dying for another pair of eyes and somebody else to talk to.

Nat caved in. "We have an extra pair in our suite. I should probably explain how they work. It's—er—not exactly a normal AI situation."

15

BASHER SQUELCHED the impulse to give Claire a hand as she scooted off the lower bunk. "Wait at the door," he said. "You have to be handcuffed when you're not in the cell."

She obediently stood still, but the muscles in her neck were stiff with tension while his Spo partner held her wrists to secure the handcuffs.

In the medical room were two cot-like hospital beds, the standard blood pressure cuff on the wall, and syringes on the counter. A large EKG machine lurked in the back, part of a failed experiment to find another way to tell fakes from humans.

"It's all so... Earthly," Claire said. "I thought this was a Spo facility."

"We deal with a lot of Rik," Basher said. "We've imported standard hospital supplies." He waited by the door while his partner had Claire sit on a cot.

"I'm—sorry I interfered," Claire told his partner. "I didn't understand that you were chasing a Rik woman. I thought she was human."

He didn't respond to that, only removed an electronic pad from the cabinet and hit a couple buttons. "First, you will be fingerprinted. Right thumb," he said.

Claire pressed her thumb to the screen, and it gave slightly. The swirls of her print showed briefly orange against the black background, then it was gone. While his partner got the rest of her fingerprints, he entered her information into his tablet. "Full name?"

"Claire Elizabeth Kindler."

"Age?"

"Twenty, I think. The Spo took me about six years ago, during my 8th grade year."

"Birthday?"

"June 11."

Basher swallowed. That fit with the data Sam and Nat had found. "Then yeah, you'd be twenty."

"How can I prove I'm not an alien?" she blurted out. "Can't you look for a slit in my neck or a parasite in my stomach or something? That must be what all this is for." She gestured to the EKG.

Basher narrowed his eyes. Wouldn't she know how the Rik turned people? It was a combination of nanotechnology inserted into the spine like an epidural, and electro-patterning. The only visible mark was the injection site on the back, and the Rik had quickly learned to erase that tiny mark.

Basher didn't realize he was lost in thought, until his partner repeated, "Basher, are you going to finish the questions?"

"Basher," Claire said. "That's an odd name."

"From Bashar. It's a nickname." While he switched to his note-taking app, his partner had Claire turn around and raised her shirt to examine her lower back.

"No obvious scar," he said, and Basher dutifully recorded it.

"Some bruising of the mid-section," his partner added. "I did that."

She pulled her shirt down and turned around defiantly. "At least I apologized."

"I have nothing to apologize for," his partner returned. "You are also malnourished. We will give you a vitamin injection."

This was part of their script, and it jolted Basher back to his duties. The standard procedure was to tell the subject that the blood test was merely a vitamin injection.

"It should improve your health in the next few days," his partner continued.

When they'd first run this test, they'd made the mistake of explaining what it was for. Basher had to endure hours of fakes pretending to be deathly ill. A few had even managed to work themselves into a light fever. It had been clear they were pretending, but the resulting red tape to prove the results weren't accurate had taken forever.

Now they simply told the fakes it was a vitamin shot. Basher noticed Claire rubbing her thumbnail, and noted that it was rippled oddly. She probably *was* malnourished; a lack of vitamins would do that to her fingernails.

He cleared his throat. It was also standard to ask a series of questions that Rik usually got wildly wrong. "Where were you born?"

"Pensacola, Florida."

"How much land did your parents own?"

"Um." Claire watched the Spo fill the syringe. "We just lived in a regular neighborhood. It was a two-bedroom house with a big back yard."

"How did you get to school?"

"Mostly my dad took me on his way to work. I took the bus home. My dad worked for the park service, so he took me out in his motorboat on the lakes sometimes, too."

Basher took quick notes. Was his partner moving in slow motion with that syringe?

"How did you get off Earth?"

"I told you, the Spo took me for their cadet program. I was

there for several years, and then one of the Spo sold me to the Merith you met today. There were two of us, sort of. The other girl died."

"What was her name?"

"Jenelle Johnson."

The Spo tapped the syringe.

"What's your favorite book?" Basher asked.

"For heaven's sake, does that matter?" she snapped.

"Just answer the question."

"Uhh—I liked mysteries. Sometimes fantasy. I haven't really kept up with the bestseller lists recently."

The Spo brought the syringe to her and stuck it in her arm without preamble.

"Favorite food," Basher said.

Claire tore her eyes away from the needle and looked at Basher. "Do the aliens not know this stuff, or what? Because I can tell you anything you want to know. When I was little my favorite food was macaroni and cheese. Later, I loved tacos and my dad's shrimp gumbo." She winced as the thick serum was injected. "Every year on my birthday my parents would take me to Disneyworld in Orlando, and we'd stay with my grandparents there. My grandma would make tapioca pudding which I also loved. When the Spo sold me, I had just eaten something that tasted like onions, and I had a bad taste in my mouth for days."

His partner finally removed the syringe and pressed a bandage to her arm.

Basher nodded. "If you are human, I'll apologize in the morning."

"In the morning?" she asked.

His partner put the syringe into a plastic disposal bag on the counter. "Figure of speech," he said, with a curious glance at Basher, obviously wondering why he'd almost told her the truth.

Basher tried to regain his professional footing. "On the other hand, if the judicial paperwork goes in his favor, Faal might be allowed to collect you tomorrow."

Basher felt bad threatening her, but he ignored his impulse to take it back. He needed to distract her from his slip of the tongue about tomorrow morning. If she *was* human, he would never let Faal near her. He would protect her as if she was one of his sisters.

"Can I at least have another room while you make up your mind about me?" Claire asked. "Those Rik don't want me in their cell. *They* know I'm human, and they were talking about me while I was sleeping. One of them said something about not having me in there tonight. I don't know why, but I really don't want to find out. See, I'm telling you the truth. I'm on your side."

"There are no other empty containment rooms," Basher said. "Or I would consider it."

"Well, who's in the other ones? I've shared cages before, just not with people who might kill me."

Basher paused at the first row of containment rooms. "This cell contains normal Spo criminals who are under arrest for everything from petty theft to assault. I wouldn't go in there if I was you."

Spo changed colors like chameleons, showing their emotion; and this room was a watercolor of frustration and barely controlled aggression. No way would Basher allow her in there.

The other room looked empty.

"How about that one?" she asked.

"Look at the ceiling."

"Are those... sentient?" Claire gasped. "They look like giant wasps."

"Not sentient. They're native to the Spo planet, and we aren't sure how they got here. Perhaps they stowed away in a cargo hold, like rats on a ship. We've been rounding them up, but we didn't have a large enough cage for them."

"Why don't you just kill them? I would."

"Just between us, I would too—" Basher caught himself on the expression, and he gestured curtly for her to keep walking. "They're endangered on Spo. We're not allowed to kill them."

In the next section, there were also two rooms—the one with the Rik she'd been with, and another room with Rik.

Basher watched her look back and forth, a guarded expression on her face.

"I don't care what you do," he said, untruthfully, "but I'd suggest your previous cell. They're unpredictable, no doubt, but I've never seen them fighting. I can't say the same for these." He jerked a thumb at a military-looking crew of Rik in the other room.

Claire sighed. "Will you at least check on me tonight? Or, I mean, maybe not *you*... But could you have someone come by and make sure they haven't killed me in my sleep?"

"I'll tell the night guard to keep an eyestalk out for you." Basher took two steps back and opened the door to her cell. "In you go."

16

CLAIRE FELT a rush of air as Basher slammed the door behind her. For a moment she'd felt like they were having a real conversation, but then he'd pulled back. Maybe she'd forgotten how to make a connection with people.

"Welcome back," Young Twin said. "They're about to bring us dinner. Are you hungry?"

Claire nodded, then shook her head. "I don't know." All she knew was that Basher still didn't believe her, and she had no way of knowing if he ever would.

These Rik, most of them anyway, were being perfectly friendly. She felt the danger of succumbing to it—of forgetting they were fiends, not friends. She'd told Basher she was afraid that they'd kill her in her sleep. But her greater fear was that she'd connect with *them*. She'd felt Young Twin's fingers on her cheek, and she'd desperately wanted to resist that with something real. She felt herself slipping down the slope.

"I know some of you don't want me in your cell tonight," Claire said, "but you're just going to have to deal with it. Basher is going to make sure the night guard keeps an eye on me. So, you shouldn't try anything."

This maybe wasn't wise, but she felt the need to distance

herself from them. They started doing that eye gaze thing again, and Claire snapped, "Stop that! I can see what you're doing, you know. It's not subtle."

There was shocked silence.

"It isn't?" Diva said. "How disappointing."

"Basher was right. You're all crazy."

"Not crazy," Diva said. "Just, not human."

"Not human," they all muttered, like a too-often repeated prayer.

Young Twin broke the uncomfortable silence. "You might as well lie down. We're not going to hurt you."

An hour later they were fed dinner, and the Rik gathered together to eat. Their knees bumped in the narrow walkway between bunk beds as they found spots.

Claire sat a little apart and awkwardly held a small food box in her lap. Sage had passed it to her with a slight smile when it was delivered.

When she cracked the lid, Claire smelled something amazing. She dug in with the spork and pulled out pasta with tomato sauce. Human food! It looked like a recently frozen meal, probably shipped here in bulk, and Claire was thrilled.

Faal had fed her the occasional human "delicacy" he'd imported, like canned corn or crackers, but generally she ate an oatmeal-like mush that was appropriate for carbon/water species like her. On the Diadina's ship she'd eaten better, but it wasn't human food.

Claire closed her eyes and savored the taste. It was a Tuesday night dinner with her mom in front of a movie. It was leftover lunch after church on a lazy Sunday afternoon. Tears filled her eyes.

"That's incredible," Diva said. "So sincere."

"The neocortex handles the sensory input, but it also connects to the emotional center of the brain," Sage explained.

Claire opened her eyes, her nostalgic moment ruined. "Are you talking about me?"

Clearly, they were. They all sat there with their food boxes untouched on their laps, watching her cry over her food.

"We've had very little chance to observe humans in natural settings," Sage explained. "What with one thing and another."

"Well, don't observe me. I'm not here for your amusement."

Sage looked hurt and Claire told herself she didn't care as she sat back on her bed, putting her back to them as best she could.

Then Diva said in her melodic voice, "Thank you for this food and bless it to our bodies. Amen."

"Amen," they all repeated.

Claire choked on her food. She coughed for a moment, but Sage offered her a bottle of water. A long drink helped. "Okay, I have to ask. What's that about? Who were you praying to?"

"The food," Athlete said.

"A spirit," Diva said at the same time.

"Our cells," Sage said.

"Nobody," Old Twin said.

They all looked at each other.

"Hmm. We've never discussed it before," Sage said. "I just assumed we agreed..."

"Why would you pray at all, though?" Claire asked. "Who taught you?"

"No one taught us," Sage explained. "We watched observational videos taken by Rik field agents. The ones already on Earth, you see. This is the human custom before meals, yes? An imprecation to remember the value of sustenance in a society removed from the primary role of food production..."

"Oh, stop him," Young Twin said. "He'll go on and on about human psychology. The fact is: we don't know why you do it, but we want to be human, so we do it."

Athlete opened his carton. "I really don't care, I'm hungry."

"I care," Diva said. "I think humans are praying to their Creator Spirit, like the Crosspoint do. Isn't that it, Claire?"

"That's the closest answer, I guess. Not all humans pray though, not by a long shot. And not all those who pray are thinking of the same god." Claire ate a few more bites. "The Crosspoint pray? That's interesting."

"Every species has a subset that believe in some sort of deity," Sage started, happily seizing the chance to explain something. "The Crosspoint are one of the only species who actively recruit... or, what's the word... evangelize? Some people estimate that half the galaxy believes in the Crosspoint god."

"Hmmm. What's their god like?" Claire asked. Her stomach was starting to feel queasy, and she stirred her food slowly.

"Dangerous," Athlete said.

"Loving," Diva said.

"Controlling," Sage said.

They looked at each other. "Clearly that's another thing we haven't discussed," Sage said. "You are so good for us."

When Claire stopped eating, with half her food still in the container, she curled up on the bed and fell asleep. And when she woke up, the room was darker, lit only by green runner lights along the edges of the floor.

"He'll be here any minute," Diva said, not even attempting to whisper. "We need to wake her up."

"I'm awake," Claire said groggily. Her face was hot, but her body was cold. "I don't feel good."

"We have a problem," Sage said. "We're escaping tonight."

"What?"

"One of the night guards is going to get us out of here, he's been paid. He'll be here in less than half an hour."

Claire forced herself upright. "That's why you didn't want me here?"

Old Twin hissed, "Turn your face away from the window. Just in case."

Claire stared at her. "Why would I care if you got caught? I'm not Rik."

Sage put a hand on her shoulder, and Claire jerked away from him. "Don't touch me."

"Sorry!" he said. "Look, I know humans have every reason to hate the Rik, but we didn't choose this. We're not evil. We were chosen for our cultural success; we're not assassins or soldiers. Diva was a singer, actually, and..."

"Yes, yes. You're all celebrities or something, I get it," Claire said crossly. "But I still don't care if you get caught. I've got my own problems to deal with."

"Clearly," Sage said.

"I don't just mean *this*. Faal of Merith II is claiming I stole from him."

Sage's eyebrows were almost in his hair. "You do have problems. *Did* you steal from him?"

"Technically, yes." Claire pressed her fingers into her scalp. "I know."

"Perhaps we can help each other. You see... we can't have you hanging around, watching us escape and ratting out our contact. And you can't wait here to be given back to Faal."

"So?"

"So, come with us."

The room stilled. Then Old Twin slapped the back of Sage's head. "What's the matter with you?"

They engaged in a furious whisper war, while Claire considered his offer. Her choices were bad either way. If she stayed, she could be returned to Faal anytime. Perhaps Basher would come to believe that she was human and protect her... But perhaps he wouldn't have time.

If she escaped with the Rik, Basher would be completely

convinced that she wasn't human, but she could get far away from Faal. If only there was some way to prove she was human *now*.

Claire took a deep breath. Her options were bad, but that was life. 'Life is not cake and choices are not candy,' her mom used to say.

"I'll go," Claire told him.

"Excellent!" Sage looked genuinely pleased and raised a hand, as if to pat her on the shoulder again, but then he remembered and put it down. "Here's the plan..."

Old Twin retired to her bunk, furious, but she didn't fight with him anymore. Claire wondered briefly what Sage's position had been and why he was one of these dispossessed Rik.

Anyway, the plan was simple. Sage had a friend on Lower Selta who was willing to employ him and the four others. This employer was willing to put up the money for their escape, in return for twelve months of service. After that, the Rik would be free to stay or go as they chose. If they stayed, they would be paid fair wages.

"What kind of work?" Claire asked dubiously.

"I believe it's a restaurant. A high-class café where they serve Human."

"They eat *humans*?"

Sage burst out laughing and Claire immediately realized what he meant. "Oh. You mean they serve human food?"

"Yes, of course. The owner wants human servers to make it more exotic, and apparently there aren't a lot of humans around. So, he decided Rik will do."

"Sounds simple," Claire said.

"It is simple."

Claire felt a surge of nausea and beat it back. "Escape is *never* simple."

17

CLAIRE CURSED HER CORRECTNESS. The guard came at midnight, as planned (a ridiculous time to escape, in Claire's opinion), but he had no intention of helping a sixth person escape. He'd gotten no money for her.

"You'll just leave me here to tell on you?" Claire's head was pounding, and she was beginning to shiver.

"No, I'll kill you," the guard said coldly. "They will think the Rik murdered you before they left."

Sage looked from her to the guard, mouth hard. Suddenly he stooped and grabbed the Spo's hand. He used one of the guard's claws to cut a thin line on his own hand.

Claire and the others gasped. The guard jerked his hand away.

"Here. The Spo like blood promises, right? I promise you, you will be paid for her." Sage offered his hand to the guard.

The guard looked at Sage suspiciously, but finally took his hand, smearing the blood. "A Spo promise I will accept. But if I don't receive payment in a week, your employer will regret it. I may not know his name, but I know how to find him."

The guard brought out tools. "This is how you escaped," he

said shortly. He had Athlete use the tools to break open the inside of the cell door and the panel next to it.

Claire followed the Rik into the hallway. It was almost pitch black and she kept a hand against the wall to keep her bearings.

The Spo guard led them without hesitation. An orange light on his belt was the only bit Claire could see. They passed the medical quarters where she'd been questioned earlier, and Claire rubbed her injection spot. It was starting to itch, and she was pretty sure she had a high fever. Had they truly given her a vitamin injection?

They passed a large desk, and a pair of rectangular glasses reflected the low light.

"Come on," Sage whispered.

"One sec!" She put the glasses on. Smart glasses were becoming all the rage just before the Hadron event. They could automatically adjust their focal point as your vision got worse or better. Was there any chance these might work for her?

She didn't have terrible eyesight, thank heaven, but she was far-sighted. She'd been without glasses for so long she was completely used to a bit of foreground fuzziness, but this might be her last chance to score a pair of glasses for a very long time.

They were nice glasses, Ray-Ban, and she wondered where they'd come from. At first, she still couldn't see anything (the hall was so dark) but she blinked and stumbled after the others. A dot began to flash on the center of each lens.

Adjusting Depth of Field.

Please Wait.

The words appeared in light green and looked as if they were hovering a foot in front of her, in thin air.

The dot began to flash and then disappeared.

Vision: Optical shortening

Adjusting Right Lens +2.5,

Adjusting Left Lens +3.0

"Yes!" Though still dark, so many details were suddenly visible to Claire. She could see the edges of the papers on the desk, the outline of doors, and the impatience in everyone's eyes.

"Sorry! I'm coming."

Sage looked dubious. "I don't know if you should take those. What if they have a tracker in them?"

"Like GPS? I doubt it. They're made on Earth. They wouldn't be calibrated to Selta, would they?"

"Probably not, but we should be sure—"

"Take them or leave them but we must keep going," the guard said.

"I'm taking them. I'm sick of blurriness."

The guard guided them to a set of stairs. "This is where you go alone." He handed a token to Sage. It was a tiny electronic cube, the size of a key fob. Basher had used one like it when he brought her into the embassy.

"Interior doors will unlock for you, but only one exterior door. It will lead you to the Observation Deck under the lower level of the embassy. Go to the third down-spinner east, and slip down ten levels." He gave them directions. "If you are caught, I will deny all this."

He paused, and in the dim light she saw the guard's eyestalks twitch toward Sage. "You owe me for her. If I don't receive payment within the week... you will owe." He shuffled away on his four legs and Claire wondered briefly how he was going to get away with this. Surely he would be suspected?

Claire didn't have long to ponder. Young Twin put a hand on her back to push her toward the stairs.

They went down in a single-file, trying to be quiet in the dark stairwell.

"Don't the Spo believe in exit lights?" Claire grumbled.

Sage shook his head without looking back. "They have excellent night vision."

Claire began to shiver as they descended the long flight of stairs. By the time they reached the bottom her teeth were chattering. "Is it r-really cold in here?"

Temperature: 78 Degrees F, 29 Degrees C.

The words appeared on her glasses.

"No, it's not cold." Diva caught her arm when she stumbled on the last step and would have fallen to the ground.

She felt a hand on her forehead.

"It works!" Diva said. "I can feel that she is very hot. She must be ill. How interesting."

"Another time it would be interesting. Not now!" Athlete hissed.

They began to go down the last hall. Sage whispered that they were almost to the door, but Claire jerked to a stop. "I forgot! I can't believe it. I forgot to get Kit."

Sage's hand was on her arm, he was dragging her forward. "I'm sorry, but we can't go back."

"But—but—Basher will give him back to Faal. I've got to go get him!"

Sage was still pulling. "More guards will be coming any moment."

The silence following his words was broken by the sound of a door opening at the end of the hall, behind them. Claire opened her mouth, but Sage clapped a hand over it. Old Twin opened a door, and they crowded into a tiny room. Sage released Claire and silently pulled the door shut behind them.

The closet smelled more than ordinarily of bleach. Must be a janitor's room, Claire thought, stifling the urge to cough. There was barely room for them all. She found herself pressed against a wall, squashed between Sage and Athlete.

Sage twisted to face her, and she could feel every motion he made. "Just stay still," he whispered, his breath on her face. She could feel Athlete's bulk, solid on her left, trapping her between them.

Despite her climbing fever and clenching stomach, she had a moment of clarity.

I am surrounded by aliens. Have I gone mad? I'm leaving the only real human I've seen in three years to join these Rik. And I only have their word for it that they won't desert me or kill me or sell me for money...

Claire could hear footsteps in the hall as someone passed their hiding place. She almost screamed. She took a deep breath and opened her mouth, but Sage felt it. He leaned his forehead against hers.

"Trust us. Trust *me*. Please."

If he'd put his hand over her mouth again, she would have done it. She would have screamed and gotten them all caught. But his simple words, 'trust me,' made her pause. She felt the coolness of his forehead against her feverish one and wished it didn't matter.

Then the guard was gone, and her feverish mind skipped a few beats. They got to the end of the hall, where Sage expertly pressed the token to the correct spot on a large door. The double panels unlocked with an audible *thunk*.

Sage jerked the doors open and blue light spilled across his handsome face. "Let's get away from here. Quickly."

AKEMI WAS SLEEPING when the new glasses came online. Her sleep mode was interrupted with a data dump from the new glasses. They'd automatically calibrated with the built-in software when they'd detected sustained body heat. Now the particulars of the calibration popped up, plus the current speed, time, and temp, along with the camera view from the left lens.

Akemi gave a mental yawn. It was fine with her if Basher wanted to try on his glasses now, but if she'd known, she would have waited to sleep until he was done. She was always groggy when she woke up. That part of her teenage self was still very much the same.

Basher was going out a door now, out of the embassy, with several others. He turned and looked back and—*what?*

Those were Rik! Akemi was wide awake now.

Basher. What are you doing? she sent.

"Shoot." It was an uncertain girl's voice, hoarse and low pitched. "My glasses are saying something to me. Or uh, to Basher."

"Trash them."

"I don't want to. I'm sick of not having glasses."

In a blink, Akemi understood the gist of what was happening, and was sending alerts to Sam and Nat. That cadet girl, the one they weren't sure about, had escaped with the Rik.

But of course, Sam and Nat were asleep. Akemi brought out the worst curse word she could think of (it wasn't very bad) and tried to think what to do. It was so *stupid* that she couldn't alert anyone to what was happening.

"You can't endanger us all," one of the Rik was saying. "Give me the glasses."

Akemi thought fast. Claire wanted these glasses, but the others were scared. She had to convince them the glasses were harmless.

Akemi needed to act dumb. Quickly.

If this is another user, please speak your name.

Or say Menu Options.

"If you can't turn it off in the next thirty seconds, they're gone," the Rik warned her.

"Menu options," Claire stuttered.

Smart mode

Simple mode

Turn off access

"Turn off access," the girl said. "There, I did it. We can go."

"Are you sure?"

Akemi made the letters fade slowly to nothing.

Shutting down now

Squeeze nose piece to power on

Then she waited, tensely.

"I've turned it off, really." Claire tripped on something and staggered a few steps before regaining her balance.

One of the Rik steadied her and touched her face. "She really is burning up."

Akemi felt a surge of fear. She checked Claire's temperature and found that it was nearly six degrees higher than it should be.

She was reacting to the blood test. She must be human.

Akemi cursed her isolated state with renewed vigor. She'd been upset that these Rik were escaping, but it was nothing to how she felt knowing they were escaping and taking a *human* with them. With every step, Claire went further away from the embassy, further away from help.

Akemi didn't exactly hate the Rik as a species, despite what they'd done to her, but she would never trust them. It killed her to see this girl fooled into following them. And *why* were they taking her with them? In Akemi's experience, the answers were never good.

Akemi could play the dumb glasses role to spy on the Rik, but she'd willingly break her pretense to save Claire. But what could Akemi say that would convince Claire fast enough? As soon as she said a thing, the Rik would toss the glasses and run. Even worse, if Akemi somehow got Claire to reconsider, would the Rik *let* her go back?

Akemi writhed in frustration and indecision. She had been in a tiny cell with her sister when four Rik scientists tried to take

Nat's body. They'd expected the transfer to go quickly and smoothly.

It hadn't.

Akemi had woken to the sound of Nat's screams, as the nanotech attacked her brain and the remapping of the Spo inoculation confused and thwarted their electronic mission. Nat's mind had been a battleground, and it had nearly killed her. Nat had clawed at her own arms, as if trying to tear her own skin off. She'd convulsed so violently she fell off onto the floor, and Akemi, in her weakened state, couldn't even hold Nat's head in her lap.

Akemi's own body had been in the midst of rejecting a new lung transplant. Those few hours in that cell were the worst memories of Akemi's life. They were a nightmare that she'd only awoken from after the Rik took her brain and installed her in a ship.

Akemi didn't know these Rik who were taking Claire with them, but there were decent odds they were as selfish and cruel as any other Rik. And yet Claire followed after them like a puppy, as if they were the ones she should trust.

When Claire stumbled again, one of the Rik picked her up. "I can get her as far as the train station."

Sage grabbed Claire's glasses and folded them up, effectively blinding Akemi from the rest of their journey. But now at least she knew they weren't trying to leave the planet. If they were going to the train station, they were headed to Lower Selta.

CLAIRE DRIFTED as Athlete carried her. The ceiling had to be ten stories above her head. On her right was an open mining shaft in which a gigantic drill turned.

"It's the—spinner drill," she slurred. "Kitteh told me."

In Claire's fevered eyes, the spinner looked ancient and almost evil. The double helix shape, easily fifty yards across, turned slowly, like a gigantic corkscrew twisting into the heart of the planet. Each metal strand was at least three feet thick. It was a lot like the spinners used to get between levels. They must've patterned them after the drills.

Soon the Rik wanted to go down a level and Claire tried to focus. Diva stepped onto one strand of the small spinner—a pedestrian one—and twirled gracefully down the hole. Young Twin and Old Twin did the same.

"I've done this already," Claire told Athlete. "I've got it."

Sage grabbed her arm as she moved to step on. "Hold on, that's the fever talking. You should ride backward, like this." He got on like he was mounting a horse and showed her how to wrap her arms around the strand and slide down backward. Like a toddler on a slide.

The vertigo she was feeling confirmed he was probably right, so she swung a leg over and slid down on her tummy. The metal was so smooth at first, it offered almost no friction. For a dizzy moment, she was afraid she'd fly off or slam into the ground. But just as she was getting afraid, the pole got rougher, almost sticky, rubbing against her pants and arms and naturally slowing her just before her feet hit the ground at the next level.

"That wasn't so bad," Claire said, putting a hand to her aching eyes.

"Good. You've got nine more levels to go," Sage told her.

After nine levels, Claire was so dizzy she couldn't walk a straight line. She slumped against a wall. "This is the perfect time for you to ditch me. I've no idea where I am. No money. Nothing."

"Do you *want* us to leave you?" Sage asked.

"I don't know. No. Please don't."

"That's enough for me." He smiled. "You're ours now."

18

WHEN BASHER BROKE down and went to check on Claire—at
three in the morning—he found the empty cell. The door was left
open, the tools they used to break the locks were left on the floor.
Hardly thinking, he entered and ran a hand over the closest bunk.
They were gone.

He stooped and looked under that bunk, then the next, more
frantically. Because surely—!

He stood and ran his hands through his hair. Because surely
she was *here*. He'd barely slept at all, picturing Claire tossing and
turning, perhaps becoming feverish, all alone with the Rik. He'd
left his room twice to check on her, only to change his mind and
stomp back, dreading to see her sleeping soundly.

Not until he'd seen the empty room did he realize which
vision had won. Only now did he realize he'd fully expected to
find Claire with a soaring fever. He'd expected to carry, er, escort
her to a guest room and do everything he could to make her sickness more bearable.

She'd be angry with him, sure, but she would understand that
they had to know for sure. He would have introduced her to Sam
and Nat, and privately requested Nat to let Claire share her room.

If Claire's story was true, she must be starved for human interaction, particularly with other women.

Basher had three younger sisters to base his guesses on, and he had been engaged, years ago, though his fiancée had passed away before they got married. Ava's death had left him angry and alone during the time after the invasion, and he'd accepted this Spo job offer cynically, half expecting that it was a suicide mission.

But even in that dark place, he'd missed people that first year. He'd missed his fiancée, of course, but also simple things: a football game at a bar, small talk at the grocery store. He'd just missed *people*.

He'd spent the last few hours wondering how Claire had made it without that.

Basher searched the room methodically, noting the missing blanket, the food boxes, and the absence of several water bottles. Then he examined the door and the tools on the floor.

Basher's partner arrived as he was gingerly using a towel to move the tools.

"What are you doing?" he asked.

"I didn't want to put my fingerprints—" Basher stopped. He'd forgotten what kind of scene he was dealing with. On Earth fingerprints might be significant, and as a detective, he'd learned to protect the evidence for forensic analysis.

But Spo didn't have fingerprints. The only fingerprints he'd find on these would be the ones of the people in the room, and he already knew who they were.

"Never mind," Basher said, tossing the towel away and picking up the magnetic chisel to examine it more closely.

"Video is wiped," his partner said.

"The night guards?"

"They're under temporary suspension, being questioned now. But it seems they were all in sight at the time the recording is gone."

"Are they protecting each other? All in it together?"

The Spo looked offended. "I do not believe so."

"That would be stupid," Basher agreed. "The night guards helped the Rik escape during the night shift? They seem more intelligent than that."

"The lower door to the spinner drill observation deck was also compromised. The logs show a token used that was marked missing two months ago."

Basher shrugged. "One of the guards could have stolen the token then, saved it for this."

His partner flushed vaguely orange with disgust at the idea. "I know all the guards personally, as do you. Do you not think them more honorable than this?"

"I don't know. But you're too inclined to think that *all* the Spo and *only* the Spo are honorable." His partner didn't say anything, and Basher sucked some blood off his knuckle. "Hey, I respect you as much as I respect anyone, but only a few weeks ago they verified that your emperor's son is a traitor. Not all Spo are above reproach."

His partner still preserved a heavy silence.

Sam and Nat arrived breathless in the doorway of the cell.

"We know what happened," Nat said. "Akemi is with them."

"What do you mean?"

"You must have left out the glasses we gave you last night," Sam said. "Claire found them and put them on."

"I—I did. I set them on the desk at the end of the hall. I planned to connect them in the morning."

"That was providential then, because she took them. Nat and I had our glasses off, so Akemi couldn't notify us until just now, when we woke up."

"Well—where is she? I mean, where are they?"

Nat handed him her glasses. "Here, she might as well talk to you."

Basher put Nat's glasses on. They were rather tight on his head, and the words began to scroll right away.

They took the Chunnel to Lower Selta, but I don't know exactly where. I'm sorry, but they tucked the glasses into a pocket. From the lower station, they walked forty-five minutes and then stopped; I think at some sort of restaurant.

Basher blinked, he wasn't used to reading with the words disappearing as quickly as he looked, but he got the gist of it.

She had a high fever and was almost delirious.

Basher barely resisted punching the wall. "I knew it. *I knew it.* But why did she escape with them? Is she an idiot? *She* knew she was human, even if I didn't."

Claire is talking about that right now. If you let me access your computer, I can display the video.

"What do you mean, right now?"

She put the glasses back on when she woke up. I can see and hear through her glasses.

Basher walked briskly to his office, letting Sam and Nat trail behind him.

This should be easy. Your computer is Spo tech, which is perfect —so am I. :)

Basher was too frustrated to smile at her small joke.

Akemi started streaming the video to Basher's computer, skimming through the disjointed escape and Claire's collapse.

"I can't believe I let this happen." Basher sat down heavily in his chair and handed Nat's glasses back to her. "I should have realized Claire was human sooner, but her story sounded so dramatic. I tried to convince myself it was just for manipulation."

Nat laughed bleakly. "Sometimes terrible stories are true."

Sam shook his head. "But why would she go with the *Rik*? She was almost in the clear."

Basher squeezed the bridge of his nose and groaned. "She didn't know about the blood test. We don't explain it in order to avoid false positives. As far as she knew, she might be turned over to Faal today."

"So she decided to take her chances with them? That's still a terrible choice."

Basher nodded. "And I can't believe Akemi *knew* it was happening and couldn't stop her."

Hey. Don't blame the messenger, Akemi printed on Basher's screen. *I couldn't exactly lock any doors. And SOMEBODY didn't give me access to their computer until right this second.*

"Fine," Basher held up his hands in surrender. "I know, I could have done it yesterday when Nat asked. But you're sure you don't know where they are now?"

From the length of time she was moving, they clearly took the train to Lower Selta. Other than that, no. I can still receive her signal through the boosters in the train corridor, but it ruins any sort of triangulation.

"How long was she out?" Basher repeated. "Like, passed out?"

Six hours.

They stared at the video on his screen. They were almost caught up to real time as Akemi skipped quickly through the video.

Here it is. This is when she woke up.

19

CLAIRE WOKE IN THE DARK, curled up under a blanket, her head on a pillow. An actual pillow. She sighed. Her bunk on the ship had been serviceable, but no pillow.

Her ribs hurt a little as she shifted, but the bed still felt heavenly. Her hand bumped into something next to the pillow, and she found the glasses.

Claire knew at once that she was over the sickness. Her head felt clear, if a bit empty, and she was no longer feverish. A pale light shone from a doorway to her right, and she could hear the voices of the others.

In the calm quiet, she faced the fact that Basher must be absolutely convinced that she was a Rik. That seemed more irrevocable now than it had yesterday in the cell. Was that only yesterday?

Someone moved into the doorway. It was Sage. "Why don't you come out, when you're ready, and we'll talk?"

"Sure." She pushed herself up and stretched her protesting muscles. She had almost forgotten what it felt like to recover from exhaustion.

She opened the door gingerly. Although she still felt conflicted about her choice of the night before, she had to admit that the Rik had been very good to her so far.

The next room was long and narrow and was clearly a kitchen. There were four stoves in a row on one side, and a sink and lots of counter space on the other side. At the end of the room was a small oval table, where the Rik sat. It was all so... mundane.

Sage idly flipped the Spo token in his hand, the one the embassy guard had given him. Diva lifted a mug to her lips. It smelled tantalizingly like coffee.

"Can I get you some toast?" Young Twin offered. "That probably wouldn't hurt your stomach."

Claire looked around the pristine kitchen. "Do we have toast? Do we have *bread*?"

Young Twin chattered to her about food, while showing her the human appliances. She was so enthusiastic that Claire didn't have the heart to tell her that she already knew about toasters and cheese graters and even blenders. Claire felt as if she'd entered an especially whimsical episode of the Twilight Zone.

Sage poured her a cup of coffee. "I hope you're not regretting your decision."

"Not right now," Claire said around a bite of toast. "This is incredible. I do feel strange, but only because you're all watching me as I eat."

Immediately Athlete looked at the ceiling, Old Twin looked at the table, and Diva shut her eyes. "Is that better?" Diva asked.

"Um. No. You can open your eyes." Claire could see that Sage was still waiting for a real answer. "I'm not regretting that I came," Claire explained. "Faal doesn't know where I am for the first time in a long time, and that makes me feel... lighter. On the other hand, the only human I know is now pretty darn sure that I'm a Rik, and that's unfortunate." Claire took another bite. "But all things considered, I'd do it again if I had to choose. I really appreciate that none of you voted to abandon me while I was sick. So, where are we?"

"Ah. Well, we're the proud employees of an Earth-themed restaurant in Lower Selta," Sage said. "The owner is an entrepreneurial Crosspoint who wanted to get into this niche while it is still fresh. As I told you, he needs authentic servers and we are the best he can do. He wanted some humans to lend to the... uh, 'ambiance of his establishment.' Seltans love novelty, and having even the grunt work done by humans would make this place very unusual."

"It's a generous deal," Athlete added. "He'll pay us a little and we can live here, too."

Claire gaped at them. "But we can't just work here, waiting for Faal to come find us! Or the Spo! Surely they'll hear about a restaurant with human staff in about five minutes?"

The door behind the table swung open dramatically, and a little Crosspoint slug waited there, framed in the space.

"Five minutes?" he said with comic drama. "You wrong me. My services are not for the masses, you see. Nor do I advertise as a common bourgeois businessman. Word of my establishment is passed strictly word-of-mouth, and my guest list is full for weeks to come. Those Spo barbarians will never hear of us, and if Faal of Merith II intended to come, I would hear of him."

If he'd had a hand he would have waved it airily. Instead he advanced into the room with that curious glide the Crosspoint had. "Let me introduce myself. I am Francois."

Claire's first thought was that he had a lot of presence for a Crosspoint barely as high as her armpit. Then her hand began to shake wildly. She pushed away from the table in panic and stood up, holding her possessed hand at arm's length. "What the—?"

Francois smiled hugely and somewhat gruesomely. "Nice to meet you."

Her hand stopped moving.

Claire stared at him, and then shook her head, her heart still pounding. "That is *not* how you shake hands."

The Crosspoint laughed with a squelching noise. "I know, but it is humorous nonetheless. Please sit, I would like to find out more about those I have rashly liberated from the Spo embassy."

Claire's chair gently bumped the back of her legs and she flinched.

"Sit!" Francois said again. "Tell me how I have acquired a sixth employee when I expected only five."

Claire sat uncomfortably. "Right. Sage told the guard he could guarantee payment..."

"I've already made arrangements—do not be concerned. If I had known there were six acceptable candidates, I would have planned accordingly."

Sage broke in. "She's human, Francois. Your investment turned out even better than you guessed."

All the cabinets in the kitchen opened and shut simultaneously with a loud rattle.

"This is superb!" Francois said. "Indeed, a rare chance for me. You will be able to aid me excessively in the authenticity of my presentation. What luck!"

Claire gave a weak smile.

"But then, while this is a luck for me," he continued, "it is perhaps not so for you. Why did you leave the embassy? There is at least one other human there, the detective they've employed these past few years."

Claire explained why she left, and Francois levitated off the ground. "I am impressed. Not many get the better of Faal in any transaction, let alone a pure theft. But that may be in your favor, he respects strength."

"He might respectfully murder me then. I also—injured him."

Francois looked thoughtful. "I will certainly keep abreast of his movements. As I said, my clients are of a select nature—but I can at least be certain that if Faal inquires about me, I will know of it. I am very well connected." He levitated himself a few more inches off the ground. "My name does not appear on any network. I operate beneath the notice of the law—and above the reach of amateurs like the Spo."

Claire told herself to be satisfied with that, but she was uneasy relying on a slug with delusions of grandeur.

"And you others?" Francois said. "I know Sage, of course, for we were acquainted before, but I do not know the rest of you."

Old Twin bowed slightly, "I was an educator—professor, you might say—in the capital city on our planet. I was an advisor to the current S.D.—"

"S.D.?" Claire asked.

"Supreme Director," Old Twin said, as if she should have known. "The leader of the Rik nation."

"*Oh.*"

"She was one of my best students—"

"We get it," Diva said, rolling her eyes. "You're brilliant and influential and don't deserve to be in this freak show. I, on the other hand, *volunteered* to become human. There were twenty thousand people at my last performance. It was chaos." She closed her eyes, clearly basking in the memory.

Athlete looked up from his breakfast. "I was an athlete. It means the same thing in English. I was chosen for the first migration for publicity reasons."

"He was great!" Young Twin explained. "The Rik are swimmers, you know, and he was champion four years in a row. Now he does weight-lifting and wrestling." Young Twin looked at him adoringly and Claire smiled involuntarily. *Total* fan girl.

But as she pictured Athlete wrestling, Claire had a sudden shock. "I know you!"

He put another bite in his mouth. "Is that so?"

"Back when I was in school my dad used to watch wrestling at night—he watched the World Wide Wrestling Federation. It's a cheesy show with colorful costumes and fake stories, but my dad still enjoyed the fights. Your circuit name was something like Ballistic Bomber or Bludgeon... You were a famous wrestler."

Claire now recalled the rest of the story. He'd dropped out of the wrestling show and the wrestling circuit all together. She remembered her dad saying sadly that those guys frequently ended up on steroids and then harder drugs until they destroyed their lives...

But apparently, he hadn't done that. He'd been abducted by aliens. Claire looked uncomfortably at the Rik sitting at the table.

Athlete nodded. "I assumed they chose a world-class athlete for me."

Young Twin seemed to sense Claire's unease. "I was only chosen for the first wave because I am the Supreme Director's daughter. Lucky me," she said apologetically.

"How old are you?" Claire asked.

She laughed uneasily. "I'm twenty-five years old, but we mature a bit later than humans. What do you call it when you're not a kid anymore, but no one thinks you're ready to do anything worthwhile?"

Claire laughed despite herself. "You're a teenager."

"And Sage—"

"I was a philosopher," Sage broke in. "That's why I can never shut up."

There was a slight pause, as if someone was about to speak and the others automatically held back. But no one spoke, and then it was gone.

"We didn't really *choose* to take these people," Young Twin added quietly. "They were going to someone, and we were selected. Now we just want to find a place to be safe. And learn to be human."

Claire impulsively squeezed her hand. "Wouldn't it be safer to... change back to being a Rik? Would that be so terrible?"

Young Twin looked shocked. "Don't you think I would if I could? We can only transfer once. Otherwise the..." she looked at Sage for help. "How do you explain it?"

"Our neural net can handle the first transfer, but it frays a bit. A second transfer invariably results in so much decay that the consciousness is lost."

"Can you transfer to other species besides humans?" Claire asked.

"Yes, but we generally don't," Sage said. "Other species know about the technology, and are on their guard. They despise us for using it but are jealous because they cannot. If we started taking bodies willy-nilly," Sage paused, and seemed to recollect himself. "Well, we do not. Francois, what work do you have for us today? The morning is not yet over! We are at your service."

Francois glided their breakfast dishes to the sink in a graceful arc. "Very well, let me introduce you to your new home.

20

THEY FOLLOWED Francois from the kitchen into the dining area of his restaurant. It was a tiny little place, but fancy. There were three low tables and an antique bar that looked like it had been imported straight from a pub. Claire rubbed her hand over the wood; it had the muted shine of age and the touch of many hands. There were even a few old initials carved into it. She traced the soft grooves of J.R. and K.S.

There were different pairs of seats for each type of the various aliens who might come: mushroom-shaped squats for the Spo, stools for the Merith, cup-seats for the Vel, and so on. At the end of the bar, furthest from the kitchen, was a door to the street, and though Francois told Claire it was currently locked, she checked it anyway.

A strange assortment of human objects were displayed on the walls. Claire could guess why Francois chose most of them, but it was decidedly strange to see an arrangement of empty wooden picture frames around a bright pink hula hoop, with a mounted deer's head in the center. That was on the back wall. On the front wall, there were two shelves. The first one held a guitar and two violins standing upright, which could almost have been normal decor. The second shelf held four pairs of shoes: one pair of children's blue sandals, some red high heels, and two pairs of brightly colored Nike trainers.

The whole room couldn't have been more than ten feet across, and perhaps three times that deep.

"Size is nothing; it is all about presentation," Francois told them, as if he'd heard her. "If you present yourself and your establishment as elite and mysterious—a haven for the connoisseur of culture—it will be perceived as such."

Claire glanced down at herself. She was still wearing the torn uniform she'd gotten aboard *Final Say,* and it was on the outer edge of grimy. She'd worn it during her last two days on the ship, the afternoon and night at the embassy prison, and today. Could it be only the second day since she'd left the ship?

Regardless, she needed a shower or some serious deodorant because she had the rank smell of someone unwashed and recently ill. She certainly didn't feel either elite or mysterious.

"Presence," Francois repeated emphatically. A cutting board resting on the bar thumped to make his point. "You must cultivate presence." A pepper mill spun lazily on the counter.

He continued to lecture, and Claire tried to wrap her head more firmly around the idea of his telekinesis. She'd dealt with that Crosspoint on the ship, but Francois moved things *all the time.* Maybe other Crosspointers trained themselves to rein in their ability. If so, Francois had despised such training. Every sentence ended with a visible period, as some plate or cutlery twitched. Claire kept catching movement out of the corner of her eye, only to see a pot gracefully swaying on its hook or grains of rice lifting and trickling through invisible fingers.

"You still haven't told me," Claire said, breaking into his monologue and gesturing at the door, "What makes you certain that the Spo won't hear about this place and grab us tomorrow?"

"For one thing—" he broke off. "You keep wincing. What is the matter?"

She sank down on a stool and her ribs gave a painful twinge as she explained her very brief fight with the Spo.

"Hmm." The top of her uniform started to slide up. "Let's see."

Claire clutched her shirt, holding it down. "Stop that!"

Francois looked blank. "Are humans protective of their pain? I didn't know. The Vel are like that, and the Spo, a little. I apologize—"

"No," Claire said. "I'm not protective of—of the pain, we just don't—you can't move someone's clothes without asking. We're protective of our space."

"Would it violate your space if I fixed the injury that is hurting you?" Several bowls adjusted themselves on a shelf behind Francois' head, as if impatient.

"Can you do that?"

"Of course. I have basic micro-medical training, after all. Just hold still for a moment."

He closed his eyes and pain flared in her rib cage.

"Ow! Yikes—ow." She rubbed her side, but the pain was almost gone before the words were out of her mouth.

"How is that?"

She gingerly stretched her arms over her head and felt only the echo of an ache. "That's incredible. Thank you so much."

"It's nothing, it's nothing," he said, but Claire could tell he was pleased. "Human bones are not much different from other calcium-fortified mammals. A few cells shifted, and it's half-healed. You should be careful for several weeks, however, not to re-injure the spot."

Then he launched into the nuances of food preparation for alien species. She'd gotten the gist of this during her work on the Diadina's ship, but she hadn't been serving it. She certainly hadn't been allowed to prepare the food.

There were supplements for everything. When an alien ate

across culture, which apparently aliens loved to do, things got complicated. Every species had standard vitamin supplements that they generally took with any meal that wasn't from their home planet. But each species had things they flat couldn't stomach, or that had to be counteracted in some ways. It was a balance —present the cuisine as close to the original as possible, but in such a way that the customer wouldn't leave with a stomach ache, hives, or newly sprouted green hair. Some ingredients could be suppressed and some had to be altered. Some were innocuous when combined with another Earth food, or only in certain amounts. Some had to be separated out altogether.

Francois had been testing all his food samples for the last few weeks as he prepared to open his restaurant.

Claire wished she had a computer, or even a notebook to take notes. She felt like she'd strayed into an advanced chemistry class without her textbook.

"You look pained again," Francois said. "It's very disconcerting."

"Sorry. I'm just trying to remember what you said. Protein supplements for Vel—?"

"No, no. You're treating this like a science, but it is an art! You mustn't just memorize this as a list, but get a feel for each species and their particular problems." The guitar on the wall strummed gracefully, apparently to make his point about art.

Francois continued to teach, and despite what he said, it was a lot of memorization. At some point a young Merith came in, whom Francois introduced as the chef. He began preparations for dinner, mixing up bread dough and forming eight loaves.

If someone had asked Claire whether she missed the smell of flour or corn meal or any of a dozen mundane ingredients, she would have shrugged. But the smell of dough reminded her of Thanksgiving when she made rolls with her Nana and watched her mom roll out pie crusts on the table. The yeast smelled like homemade pizza, her dad's specialty. The cinnamon was for winter, in oatmeal and hot chocolate.

"Francois, you never told me. How do you get all this?" Claire asked. If someone was bringing him supplies from Earth, then someone here was regularly *going to Earth*. Why shouldn't she use that ship to get home?

"I have contacts in Spo mainspace who put me in touch with a supplier. Earth restaurants are going to be the next big thing. From what I understand, shipments are still controlled by the Spo supervisors on Earth, but I bought a start-up shipment which should last for some months. Now look here and tell me, is this food or paint? I tried some in a mixed drink only two days ago and it turned me pink for twelve hours."

Several kinds of ketchup sat in the cabinet, and Claire laughed in spite of herself. "It *is* more like paint than food, but we eat it. It's supposed to go on certain things... mostly salty, fried things."

"Ah, see, already you help me." He smiled, and his flat, leaf-grinding molars flashed again.

"I would like you all to take part in the food preparation eventually," Francois added, "to add to the authenticity of the experience. But authenticity goes poorly with bad food, so that will wait. Tonight, you will merely serve food and speak to the customers. The timing of our opening couldn't be better; humans are all over the news reports.

Claire licked her lips. No one seemed to be concerned about having a high-profile job after escaping from the Spo.

Sage pulled her aside. "We can make a fortune if we stick with this. I know he's a little overwhelming, but hang in there. Your share for tonight alone would be..." and the amount made Claire's eyes get wide. "We have to pay off our escape first, but then we'll earn quickly."

It was more than a week's worth of pay on *Final Say*, for a few hours of serving food and chatting up the guests. Surely she could silence her nerves for such a good cause.

Sage showed her back to a small staircase.

"Straight up there are our living quarters. Girls on the left, boys on the right. Diva said that would make you more comfortable."

The "girls" room was fitted out with Spo cots, but they would do fine for humans. Next to each bed there was a hook on the wall, and Claire could see that the Rik had already hung their extra clothes up.

She went to the unclaimed bed and sank down on it, grateful for a moment of quiet reflection. Was she a fool to stay and trust Francois? Was she a traitor to enjoy the company of her new friends?

Because yes, she was enjoying them. They might be aliens, but they also seemed like decent people...

After Claire showered, she spied a stack of clothing waiting for her. Claire picked up the top item, a cherry-red, satin something, and unfolded it. "Ha! A kimono?"

She ran her hand down the pretty wrap-around dress, admiring the gold and black thread on the red background. It must have been part of Francois's shipment.

When she was dry and dressed, she stared in the mirror for a long time. It had been so long since she'd really looked at herself. Years.

She didn't know this person very well. It wasn't that she was so much older or taller than she had been—the physical differences between fourteen and twenty weren't that obvious. It was more the expression that was different. The seriousness of the eyes, the firmly compressed lips.

It was bizarre to feel so little connection to the person in the mirror. Her light brown skin was so pale it was almost yellow. Lack of sunlight was probably to blame for that, Claire supposed.

She had a lot of dark, curly hair and dark brown eyes. And, of course, the wretched Spo tattoo on her cheek.

She didn't know if she was still pretty or not. She was too thin; she didn't look healthy. Basher was probably right about a vitamin deficiency. And this girl looked so—guarded. She looked like a cautious, well-trained Spo cadet.

Claire always thought they made a weird mistake selecting her and giving her this tattoo, but now she looked exactly their sort.

21

IF AKEMI STILL HAD LUNGS, she would have watched with bated breath. Claire's story was better than a movie. Akemi totally loved Sam and Nat, but there was no denying that two was just *not* enough company. During the last few weeks, Akemi had grown sick of seeing Senator Fontley's angry face, Sam's frustrated one, and Nat's blank, politically pacifying one. Watching Claire's life was a breath of fresh air.

And goodness, those kimonos were beautiful. Akemi was from Japan, and she knew good craftsmanship when she saw it. That Crosspoint hadn't been exaggerating; he must expect his restaurant to be super exclusive (and expensive) to afford exports like that.

Francois was briefing them on the dinner guests now. He'd planned who would sit in each of the twelve chairs, and he wanted it all to be perfect.

"The two Tergre here, the Vel family at the other end, single Crosspoint here and here..." He removed the chairs to leave empty spaces for the Crosspoints, and arranged the cup chairs for the Vel.

When he mentioned any specific names, Akemi immediately searched for them in the Seltan databases she could access.

He wasn't kidding about having exclusive clients.

The Tergre family was listed as one of the founding names in Seltan history. They currently owned 64% of the mining capabilities on the planet... They were like the Rockefellers of New York.

Akemi also stored the list of names on Basher's computer. Perhaps he could track down this restaurant through them.

Suddenly Claire tripped and her glasses flew off. Akemi heard Claire groan.

"If these break, I'm going to kill myself," she said.

Akemi wasn't worried. The frames were titanium—light and very strong. Claire would have to do more than drop them to bend those babies.

However, in the moment it took Claire to stoop and grab the glasses, Akemi saw an opportunity. It was probably a bad idea, but...

Safe mode initialized. Are you injured? Akemi sent.

Nat and Sam would smack her if they knew the risk she was taking, and Basher would be very angry that she disregarded his directions, but Akemi didn't care. She wanted to be involved, and she would be careful. Besides, what could they do to her?

Claire went still when the words showed up. If the others knew they had turned on, they'd freak out again.

Akemi smiled to herself. She could give Claire a way out.

Please clench your jaw for yes

Or blink for no

Claire blinked slowly, looking guiltily around, no doubt to see if anyone had noticed.

Good enough for now. Akemi faded out. She didn't want to overwhelm Claire or she might change her mind and do without the glasses. And this was too fun.

. . .

Claire surreptitiously took off her glasses as if to clean them, looking for a tiny switch or camera, or *anything* that would indicate how to turn these off. She would have tried speaking a few random commands, but then the others might realize what had happened.

Claire heard them coming back down the stairs, and put the glasses back on as they entered the room.

The Rik women were wearing the same kind of kimono she was, but they did it way better than she did. Diva looked regal and beautiful, large and proud. The twins wore matching black kimonos and pulled their hair back identically, which might have made it hard to tell them apart if they weren't so different. Young Twin seemed like a bubbly teenager, crushing hard on Athlete, while Old Twin was an arrogant and cynical old woman.

"We really have to work on this Young Twin and Old Twin business," Claire said. "Those names are awkward, and they don't suit either of you."

Young Twin grinned. "I know, they're terrible! Do you have any suggestions? Sage kept calling us that, because he's a stick-in-the-mud scientist, but I'm sick of it."

Old Twin rolled her eyes. "Is there a name for someone light on intelligence who never closes her mouth?"

Young Twin stuck out her tongue. "I want a name that's young and romantic and beautiful..."

"How about Juliet?" Claire offered. "She was a character in a famous play who fell in love with a boy she couldn't have."

"Juliet—I love it!" She looked genuinely pleased.

"What did people call you?" Claire asked Old Twin.

"Madame Professor," she said shortly. "Don't try and give me a cute new name. I've expelled students for less."

"But don't you want—"

"No. I've been Old Twin for a while now. That will do."

Sage and Athlete came back in traditional Asian garb, which

looked more than a little funny on Sage's gangly frame and Athlete's quiet bulk.

Young Twin, or Juliet, Claire corrected herself, told them her new name and embraced Claire again. "Thank you!"

By the time Francois unlocked the front door, Claire was stationed at the bar to serve the two Tergre guests. Her stomach was in knots.

The Vel arrived first; a grandmother, her daughter, and a granddaughter. Their scaled skin was shiny, and certain scales had been painted in complicated patterns. They were Juliet's responsibility, and she bowed shakily and greeted them.

With surprise, Claire realized Juliet was sweating. A quick glance showed Diva swallowing compulsively and a muscle in Athlete's neck twitching spasmodically.

They were nervous, too! Claire felt better. She was the only *real* human here, after all, she should be proud. They had to fake it, but she was genuine. Claire's assigned guests, a male and female Tergre, were the last to arrive, and she held out a hand and bowed.

"Welcome to a vignette of Earth." She'd memorized the phrase in Tergre, which was a common language on Selta, but not one she'd learned.

As soon as the patrons were seated, the kitchen door swung open, and Francois made his dramatic entrance, announcing the menu options for the evening and introducing the servers.

When he was done, the two Tergre began to study her. They spoke in their language, so Claire didn't even try to follow. They knew to order in Spo or Merith.

But after a moment of conversation, her glasses lit up.
Translation: Colloquial Tergre to American Standard English
Blink twice to turn off.
"She's kind of a bony thing, isn't she? But I like the fur."

"What is its anthropological origin? Does it have a heraldic tradition?"

Claire didn't even know what those words meant in English, let alone Tergre, but the translation was amazing.

"I've heard very little. The Spo kept such a tight lid on the planet during their probation."

"I pity them being at the mercy of the Spo for so long."

Claire choked.

"Somewhat inarticulate, isn't it?" the male said.

"Be nice, they are new to the Council." The female switched to the Spo language and said loudly, *"CAN YOU UNDERSTAND ME?"*

Claire nodded. "Yes, yes. I—speak Spo and some Merith. I didn't realize you were speaking to me."

"Very good. You speak well," the female shouted at her.

Claire laughed. "Thank you very much. What may I serve you tonight?"

They made their selection from the limited menu, and Claire went to the kitchen to tell the chef. After she returned to her station she tried to be unobtrusive while the couple gossiped about the other guests in quiet voices, but now that she knew what they were saying, it was harder to keep a straight face.

"Oh, my dear—will you look at Enrithsco? No, don't turn your whole self, she'll see!" <Giggle>

"Is that an extra pouch?"

"It is! Another little one, at her age. Can you imagine how angry her daughter is?"

"Shh."

Claire was so busy following their conversation (a few lines behind) that she didn't immediately realize when they asked her something.

"I'm sorry. What was that?" she asked.

"Art," said the male Tergre. He spoke in Merith, but her glasses kept translating anyway, which was a darn good thing because he spoke with a strong accent. "I'm an art dealer, and I recently saw a most interesting catalog of human art. You've seen it?"

"No, not yet. But if you have questions about human art, perhaps I can help?" Claire stumbled over the words and a pronunciation guide appeared in her glasses, prompting her. These glasses were so incredibly awesome.

"The auditory portions were my favorite," the Tergre said. "Would you give my mate an example?"

"Auditory portion...?"

Her glasses came to her rescue again.

Reference log:

Auditory portion of the Catalog of Human Culture, Section 34: Singing and dancing.

"Oh, you mean singing?"

The Tergre lifted his long nose and made a muted hooting sound. It hit a few vague tones—sort of familiar.

Translation uncertain. Best match from catalog: Stille Nacht or Silent Night.

"I do know that song. We sing it during Christmas—a holiday." Finally, something she understood.

They waited.

"Oh, you want me to sing it?" A week's pay, she told herself, it's worth a week's pay. Her throat tightened. She wasn't sure what was worse—the silence before or whatever was about to come after.

Claire sang the first line softly, so as not to interrupt the fragile buzz of conversation in the room.

No such luck. Dead silence fell. Claire cleared her throat, feeling her cheeks warm. "All is calm, all is bright..."

She only knew the first verse, the one she'd sung in school

choirs since she was in preschool. How surreal to sing it for a room full of aliens.

She finished quickly, but when she was done Diva held up a hand like a conductor. "If you sing it once more, we can accompany you."

"Oh, no, that's—"

"An excellent suggestion for our guests!" Francois said. "Once more, please Claire."

Claire sang it again, but better this time. She'd started too high last time. She glanced at Diva, when she was done, who was waving her hand with an ecstatic smile on her face.

"Yes, I have it now," Diva said.

Claire started for a third time, and this time not just Diva, but all the others joined in. Juliet and Old Twin followed Claire exactly, and Diva sang a soaring descant she'd apparently made up on the spot. Sage's voice was a nice baritone, and Athlete had a surprisingly rich tenor. He followed Diva when they did it the last time, and it was beautiful.

The guests applauded/honked/twizzled their appreciation, and Francois was so pleased, he couldn't stop twirling a frying pan above his head.

22

THAT NIGHT, Claire lay in bed with her glasses still on. The glasses had saved her tonight. Translations, hints, pronunciation. She was never letting them go. They must be worth a fortune.

Being adrift for so long, she'd learned to pidgin or mime her way through conversations that got out of her depth. But it was so *exhausting* to never know for sure what someone was saying. Just speaking to the Rik in English had been an enormous relief, but it paled in comparison to what her glasses could do.

Even if something terrible happened and she ended up on her own again, still hunted by Faal and his people, at least she could *communicate* with the people around her. She could ask for help in ways people would understand. As long as she had these glasses she would never be so alone and vulnerable again.

The other Rik were still down in the kitchen, so Claire was alone with them. "Um... Glasses. I'd like to see a map," Claire said, softly.

Specify location, please.

"Map of Selta?"

A revolving moon appeared before her, light blue lines marking the spatial approaches to Selta's main shipyards on the surface. Just under the surface, spreading in layers like an onion was Upper Selta (neatly labeled). A thick blue tube extended from the upper sprawl straight into the planet. It connected to a similar layered onion of civilization in the middle: Lower Selta. That tube must be the train, but Claire didn't remember traveling through it.

She squinted at Upper Selta, trying to see where the shipyard connected. The map zoomed in, exactly to where she'd been looking.

"Wow."

She could see the individual elevator shafts leading down from the loading bays, and she thought she could roughly trace the path she'd taken when she'd gotten off that first day.

"Can you tell me what ships are docked?" she asked.

There was a pause. Then neat labels showed up, hovering over and around the different ports. Nothing she recognized. *Final Say* was gone, and that left a strange emptiness in her chest. "Is the Diadian still on Delta?"

Yes. The Diadiana stays to perform at the Herayung.

"Can you show me my current location?"

More data needed. Please speak address or sector.

So, the glasses had no GPS or positioning system; they didn't know where she was. She exhaled in relief.

"Is this an AI? Do you have a name—like Alexa or Siri?"

There was a slight pause, then: *You can call me A.K.E.M.I.*
Artificial Knowledge Engine for Machine Intelligence.

"Akemi, great. Whose glasses are these?"

Yours. Please speak your full name and address to verify ownership.

"I'll do that later." She tried a different subject. "News reports."

An image popped up in front of her, a Seltan news channel. There was no sound, but the subtitles appeared, in English no less! These glasses couldn't be standard. Did they belong to Basher? They were clearly meant for human use. But if he had these, why had he come to *Final Say* without them, speaking in his less than stellar Spo accent? If these were his, why would he ever take them off?

That gave her another thought. "Show Earth?" she asked.

AKEMI WAS HAVING so much fun. Sure, it was limiting to pretend to be an AI, but she was starting to get the hang of it. She could show Claire rather complex things, if she waited for Claire to ask the right questions.

Now this one, "Show Earth," was tricky. She didn't have access to the full "internet" of Selta, only what was downloaded at the Spo embassy. It was a lot, but not everything. The only good videos were from the art catalog that she and Shara had put together to showcase Earth's culture.

But Akemi could hear the repressed shiver in Claire's voice when she asked for Earth, and Akemi wanted to give her something more personal. Something to remind Claire that she was human and not Rik. Searching around through the various subsystems, Akemi came across several video files on Basher's computer.

Ah. This was perfect, it seemed to be a vacation video. She heard Claire sigh when it started. It was a phone video, a little shaky, of a campus in Boston.

"I still don't know why you wanted to visit Dartmouth," Basher was saying. "You lured me up here with promises of a hike." He was in the foreground of the video, talking to whoever was holding the camera.

"Don't you feel smarter already?" It was a woman's voice, teasing and fun. "Anyway, we'll go for that hike, but I've never been here before." The phone moved around, taking in stately, tree-lined pathways and ornate, brick buildings.

"Hey, look at this squirrel," Basher said. He crouched down

and pointed to a big, gray squirrel that was inching towards him. "It's as big as a cat."

He put out his hand and chirped and the squirrel crept a few steps closer.

"Well, give him something," the woman said.

Basher reached slowly in his pocket and pulled out a stick of gum.

"Not that, you'll make it sick!"

"Not that sick—haven't you ever given gum to a squirrel?"

The video went sideways as the woman behind the camera handed him half a muffin.

"That cost four bucks," Basher protested.

"My video. Feed the squirrel."

Basher rolled his eyes, but obligingly pinched off a piece and gave it to the squirrel.

"Your turn, Ava," he said. They traded places and now a dark-haired woman fed the squirrel. She had an engagement ring on her left hand.

"Hey, please don't feed the squirrels." A campus security guy came into view and the video cut off abruptly with the sound of their embarrassed laughter.

The next clip was a view of a harbor, although Akemi didn't know exactly where—perhaps they were still on vacation in Massachusetts. The sky was cloudy and gray, and a strong wind was whipping up the waves. Ava was in the video again. She held her arms out and the wind blew her hair wildly around her head. "This is so great!" she shouted over the wind. "I think there'll be a storm. I already feel the drops."

"We should go in," Basher said. "I don't think I have any more clean pants in my suitcase."

She made a face, and took the phone, panning the length of the coast, showing dark rain clouds massing above the rocky shore, broken by an unexpected shaft of sunlight that momentarily formed a rainbow prism.

"Did you see that?" Ava asked. "It was beautiful."

"I did," Basher said. "But we really are getting wet now!"

The rain was coming down faster, and his hair was dripping. Basher kissed her cheek and then grabbed for the phone while she tried to hold it away. She was laughing as the clip ended.

Claire wiped away a tear and mouthed Ava's name.

23

BASHER WATCHED the video recording of Claire receiving her injection in the medical room—again.

"I can't believe it's been a week, and we *still* can't get a location on them. A week!" Basher said to Akemi.

He knew she could hear and see him through his computer. He'd given her access to it, and at first, he'd been self-conscious that she kept the tiny video recorder going non-stop, but he'd gotten used to it. He felt bad for her, trapped in a computer with only a few visual outlets.

He knew she was no longer human, exactly, but he kept picturing a real girl, stuck in her room, bored out of her mind, texting everybody she knew.

He'd gotten used to her presence.

Sorry. Akemi printed in a small text box on his screen. *She really hasn't given me much to work with.*

"I would go stir-crazy stuck in a tiny apartment above a tiny restaurant for so many days," Basher said. "Why doesn't she step outside? Ever?"

She's used to confinement. And she's... happy.

"Don't even get me started on the Rik. They're taking advantage of her."

But they look human and they're nice to her. It's more than she's had in a while.

"You don't think she's going to leave any time soon?"

She could take a walk tomorrow, but I doubt it. Nothing new from the videos?

Basher rolled his eyes. "No. And don't say 'I told you so,' please."

Basher's partner entered their shared office. He carried a cloth satchel, as many Spo did, and now he unfastened it from his torso. He flushed a vague color of embarrassment, somewhere between pink and peach that Basher had never seen on him before.

When the Spo released the catch on the bag, the lemur sprang out of it. It chittered happily and jumped onto one of the Spo's knees.

Basher laughed in surprise, and his partner turned a deeper pink. "It is only that I felt...perhaps it requires company." He looked sheepish. "Walking past it every day, I had a feeling—like —" he struggled for words, "like a father who is ignoring the youngest of his litter."

Basher stared at the alien. He'd been his partner for two years and he just learned more about him in one sentence than he had in all that time. "I guess this is fine, as long as it doesn't bite."

"I believe it only attacked in defense. It does not seem violent."

Just then Sam appeared in the open doorway, knocking perfunctorily on the door frame. "Cute animal," he said, rubbing the lemur. "I brought my pet trouncer, but the Seltan authorities haven't given permission for him to join me yet. Any chance you could help me with that?"

"Your pet *trouncer*? Those are not tame," Basher said.

"Nebbie is. I bet he'd even get along with this little guy."

"Okay... I'll see what I can do. Was there something else?"

"We just got a tip from a Seltan constable about the Rik we followed here. Coming with us?"

Basher stood and pushed in his chair. "Of course, let's go." The *real* investigation he should be worrying about was the attack on the space station. It had taken a back seat in his mind, although he knew that Sam and Nat had been using diplomatic channels to trace the Rik delegation. So far, they had only confirmed that the ship of Rik diplomats who had left the space station (a suspicious *hour* before the explosion) had arrived here.

"What tip did you get?" Basher followed Sam out of the embassy.

"It's not a tip so much as a... crime. A Seltan officer found an apartment full of dead Rik."

"Woah."

"And since we'd asked them to let us know if there was any strange Rik activity... they sent me a message. They really should have sent it to you," Sam said frankly. "But you don't seem very popular with them."

Basher sighed. "Yeah, the Seltan constables don't appreciate that I'm allowed to walk around with a weapon and arrest people while they have to get permission to wipe spit off their shoes."

"Well, that would be annoying," Sam said. "Do people spit on them often?"

"You'd be surprised. On Selta, they want order and security for their visitors and their residents, of course, but they want their rich criminals to be happy, too."

"They do?"

"Yes. For instance, if a Vel woman shot her chauffeur for wasting time, she'd be fined for taking a life and endangering the lives of those around her. But if she happened to have caused a revolution that cost the lives of thousands of people on her home-world, well, that would be completely her own business. Selta has few extradition treaties with anyone. We are an exception because of the Rik problem. So long as she didn't use her insurrectionist talents on Selta, that woman would be a model citizen. Speaking of model citizens, isn't Nat coming with us?"

"Not today. She's dealt with enough dead Rik, she doesn't have any desire to see more."

"Has she?"

"She—er—killed three Rik when she was trying to get to the trial. It was ugly."

"I'm sorry."

"Shara wants to come," Sam added. "She'll meet us there."

Basher clenched his jaw as he and Sam left the main entrance of the embassy. He knew now that Shara was a 'turned' Rik, one of those who'd sworn allegiance to humanity and supposedly proved her usefulness, but he still didn't like working with her.

"If you ignore her flirting, she won't bother you so much," Sam said. "She does that to everyone."

"I don't care about that," Basher said, which was true, though he admitted to some relief that she was beginning to pick up on his dislike of her. "The problem is investigating a Rik conspiracy *with* a Rik. It's a conflict of interest. Besides, Nat can't stand her. Why did she come?"

"Believe it or not, it was Nat's idea. Akemi and Shara are friends, and Nat will do anything for Akemi." Sam laughed, a little sadly. "In fact, if you ever see Nat do something irrational, you can bet it's about Akemi."

Sam paused and put a hand to his glasses. "Now Akemi's chewing me out," he explained to Basher. "Akemi—No, you know it's true, I'm just explaining to Basher. No, don't tell Nat I said that..."

The apartment was in an upscale Vel establishment. A large central courtyard was complete with synchronized fountains and ornamental trees. It was surrounded by three levels of private dwellings, and Basher easily guessed that the apartment they wanted was the one with two Tergre constables outside the door.

There appeared to have been no serious conflict in the front room, but there were five dead bodies, and the smell was not good. They'd probably been dead at least forty-eight hours, though Basher would need more evidence to pin it down. The rigid temperature and moisture control on Selta made decomposition slower than on Earth. He wasn't a medical examiner, and he didn't often deal with murder, so he'd have to ask the embassy physician to help him out. Three of the Rik were slumped in chairs, two seemed to have fallen off stools onto the floor.

Sam's face blanched as he came to the door. He started to walk into the room, but Basher stopped him. "Hang on a second."

Basher mentally cataloged the scene while taking pictures with his tablet, appreciating again that Sam was willing to do as he asked with a good attitude. He'd been pleasantly surprised to find that Sam consistently deferred to Basher's judgment, even when it wasn't a big deal. Listening to the Tergre talk about Sam, Basher had wondered if he was going to be a real pain.

"Thanks for waiting," Basher said when he was done. "Let's go on in, but try not to step on any blood, even where it's dry—there may be hairs, footprints, or other evidence in it."

Sam looked grim.

"Are you okay?"

"I met these people on the space station. Nat and I spent several days negotiating the terms of the lunar colony with them. Well, technically Senator Fontley was doing the negotiation, but he hates aliens, so it was mostly us. It's frustrating how... how lately the people I meet keep dying."

"No offense, Sam, but this isn't about you."

"That sounded self-centered, didn't it? But I'm the one who made the treaty with the Rik in the first place, so if it's not my fault, whose is it?"

Basher grunted. "You can't compare their deaths to your friends who died on Earth. These are just Rik."

"Yeah, but to the rest of the galaxy we're *just humans*. Murder is murder." Sam shook his head. "Are you thinking poison? It's a Rik specialty."

"Probably, but we'll need an autopsy to find out." Basher wrinkled his nose. There was a strong smell of blood that didn't seem entirely explained by the scene in front of him. He went on into the next room and found the reason. Three more dead Rik in this room, and it clearly wasn't poison. There were pools of dried blood under the bodies, stab wounds, and clear signs of struggle.

"Just Rik?" Sam repeated.

"I'm not saying this is all right. But in my book they're already murderers." Basher took more pictures. "Legally, does the agreement you negotiated with these people still stand if they're all dead?"

Sam touched his glasses, indicating that Akemi was talking to him. "Akemi says yes. Our agreements about the partnership and the moon colony have already been ratified by the Rik government. That's good news, I suppose."

Basher stared at him. "Do you still *want* to have a treaty with the Rik? I understand why you did it to begin with, but now?" He gestured at the slaughtered Rik. "*All this* means it's likely they were involved in that explosion. They would've killed you on the space station if they could."

Sam grimaced. "The fact that they're dead doesn't prove they did it."

"It doesn't make them look strikingly innocent either."

"You're right. It doesn't. But even if a few Rik did do this, that doesn't mean the whole species is responsible."

Basher shook his head. He and Sam weren't going to agree on that any time soon.

"Defensive wounds on his hands," Basher said, pointing to one of the men who was further in the room. "I think this short guy was killed first, the stab wound is in his back. Then the other two fought back... but they're not positioned like they fought each other, so the killer might have walked away."

"But we're only looking for eight Rik," Sam said. "I mean, all the Rik who were on the space station are here. Are we looking for a ninth person?"

"We'll ask the neighbors if they heard or saw anything..." Basher trailed off. The neighbors here would most likely tell him nothing. Seltans were definitely of the *live and let live* mentality— particularly where he was concerned. Most kept their mouths (or beaks) shut when Basher came around. Maybe he would send Sam and see if he had any luck.

Basher conferred with the constables about where the bodies would be taken. He would prefer to take them back to the embassy to examine, but they didn't have the room for this much cold storage. Seltan law was strict about dead bodies in their pristine closed environment.

Shara arrived soon after, and if Basher had expected the sight of eight dead Rik to subdue her he was disappointed.

"Ew," she said. "This's gross."

"Thank you for the critical analysis."

"Well, it *is* gross. And I wasn't chosen to be a Rik assassin for my compassion, so if you expect me to cry over people I never met then that's silly."

"Clearly."

"Would you like me more if I cried over them? I can." She focused intently. Tears overflowed and ran down her cheeks. "See?"

Basher turned away without replying, vaguely disgusted. He began to go through the contents of the small locker in the bathroom.

"Fine, be that way." She went back to the front room.

There was nothing personal in the locker. He went through their pockets and the other cabinets in the main room. If these people had anything with them besides extra clothes, it had been taken.

"Definitely sasoikeo," Shara called from the front room. "I can smell it."

"Are you sure?"

"Of course I'm sure." She joined him again. "I'm an *assassin*. Do you know what that means?"

"It means you should be in prison."

"It means..." She lifted the fingers of the man who'd been stabbed in the back and sniffed them. "It means I can tell you that this guy administered the poison to the others. He'd had on rubber gloves to avoid getting it on his skin. That means the poison was probably in liquid form and administered in a drink. The solid and aerosol forms are safe to touch. I can smell the latex and there's a bit of that powdery residue on his skin."

Basher sat back on his heels. "Alright, what about the stabbing?"

"I'm not as sure about that part. We are usually trained in all types of weapons, I wouldn't consider knives a Rik favorite. I would guess..." she looked around the room. "I would guess that there was a ninth person here who stabbed this guy when he got back from poisoning the others, and then killed the other two. But that part is a guess."

Her admitted ignorance made Basher give more credit to her other surmises. It was the mark of a professional to know where the line lay between deduction and guesswork and not to pretend to know more than they did. It didn't lessen his dislike for her, however.

They both heard the front door to the apartment open again.

"Sam, is that you?" he called.

"We have a guest," Sam called back. "Faal of Merith II."

"Ah, young Sam," Faal said. "It is a pleasure."

Shara's eyes opened wide, and Basher jumped to his feet. He'd not seen Faal since the day he arrested Claire.

"Faal," Basher said, nodding to him and his five bodyguards. They'd already come into the room and Faal was leaning over one of the Rik.

Basher gestured to the door. "Please step outside, I would rather not have the scene... exposed to so many people." He didn't want Faal sniffing out clues.

Faal didn't move. "I have not heard from you concerning the thief and my property. Have you not educated yourself on the diplomatic law that governs this situation?"

"I apologize for not contacting you," Basher said formally. "My time has been quite full of late. If we could step *outside,* I will update you."

Faal relented, but not without letting Basher feel the weight of his arrogance. Following him outside, Basher started over. "I should inform you that there was a regrettable lapse in security and several Rik escaped from the embassy." He knew there were rumors about an escape, and he suspected that Faal already knew.

"Well for you that you did not lie; you are forthright for a human. Have they left Selta?"

"No. We have reason to believe they are still here."

"Ah. Do you? Lower Selta then."

Basher twitched. "I didn't say—"

"No, of course not. But if they have not escaped the planet, the only logical refuge is Lower Selta. You should have sought my aid sooner. I have several excellent contacts there. I am in a much better position to discover them than you are."

Basher felt cold. "And of course you will inform us of their location, should you discover it?"

Faal gave him an amused glance, as if he knew exactly what Basher was thinking. "Certainly, cooperation is always best, is it not? Meanwhile, I was informed that these Rik from the space station were found. What is the situation?"

Basher gave him the bare basics as he didn't see any purpose in subterfuge. "Do you have any thoughts on this?"

Faal bristled. "You do not ask a Merith if they have any thoughts. It is akin to asking if you have any brains."

"I apologize. I meant, would you like to make any suggestions?"

"I believe I may have a few suggestions, but I must ponder. I will call on you at the embassy to discuss this further."

Basher didn't like the idea of letting Faal into the embassy. It was the only conceivable place he might gain a clue to Claire's location, though admittedly it would have to be a clue that eluded Basher. But could he afford to alienate Faal by refusing his help?

"Anyone is welcome to visit the embassy," Basher said. "By the way, concerning your Rik thief: how *did* she infiltrate your zoo in order to steal that animal?"

"I never said she was Rik."

Basher nearly gaped with shock. "You *admit* she's human?"

"Yes. I referred to her as a *fake*, and she is, though not as you assumed. She is a criminal and a fugitive." Faal blinked his large eye. "So I'm sure you will accept my help in her recovery."

Basher raged inwardly. Faal didn't care that Claire's humanity was common knowledge! He knew that he was better positioned to find Claire than Basher was, and he'd guessed (correctly) that Basher would continue to work with him if there was any chance he might find her. Faal was playing a game, and he didn't care that Basher knew it, because he held all the cards.

"How long was Claire in your zoo?"

The amused expression disappeared. "Long enough that her sudden and violent attack on me is one of the greater insults I have received." Faal fingered a silk cord tied around his robe. It was intricately knotted into a loose chain. His inner eyelid half closed and for a moment his hand clenched in a fist around the cord. "She will be honored to know she achieved a feud knot."

Basher felt a sense of urgency, even as Faal regained his calm and took his leave. His hand trembled slightly as he opened his tablet. He *had* to find Claire before Faal did.

24

FAAL LEFT THE RESIDENCE, aware that Basher watched him until he was out of sight.

The whole building reeked of dead Rik. Even with their inferior sense of smell, the Vel and Tergre residents must have been unusually apathetic.

Faal exhaled sharply as he reached the public corridor, but it did little to dislodge the smell. His robes were no doubt inundated with it; he would dispose of them.

He compulsively twisted another knot into his sash. Was there no end to the inconvenience Claire would cause him? First, she dishonored him by rejecting his hospitality and causing injury. Next, she took refuge with the Diadina, curse the woman. Then, Claire had gotten the human detective, Basher, to take her back to the embassy. Faal had known then that it was only a matter of time until they realized she was human. The Spo had developed a new blood test that was being used at several embassies.

Faal had made new plans to reclaim her—either to extradite her legally, or to kidnap her illegally if need be. It was only a question of money. The Spo embassy was no match for him.

Her escape from the embassy, on top of the rest, was another insult. Now he had to go to the trouble of tracking her down in

Lower Selta. And despite what he had said to Basher, even his contacts might have trouble locating a single alien in the warren of that sprawling city. They might discover her tomorrow, but it was more likely to be several weeks.

In the meantime, Claire had caused him to significantly alter his strategy with Basher, which threatened to complicate his plans.

Still, he was Faal of Merith II. He raised kingdoms with a word and ended lives with a frown. He would not be thwarted by *her*. He would leave this planet with Claire.

Meanwhile, he had a secondary goal as well. The rumors of the human biocomputer on the Spo space station, the one called Akemi, had proved true. Faal had been intrigued during the trial. He had been fascinated on his second visit.

Had it retained memory and personality? If so, was its personality influenced by the Spo technology or not? How long would it last before it burnt out? How did it retain its sanity with no physical body? It could arguably be the next step in artificial computing, as it sidestepped the Merith rejection of *pure* artificial intelligence.

Most importantly, was it reproduceable?

When Faal was fascinated, he took what he wanted. If things had gone *well* with the explosion, he would already have it in his possession. He had planned to take the biocomputer from the wreckage during the confused aftermath of the space station destruction. Unfortunately, those arrogant children had gotten the computer to their escape capsule and prevented him from salvaging it like he'd planned.

It was a setback, he did not deny it.

Now that Sam and Natsuki were here on Selta, he was certain the computer was as well. He needed further access to the embassy to find out its exact location.

Faal was passing through a Merith neighborhood now. He

could feel the slight differences in the air of the corridor that mimicked the salty, argon-rich atmosphere of Merith II. A sushi restaurant was just ahead, and he found himself hungry.

Faal took two of his men to accompany him into the establishment. It was not up to his usual standards, with strings of fake jewels sewn into the synthetic curtains. There were clean, if threadbare, cushions on the lounge chairs, and small chipped tables between each. A handful of Merith already occupied the small space, which had the sole benefit of informing Faal that the food was not terrible.

He sat in the one available chair, and his men stationed themselves behind him. All eyes were on him, of course, no doubt shocked that a Merith of his obvious substance was to dine there. Faal did not often patronize such places, but he had had a wild period in his youth when he gained great familiarity with the low places of Merith society.

A server appeared and bowed deeply. He correctly did not address Faal, however, but spoke to his bodyguard. "What may I have the honor of serving your master?"

"Whatever of your offerings is the best. Faal of Merith II has not yet had his midday meal."

The skin around the server's eye blushed red as he took in the identity of the guest. "Absolutely. The chef has just received a fresh shipment of fish from Comboda, if Faal would care to wait for a fluted *gretish*?"

Faal waved his hand, dismissive. "That will do."

He was not sorry to have some time to rest his leg. When Claire had dropped a branch on him, she had been even more effective than she knew, fracturing a small bone in his ankle. It still pained him when he traveled more than a small distance. He did not allow the pain to dictate his movement, but a small rest would improve the walk back to his residence.

Soon he would call on the Spo embassy to initiate the next

step in his current plan. Basher saw him as an adversary now, but this was the sort of game Faal enjoyed most. It was child's play to manipulate someone who saw you as a friend. But manipulating someone who knew you for an enemy—that was satisfying.

The server returned with a slightly bubbling beverage in one hand and a tall, cold goblet in the other. Faal could smell herbal tea and a sweet scratchwet.

"I don't suppose you carry any of the new Melifleuran wines?" Faal inquired.

The server bowed his head abjectly. "I'm afraid we do not."

"Then take this mess away. I'll have mineral water."

"At once!"

Faal pondered his course of action. The explosion of the space station had gone well enough. He'd been disappointed to miss his opportunity for gaining the computer then, but the explosion was also planned to drive a wedge between the humans and the Rik.

No serious suspicion had been directed his way as yet, despite his immediate proximity to the space station. His Council status and his immediate help to find survivors had closed the first window of suspicion, and he would arrange the coming evidence to point more damningly than ever at the Rik nation.

The most perfect part of the plan was that the Rik actually *had* committed the sabotage. He'd blackmailed them into it, which was not difficult for a Merith with his influence over eight nearly powerless Rik. In fact, he probably could have bribed them into it, but he found the idea of bribing a Rik morally distasteful. There were lines he would not cross.

The server returned with his mineral water, and Faal took some in his beak, throwing his head back to swallow.

It'd been necessary for the actual perpetrators to die, of course. They knew the truth and they should have known that Faal would never let them live with that much power.

Also, he did not want the humans to think the sabotage had

been an isolated event. That would do him no good because the humans were just irrational enough to 'forgive' that sort of crime and continue their abominable sponsorship of the Rik.

No, Faal wanted the Rik/Human alliance destroyed, and so the sabotage must appear to be an organized attack by the entire Rik government. He had the evidence in place to lead Basher to that conclusion, and if Basher proved slow to take the clues, then Faal would make it plainer.

Faal's own desire to make a breach in the Rik/Human alliance was as much for the humans' good as it was to punish the Rik. It was quite generous of him really. The humans were not a bad species. Indeed, they had a strength of purpose and resilience he found refreshing. Even Claire, as inexcusable as her actions were, displayed a boldness and intelligence he grudgingly respected. When he caught her, she would be punished as an enemy, not a slave. She would probably not appreciate the difference, but it mattered to him.

Sam Locklear, the human boy who'd somehow brainwashed the Spo into allowing him to run the trial, was a perfect example of humanity's potential.

The boy had accomplished wonders during that trial. He had proved the emperor's son to be a traitor. He had uncovered a Rik plot to assassinate the cadets and even wrung a confession from one of their assassins. To top it off, he'd managed to show proof of the Rik fleet closing in on Earth. The boy had annihilated the Rik prosecutor and everyone knew it.

And then! Then Sam's humanity betrayed him and he threw it all away by affiliating with the Rik. His ostensible reason had been the valuable expertise the Rik could offer to humanity, as well as partial ownership of their large space fleet, but that was idiotic. The humans could have taken whatever they wanted from a gutted Rik populace.

Faal had not immediately decided to undo this ill-favored

alliance, but when several other pieces fell into place, he'd wondered if he might not try his hand at galactic politics. It would be a benevolent kindness toward the misguided humans, as well as gaining his own ends, namely the Akemi experiment.

The server finally returned with his meal, setting the deceptively simple dish on the table at Faal's left hand. It was a medium-size fish, about two of Faal's fists, and did indeed smell fresh, which he had somewhat doubted. The fish had been filleted and skewered with hot glass rods. Most of the rods had been removed, though two remained for him to hold. A pure, bacterial-fermented solution had been poured into the 'flutes' or holes seared into the raw flesh by the glass rods. A sprinkling of sea salt and, he noted with approval, flakes of silver, topped the light pink flesh of the fish.

"May I bring your master anything else?"

Faal waved his hand. "I have everything I require." He bit into the fish and the strong sauce dripped from his beak. Not as pure as it should have been. A disgrace, really. The flavor of the gretish was almost entirely dependent on the quality of the fermentation, and this one was slightly lacking.

Faal grimaced and took another bite. Many people thought he was above compromise, but they were wrong. Obsession with small disappointments was weakness. Every good strategist knew that. Self-control was essential to perspective, and Faal had excellent self-control. He took another bite of the gretish, pondering what interesting experiments he would do with that biocomputer.

25

AFTER NEARLY TWO weeks of serving the high-end aliens that came to Francois's restaurant, Claire woke in a cold sweat. She'd had a terrible dream, and she stumbled from her bed in a panic.

Claire stumbled into the wall and followed it to the bathroom. She collided with the waist high cabinet and a light automatically turned on. Her wild reflection faced her in the bathroom mirror, and she was half-surprised to see her own face, and not Jenelle's. It had started with the usual dream, but the rest of it had been new.

Sage came to the open door, blinking in the light and looking concerned. "Claire, are you alright? I thought I heard someone fall."

Claire laughed, somewhat hysterically. "No, I'm fine... just a bad dream."

She touched the plate to turn off the light and Sage stepped back to let her come out. He put his hand on her forehead. "Do you have another fever?"

"No, I—" Claire broke off into a sob. The soft feel of a human hand, from someone who knew her name and cared whether she lived or died was too much. "I just..."

Claire stepped forward and wrapped her arms around Sage,

hugging him tightly. She was crying in earnest now, and she muffled her sobs against his shoulder.

"It's good to cry. Your body is finally releasing stress." Sage rubbed her back.

"I dreamed about—all of you."

"Was it bad?"

"There were six cups on a table, and I came to pour Francois's wine into them. One was for me—it was silver, I think. The other five were ceramic. And when I had filled them all, Faal came to the table. He—he knocked my glass off but he *smashed* Juliet…"

"Shh. Dreams don't mean anything except that you are worried," Sage said. "You should get back to bed." He led her by the hand back into the 'girls' room.

Claire sat on the edge of her bed. "I guess so."

"Do you want me to stay?"

Claire knew she should say no. "Yes."

Claire curled under the blanket and Sage lay behind, wrapping an arm around her. "I've got you, you're safe." He rubbed her hand with his thumb. "You have PTSD—the key word being 'post.' I've seen—I've *read* that while humans are in trauma, they can function well, with bravery and resource. It's only *after* that their body betrays them."

"Probably. I know it sounds stupid, but when those cups shattered—I knew it was Juliet, and you, and—" She broke off. "The first part of the dream was with Jenelle. I haven't told you about her yet. It's a depressing story."

Sage stroked her hand. "Tell me everything."

CLAIRE WOKE in the morning to the sound of an argument. She was alone in the bed, facing the wall.

"What are you doing with her?" Old Twin said in a low voice.

"That's none of your business," Sage said. They were on the small landing between the sleeping rooms.

"You can't keep experimenting."

"I'm not experimenting. I like her very much."

Old Twin snorted.

"You would have let that guard kill her," Sage retorted. "You lost your right to interfere."

"That would have been cleaner than this."

Claire closed her eyes when she realized Old Twin was coming into their shared bedroom. Old Twin pushed the door open roughly and walked over to grab her clothes.

Claire knew Sage was an alien. Why didn't that totally disgust her? Maybe something was wrong with her...

She heard the shower turn on in the bathroom, which meant Old Twin was occupied, so she swung her legs over the bed and sat up, hugging her pillow. She made herself say it out loud. "Sage is an alien."

Still nothing. It's not that she didn't care about the people who they'd stolen... but Sage hadn't done it himself. If they'd turned the offer down, those bodies would still have been used, they'd just have gone to someone else.

Still, they *should* have turned it down, if they really cared about killing people. She knew she should hate him for what he'd done. But when she thought about his thumb rubbing her hand, she couldn't summon the hate.

After all, the Rik were *taught* that it was perfectly okay to take another body. Surely the fact that Sage had developed a conscience, even if it was a little late, was evidence that he was a good person.

Claire looked out the tiny window in her room to the slanted pedestrian walkway outside. The roof in this tunnel extended diagonally down from just above her window to the far side of the street, meeting the ground at a sharp angle.

Nobody could walk in the last three feet of that space, where the roof was so low. At 'nightfall', when the streetlights switched from yellow/orange to green, aliens would come and sleep in the gap. She would have assumed they were homeless if she'd seen that type of thing on Earth, but she didn't know if that was the case here. Maybe they rented the space. With the constant climate control on every bit of Selta, it would never get too cold or rainy or windy to sleep 'outdoors.'

While she waited for the shower, she watched two Tergre in the street wake up and pack their bedding. She'd seen them before. They always spread out one blanket and lay very close to each other, like two dogs curled up in a single doggie bed. This morning the reddish-furred female began to stir first, and Claire watched her rub her mate's furry back with her long snout until he woke up. Even from up here, looking down on the two of them, she could see his eyes open and a sleepy smile lift his eyes.

So what if Sage was an alien? Clearly lots of aliens were affectionate and kind and... Claire turned away from the window, and sank back on her pillow. She needed to get a grip on herself. She had one night of comfort, and now she was picturing growing old with Sage.

She got up and ruthlessly straightened her bed.

FRANCOIS OPENED the restaurant to guests every other night for dinner, but he served a mid-day meal only twice a week. He said it drove up demand to keep down the supply, and it also meant that they could have lazy mornings before helping in the afternoon and evening.

She helped herself to a can of corn (she had the weirdest cravings now that she had access to real food again), and she added water to some powdered milk.

Sage, Juliet, Old Twin, and Diva were eating breakfast at the little table in the kitchen, very silent. Claire felt awkward as they watched her open the can and dump it in a bowl. She wondered if they'd all seen Sage with her.

"Did you guys sleep well?" she finally said to fill the silence.

"Yes. I suppose. What does bad sleep feel like?" Diva asked.

"When you wake up a lot, I guess."

"Ah. Then I slept badly. Do humans usually talk about their sleep? We usually talk about what we do when we're conscious."

"But if we should talk about sleep—we will talk about sleep!" Juliet added with enthusiasm.

"It's okay. You don't have to talk about anything; not all humans are talkative in the morning."

"But what would they talk about if they were?" Juliet asked. "I think I'm talkative."

"No!" Old Twin said sarcastically. "We never would have guessed."

Juliet rolled her eyes, "You're so grumpy."

Claire ate her corn slowly. "My dad always talked about weather, which is kind of an empty topic here. My mom would talk about her students, and I would talk about my friends..." She had a moment of nostalgia, thinking about Jenelle.

Sage put his hand over hers. "We're your friends, too."

Francois came in the back door just then, and the room suddenly came to life. Three cabinets opened and closed, the empty chair by the table scooted itself in, and the tins on the counter began restacking themselves.

"Good morning, my fine friends and servitors. We received another shipment today!"

Three large crates rolled in the door after Francois, and soon Claire and the others were excitedly unpacking the contents, surrounded by bags of rice and potatoes, canned food, McCormick spices, and princess birthday napkins.

Claire could practically see the grocery aisles that had been pillaged to get this assortment.

"And what are these?" Francois said next, levitating a small plastic package in the air. "Some sort of food preparation item?"

Claire usually tried to let the others have a chance to identify things. Juliet really enjoyed trying to match items with various commercials she'd seen, but these made Claire laugh.

"No, those are razors. They're for shaving your legs."

Juliet immediately pulled her pants leg up. "The Tergre sometimes shave their noses and paws, at least I think some of them do —it looks like that. But I didn't know humans did." She rubbed her leg which was, by Claire's American standards, very hairy. "Other humans must be hairier than I, I suppose?"

"In some countries they don't shave," Claire hedged.

They were all examining their legs now.

"You certainly need to shave," Juliet said to Sage and Athlete, looking at their hairy calves.

"No—only girls shaved in my country. Well, sometimes athletes do, I guess." Claire laughed again at their confused expressions. Maybe she was losing her mind. Last night she'd cried herself to sleep, and now she was teaching aliens to shave their legs.

"Ah, another gender specific habit," Sage said. "And why—"

"Never mind," Old Twin cut him off. "What else is in that box?"

FRANCOIS GAVE them another lesson in food additives, so that they could put the final touches on the food themselves.

He lifted something that looked like the offspring of a pepper grinder and a clarinet, showing them the different compartments and how to open and close them.

"Of course, you could do each individually, but where's the art in that?" Francois asked. "Much better to mix the supplements in the main chamber first, say a prostaglandin-damper with a protein-acid, and then dispense at once... like this." A silvery blue dust wafted out the bottom and onto the floor. "And what would that mixture be appropriate for?"

There was silence for a second.

Claire's glasses printed: *Nut protein. Spo additive.*

"Oh, right," Claire said. "We did that one yesterday... peanut butter for a ... Spo?"

"*Ding! Ding! Ding!* Correct," Francois said. "Any kind of nut would require this." Somewhere Francois had seen a human game show, and now he liked to make his own sound effects.

Sage held the pepper grinder and struggled to open the right valves. "Just think," he said. "In a thousand years, we'll have evolved to tolerate each other's food. Won't that be... nice."

He twisted the release and an orange powder wafted out the bottom and exploded on the floor with a small, but emphatic *pop*.

Francois laughed. "Evolution may need some help." He passed the grinder to Juliet, who took her turn with a determined look in her eye.

Sage rolled his eyes. "Seven of the ten Council species deny the existence of a creator, Francois."

"There's twelve species, now, and more coming," Francois said, shifting the grinder to Claire. "What with the Melifleurs and the humans. What story do humans have for their existence?"

Claire placed her fingers carefully on the grinder, depressing the thumb piece, pointer, and pinkie on the side... blue dust, just right. She smiled. It was cathartic to have a job to do and learn to do it well. "I don't know. Evolution, I guess. I mean, here you all are..." She handed the grinder to Old Twin and gestured at them.

Francois wriggled his thick, fleshy body. "Adaptation alone? We are giant slugs—with no hands, flippers, or cilia. Did we simply *slither* into intelligence? And look at the Tergre, lovable, overgrown ferrets that they are—no! They're sentient. Evolution is a tool, but someone is wielding it."

Sage groaned, and Francois laughed, jiggling his translucent skin and the fiery orange body paint he'd opted for today.

As he continued, the dust on the floor silently collected itself and flew to the trash. It was so weird that she was becoming used to this—it was like living at Hogwarts.

Though Francois would definitely be one of Hagrid's strange creatures.

26

BASHER COULDN'T SLEEP that night. He tossed and turned and finally went to his office, letting the lemur ride on his shoulder.

"Hey, Akemi, you awake?" he said. There was no response on his computer.

He opened some paperwork he needed to complete for the other Rik he'd caught recently, and he also opened a chat box to speak with Akemi.

"I'm up if you want to talk," he typed.

Okay, Mom.

"Sorry what?"

No, it's okay. I feel good today.

"Are you talking to me?"

A huge chunk of text followed that looked like gibberish.

Basher frowned. Was Akemi asleep? The human brain wasn't designed for constant awareness, and she'd mentioned that sometimes she accidentally did stuff in her sleepstate.

Then came another segment—phrases and sentences spliced together. Snippets of their research seemed to be mixed with things she'd been reading about philosophy.

Faal is suspected of illegally visiting the Velvidian Enclave weapons do not cut this Spirit, fire does not burn it, water does not make it wet, and the wind does not make it dry Faal's underground zoological research—is he bribing the planetary inspectors? Inquire. That is why the good news was given to those who are now dead, those who are now dead, those who are now dead...

She was pondering the nature of death. Of *course* she was. While incredibly positive about her situation, it had to prey on her mind. Basher was ashamed he had not thought of that, nor did he know how long she would last in her current state.

He would have closed the connection then, but Akemi's stream continued into a video.

Nat was in it. Basher recognized her, though she looked younger and healthier and had no tattoo on her face. She was riding down an escalator in a huge mall, and all the signs were in Japanese. Near the bottom of the escalator she jumped off the last two steps and ran to hug a smaller Japanese girl.

She looked like Nat, but her black hair had light brown highlights and her eyes were more almond shaped. Designer sunglasses held back her hair.

That must be Akemi, Basher realized, rather stunned. He wondered if this was her memory of something that really happened, or just a dream.

He had his answer when they waved at Sam, passing by on the other side. Another man waved as well. He was a little shorter than Sam, with dark hair and a five o'clock shadow...

Oh, it was clearly supposed to be *him,* only better looking— like a Bollywood actor version of Basher.

But the mall began to shake. A crack split the floor and Nat slid toward it, grasping desperately for her sister's hand.

He could feel Akemi's horror as Nat's fingers slipped and she disappeared into the void. Akemi's mouth opened in a soundless cry. She ran forward and threw herself into the crack after her.

Basher had read once that people who dream of falling never

actually hit the ground, but apparently Akemi hadn't read that. The landing looked painful.

Akemi's life certainly hadn't taught her that you get rescued at the last moment. It echoed what Nat said when she first saw Claire: "Sometimes the terrible story is true."

Suddenly Basher realized what he was doing—spying on a teenage girl's dreams. He closed the connection immediately.

She deserved what privacy she had, though he was glad to have a face to put with his mental image of her.

Basher was surprised when Nat wandered in his office a few minutes later. It was after midnight.

Basher wasn't usually one to notice, but she looked even more exhausted than when she'd arrived at the embassy two weeks ago.

"Are you alright, Nat? Can I get you something?"

She shook her head with an attempted smile. "No, I just can't sleep, and I saw that you'd opened a connection with Akemi, so I knew you were awake."

"I didn't mean to watch her dream," Basher explained. "I thought she was awake for a moment."

"It's okay, I didn't think that. I was just surprised to see you in her dream."

"I was, too."

Nat sat in his partner's chair. "I know she's lonely, with only us to talk to. I'm glad you've become friends with her."

"It's not hard. She's a lot of fun, and she certainly is great with the research."

"The research..." Nat said vaguely. "Right."

"We've uncovered a decent bit about the eight Rik in the apartment. Nothing would indicate that they had particular terrorist leanings, but there were a few interesting things."

"Do tell."

"They bought entirely new wardrobes and personal items when they got here. Akemi found the records. Looks like they were concerned that their clothes might be evidence, which would be the case if they had those explosives with them for any length of time. They also paid for Vel deep-cleaning, which is really unpleasant but would effectively destroy the top layer of their skin that might hold trace elements or even burns from when they wired the bombs."

Sam entered and Nat jumped, looking a little guilty. "Basher was just telling me about the progress Akemi has made."

Sam rubbed her shoulders. "Okay. But you really need to sleep."

Basher continued. "There's not much else yet. Except Akemi says that she was lucky in the way they set the bombs. Even if you hadn't been able to get to her, she probably would have survived the explosion. The engine room was nearly untouched, though of course without breathable air. You probably would have been able to retrieve her from the wreckage."

That finally got a little reaction out of Nat, who smiled. "You had to tell me that now? Sam'll never let me live it down if it turns out I dragged him through all that for nothing."

"I'll hold it in reserve for a rainy day," Sam said.

ONLY A FEW HOURS LATER, Basher stood squarely in front of the Merith entourage surrounding Faal. They were bigger than him, armed, and confident.

He couldn't do anything about their size or attitude, but he refused to admit the five Merith bodyguards until they submitted their weapons. That was standard at every embassy.

They weren't thrilled.

Faal was richly dressed in a deep orange robe hanging from his sloping shoulders. He was in complete control of himself this morning. Heck, he was probably in control of the traffic in the tunnel behind him as well. From what Basher and Akemi had uncovered about this guy, he'd been a crime lord in Merith main-space until he'd turned his considerable resources toward politics.

"I don't doubt your intentions," Basher said, which was a total lie, "but we've had several security episodes in recent days and must be extra cautious. We cannot allow any weapons into the embassy in case they should fall into the wrong hands."

"We are not armed," said one of the bodyguards. "We were instructed of the requirements."

Basher smiled and then lunged forward a step.

Faal's bodyguards shifted in a lightning-fast blur, ending with three weapons pointed at Basher's head.

Before he'd even finished the movement, Basher had shifted his weight and retreated a step. He held out empty hands.

Faal's soldiers growled low in their throats at the trick.

"'No harm, no foul,' as we say on Earth." Basher tapped the closest gun with one finger. "My partner will need to collect these. Welcome to the Spo embassy. I shall meet you shortly in the reception hall."

Out of sight, Basher leaned against the wall for a moment, his heart pounding like it wanted out of his chest. That was a trick he'd learned on Earth, back when they'd worked security for Spo events a couple times. Basher's mentor had said, "If you think someone's entourage is overly armed, and you can't throw them in jail, give them a low-grade threat before they get inside. They show their weapons, you confiscate them... Minimal danger, and you've avoided a possible incident."

Except for the possibility that they freak out and shoot you. And for just a second there, Basher had thought perhaps he'd gone too far. But his friend always said that the more professional the help, the better your chance of walking away.

Basher had wagered that Faal would have extremely profes-sional guards, who wouldn't kill without being sure of the situa-tion, and he'd won his gamble. Barely.

Now Faal had been slightly humbled. He was clearly an alien used to dominating his inferiors, and a reminder like that never hurt.

Sam, Nat, and Shara joined them in the reception hall, along with Basher's partner and the ambassador from Spo, who formally welcomed Faal to this outpost of Spo territory.

When the ambassador left, Faal surveyed them with satisfaction. He seemed to take particular note of Sam and Nat, who sat close together, their glasses occasionally winking in the light.

"It has been my desire to meet you both," Faal said. "Since I had the honor of presiding over your rather remarkable trial."

He ignored Shara, who looked a little piqued. She'd been at the trial, too. Her confession had changed everything.

Faal added something in the Merith language that Basher did not quite catch. Sam nodded and responded formally in the same dialect, putting a hand to his glasses, as he often did when Akemi was translating or talking to him.

Faal clicked his beak in appreciation and switched back. "Very prettily said."

"And your English is excellent," Sam returned. "You sound like you've had a native tutor."

"Yes, a truly exceptional one."

Again, Basher felt the familiar surge of helpless rage that hit him whenever he thought about Claire in Faal's clutches.

Faal continued. "I do not know what you have uncovered about the dead Rik as yet, but I have come to offer my aid in supplying a Crosspoint to examine the bodies. A Crosspoint who is trained in micro-manipulation can perform a better autopsy than anyone else."

Basher mentally saluted Faal. That was a good move. He'd offered something so valuable they couldn't refuse, even if they wanted to. "Thank you. That would be very valuable in our investigation. The Tergre have still not verified if there was poison in use."

Faal smiled. "Of course not. I will send you the name of several respected Crosspoint practitioners. You may select whichever you wish and send me the bill."

"That's very generous of you," Basher said flatly.

Faal inclined his head. "Perhaps in turn you would generously offer me a tour of the embassy? I have never had occasion to visit the Spo embassy before. These skylights are quite spectacular."

Sam made eye contact with Basher and shrugged slightly, as if to say, "What can I do?"

Sam gave the tour. Basher thought Faal wanted an excuse to find out about Claire's escape, but he was wrong. Faal made no push to see the containment cells and asked no questions about the escape. He did comment favorably on the guest rooms.

"Very spacious. Do you all stay together?"

"Shara and I have our own suite," Nat answered. "The same as this."

Only at the end of the tour did Faal bring up Claire.

"No word on our fugitive?" he asked casually.

Basher stiffened. "Legally, you may have the animal, but the matter of the human is dependent on international law."

"Yes. I've spoken to the Seltan judge to whom you submitted the case. The human stole from me personally, therefore, I can press civil charges on my home planet, since Selta has tight limits on criminal extradition."

Unfortunately, there was some precedent for Faal's claim. Basher and Akemi had been researching that as well—but it was a gray area. Private property was a big deal in Council law, and Faal was right that it trumped a lot of other things.

Claire's status at the time of the theft would be critical. Would she be considered Faal's slave, a prisoner of war, or a victim of private criminal activity? Akemi said arguments could be made for all three. It would depend on the judge.

"It's rather a moot point right now, isn't it?" Basher said. "I suppose we'll have plenty of time to figure that out once our *fugitive* is found."

They escorted him to the exit and Shara shook her head when he was gone. "That guy is creepy. And I'm an alien assassin, so when I say creepy, I mean that I wouldn't mind killing him for you."

For once Basher didn't roll his eyes. He just nodded.

27

THAT NIGHT, during the supper service, Francois had a surprise for his guests. He levitated twelve tiny bowls filled with crème brûlée toward the guests.

Claire had tasted a tiny bit with her finger earlier and found it delicious. Unfortunately, her esophagus also burned like fire and Francois scolded her for trying something after he'd put in the special additives. He'd given her a shot glass full of something that tasted and felt like chalk dissolved in water, but it had soothed her burning throat.

Francois addressed the guests. "Please be so kind as to observe the delightful smell of the delicacy in front of you." He paused while they audibly sniffed. "And then direct your attention to your server, to see the final step of preparation."

Francois brought out several small torches to caramelize the top layer of the dessert. Claire picked one up and saw Francois turn off the heat sensor above the bar. He wasn't supposed to access the sensor, but he'd called in a favor to disable it just for this. He always seemed to have friends where he needed them.

Claire flipped on the tiny torch and proceeded to caramelize the first dish. About twenty seconds was all it took. She spun the ramekin with her hand as Francois had shown her, getting all the edges even. The Vel rubbed her hands in anticipation, her forked tongue darting out delicately.

Claire smiled as she finished the first and moved to the second dessert. This wasn't rocket science, but it was fun to have a rapt audience.

Francois gave a short lecture to the guests while Claire moved down the bar.

Her glasses translated his speech as she went.

As you will now see, the open flame has caused the sugar particles to undergo a chemical change. Combined with the flavor of vanilla...

Claire loved her glasses—especially moments like this when they allowed her to connect with everyone around her.

Francois turned to Claire. "Could you please tell our guests some of the other uses of vanilla while they eat?"

A few weeks ago, that would have put Claire in a cold sweat, but now she simply waited for her glasses to look it up.

Uses of vanilla:

Baking

Drinks (i.e. white hot-chocolate, vanilla smoothie)

Non-cooking uses:

Potpourri

Cleaning agent, to reduce food odors

"Thanks," Claire whispered under her breath.

You are welcome.

Claire talked about making banana bread with her grandmother (which made the matriarchal Vel customers happy) and having vanilla ice cream while watching sports. She glanced at Athlete, remembering watching reruns of him on TV, but he didn't notice.

. . .

AFTER CLEANUP THAT NIGHT, Claire waited until the other girls were asleep and then got her glasses out again. Talking about her grandmother made her homesick.

"Show me Earth, Akemi," she whispered. "More videos of Earth or Basher's videos, if you have them."

Accessing downloaded videos. Please wait.

When the video started, Claire could tell it was another of his. The video moved in a clumsy panorama shot of a police station while an older woman narrated.

"Here I am in front of Basher's station. He graduated from the academy last month, and now he's working here."

There was a large parking lot with three cop cars parked by the front door. A rack held several black police bikes. An American flag waved from a flag pole.

The lady walked closer to the door still filming. "I asked him if I could come visit him today, and he said to come on his lunch break. I knew you would want to see it all, Ava, so I'll text you the video."

Just then the front door opened, and Basher walked out. He looked a lot younger then; more relaxed and without the coiled tension Claire had felt in him when they met.

"I thought I saw you out here," he said with an easy smile.

"Say hello to Ava," she said. "I am going to send this to her."

Basher smiled. "She'll be home in a month when her semester's over. She could see it then."

His mother ignored him. "Which car is yours?"

"None of 'em. I'll be on bike patrol for a while. If I do go out, it'll be ride-along."

"Well, a policeman on a bike is still a policeman. I'm so proud of you."

Basher hugged his mom, and then said, "But can you please put that away while I show you around? They'll give me a hard time..."

The next video was dated years later, and now that Claire thought about it, only a few months before the Hadron explosion changed everything. It felt surreal to see this window into the world, knowing how radically everything was about to change.

This time the phone or camera seemed to be mounted at the back of a huge church. A polished, wooden crucifix hung below a stained-glass window. For a moment Claire wondered if this was a video of Basher and Ava's wedding, but then she realized the pews were filled with people in black.

Several people in front of the stage moved to sit and revealed a closed, blue casket.

"Are you sure you should film this?" someone whispered off the screen.

A sniff. "I don't know. But I already had the tripod for the wedding, and now..." A broken sob. "I don't know. I just think Basher may need to see this again. After he's had time for it to sink in."

"We are here to celebrate the life of Ava Marie Hendrickson," a priest began. "A girl who we all loved, and who we look forward to embracing in heaven."

He gave a short eulogy, followed by a woman who was Ava's cousin.

By the time Basher got up to speak Claire was already crying. She crept into the bathroom so she wouldn't wake anyone up.

He didn't speak long, but gave a heart-felt eulogy for his fiancée, who had died in a collision with a drunk driver a week before their wedding. When the funeral was over, the video stopped.

Claire sobbed into a towel, gripping the cold sink. She wasn't crying just for Basher or that girl's family; she was crying for all the people who were about to die in the Hadron explosion. How many people at that funeral were still alive? How many loved ones had they lost in the aftermath of the explosion and the Spo purges?

"Claire, are you alright?"

She jumped. Sage was knocking at the bathroom door. She used the towel to wipe her eyes, and she vigorously blow her nose.

"One second." She forced herself to breathe deeply and then washed her face before opening the door. "All done."

Even in the dim light, Sage could tell she'd been crying. "Did you have another nightmare?"

"No, I was only..." What was she doing? Watching the private videos of a man she'd barely met and grieving over everything they'd lost?

"Were you thinking of Jenelle again?"

Claire jerked. She'd told Sage the story of Jenelle in the safety of the dark that night. Somehow having him bring it up now, face to face, felt like a slap.

"No, I was homesick."

She knew Sage would be happy to comfort her again, but something in her recoiled. Basher's videos reminded who she was, and who Sage wasn't. She may not blame him for everything the Rik had done to humanity... but she was human and he was Rik.

"I'm fine," she said weakly.

"You know you can trust me?"

"Of course. Goodnight, Sage."

28

BASHER HAD DELAYED CHECKING Akemi's latest surveillance footage until the morning after Faal's visit to the embassy. He'd spent the rest of the day investigating the names of the Crosspoint who might provide a more detailed autopsy.

Akemi had standing orders to alert him if Claire left the café or saw anything that might pinpoint their position, but other than that, he just caught up on the highlights every few days. It felt intrusive to watch too much from Claire's glasses. He didn't want to grossly invade her privacy unless he had to.

He often let the lemur out of the cage when Akemi was bringing him up to date. Since the first time his partner had brought the little animal into their office, they'd had a tacit agreement that whoever had time off would feed the little guy and give him some time to climb around. As often as not, after a brief and energetic fling around their desks, he'd settle into Basher's lap to be petted, purring softly like a very contented lemur-kitten.

Today Akemi showed him a fast-cut, high speed version of the previous few days like usual. Akemi skipped around in the video, but in one shot, it looked like Sage was lying next to Claire in bed.

"Hang on," he told Akemi. "What was going on there?"

Claire had a nightmare. Sage stayed with her.

His face must have shown exactly what he thought of that.

They just talked. She probably needed human contact.

Basher forced himself to leave it. "Never mind. Keep going."

It infuriated him to see the Rik comforting her. Claire shouldn't have *any* man in her bed while she was recovering from everything she'd been through. Basher had three sisters, and he would beat anyone who took advantage of them while they were lonely and vulnerable.

Akemi slowed the video when Claire faced down the big, black Rik, the one called Athlete, while he gave her a lesson in self-defense.

"I learned some techniques from the Spo," Claire said, "and some from a Merith on *Final Say*. But I'm always up to learn more."

Basher was grudgingly appreciative of his efforts. Now that Faal knew Claire was in Lower Selta, they were on a ticking clock.

There was no doubt that Faal was looking for her, and based on his previous illegal activities, he probably did have very good contacts in Lower Selta. Would they know of an exclusive, invitation-only restaurant featuring humans? Maybe, maybe not. Lower Selta held roughly two million aliens—surely that was enough for Claire to remain anonymous for a little longer.

He just had to find them first. He could get the other Rik safely back in custody, and he could help Claire get somewhere Faal would never reach her. After less than five interactions with Faal, Basher had decided that whatever Claire had done to get away from him was warranted. The Merith was powerful, arrogant, and cruel.

They watched Claire's foot try to smack Athlete's gloved hand and then the video tumbled to the side as she lost her balance and fell over. He could hear Claire's laughter about it, and he might have laughed too, had he not also had to watch Sage giving her a hand up. His hand slid up to her shoulder and squeezed lightly.

"You're doing fine. I told you."

Claire laughed again. "I'd be better if you stopped watching us practice, you're making me nervous."

Basher grimaced. Claire had no idea how many people were watching her practice. He gestured curtly for Akemi to stop the video. He knew Akemi could see him through the camera in his screen.

"We've got more important things to do this morning." Basher tried to curb his bad mood. "Did you have time to requisition the data we talked about last night?"

Yeah, of course. She pulled up the raw files.

Basher slowly scanned the data. "You want to summarize for me?" He wouldn't have asked her that a week ago, but the more he interacted with her, the more impressed he was with her capabilities. At this point he would trust her summary as much as his own, and it would save him several hours of reading tiny text translated to English by his Spo computer.

Good news: they Rik were here before the attack and it's pretty conclusive they came directly from their own planet. We have a ship ID for four of them, and the others could have come under 'misc. crew.' Bad news: We traced the payment for their clothes and cleaning—it was hard to do, but it looks like a member of the Rik government paid their bills.

"Sam is going to be crushed."

Further bad news: I just got back the coroner's report, and we're getting into deep political waters now.

Basher began to look it over while Akemi summarized.

The medical Crosspoint confirmed trace amounts of explosive residue in some of their deeper tissues. We have to involve the Human Coalition Government if we continue to pursue the investigation and request records from the Rik planet. We are on the verge of accusing the Rik government of a terrorist attack. I sure don't have the authority to do that, and I don't think you do either.

If we go much further, this will threaten the validity of the Human/Rik treaty.

Basher whistled. He'd known that was where the investigation was headed, but he hadn't expected it to be confirmed this quickly. Sam was not going to be happy. He still seemed to think the Rik treaty was worth preserving, and even that the Rik were innocent, which it was becoming increasingly clear wasn't true.

When Basher laid the case out to Sam that afternoon, he wasn't surprised at Sam's frustration.

"Look," Basher was honest, "I believed from the beginning that the Rik were guilty. But you've seen the same evidence I have. Do you honestly think I should offer a different report to the Coalition?"

He and Sam were alone in his office. Basher's partner was checking out another Rik sighting, and Nat was catching up on sleep in her room.

"The evidence is *too* clear," Sam argued. "The Rik are smarter than this. If they went to the trouble to secretly sabotage the space station, couldn't they cover their tracks better than this?"

"Like they covered their tracks when they tried to invade Earth?" Basher countered. "They're not geniuses, Sam. They make mistakes and breed traitors and overreach their capabilities. Tell me how this contradicts any of that."

"I suppose that's possible..." Sam sighed sharply. "In any case, I understand that you need to file the report as is. The Rik Supreme Director will get involved. Our provisional government is already sending a Coalition Representative to handle communication with her."

"It's Senator Fontley, isn't it? He's already sent special requests to the Spo for his visit."

"Yeah, just my luck. That guy hates me."

"Do you—resent that you're not part of the Coalition government?"

Sam smiled unexpectedly. "No, I'm not that stupid. I might be an arrogant teenager, but I truly don't want to oversee the world. I had a little taste of that responsibility, and it's not as fun as it's cracked up to be."

Basher made an equivocal noise and Sam laughed. "It's okay. I already know how much you dislike my treaty with the Rik; you've never hidden it. I appreciate that you've given me the benefit of the doubt."

Basher grinned. "Then I'll admit that you're not nearly as arrogant a teenager as I was at your age."

"Don't be too sure about that," Sam laughed. "Senator Fontley will be only too happy to tell you what a conceited and dangerous freak I am."

Basher and Sam looked at his computer when it beeped.

I know where Claire is! Akemi sent. *Look!*

She pulled up a 3D map of Lower Selta and put a red dot on one of the onion layers that made up the city. *They're here. I had a brainwave. They made a dessert a few days ago which used an open flame. Francois turned off their heat detectors. I hacked into the records for Lower Selta and cross-referenced blips in the environmental controls—there's more than you'd think—with shipments of Earth-related goods.*

I found them!

"That's incredible," Basher said. "Good job. Inform the ambassador immediately. Purchase five tickets for the next train down to Lower Selta and wire them to my tablet—"

Oh, no. No, no, no. There's something else. This shipment from Earth which helped me track them—it was part of a huge order. Over 200 pods and crates. The whole ship was delayed and rerouted before it got to Selta. There have been a lot of complaints logged about the delay. You want to guess where it was rerouted? Merith II.

"You think Faal did something to it?"

Yes. I think he delayed an entire SHIP and then put trackers in every single one of those pods.

"To track each of them when it got to Selta." Basher gripped the desk to stead himself.

He could be there any minute.

29

FRANCOIS'S latest shipment had been delayed, but it had finally arrived, and it included a huge case of off-brand soda. Claire and the others sipped one appreciatively, passing it back and forth before they got ready for dinner.

Sage spun the electronic token in his hand again, while Diva fiddled with a set of chess pieces that had arrived in the last shipment.

Claire leaned back in one of the Vel chairs and took a sip of warm soda. If this place had been on Earth, the late afternoon sun would have been shining through the windows, lighting up motes of dust in a slow, golden display. It was a warm and lazy afternoon.

Sage took the can from her and took another sip. "I think this body used to like this."

Claire stiffened slightly. She didn't want to think about that. Only this morning she'd come across Juliet weeping in the corner of their bedroom.

"What's the matter?" Claire had asked, crouching down to touch her shoulder.

Juliet met her eyes and then sobbed harder. "I've finally realized... she was like you. This girl they killed for my body. She was someone like you."

Claire bit her lip. "She was. But I know you wouldn't have done it if it was up to you."

"Does that matter? I *knew* everything I know now, but I hadn't *felt* it."

"We've all done things we regret."

"But there's no way to go back. I'll always be guilty of her death."

Claire was silent.

"I'm sorry," Juliet said. "I shouldn't make *you* of all people comfort me. It just overwhelmed me. I'll never be free of this, now that I know you."

Juliet was in the kitchen with Francois now, listening to him expound about the nature of guilt and forgiveness.

Claire had escaped into the outer room with the others.

Sage's hand was draped over hers on the bar, casually rubbing her palm with his thumb. She still wasn't over her deep reaction to human touch. Apparently it took longer than a few weeks to make up that sort of deficit. Athlete had rubbed her back after they'd sparred the other day, and Claire had just about melted.

She'd missed a lot of things while she was with Faal: good food, someone to talk to, socks, music, books, the ocean... but she hadn't realized that the touch of human skin was so unique. She knew the clammy touch of Spo skin, the warm roughness of the Merith, even the feel of the furry Tergre who sometimes clumsily shook her hand when they left the restaurant; but anytime she felt the fine grain texture of human skin, her nerves thrilled.

Francois hovered in the door. "I need a few of you with actual hands to assist me in organizing the storeroom."

Athlete and the others followed him through the kitchen door, but when Claire stood to go after, Sage pulled her back down.

"Take a break. He said he only needs a few of us."

Claire hesitated, but the door was already swinging shut. She shrugged and plopped back down, enjoying the quiet and her soda. Sage started to say something, but Claire didn't hear him. Her glasses were suddenly going a mile a minute.

Claire, Faal knows where your restaurant is. He put a tracker in the delayed shipment. He could be there any time; he already knew you were in Lower Selta—

Claire bolted to her feet. "What? Are you sure?"

"What's the matter?" Sage demanded.

"He's found me." Claire's throat went tight, and her vision tunneled in panic. "He could be here any minute—"

The front door opened with a load *crack*. It had been locked, but a well-placed crowbar and a heavy kick broke the hinges.

Faal stood in the doorway, completely at ease. The soda can fell from Claire's numb fingers.

Followed by several bodyguards, Faal entered the restaurant. Two of his thugs shoved the broken door closed behind them.

Run to the kitchen. Francois may be able to help you. Rear exit. GO, Claire.

Claire was around the bar to the kitchen door in a matter of seconds, and slammed it open with her hand as she crashed through. "Francois!" she cried.

But he wasn't in the kitchen, and neither were the others. Instead, her least favorite zookeeper and another of Faal's guards waited for her.

She tried to check her momentum, but her feet were still moving. She slammed into the zookeeper's thick chest.

He grabbed her wrist and spun her around, locking an arm around her neck in a modified headlock. He pulled her against him. His beak was next to her ear. "We've missed you, Claire. Did you know Faal punished me for your escape?"

She clawed at his muscular arm with her fingernails, but he just tightened his elbow until her vision tunneled and her knees went limp.

"Francois...Athlete..." Claire choked out. The zookeeper must have locked Francois and the others in the storeroom? She hoped so, and that they weren't hurt.

"Bring her in here," Faal said.

Sage was untouched. He was coolly appraising Faal, while yet another guard pointed a pellet gun at him. That made four—Faal and his guard by the door, and the zookeeper and another guard with her. Were there more? Claire suspected there might be, but then, Faal might assume that regaining her wouldn't be very difficult. Her only escapes from him so far had been extremely lucky.

Faal ignored Sage and his gaze raked Claire up and down. "You injured me," he told Claire, as if she'd asked a question. He flicked his knotted feud belt at her. "You fractured my leg with that trap you engineered. I've ended families for less."

Claire wanted to retort, but the arm around her neck was too tight.

"You made a trap, Claire?" Sage said calmly. "You never told me that part. Very impressive."

Faal gave Sage a cursory glance. "You are one of the Rik/humans, yes? Then you will know my name. I am Faal of Merith II. If you don't become a problem for me, I will not become a problem for you. Bring her." This last was to the zookeeper, who began to edge Claire towards the front door.

"No, I'm afraid not," Sage said. "She works here, and the Crosspoint who owns this establishment will not appreciate her kidnapping."

Faal smiled. "Normally I would never bribe a Rik, but I would like to make a point to Claire. I will make this easy. You need to get off this station, correct? Headed to Earth?"

Sage inclined his head.

Faal pulled a clip from his bag, removed a card, and flicked it contemptuously to Sage. "If I endorse that credit, you could afford a private ship to Earth."

Sage looked slowly from the card to Claire, and her chest

clenched in pain. She felt as if a giant air bubble was trapped around her heart. This was the same moment, happening again.

He could do it. He could take the card, and take the others to Earth. He would feel guilty about her, possibly heart-broken, but she would be betrayed again. When Jenelle turned on Claire, her face had screwed up with fear and hate. Would Sage do the same?

Faal's beak twitched and she knew he was loving this. He knew all about Jenelle.

Sage's eyes were wary, and he held the card carefully.

"She's worth that much to you?" he said.

Faal gestured to his stiff leg. "She injured me. I was going to release her that day and instead she injured me."

Claire finally got her voice back. "No, you weren't."

"Oh, but I was. I would never keep a sentient being as an animal. Once they become common place in the galaxy, they lose all value. I was indeed going to give you up when I returned from humanity's trial. I'd broken you down, of course, but you were an interesting study. I was curious if you would heal. Imagine that; if you had only waited another day, you could have been spared all this."

Claire reeled, only held up by the zookeeper. It was true, she could see it in his eyes.

"But now we shall begin again," Faal said. "Perhaps much like the first time. What do you say, Rik? Survival is sanity."

Sage looked at Claire and the whites of his eyes reflected in the light.

"It's not worth it." A tear slid down Claire's cheek. "Believe me, I don't blame you for selling me out, but I know how you'll feel tomorrow. You'll regret it; I think Jenelle did, at the last moment."

The zookeeper began to push her forward, and Claire tried to brace her feet against the floor. Her slip-on shoes skidded uselessly.

Sage made eye contact with her, and his face wasn't conflicted at all.

"No, thank you." His answer hung in the air. "I'm afraid I must decline your very generous offer," Sage said. "See, the human has value to us as well, and—"

Faal snapped his beak, "Be silent. I won't negotiate with the bastard son of a bastard species." He gestured to his guard. "Kill him."

"You won't leave with her." The certainty in Sage's voice demanded attention. "You've misjudged your opponents. You've played the game badly this time."

Faal's eye slitted in anger at this supreme insult, but before he could reply, the front door flew open again on its broken hinges. Athlete barreled through. He ducked his head and tackled Faal's nearest bodyguard like a defensive lineman. They seemed to fly several feet through the air before crashing to the floor in a tangle of blows and falling bar stools.

Juliet came low through the door just behind Athlete. She snaked to the left in a blur, tossing a gun to Sage. She rolled over the bar and disappeared behind it just as the zookeeper began to fire at her.

In drawing his gun, the zookeeper released Claire and she slipped down. She landed hard on her bottom on the slick floor, and scrambled away. Another bodyguard reached for his weapon, but it was floating out the door.

Sage covered the distance to the zookeeper in two strides, leaping over Athlete and using the butt of the Merith's own weapon to strike him at the base of his neck.

Athlete and the other guard rolled toward Claire, exchanging vicious blows. She flung herself away and kicked at the last body-guard, tripping him to the floor.

A muffled, *thu-u-uh* came from the injured diaphragm of the one Sage was fighting. Sage kicked the gun out of his hand as he crumpled. He immediately swiveled to cover Faal, who was also at the point of Old Twin's weapon.

Only Athlete and the second bodyguard were still active, as they tussled among the chairs. The Merith rolled and pinned Athlete between the floor and the bar. He got a knee onto Athlete's chest and used his sharp hands to jab at Athlete's abdomen. Claire whimpered, but before she could decide what to do, Juliet vaulted back over the bar. She jumped on the bodyguard's back like a monkey and pushed her gun flush against his domed head. He stopped.

Faal stood perfectly still, a look of unearthly rage and surprise on his face.

Everyone was still for a moment. Only the sound of harsh breath broke the silence. Claire backed up against a wall. Sage covered Faal and the zookeeper.

Sage took a deep breath. "That was unfortunate. I honestly don't wish to antagonize you. Please take note that we refrained from killing any of your employees. I hope that might in some way mitigate this insult. However, the Claire is with us, and we will defend her right to stay."

Claire sagged against the wall.

Faal's eye was bloodshot with rage, he blinked and it looked like on oncoming train signal. Finally, he spat on the floor. "Every Rik has a price."

"Generally, yes, we do. You caught me on a bad day," Sage said.

Faal seethed within a scenario he no longer controlled. "What is your plan, Rik scum? You weren't bred for loyalty—"

"She inspires me to new heights."

With a curt snap, Faal gestured for the two less-injured Merith to assist their fallen comrade. Claire quickly grabbed the knife that one of the bodyguards had dropped. She held it defensively while they picked up the limp body of their comrade. The zookeeper already had a purpling bruise on his throat. Sage kept his gun on Faal.

Before he left, Faal looked back at her, and Claire bit back another whimper, steadying the knife in her hand. She could feel his hate envelope her like a cold bath, and she shuddered until the door shut behind him.

For several minutes, there was silence in the restaurant. Sage cleared his throat. "Juliet, you want to check the street, make sure they're gone? And barricade that door while you're at it. Claire, we should get Athlete some ice."

"Uh. Right." Claire's brain was in slow motion. She went to the kitchen in a daze, but just stood there in the empty room, in front of the low freezer. Eventually she opened the freezer door and the cold air seeped around her. She didn't know how long she stood there, but then Sage's hand was on hers, easing the freezer door shut.

"I think he's alright after all," Sage said.

Claire turned to him to thank him, but her throat filled. "I've never—When he offered—I thought you would take it."

Sage wrapped his arms around her and pressed her head to his shoulder. "I would never give you up."

Her hot tears burned her raw cheeks, frozen from standing in front of the open freezer. Claire wiped them, with a slightly hysterical laugh. She pulled back slightly and looked at Sage. "Thank you—"

Sage kissed her, and Claire was so surprised she almost pulled away. Only almost.

He drew back a bit and stroked her forehead with his fingers. "I'm sorry. I was terrified for you."

"It's okay..."

He kissed her again and Claire leaned in to meet him this time. She wrapped her arms around him again and enjoyed her first kiss.

She didn't even shudder at the thought that he was an alien. He'd just proven his loyalty in a way she'd never expected.

30

AFTER SEVERAL LONG moments of kissing Sage, however, Claire began to feel a little awkward. How did you end it? Because, well, you couldn't kiss forever. Or even very long, if you had no idea what you were doing.

Then you're just standing near a huge freezer with cold lips and red cheeks.

Sage sighed. "We can't stay here."

"No." Claire was still reacting, but didn't want sound like an idiot. "It's cold."

"I mean, we can't stay at the restaurant."

Francois agreed. Claire could tell he was upset because he hovered nearly a foot off the ground when they all gathered in the kitchen, rather than his customary half inch.

"I failed you all," he said. "I cannot apologize enough." Pots and pans were rattling around Francois, and in his agitation, he began turning the hot water in the sink on and off. "I did not know. I have failed you. I truly believed I could give you warning if he made inquiries. I don't know how he found us."

Steam was rising from the hot water in the sink, making the air moist and warm. Claire went to sit at the table with Juliet, as her legs were a little shaky. "You were so fast," Claire told her. "How did you learn to move like that?"

"I told you; I'm the Director's daughter."

"She doesn't know what that means," Sage said to Juliet.

"Oh," she paused. "The Rik are *ruthless* politicians. They make Earthly politicians look like good-hearted children. Manipulation, collateral, blackmail, hostages..."

"I'm still not getting—"

"I had extensive training so I could avoid being kidnapped or killed by my mother's enemies."

"Wow. And that carried through to your human body?"

"No, I was changed... a long time ago." Juliet's eyes shadowed. "I've had a lot of practice in this body."

"And Athlete and Sage, too, you all worked so well together." Claire narrowed her eyes. "I feel like you've been holding out on me."

"We've been together for a while," Juliet said. She smiled at Athlete, who was holding an ice pack on his face after all. The part of his mouth that they could see turned up, and he gave her a thumb's up.

"Together doing what? Military training?" Claire was half-joking, but the furtive looks they cast at Sage made her raise her eyebrows. "No, really?"

Sage was busy talking to Francois, so Juliet shrugged uncomfortably. "Anyone who was going to Earth in the next few years had extensive training... We were planning an invasion, you know. Athlete and I had extra training, because of who we were, and Sage is... Sage."

Sage was speaking to Francois, "Faal kept repeating that Claire had injured him. I had no idea it had become a personal vendetta, or I would have warned you."

"I did try to tell you," Claire said.

"I know. I should have taken you more seriously."

Francois looked sadly at Claire, and she realized how fond she was of the little alien. He looked deflated. "You mustn't be here when he returns. I can protect myself. I have contacts as high as him, and that'll keep him in check. But I don't have enough pull to protect all of you." He looked downright heartbroken.

Claire rubbed her eyes. "I'm so sorry."

Sage squeezed her shoulder, almost painfully. "No. Don't waste time being sorry. You should be angry at Faal. How dare he come after you? How dare he treat you like an animal now that humanity is declared sentient? Don't feel guilty."

"Where will you go?" Francois asked him.

"We don't all need to go," Claire said. "*I* can leave. I bet I can get another job on a ship, particularly if you refer me." She tried to smile at Francois. "I'll save money, and I'll avoid any Merith..."

"That's ridiculous," Sage said. "They'd catch you right away. I think we should go back to Upper Selta and try to find a ship. We have what we've saved these last few weeks. Between all of us, it may be enough to charter a smuggler as far as Earth."

"But if Faal is still hunting me, he'll keep searching even if I get off Selta," Claire said.

Sage rubbed her neck. "I know. We need to get all the way to Earth. That's the only place we would be safe, and the only place for you to stay out of Faal's hands."

BASHER just about broke his keyboard watching Faal's attack. He still wasn't entirely sure what had happened because Claire kept turning her head in the wrong direction. What it boiled down to was that the Rik had overpowered Faal's guards and Faal had temporarily withdrawn.

Grudgingly, Basher was impressed. "Okay Akemi. What's next? Are they leaving?"

There was a slight pause. *They're still talking.*

The video jumped a few minutes and they watched the discussion.

"She's not even considering coming here," Basher noted.

Akemi tactfully ignored that. *I can watch their entire route through the Chunnel, and you can pick them up when they get off.*

Basher nodded slowly. "Faal will make another attempt soon. Or set people to watch this end of the Chunnel."

This would be an opportune time for me to let Claire in on my presence. I can explain that we know she's human and that she'd be safe here. In fact, I already broke my cover trying to warn her.

"But she didn't say anything to the Rik. Are you sure she saw it?"

She did, but I think she's been too... distracted to realize. It'll probably hit her soon.

"It's time to tell her, then."

Maybe now she'll be scared enough to leave the Rik and come back.

THE OTHER REASON Akemi wanted to talk to Claire, the one Akemi did not share with Basher, was the kiss. Akemi had *not* enjoyed watching Claire kiss Sage.

That is, she had not enjoyed the close-up of Sage's face which she got while they were kissing. It was creepy as heck, and worse, Sage had not closed his eyes.

Who keeps their eyes open while they're kissing? Somebody not that into a kiss, in her opinion. Putting aside that trusting a Rik was usually a horrible idea, the way Sage's eyes stayed open the whole time was *unsettling*. It looked like he was staring right at Akemi, into the tiny camera on Claire's glasses.

It was bad enough when Claire let Sage hold her as she fell asleep, worse when Claire was telling him her story—her secrets and her trauma. This kiss was the worst, though. She couldn't allow this to happen to her friend.

Akemi had had very few proper friends in her life due to her illness and isolation. She felt almost as close to Claire as she did to her sister.

Akemi sighed. If only Claire knew that there was a perfectly good guy *here*. Basher didn't say anything, but she'd been watching him through his computer monitor. He didn't really know Claire yet, but Akemi was still human enough to feel the potential there. And Basher was great company. Matchmaking Claire with Basher was a long term plan, however.

Detaching Claire from Sage, on the other hand, was urgent business. As Claire's friend, she had to step in now. What was the point of being a computer and seeing everything if she wasn't going to do anything about it?

Hey, Claire, Akemi sent.

Do you have a minute alone? I need to talk to you.

31

CLAIRE WAS THROWING her clothes into a bag and the words waited patiently on her glasses. She looked furtively to the door. No one was nearby.

"Akemi?" she repeated tentatively.

Yes. I have some things to tell you. A confession of sorts. I am not actually an AI. That is, technically I am partly artificial, but it's a long story involving a trouncer, a Rik assassin, and a computer. The crux of the matter is that I'm a person, a teenage girl, actually. These glasses are directly linked to my computer, and I've been keeping tabs on you since you put the glasses on. I've been updating Basher, Sam, and Nat on your—well-being.

Claire hadn't known what to expect, and now she couldn't even decide where to start questioning. "Sam and Nat? The cadets? Are they at the embassy?" she said stupidly.

Yes, I came with them. They can communicate with me, too. These glasses were going to be for Basher, but they hadn't been calibrated yet. I'm glad you took them instead. I've enjoyed keeping you company these last few weeks.

"Er—I appreciate it? I couldn't've made it without all your translations and tips." Claire's brain was working faster now. "If you're at the embassy, why hasn't someone come and arrested us? Don't you know where I am?"

We do now, but we only realized as Faal was arriving. He put a tracker in every single shipment that reached Selta from Earth today. I'd tell your Crosspoint to search it.

I would have warned you sooner if I could. If you'd ever gone outside that would have simplified things a lot; we'd have found you weeks ago.

Claire smiled involuntarily. Her reclusiveness had served an extra purpose then.

More importantly, Basher knows you're human, Claire. You can come back to the embassy at any time and be safe. Basher would never let Faal take a true human, especially you. Nat and Sam agree completely.

Claire felt no desire to smile now. Was this the truth—or a ploy to get her to walk back into captivity and betray the people who'd protected her?

I wouldn't lie to you. I know you thought I was just an AI, but don't you have some sense of who I am? I'm your friend.

"It's shockingly easy to think of you as a teenage girl," Claire admitted. "But that doesn't mean you want the same things I do. What about the Rik? I assume they won't get a free pass?"

I admit, Basher still has every intention of arresting them. But this isn't about them. You can come to the embassy on your own. They can go wherever they need to, and you can be safe.

Claire had the feeling that Akemi was being extremely careful in her phrasing.

I saw what happened. The Rik rescued you from Faal, and that was amazing. But will they be able to do it the next time? Faal is out to get you. You belong with your own kind. Basher can get you safely back to Earth. Isn't that what you want?

"Yes, that is what I want... eventually," she said. "But I need to think. I'm going to have to take the glasses off. My friends won't trust you."

Yeah, I get it. But before you go, Basher wanted me to warn you. Faal will send more people to get you. You need to leave immediately.

Claire folded the glasses quickly and tucked them under her pillow.

Downstairs, in the kitchen, Sage was packing a satchel and talking to Francois about various methods of getting to the Chunnel. "Suppose they have watchers—the twelve main thoroughfares offer some options..."

"Better I go with you," Francois said. "Stealth is all well and good, but wealth is better."

Claire held up her hand to interrupt. "I have another complication to add." She explained the conversation she'd just had, but leaving out the part about Basher knowing she was human. Plenty of time to think about that. Sage seemed perturbed enough as it was.

"You didn't know?" he demanded.

"I'm sorry! The glasses usually only—"

"*Usually?*"

Claire bit her lip guiltily. She hadn't told Sage what her glasses were capable of because she'd been sure he would overreact. "Do you think it's true—the part about her being a girl?"

Sage rubbed his head. "It's possible. We were experimenting with—" He cut off. "It's possible. I can't believe Basher hasn't come for us yet."

Juliet was looking thoughtful. "Claire was ill the whole way here, and the glasses were put away. And she hasn't left this café since we arrived. If those glasses don't have a positioning system that functions on Selta, then they have nothing except distance to pinpoint our location."

Sage looked puzzled. "But if she even looked out the window..."

"Not enough," Juliet said positively. "I know. I was trained in how to pinpoint a location. If someone kidnapped me, you see, and disabled my tracker, I would have had to find a way to tell my mother where I was, without giving myself away. There's things – electrical infrastructure, construction material, even the type of foot traffic – that can help someone fix a location. But this part of Lower Selta is so homogeneous..."

Sage nodded slowly. "Of course, you're right." He laughed unexpectedly and dropped a kiss on Claire's cheek. "Thank heaven you stayed inside."

Athlete frowned. "But they know our plans now. Won't that human catch us as soon as we get to Upper Selta?"

Sage shook his head. "*If* we can get to Upper Selta, I know more than one way out of the train depot. We can disappear. We'd better leave the glasses here though."

"But now *we* can control what *she* sees," Claire argued. "That could be useful."

She couldn't bear to leave the glasses behind. Akemi had helped her and guided her and brought her tidbits of real humanity. Claire knew instinctively that she couldn't explain any of this to Sage, but thankfully she didn't have too. He nodded thoughtfully and grabbed a thick hand towel from the hook on the wall.

"That should muffle the sound enough, but let's all watch what we say."

Claire wrapped the glasses and stuffed them in her backpack thankfully.

After all that, the start to their trip to the Chunnel felt like an anticlimax. They slipped out the front door into the small, slanted alley and went right, following Sage in single file, with Athlete bringing up the rear.

At first they only passed a few aliens, all (probably) heading home for their nightly meal, and Claire was feeling silly about her weeks of hiding in the café. Was this what she was afraid of?

She only felt that way until they hit the first major thoroughfare. It was as wide as a six-lane highway, and packed with aliens. The traffic roughly flowed in two directions, with the center reserved for vehicles and the edges for pedestrians.

They edged closer to the middle, and Claire was jostled by four-legged Spo and furry Tergre. Paths opened before big Merith striding along. Vel, Crosspoint, and even Renchins, which she'd never seen in the café, trudged along with her. She couldn't help squinting at each Merith, straining to identify Faal or one of his minions.

Unfortunately, she couldn't see any aliens clearly unless they got quite close to her. She'd just have to trust her friends to spot her enemies.

They moved into the walking 'lane' closest to the vehicles, and Claire's nose began to run from the smell. None of the vehicles were the small ground-cars she was familiar with. Some were wagons pulled by aliens, like rickshaws from India. Others were like coaches and carriages, pulled by strange alien animals. The odor was... impressive.

"Aren't there ground cars on Lower Selta?" Claire asked Sage.

"No. Didn't you—but, of course, you haven't been out until now. No, Lower Selta banned ground cars for general use. They prefer animals." He wrinkled his nose. "It's a purist thing. The first colonists here were a throwback group of Tergre. They believed in living simply and naturally. They eschewed the use of technology for personal gain, only using it for the mining process. Now it's become tradition."

Two large, brown animals drew abreast of Claire, reminding her of horses, but with membranous wings folded on their backs. They were sleek, with a kind of aerodynamic quality that seemed out of sync with their size, and Claire wondered in awe what planet they were from.

One of them suddenly reared, with a screaming neigh that made Claire clap her hands over her ears. Several other animals responded and the noise in the huge corridor, already loud, became deafening. The ceiling, high over their head, made everything echo louder.

She followed Sage for another half a mile before he guided her away from the center, and towards the slower dregs on the edges of the hall. They went through an archway and Claire gasped. The last thoroughfare had seemed huge, but this one dwarfed it. Easily five times as wide, this one was partly dedicated to an open air market. Past the market were several huge tracks, where she could see Vel and Merith riding large mounts in a fierce competition. Sage skirted the crowds surrounding these tracks, and Claire noticed that he kept looking behind them.

"What? Do you see something?" Claire asked, uselessly looking over her shoulder.

"Maybe. We're going to get to get somewhere a little less crowded. They'll have to either follow closer or fall back."

Sage led them into increasingly smaller caverns from there. Claire lost all sense of direction, as they often veered left or right with the natural flow of the warrens of Lower Selta. They were clearly off the 'highways' now; it was more inner-city. There was even an inner-city park, a small area lush with greenery.

False sunlight shone from the false 'sky,' and it reminded Claire unpleasantly of Faal's zoo. Beautiful, maybe, but not to her. Many Seltans sat or lay on the spongy rock, probably soaking up the UV rays, but Sage led them steadily through. "There's a sort of chapel through here, a Tergre place, and we're going to spend the night."

"We are? I thought we were in a hurry."

"We were. Sort of. I didn't want to mention this before," Sage explained, "but Francois recommended it. We need to change our timing. Too many people are waiting for us. It's better to kill ten or twelve hours than rush right into a trap."

"You didn't tell me in case I blabbed it to Akemi, didn't you? I don't want you to get caught either."

"I know. I trust you."

"Do you?" Claire asked.

"As much as I trust anyone." He kissed her and slipped her bag from her shoulders. "Don't worry, I'll take care of you."

32

BASHER LEANED against a wall at the Chunnel station on Upper Selta, waiting for the next train. He held his tablet in his hands to communicate with Akemi.

I'm sorry. The Rik have been gone from the café more than ten hours. They should have taken the train hours ago. Perhaps I miscalculated, or we missed them already. I really screwed up.

Basher knuckled his eyes. He'd been at the station all night, since Akemi's warning last evening.

I just can't imagine where they are, Akemi also said for the third, or possibly fourth, time. *I guess they might have decided to stay in Lower Selta? Or else we've missed them... or else, Faal has them.*

"I don't think Faal caught them," Basher reassured her. "Surely Claire would pull out the glasses if she was in trouble. Either way, I have to get back to the embassy. Senator Fontley is supposed to arrive today. And he is supposed to meet with Faal, ironically enough."

It doesn't seem right that Faal should come openly to the embassy when we know he's trying to kidnap Claire. He doesn't even pretend otherwise.

"He doesn't have to pretend and he knows it. If I arrest him, he has enough clout to begin a war between the Merith and us. It'd be catastrophic."

"He sure is taking his time," Sam said, pushing his glasses up his nose. "It's been more than twenty minutes."

Sam and Nat and Basher waited in an alcove off the central shipping cavern, waiting for Senator Fontley to come down the elevator from his ship. Many ship berths had private lobbies and waiting areas like this, so at least the three of them could sit.

Sam had confirmed the time they would be there to escort the Senator to the embassy, but Fontley hadn't made an appearance yet. "He probably enjoys making us wait," Sam added.

"Maybe he's just reluctant to get off," Nat said. "This has got to be his worst nightmare."

They'd heard through other channels that the xenophobic senator had expressed grave concerns about this trip. He undoubtedly would have shoved it off onto someone else if he could have done so while avoiding political suicide. He was one of the most popular Coalition members on Earth, but if he appeared too terrified to represent humanity out in the galaxy, he would rapidly lose that popularity.

Finally, the elevator descended and Fontley stepped out.

He looked as camera-ready as Sam remembered him, as if he'd just stepped out of a hair and makeup studio off Hollywood and Vine.

He looked around quickly, and Sam wondered if he was looking for Shara, whom he despised. Sam and Nat had tactfully sent her away for a time, for just that reason. She was on a trip to visit the cadet facilities on the Spo planet and to research Claire's "death." Sam envied her.

Sam tried unsuccessfully to inject welcome into his voice.

"Senator Fontley, welcome to Selta." He held out his hand and Fontley shook it perfunctorily.

Fontley was affable during his introduction to Basher and greeted Nat more warmly than he had treated her before, but his manner toward Sam was as cool as ever.

"Sam, can I speak to you for a moment alone?" he asked.

After Basher and Nat awkwardly retreated from the alcove, Fontley turned to him. "I would like to get a few things clear before we get to the embassy."

"Of course." Sam was pretty sure he knew what was coming.

"Now that I am here, I am the ranking representative of humanity. I expect you to behave with all respect and compliance during my stay."

Sam's jaw clenched. "That's fair enough."

"I am serious, young man. You've attained your position of authority through the merest chance, and I will not tolerate any insubordination. If I am not much mistaken, the treaty you so rashly thrust us into with these liars and terrorists is on the brink of termination. If you attempt to undermine my decisions, I won't hesitate to send you to the penal colony on the moon until Earth is more stable."

Sam raised his eyebrows. "I hardly think you'll be allowed to send me to prison unilaterally, but," he raised his hand as Fontley began to speak, "I understand what you're saying. I won't attempt to undermine you during the remainder of the investigation and negotiation."

AKEMI WINCED at the sight of Senator Fontley's strained neck and bulging eyes that she was seeing through Sam's glasses. Sam was taller than the senator, and Akemi was sure the smaller man resented the heck out of that, in addition to the other reasons he'd taken Sam in violent dislike.

Sam's temperature (which Akemi recorded through the glasses) was rising. "I do, however, know a lot about the Merith and the Spo," Sam was saying. "I'd be a valuable source of information, and it'd be foolish to ignore what I can offer."

"That's what I'm talking about. You'd better not correct me," Senator Fontley jabbed Sam's chest with a finger, "question me," another jab, "or disagree with me in front of them." Jab.

Sam slapped the senator's hand away and stepped closer, leaning over the man. "Don't touch me again. I don't know how you got this far, but it certainly wasn't on professionalism."

Akemi sighed. Poor Sam. He was about to see what he'd accomplished undone, and his ego had taken a beating. Akemi didn't blame Sam for getting a little defensive at this renewed attack.

He stalked away from the senator and gave a forced smile to Nat and Basher. "Ready to go?"

Senator Fontley rode in the passenger seat next to Basher, while Sam and Nat rode in the back. The senator eyed Selta with barely restrained disgust.

"When will the Rik Director arrive?" Fontley asked abruptly. "Will she be housed at the same facility as us, and how many are in her delegation?"

Sam rested his forehead against the window.

Don't hurt the glasses, Akemi reminded him. *I have few enough inputs as it is.*

"The Supreme Director won't be staying at the Spo embassy," Basher explained. "We are housed there as the Spo were our sponsors and are now our allies, but the Rik have no such arrangement. I imagine she'll come directly from her ship."

"Good, good," Fontley said. "The talks will be on our turf, so to speak, and we'll be there first. I'd like a full tour of the facility as soon as possible. And I'd like to examine the negotiation room and possibly make changes there."

"The tour is already planned. And the Spo are pretty particular about their negotiations," Basher said.

"Well, *I'd* like to be sure we don't present a weak appearance."

"The Spo are territorial, so believe me, their negotiation room will be everything you could want," Basher said.

Nat spoke up, clearly trying to cut the tension. "The Spo call them 'rooms of decision,' and they model them after the desert in summer, when all things 'slow and run together,' but they usually throw in a skull or two. Do I have that right, Basher?"

"Yeah. It's pretty intense. They have a sort of altar where they put a small death glass, a sacrificial knife, and the skull of a trouncer. Pretty macabre, if you ask me."

Fontley grimaced. "*Aliens*, ugh. I cannot wait to finish this and get back to Earth. Speaking of which, Faal of Merith II contacted me. He's a real force in the galaxy, isn't he? I'm looking forward to meeting him."

AFTER THE TOUR, Basher made himself some very strong coffee. The grounds had been a gift from his partner on Basher's birthday. Basher still hadn't figured out how to reciprocate, as Spo didn't celebrate birthdays, but he'd certainly been enjoying the coffee. He hoarded it for special occasions or days when he felt particularly sick of aliens.

With no sleep and a day of Senator Fontley and Faal ahead of him, Basher figured this qualified as special occasion *and* a day when he was going to be sick of aliens. He sipped the fresh coffee and groaned unintentionally. *So good.*

The only redeeming factor of this coming meeting was that Faal couldn't be terrorizing Claire somewhere else, if he was schmoozing with the Senator *here*.

Basher made his way tiredly to the negotiation room where he was to meet Senator Fontley.

Sam and Nat were leaning against the wall, with a careful amount of space between them. Basher wondered in passing if something had happened with them.

At the end of the room was a raised platform, the altar that Basher had described. The skull of a trouncer was there alright, along with several other symbolic items. This room also had a mirrored skylight that was just over the altar, shining a pale light on the items. The whole room gave Basher the skin-crawling feeling of being watched by something long dead and disapproving.

Today, it was enlivened by the presence of Sam's pet trouncer, who'd finally gotten permission to leave their spaceship several days ago. The trouncer was an ugly, predatory animal, but it was crouched amicably enough next to Sam, who rubbed his bony head. *That* was a weird sight.

Sam nodded a silent hello to Basher and tapped his glasses. He probably meant that Akemi had told him about their lost quarry.

Senator Fontley greeted Faal in an overdone and somewhat theatrical way when he arrived. Basher thought of it as his CNN persona, but perhaps he was just making up for the trouncer.

"I have just finished reading the report on the dead Rik," Fontley said to Faal, bowing low. "Very disturbing to someone with my nerves, let me tell you, but very clear. I cannot thank you enough for using your influence to get us a full autopsy. Your help has been most appreciated by the people of Earth."

Faal inclined his head, but Basher noted a bit of cynicism in his eye. Senator Fontley would have done better not to mention weak nerves in front of a Merith. Faal didn't even look down when Sam's trouncer growled at him, but Senator Fontley flinched back.

Faal waved a clawed hand. "You are welcome. I had plenty of time to peruse the documents myself during my recent trip to Lower Selta. They are indeed, as Senator Fontley says, clearly damning of the Rik. But then, I cannot believe that their guilt would shock you, as familiar with their vices as you are."

Basher opened his mouth to reply, but Senator Fontley broke in. "Their vices, indeed, are well known to us. Their deceptive impulses and violent tendencies are ubiquitous."

No sign of our Rik yet, Akemi sent to Basher's tablet. *Is Senator Fontley listening to himself talk again?*

Basher knew she didn't really expect a reply. He couldn't speak out loud to her, and it was rather distracting if he tried to type too much. Mostly she just kept up a running commentary on the proceedings.

Yep, the good senator didn't waste any time today. How do you think he gets his teeth to sparkle like that? Maybe you should ask.

Basher involuntarily licked his teeth.

Ha, I saw that. I'm just kidding. Your teeth are fine.

Basher tapped the screen twice. Little imp.

Senator Fontley was still talking after they'd all sat. "Indeed, I'll confess that this news is a relief. I originally suspected Nat's computer of the sabotage and the explosion. It was a Rik experiment with a biocomputer, you see, which must excuse my suspicions. I am not often wrong, but I admit it when I am." He nodded to Sam and Nat.

Hey, he's talking about me, Akemi said. *I don't like it.*

Faal had tensed at these careless words. "Fascinating. And the computer yet lives? I don't think a biocomputer has ever lasted so long."

"Strange, isn't it?" the Senator agreed. "Personally, I prefer simple technology. I don't trust anything the Rik or the Spo create."

Basher didn't like the direction of this conversation, or the keen sense of satisfaction from Faal. Sam and Nat were frowning as well.

"Let's return to the point," Sam said briskly. "The Supreme

Director of the Rik arrives on Selta tomorrow. The investigative report has been filed with all three governments. Any official decisions regarding the Rik should be made after we present the charges in person, and the Director has her opportunity to offer a defense."

"I offer my services a Council member to facilitate the hearing," Faal said.

"Actually," Sam said, "while we appreciate all your help, the remainder of this investigation is a uniquely human and Rik issue. I have examined the legal precedents, and to allow a non-affiliated, non-species member to attend the hearings would be objectionable."

Senator Fontley looked vexed at this, and Basher quickly backed Sam up. "I've sent all the pertinent files to your computer, Senator." He nodded at Faal. "We thank you for your—services and assure you that you are free to continue your travels. We won't be wasting any more of your valuable time."

Faal looked amused. "As a member in highest standing of the Galactic Council, I planned to offer a very different service to Senator Fontley. If there is a legal dissolution of the contract between the Humans and the Rik, it will need to be ratified by the Council. As I was the acting judge at the time of the human trial and the original treaty, I am uniquely positioned to do so."

Senator Fontley slapped the table. "Of course! I'd be glad to have the help of a neutral party in this mess. I only hope this may be the start of a long and prosperous relationship between our two species."

"Senator," Basher said, "there are extenuating circumstances that we haven't had time to apprise you of yet—"

"I did my *own* research, and I am perfectly satisfied."

Basher understood Senator Fontley. He was a politician and he was more than willing to suck up to Faal for the patronage of such a powerful Merith. It was disgusting to watch his blatant sycophancy, but Basher could understand his reasoning and his priorities.

Sam's jaw was rigid, but he remained silent. Basher assumed he'd made the same conclusion: the Senator's mind was made up.

Faal looked smug. "I see there are no objections. How lovely."

DURING THEIR LUNCH BREAK, Nat excused herself from the negotiation room. She could feel a pressure in the base of her neck that meant another migraine was coming. Sometimes they were brought on by stress, and she'd been horribly tense after Senator Fontley mentioned Akemi.

Sam followed her out, bringing his trouncer with him. "I really want to leave Nebbie alone with Senator Fontley and Faal see how it goes, but that might be crossing a line."

"Maybe a little."

"Another headache?" he asked.

"Not quite yet, but it's coming."

He walked her back to her room and Nat felt guilty for taking him away from the action. He probably saw it as another duty: Walk Nat back to her room. Check.

"You don't have to walk me back every time," Nat said. "I can take myself."

"Are you kidding? I savor any moment to talk to you alone. What did you think of all that?" Sam asked.

"I wasn't happy about it, obviously, but I don't think there's any overt danger in Faal knowing Akemi is here. He might have heard rumors about her anyway."

Sam only looked at her, a slight frown between his eyes.

"What?"

"That's all?" Sam said. "What about the rest of it?"

"I'm not too fussed. I thought the Rik were guilty all along. Look what they did to Akemi—"

Sam threw up his hands. "The treaty is about to be dissolved, and if Fontley has his way, we'll be neck deep in a Merith alliance before we know it. Don't you *care?*"

Nat flared. "Of course, I care."

"Then—help me? You were at the top of all our political science classes on Spo, and you haven't said a thing to me about any of this. I hate that your head hurts, but you spend half your nights watching Akemi's dreams. That might be triggering some of your migraines. It's not healthy, Nat."

"I think she's struggling. She never *says* anything, but she's afraid—"

"I'm sure she is, and I want to help her too, but the obsessive thing you're doing isn't working. Have you slept more than a few hours at a time since we got here?"

"Are you keeping tabs on me?"

"Should I be?" Sam took a deep breath. "I didn't mean to argue when you're in pain, but I could really use your help. You're good at thinking through these things."

"You want my help? I *want* the treaty dissolved, Sam. I don't know how else to say that. The Rik are a despicable race, and I don't care what happens to them. Last night in Akemi's dream, she dreamed about the surgery—"

"Please don't. You have got to quit watching those. I think they hurt you more than they hurt her. She probably doesn't even remember."

They reached Nat's door, and she used her token to open it. "If your sister Claudia had been the one hurt, the one *murdered,* you'd feel the same."

"Maybe I would, but I—miss you, Nat. You're here, but not. Ever since the explosion, you're slipping away."

Nat went in without saying anything, and as the door slid shut, she heard him say, "Take something and sleep, please."

33

CLAIRE WAS unnerved to realize that Sage's 'contact' in Upper Selta was another Rik in a human body. He was a handsome middle-aged guy with thick blonde hair and a Dutch accent. How many Rik were on Selta? How many people had been kidnapped from Europe before they bombed the Hadron Collider? She didn't ask, because she didn't want to know.

After they'd surreptitiously gotten away from the train station during the midmorning slump, Sage had led them to a huge block of residential suites. Pleasant, carpeted hallways led deep into the quiet structure. He knocked on a numbered door, and his friend had opened it.

He clapped him on the shoulder in a friendly way. "Sage, you have arrived! How long has it been? I was happy to hear that you are alive and well—"

"It's been a long time, Karel," Sage said, cutting him off. "Thank you for arranging this flat for us on short notice."

"Of course, of course, it's the least I can do. Have you seen—?"

"Here's the price we agreed on," Sage said, handing him a roll of Seltan currency.

Claire didn't like that they were using up so much of their money, essentially for nothing, but Sage had reminded her on the train how much they'd earned from Francois and laughed at her worry. "It's not so much to pay for a good favor," he'd said.

"It isn't much of a favor if you have to pay for it. Isn't this guy your friend?"

"What does that have to do with it?"

Claire shook her head. She already knew Rik ideas of friendship were cold and calculating, but sometimes she forgot.

"Karel, we're dead on our feet," Sage told his 'friend'. "We spent all night keeping watch, so I think we just need to crash now. Can I meet you for dinner tonight? To catch up?"

Claire wasn't blind to the significant look being passed between them but she was too tired to do more than note it. She wasn't surprised that Sage didn't want to *catch up* with her around. That would be more than awkward for everyone.

THAT EVENING IN THE FLAT, Athlete and Juliet were watching news reports on the big screen. Claire settled next to Juliet, who obligingly translated for her.

Claire *really* missed Akemi and the ease of her glasses.

It was tabloid television. There were affairs, scandals, and big secrets revealed. One of the breaking stories didn't even make sense. Septuplets born with double-faceted eyes? It turned out to be a scandal, as the eyes were proof of infidelity on the father's part. Selta was a mixing pot of the galaxy, full of celebrities, all the way from emperors to white-collar criminals.

Soon there would be an athletic competition, something like an Olympics, and Athlete explained several of the sports to her when they popped up on the news reports. There was longing in his voice, and she wondered if he would have competed for the Rik, had things gone differently for him.

She kept expecting every culture other than hers to be simpler; easier to stereotype and catalog in her brain, but it wasn't.

Faal was evil, no doubt about it, but Kitteh and the other Merith on the ship had been kind. The Rik were painted as evil scavengers of society, but her Rik were loyal and brave.

It was just a confusing galaxy. So, while Sage had dinner with his friend, and Juliet tried to flirt with Athlete, Claire watched the reports.

That's when she saw Sam and Nat on the news. They stood on the observation deck in front of the huge spinner drill. Both cadets had the Spo tattoo on their cheeks, and when they waved, she saw the other tattoo on their wrists.

"The human delegation has been investigating the sabotage of the Spo space station," the Spo announcer was saying. "They agreed to a public press conference this morning, however, it entirely concerned the Rik problem, not the space station. Many speculate that the brief Rik-Human alliance is at an end."

The screen flipped back to the cadets, and Basher stepped up between Sam and Nat to speak. "We wish to warn all Seltan businessman and security that true humans have a Crosspoint tattoo on their wrist," the screen flicked to a picture of the intricate tattoo. "And that any human without this tattoo should be treated with all caution and reported to the Spo embassy immediately. Any and all ships suspected of transporting humans or Rik off Selta will be searched at temporary checkpoints."

Juliet looked at Claire. "That's because of you. Or us, I guess. He's making sure we don't leave the planet."

"Why does he have to be so difficult? He's making it *harder* for me to escape Faal."

"I think he's trying to protect you," Juliet said. "He doesn't know where you are, but with these searches, he can at least try to make sure Faal doesn't leave with you."

The newscaster came back on. "The cadets are staying at the Spo embassy, and if you want to catch a glimpse of these true humans, they can occasionally be seen entering and exiting the embassy on level H. Our reporters were disappointed to see, however, that the true humans are very like the Rik we are all too familiar with—not much to look at."

"The humans have not issued a report on their investigation, but inside sources say the prime suspects are Rik. It is also rumored that Faal of Merith II is assisting with the investigation. This surprising species has certainly dived into the deep end of galactic politics."

"You must get away," Karel said. "Your only hope is to get to Earth and blend in. We just need a ship—"

"No one will risk it," Sage said. He sat across from Karel, his former protégé, in a small, dimly-lit diner. The smell of fish permeated the air... fish roasting, frying, sautéing, and chilling. Not really fish, of course, but the salt water equivalent grown in tanks on the Lower Seltan levels. Sage and Karel sat at one of the many small tables in tiny chairs that put their knees uncomfortably high.

Sage sighed. "Even if we found a pilot and ship willing to take us all, we couldn't get through the port now."

Karel rubbed his forehead. "We're back to that stupid tattoo. I can't believe a little bit of ink is going to be the death of us."

"It's the real thing or nothing," Sage agreed.

He became lost in a half-formed idea, but Karel interjected. "Why were you so anxious to shut me up, by the way? When you arrived this morning?"

"What? Oh, that's because the new girl—she's human."

Karel's eyes got wide. "Oh, indeed?"

"It's on her account I'm in a rush. She's managed to make a personal enemy of Faal of Merith II. If she doesn't get off Selta soon, Faal will take her."

Karel raised his eyebrows. "That makes her a dangerous resource to cultivate then. Hadn't you better cut her loose?"

"She's valuable." Sage fell back into utilitarian ways of speaking, but the truth was—he cared more about Claire than just her utility. "She's useful," he reiterated, nonetheless, "but I'm not sure how to make it work."

He pulled out the old token from the embassy absently. "The ink is in the embassy. The human detective at the embassy is looking for us. Mostly looking for her," Sage was thinking aloud. "He has access to the embassy and access to the ink. Perhaps we could use that. Claire could get near him, I'm sure of it. Maybe even... steal his ID token? Could we steal the ink? Francois could administer the tattoo—only the Crosspoint can do it at the cellular level."

Karel stroked his blonde mustache. "But betraying her own kind to help us—would she do it?"

"Yes."

"That's impressive, Sage, even for you. How did you break her so fast?"

"I *didn't* break her; she cares about us. It's different. Stealing a token is useless though—Basher would realize as soon as he got back to the embassy."

"Maybe we could copy it? It's the digital signal we need."

Sage finished his fish. "Can you check with one of the others—maybe Joan? She would have the tech if anyone would."

"We all thought you were crazy, you know. Your fascination with human psychology. But all that testing is paying off for us now."

"I regret what I did to those people. Claire's helped me understand humans better than I ever did before. She did so without any coercion."

Karel raised his eyebrows. "Claire? Is that her name? I don't recall you being much interested in names. Is she something special?"

"Yes. She is."

Karel's eyebrows went up. "You're willing to cross Faal for her?"

"I know, I can't believe it myself."

"Fascinating. Have you—"

"Drop it, Karel." Sage didn't want to discuss Claire. Karel had a simple mind even when they were Rik, and his human host did not seem to have helped. Sage had hand-picked the humans for many of his associates, but he hadn't done Karel any favors. "If Joan can figure something out, we'll have to make a play for the ink right away. Have the others ready to go on my word."

Karel threw some money on the table. "But Faal—if he takes issue with this girl, we could all be in danger."

"I know. I'll deal with it."

"How will Claire react when she realizes she's helping a lot more than five Rik get to Earth?"

"I think I can bring her around," Sage said. "I'll get Francois to join us. We'll have to work fast if we manage to get the ink."

Karel grinned. "That's the old Sage, I know. Always collecting resources."

Sage nodded a curt goodbye and walked briskly down the small street away from the fishy smell of the place. This alley was similar to the one they'd carried Claire through the night they'd escaped and she'd been so ill. That had been a stroke of genius on his part, to bring her with them.

Claire's long imprisonment had left her uniquely vulnerable. She was so starved for affection and security that she accepted all five of them almost without hesitation. She'd also been traumatized by that business with the cadet girl who died. She felt both betrayed and guilty which left her even more vulnerable to correctly applied psychology.

He'd taken advantage of that, up to a point, because Claire's presence was undoubtedly an advantage to them. At least it had been, until he realized Faal had a vendetta against her. Faal's determined pursuit of her had truly shocked him. She'd told him that she escaped, but he hadn't realized the depth of insult Faal had taken from that.

Still, the more her allegiance was with them, the better. The details hadn't come together until now. But he'd had this ink theft in mind for some time. He'd known Claire's loyalty might make all the difference.

But he *did* care about her, he wasn't faking that. When he was a Rik, he'd been consumed with his research. He'd barely allotted time for rest, let alone forming a relationship. But with Claire...it was suddenly easy.

He had been shocked to find himself standing up for her against Faal. It went against every bit of his Rik personality to give up what Faal had offered.

In that moment, he'd considered Claire more important than himself, and that just wasn't the Rik way. What did that mean? Love wasn't something the Rik valued, but humans did. Did he love her? He was pretty sure she loved him.

Sage knew from his studies, when he'd been part of the national research team focused on learning about human psychology, that girls who'd been locked up for a long time were often ready to fall in love...

Sage walked briskly into the flat. The next two days were going to be tricky, but if they could only get to Earth, he could put all this behind him. Maybe he and Claire could be together for good. No manipulation, no past. Just two humans making a new life for themselves.

Sage watched Claire's face carefully as he explained the pertinent details of his conversation with Karel.

"So, we need the ink?" she said. "And we need a token to get into the embassy?"

"That's the gist of it. No one at the embassy will be letting us in the front door." Aha, he saw a flicker in her face that confirmed his latest guess. The thought of the embassy was more appealing to her now.

"You *can* go back, can't you?" Sage said gently. "Did they finally figure out you are human?"

"Yes... Akemi and Basher believe me now."

"She said they'd protect you?"

"Yes. But I wasn't going to go! Not unless something terrible happened. I want you to get off Selta, too."

Sage took her hand in his. "Maybe that *would* be the best option for you now. If we can't get off Selta fast enough, Faal could find us at any time. Perhaps you should go to them."

Claire opened her mouth, but Sage held up his hand. "It wouldn't be like your friend—you're not betraying us. Whatever happens to us isn't your fault." He hated manipulating her, but he wanted the association to be clear.

Claire made a strange face which sent a frisson of fear down his back that he'd overplayed his hand, but her words were a relief. "It doesn't matter, because I won't go. Or if I do, it will only be to help you steal the ink. You're my friends, and I would *never* abandon you."

Sage smiled, though not without pain, appreciating how straightforward her mind was, how inflexible her trauma. "Thank you, Claire. With your help, I think we can work something out."

34

SAGE WRAPPED his arm around Claire's shoulders while his friend Joan explained her plan. She was short and—of Korean extraction, if he remembered correctly. Claire had taken the introduction well, but she had to be wondering how he had this network just waiting for him in Upper Selta.

"This isn't very good technology," Joan said, waving Sage's old token. "Which means we're in luck. The Spo have used an older type of authentication."

"You think we can copy the token?" Sage asked.

"Not this one. It's dead. We need one that's actively sending and receiving electronically for us to copy it. In short, we need a live one, which Karel tells me you can get."

"It depends. What would we need to do?"

Joan tapped a small tablet computer. "You would need to get this near a live token for at least five to ten minutes. Maybe longer. And you would need to... er, distract the person holding the real token, so they don't notice it buzzing."

"How near would I have to be?" Claire asked.

"Within a foot, or so." Joan brought the token closer to the tablet and when it was about twelve inches away, the tablet lit up. "See, I've set up the tablet with the same software as the embassy uses in its doors. When a token gets close enough, the tablet sends a challenge to the token. This token is dead, so it won't work." She waited about thirty seconds, until the tablet vibrated and printed, 'Invalid authentication.'

"But if the token was working, it would receive the challenge, multiply it by the authentication code, and return it. Usually the authentication code is a super-large prime number, very hard to figure out. But if you challenge it enough..."

Sage's brow furrowed "So, Claire must get within a foot of Basher, for ten minutes or so, and keep him from noticing that his token is trying to open something?"

"You're so skeptical," Claire said. "This actually sounds easier than I expected. I did a similar thing with Faal's zookeepers, you know, before I escaped. You have to be near someone and distract them to—take their stuff. This time I don't even have to steal anything, plus Basher is a lot less terrible than Faal's guys."

"Then I guess we should get the ball rolling." Sage seemed strangely subdued considering this was his plan.

Claire's confidence faded a little. "The only problem will be getting away again. If I'm that close—what's to stop him from just grabbing my arm and cuffing me again? I'm guessing he won't let me walk away."

Juliet clapped her hands. "I know! Oh, I know how to manage that part of it." She explained her idea, and Claire's confidence returned.

CLAIRE WENT into the bedroom and turned off all the lights, as they'd discussed, making it pitch dark. Then she got the glasses out of her backpack and carefully unrolled them. She was excited about this part.

"Akemi, can you hear me?" she said softly, putting the glasses on her nose by feel. "Are you there?"

Claire! Hello! I'm so glad you decided to talk to me. I was frantic when you didn't arrive on the train. Did Faal find you?

"No, he didn't. We're okay. Is Basher looking for us?"

I had to alert him. He's worried about you. He knows Faal is bad news.

"I figured, but—Oh, no! Did Basher give Kit back to Faal? Have you seen Kit at the embassy? He's like a climbing cat—"

He's fine, don't worry! Basher and his partner dote on the little guy. He's in Basher's lap half the time, but don't tell him I told you. ;-)

Akemi's smiley face made her laugh. "You really are a teenager, aren't you? I feel like I know you, but I don't know if that's real."

It is real. I was so upset when I realized Faal found you.

"I appreciated your warning. You don't have to tell me the whole story, but how did you become a—computer?"

The Rik like to do interesting experiments, and I got caught up in one of them. They had an idea about creating a supercomputer by using a human brain in place of a Spo trouncer.

"Oh my gosh. I'm so sorry."

It has pros and cons, for sure. The Rik who did this to me also nearly killed my sister, Nat. You need to be careful how much you trust them. You need to come back to the embassy; we can help you.

"I'm considering it, but I want to talk to Basher first. I know *you* believe me, but he was pretty convinced I was Rik."

"I can patch him through—"

"I can't talk here. I'll—I'll meet up with him, but not at the embassy. I'm not agreeing to go back yet."

I assume your friends won't be joining you?

"What would happen to them if they did?"

They'd be held at the embassy until the negotiations are settled. There's a temporary colony on Earth's moon for Rik criminals. It's not a bad place, actually."

And that was quite enough for Claire; her friends were not going to prison. But Claire said none of this to Akemi; this is where the real acting began.

"I don't want them to be hurt," Claire said softly. "I just don't know what to do."

Talk to Basher. Where do you want to meet?

Claire gave the directions to the spot Sage and Juliet had carefully selected. It was usually deserted, and it was near their current hideout, but not too near.

The idea was for her to talk to Basher about turning herself in. She was supposed to act conflicted and confused (which would be easy, since that's pretty much how she felt). At some point, she would ask Basher to give her time to make up her mind. Of course, he would try to follow her, but they now had several contingencies for that.

I suppose you're going to put the glasses away again? Akemi said sadly.

"I have to. You or Basher might see something to pinpoint our location."

What if I promise to be good? I'm so bored.

Claire laughed, somewhat painfully. "I know how that feels."

That's true, you do. If anyone can understand what it's like to lose their freedom to an alien, it's us.

Us. The word seemed to linger on Claire's glasses. Was there an 'us' between her and Akemi? She'd only just found out that Akemi existed, and she had no way to verify anything...

"Someday I want to have a real conversation with you." Claire's momentary lightness faded. "But that's not today."

I understand. Be safe, Claire.

CLAIRE STRODE QUICKLY to the rendezvous point, feeling appropriately nervous. Could she really deceive Basher long enough for her tablet to get the codes from him? She wasn't sure anymore.

And *should* she deceive him? Now that she was alone, it felt a lot more like betraying Akemi.

The service corridor was narrow here, only nine or ten feet across, and at this time of night, rather dim because the lights had switched colors. The metal ribbing in the rounded walls was rusted and flaky, and a sheen of scummy moisture coated part of the floor. This corridor was scheduled for maintenance sometime in the next week, which was part of the reason they chose it.

Basher was already there. He leaned against one wall of the corridor, seemingly relaxed, but his eyes snapped up the moment she turned the corner into view. He remained against the wall, but she could tell it was a choice. A bulky bag sat at his feet, which she eyed warily.

"Hello, again," she said. For all her planning, she hadn't considered how to start this conversation. She'd seen those videos of Basher and his fiancée, which suddenly seemed too personal a thing to know about him. And since he'd been involved with her glasses situation, he knew too much about her as well. Despite all that knowledge, the only interaction they'd had was decidedly negative.

He nodded. "I don't feel like we really met before. I should introduce myself." He extended his hand with a cautious step forward, like he was afraid she would run.

She wouldn't, at least not for ten more minutes. She gripped his hand firmly. "Claire Kindler, nice to meet you."

"Basher Kapur. Likewise." His hand was warm, and his grip was subtly different than Sage's.

"I hear you've been taking care of Kit. I appreciate it." Claire leaned against the wall next to him. She tried to look casual, but she felt like she was standing way too close. "I'm surprised Faal didn't demand him back yet."

"I don't think he cares, except as it proves your theft. It's you he's after."

"No kidding," Claire responded.

"I'm sorry I didn't believe you. I had to follow protocol to find out if you were a Rik, I can't apologize for that, but I shouldn't have threatened to turn you over to Faal. I understand that you were scared, and my words played a big part in causing you to go with the Rik."

"I appreciate it. But what do you mean about following protocol to discover if I was a Rik?"

"I thought Akemi explained it to you. There was a blood test. As soon as she realized you were feverish, we all knew you were human."

"Oh, wow. You knew way back then? I really could've stayed."

He winced. "Yeah."

"Maybe it was for the best. At any rate, I forgive you for doubting my story. I didn't realize *then* how many Rik were on Selta and how many times you'd heard a similar story." She idly kicked the wall with one foot, hoping to disguise any slight vibration he might feel from his token. "So, you know I'm in trouble with Faal. The Merith have these belts that they tie knots in. Have you seen one? He's got a number of knots for me."

"I've seen it. At the embassy, we can protect you. He can't take you from there."

"But isn't Faal there *right now*, helping with the cadet investigation or something? That doesn't make me terribly inclined to go with you."

"He's left today. He'll be back tomorrow when we talk to the Rik Director, but he doesn't need to know you're there. He comes to the negotiation room, he leaves. That's it. They're not allowed to bring weapons in."

"When does he get there? What time does he leave?"

"I can't tell you exactly, it depends on Senator Fontley. I think he'll arrive around nine and stay for several hours. It depends."

"That doesn't reassure me. I've done okay on my own so far."

Basher shook his head. "You got lucky in Lower Selta because he underestimated the loyalty of your Rik. It won't happen again. Just come back to the embassy. We can send you back to Earth on the Senator's ship." Basher laughed. "He's kind of a pain, but you would be safe with him and Sam and Nat."

"Okay—that's tempting." The small puddle by her shoe quivered as the ceiling dripped into it. "But that would only solve half my problem. The Rik I escaped with have become my friends. They protected me from Faal, and I want to help them, too. I owe it to them."

He made a wry face. "I guess I can understand that. What do you want to do for them?"

Claire hesitated. She hadn't wanted to state it quite so boldly, but this was the opening she'd been hoping for, and he'd taken it better than she expected. Maybe he was more reasonable than Sage gave him credit for...

"I want the ink," Claire blurted out. "I want to get them the tattoo so that they can be safe." She knew it was madness to divulge what she was after, but maybe he would understand. It would be so much better than the danger of breaking in and out of the embassy.

Basher's eyes got wide, and he laughed in surprise. "You're kidding. There's no way that will happen. It would be a lie—the worst kind of lie."

"Is it? They are human... now. They certainly aren't Rik anymore."

"Yes, they are."

"Excuse me, I've lived with them for six weeks. They don't just get new bodies, they get something else, too... They're more human than you think."

"Which they achieved by murder. They don't get a free pass."

"Not a free pass—but how is it fair if Faal kills these ones just because they helped me?"

"There's a base on the moon, and they'd be safe there. The Spo have organized—"

"The Spo? Are you kidding me? The Spo aren't any more incorruptible than anyone else. One bribe in the right place and my friends would be dead."

"One bribe..." Basher said, "Is that what happened to you?"

"Never mind. If we got a ship, would you let me leave the planet?"

As they'd talked, Basher had stepped away from the wall. At this, he grabbed her arm, not painfully, but firmly. "You can't go with them. They're *Rik*. They destroyed half our planet. They kidnap and kill and... you don't belong with them."

His hand moved, still restraining her, but more gently. "I know you've been through a lot, and I treated you like trash, but you can trust me now. Sam, Nat, Akemi—we're all ready to help you."

How she'd dreamed of a moment like this! Not Basher, specifically, but to have *any* human sincerely offering to help... And she had to disappoint him.

"They're not as bad as you think, at least these ones aren't. If they make it to Earth, they'll tell stories and learn sports and generally pretend to be human. Because they *want* to be human. Is that so horrible?" Claire stopped pulling. "I know some of the Rik have done terrible things, but every species has. Do they all deserve to be punished?"

Basher's jaw flexed.

"They were taught that this is okay," Claire said. "They're trying to be better."

His hand got tight again, but Claire finally felt the buzz she'd been waiting for; her tablet had finished getting the code. Now it was time to get away. Her faint hope of talking Basher to her side was bust. He would never help the Rik voluntarily. If she got away herself, it would be amazing.

"Akemi told me how you felt, but I still don't understand. How can you think of them as normal people? I'll tell you what they'll do on Earth, they'll hurt people like they've done here. They'll study them like rats, or worse, deceive them and have children..."

Claire thought of how Sage had kissed her and felt her face flushing. But it wasn't the way Basher described it. Sage was human, why shouldn't he—have someone? He wasn't deceiving her.

Basher suddenly looked furious. "Did Sage—"

"It's none of your business." He wasn't hurting her, but Claire tugged at her arm. "At least Sage doesn't treat me like this."

He loosened his hand. "I'm sorry—"

Claire twisted free, stumbling back a few steps. "Stop! Don't move." She held the torch toward a flat, gray panel on the wall. "I don't want the gate to hurt you."

"What gate?" Basher looked up just in time to see one of the environmental control gates. It slammed to the ground between them.

Claire turned and ran. Since the flame was only on the panel for a moment, she wasn't sure how long the gate would stay shut.

Sage had shown her several ways to get away quickly, so she headed toward the nearest small spinner—the ones people used to go down a level without waiting for one of the slow escalators.

Claire had mastered the knack of standing on the lower pole and holding onto he upper one, and she was ready for the friction that slowed her. She hopped off at the next level and disappeared into a crowd.

35

BASHER STARED at the safety gate in consternation. He'd been too distracted to notice it, whereas she must have planned that getaway from the beginning.

He had no idea how long it would take for the heat system to reset, so he immediately backtracked. It took him ten minutes to get to an alternate tunnel and back around to that level, and he wasn't even bothering to run by that point. If she'd planned to use a torch to set off the safety system, she must've planned several escape routes as well.

He looked around, just to be thorough, but nothing popped up. Basher kicked the wall. Why had he gotten so emotional with her? A sleepless night at the train station and a long session with Faal and Senator Fontley had left him edgy and tense, but he should have kept his cool.

Claire wouldn't be contacting him again any time soon. Maybe Akemi could get something.

The closest entrance to the embassy was the main door on the top level, the one under the arch with the guard out front. Basher was familiar to him, and the guard opened the door for him with a business-like nod

When Basher sat heavily at his computer, Akemi instantly opened a chatbox.

What happened? What happened? WHAT HAPPENED?

I don't appreciate being kept in the dark. Literally and figuratively.

"I blew it," Basher told her, shifting to face the camera so Akemi could see him better. "She came to plead for the Rik, as I should have expected, and I got upset..."

But why didn't you bring her back? In cuffs if you had to?

"She had one of those torches from the restaurant. She tripped one of the safety gates to get away."

Wow.

"I underestimated her. And I didn't understand how committed she was to the Rik."

I told you so.

"Thanks. That's really gracious of you."

Well, Claire still has two problems. She wants to help the Rik and she wants to avoid Faal. I think she'll have to contact you again. I mean, who else does she know on this planet?

CLAIRE SPREAD OUT A LARGE, hand-drawn map of the Spo embassy. Sage's friend had provided it, and it nearly covered the plastic table in their flat. Next to the map sat Sage's dead token, and the tablet she'd used to hack Basher's signal.

"Alright," Sage said, "We can get into the embassy. We need a plan."

At first Claire could make little of the map, just a jumble of rectangles and lines, but as Sage outlined their options she began to make sense of it. The Spo embassy stretched through three levels of Upper Selta, though they weren't exactly one on top of the other, like a layer cake. Each level of the embassy occupied a slightly different portion of the Seltan layers—making the edges of the map an uneven jumble of stairs, storerooms, and dwellings that didn't really match up to anything else.

The highest level of the embassy, the one closest to the surface of Selta, contained the embassy's formal reception hall, the negotiation room, and the ambassador's quarters. The second level was bigger, containing many of the offices and living quarters of the Spo and embassy guests. The third and lowest level was the one Claire had seen: containment cells, medical quarters, and storage. As Sage explained this, he drew a big D on the room that he understood was Basher's apartment.

"What does that stand for?" Claire asked.

"Detective."

"Oh, sure."

"These are the guest rooms here. Most of them will be empty so they might provide a good temporary hiding place. Anyway, the medical quarters are these two rooms." He marked the last with a small 'I.'

"I is for...?" Claire said.

Sage paused. "Ink. That's the room where the ink is stored."

"Oh, okay."

"With a working token, we should be able to get through all these interior doors, once we get through this outer door here," which he marked with a G.

Claire opened her mouth.

"G is for guard," Sage said. "Do you want to do this?"

Claire shook her head. "It's just a little confusing."

Sage took a deep breath. "The real problem will be getting back out, because by then someone will have noticed that the guards at this door are gone."

"What about that exit we took last time? The one that leads to the observation deck of the spinner drill?" Athlete asked.

"That's probably our best bet," Sage agreed. "It's kept locked, but it's on the interior door system, so it should still open for us, even if they've ice-locked the exterior doors. The observation platform has a lot of security in its own right, which is why the Spo are less concerned about it. The platform can be locked down also." He put a T on the door.

Claire didn't even bother to ask.

"To start, we'll have Juliet and Athlete overpower the guard *here*, then we'll get the ink, take these stairs here, and exit to the observation deck."

Athlete nodded slowly, "That seems like the simplest way."

"The *simplest* way?" Claire repeated. "If we can open the door by the big spinner, why not go in that way as well as out?"

Sage looked down at the map. "That observation platform will be deserted all night. We'll be too obvious."

"Then let's not go at night." She held up her hands as they all started to object. "I know, we have to go before Basher realizes his token has been hacked or has time to realize what I was doing. But what if we wait until tomorrow morning while he and the others are busy in the negotiation room? The observation deck will be crowded with people, we'll blend in and with any luck, get in and out of the lowest level without having to 'deal' with any guards at all."

There was silence for a moment, and then Juliet burst out laughing. It was so unexpected that Claire looked behind her, to see if something in the kitchen had amused her.

Juliet wiped her eyes, still laughing. "Sage, you look so disappointed. Admit it, you overcomplicate things. And she saw right through it."

Sage laughed reluctantly, and then more freely. "Okay, okay. Claire is smarter than me. She's right. If we wait until morning, we could safely use the observation deck. But there's risks, too. There'll be more Spo coming and going from the embassy during the day."

He went back to the map, outlining different escape routes, and how many Spo they might expect to find on each level.

They kept planning, and the reality of what they were going to do began to dawn on Claire. They were talking about weapons.

"We shouldn't kill anyone," Claire said. "Can't we, I don't know, stun them or something?"

Sage put his arm around her and kissed her cheek. "Hopefully we won't be seen, and we won't have to hurt anyone. But sure, I agree, we'll try to get weapons that don't kill."

Claire smiled at him, but her stomach began to ache.

36

IN THE NEGOTIATION ROOM, Sam sat at the foot of the table and prepared himself to read the formal charges to the Rik Supreme Director. She was a tall, majestic woman with graying hair in a neat cap around her head. It was strange that a Rik had chosen such an old human body, but Sam ventured to hope that it showed practicality or even humility.

Based on her attitude so far, that was wildly wishful thinking.

She sat on the left side of the table, across from Senator Fontley.

Nat had elected to stay in her room for this negotiation, and Sam hadn't argued with her. She was still in a sort of exhausted, half-asleep reality in which Akemi was more real to her than anyone else. She wasn't sleeping or eating well, and worse, she was withdrawing from him, too. Depression, maybe? Sam wanted so badly to help her, but he was afraid he was only making it worse.

Even if Nat had been fine, though, he wouldn't have wanted her to meet the Rik Director. This woman must have approved the actions taken against her and Akemi.

Basher followed Faal into the room, and if looks could kill, Basher's would.

Faal walked right up to the altar and withdrew from his

satchel a crumbling, rolled parchment. He raised the parchment to his forehead and then placed it with ritual slowness on the altar next to the skull and the deathglass.

Sam's eyes were wide as he whispered to the Spo near him, "Is that a Merith Corollary?"

The Spo nodded, faintly blue with surprise.

Sam typed a quick message to Basher's tablet. "One of their ancient documents, like... a Gutenberg Bible, or a Magna Carta. The original."

"Why?" Basher sent back.

"He's entering this talk as a representative of his own species, the Merith, not just the Council. It's not good."

Faal had also brought his five bodyguards who looked more and more like thugs to Basher. They hulked silently behind his chair at the foot of the table. One had a yellowing bruise at the base of his throat.

Five Spo stood at attention around Sam's end of the table. Basher had texted him, when Faal arrived with his entourage, that it was appropriate to match his show of authority with their own. Sam brought Nebbie for good measure.

Sam took a deep breath and began to read the report. It was largely to do with the explosion of the space station and only the final portion concerned their brief investigation on Selta: the killing of the Rik delegation, the money trail, the residue found on their bodies, and the records of their previous associations. Then came the formal charges. This had been composed by the Spo ambassador, Basher, and himself.

"Having heard this summation of our investigation and the conclusion of evidence against your fellow Rik, who we have confirmed were currently employed at the highest levels of government, what defense would you make?"

He tried to inject his voice with a bit of invitation. He sincerely hoped she *did* have a defense to make. The treaty was all but shredded unless this woman could make a darned good case for their innocence.

"I have a request to make of Senator Fontley," she said.

"Go ahead."

Senator Fontley did not look well. His face was flushed, and he was sweating.

"Do you have any desire to save this treaty?"

"The evidence is clear," he said. "Your people committed an act of terrorism against the Spo space station, an act of war."

"That is not my question. Do *you* personally, Senator Fontley, have any desire to save it? There are other alliances that humanity might make," she nodded at Faal, "but none would be so grateful to you as the Rik. In any other alliance, at least at this present time, humanity would be the junior member, not the senior."

"I believe we will take our chances," he said. "I *personally* have no desire to work with your species."

Sam had a text from Basher. "Have they met before? Feels like there's some history here."

"Not that I know of," Sam sent.

The Rik Director folded her hands on the table. "Then I have no reason to keep your secret. This man is a Rik. He was embedded in your society before we had the Hadron plan, but he failed to achieve what we wanted. Now he tries to regain power and cut us off, since we know who and what he is. He would throw us to what annihilation the galaxy will mete out."

Sam blinked. "That—is your defense? You claim that Senator Fontley is a Rik?"

Senator Fontley rose to his feet. "How dare you? I am an elected representative of the Human Coalition Government. You might as well accuse Faal of being a Rik!"

Faal snapped his beak in anger. "Let us refrain from entering into absurdities. Is this all you have to offer?" he asked the Director. "Do you admit that the Rik who sabotaged the space station did so as an organized effort of your government? Do you admit to having them murdered to silence their confession?"

"Absolutely not. They *were* my delegates, and they *would* have been arraigned for their crime, if they were still alive. I do not know why they acted as they did, who sponsored them, or who murdered them."

"They didn't communicate with you after the explosion?" Sam asked.

"No. I had no intention of targeting the Spo station. Why should I? I don't deny my people committed the attack, but I also know that that makes no difference." She glared at Senator Fontley again. "I'm positive that the *Senator* already made up his mind to dissolve the treaty. Nothing I can say will make any difference."

Senator Fontley had regained his complexion. "Whatever my previous opinion was, your outrageous accusations have certainly made up my mind. As representative of the Rik people, you have demonstrated a complete indifference to the loss of life on the space station, and a vicious inclination to turn on your human allies. I can do no less for my people than to dissolve a treaty that chains us to the vicissitudes of an ungrateful race."

Basher looked to Sam, "Could it be true?"

"How dare you—!"

As much as Sam disliked Senator Fontley, or maybe *because* of it, he didn't think the man was Rik. The ones Sam had met, even the really knowledgeable ones like Shara, made mistakes. There was just something off about them. Wasn't there?

"I don't think so," Sam said, a little sadly. "As little as we get along, he's never given me reason to doubt his humanity. He's definitely been on Earth a long time—I think my parents voted for him twenty years ago."

"He was an early plant," the Director said. "You can't trust him."

"That's nonsense," Fontley said. "You could make this accusation about anyone, because there's no way to disprove it."

Sam studied the senator. Fontley didn't know about the new blood test.

Basher sent him another message. "It'd be a good idea to start testing everyone in government circles so these sorts of accusations won't plague the new human government for the next thirty years."

Senator Fontley rose from his chair and spoke in his CNN voice. "If you have nothing else to say, I hereby, with the power given me by the Human Coalition Government, utterly dissolve the treaty between our two species. Humanity will not sponsor the Rik into the Galactic Council. The Rik may survive or not, as circumstances allow, and humanity bears no responsibility to aid or protect you in times of crisis."

The Director stood. "A well-played farce, Senator."

"Can we get her out of here?" Fontley demanded.

Sam felt a deep sense of loss. This was the end of his very brief attempt to rehabilitate the Rik and springboard humanity to a stronger, more compassionate place in the galaxy. It had been a crazy idea to begin with, and perhaps he had been wrong to try it. Certainly Nat and Basher had thought so.

Faal tapped his thick tablet with a claw and showed the translation of the judgement to Sam and Fontley. "I believe I have that here correctly. I shall submit it directly to the Galactic Council at your command."

It was in Spo and Merith which Sam doubted Senator Fontley could read. Nat was the best at this sort of thing, but she wasn't here, so he gave it his best shot. Sam perused it carefully, and finally nodded his head. "It is as correct a translation as the senator could wish."

"Then please submit it," Senator Fontley said. "And let us be dismissed."

Faal reclined a little further in his chair and smiled faintly at the Director. "This will be a dangerous time for the Rik, without sponsorship or ally. Without *sentient* status or protection."

The Director's reply was such a combination of animosity and bleakness that Sam winced. "I'm certain you'll give it your full attention."

"Oh, perhaps not quite that," Faal answered gently. "But some large part of it, yes. I have many ideas."

The Director walked to the door. "I believe there is no reason for me to stay. I would wish you all good day, but that seems to be a mark of sentience I am no longer required to fake."

Basher jumped up to usher her out of the embassy. He gestured to Faal as well. "I will show you both out. We are done here."

"Not entirely," said Faal. "You may have noticed my contribution to the table is on my own account, not as a Councilor. I should be honored to discuss an alliance between my species and humanity."

"Frankly," Sam said, "if we were going to enter another alliance, it would not be with the Merith. We have—er—differing values. Slavery and human rights being a large one."

Senator Fontley sat back down. "Frankly, *Sam,* it is not up to you. Despite our differences, I believe Faal and I have things to discuss."

Sam swallowed his frustration. "Could we speak in private first?"

"I don't feel any need for that." Fontley raised his eyebrows. "The adults need to talk, son."

"Senator, I'm afraid I have to insist," Sam said.

Faal rumbled a laugh. "You should hear him out, before he hurts himself. I must excuse myself for a moment anyway."

37

SENATOR FONTLEY GLARED at Sam after Faal excused himself. "I suppose I can spare five minutes. *What* is so pressing?"

Sam explained the situation with Claire as succinctly as he could. "So, you see, Faal has already enslaved a human, and he is practically taunting Basher with it. He doesn't respect us—not as individuals or as a species."

"The cadets, maybe; I venture to think I am in a different category."

"Only because you'll be more useful to him. I know you don't like me, but *please* consider what I'm saying. I'm not trying to embarrass you. I truly think Faal is a danger to all of us."

FONTLEY DID DISLIKE SAM, but not for the reasons Sam thought. Fontley had tried to avoid taking this assignment to Selta, but his fellow committee members had insisted, and there had been no way to decline without losing serious credibility.

He'd been afraid, but again, not for the reasons Sam thought.

It was quite simple, actually. Senator Fontley *had* been one of the first Rik on Earth.

He'd gotten his human body over twenty years ago. The invasion plan was in the first stages then, long before they'd targeted the Large Hadron Collider to cause a sentience trial.

Fontley had blended into an Earth that had no idea extraterrestrials even existed (outside their ridiculous movies). He'd enjoyed it, too. After a few years, he'd been a state representative, then a Senator. He might've become president if he'd had more time. People had praised his detached, unbiased viewpoint. No partisan politics here, they said, just good, plain solutions.

Unbiased—they had no idea. He'd been frustrated when the Supreme Director decided to take a different approach and sent him news of the Hadron plan. He'd taken careful precautions to be in a safe location from the storms and tsunamis. All had gone to plan, but then the Spo came.

He'd had to drop out of sight completely. The Spo felt justified killing as many politicians as needed to establish a new order, so he'd conveniently gone to South America for a few years. He'd nearly died in a fire storm in Sao Paolo, but he had a talent for survival, and he'd escaped again.

He'd been waiting and waiting for Earth to lose their trial. Then the Rik would come flooding in, and he'd be in a perfect position to be—oh, maybe the Deputy Director of Earth. He'd earned it.

But no. Instead Sam had ruined *everything*. He'd uncovered the Rik plot with the help of that unspeakable abomination of a computer called Akemi.

In two hours, he undid twenty years of Fontley's life.

Then Sam had the gall to make a treaty with the *Rik*. True, a treaty that would keep the Rik from being annihilated out of hand, but also one that made them debtors to Earth for a lifetime. It was an act of such arrogant condescension that it made Fontley sick.

He'd been outraged, but he'd quickly realized that his best hope lay in completely submerging himself into human culture. As one of the few former senators still alive, he had every chance of making an excellent future for himself in human politics. He was the stuff a good politician was made from. Literally. He would rule Earth in his own right.

However, that all depended on a ragged and paranoid humanity *never* finding out that he had been Rik. Sam's treaty was a direct threat to him, and Fontley was completely willing to sacrifice his people in exchange for his own survival. In fact, he would be less than human if he *didn't* consider his own needs first—and he was absolutely determined to be human.

The space station explosion was unexpected.

On the one hand, it offered the chance of driving a breach between the humans and the Rik, which he wanted. The people of Earth were already conditioned to hate aliens (thanks to the Spo), and by playing into that, people flocked to support Fontley.

On the other hand, the actual investigation of the explosion was bound to involve encounters with many Rik. He had wrangled as best he could to avoid that, but it was not to be.

The one bright note in this whole mess was the presence of Faal of Merith II. He was a Merith of renown who also had a passionate dislike of the Rik. Senator Fontley planned to cultivate that relationship for all it was worth. First, because it would be completely unlike a Rik to cultivate a Merith relationship. Second, Faal was a member of the Galactic Council. If he was convinced of the senator's bona fides, he would be a powerful and ruthless ally. And third, Sam disliked him.

It was perhaps part of Fontley's irrational human nature, but he could not forbear hating Sam. Sam was immensely popular and known around the world. In another few years, Sam would be an unstoppable political enemy.

In fact, Fontley had put another plan into motion during his stay on Selta. Was it not the perfect time to be rid of Sam for good? It would be madness to attempt an assassination out of hand on Earth, but on Selta there were many more possibilities. And a good Rik always had an assassin on his payroll. Fontley certainly did.

Sam looked at him across the table with his stupidly sincere face. "The Merith have even less in common with us than the Spo. They are a vicious species. They still allow slavery, like I said, but they also don't appreciate rule of law or due process unless they are forced."

"I will take that under consideration."

"I don't think you understand—"

"You had your chance, Sam. Don't be a sore loser. Even your Rik assassin didn't whine when she was beaten."

"I know, I wasn't—" Sam cocked his head. "You've never liked Shara."

"No, she's Rik."

"Yes... And maybe you were afraid she would recognize you." Sam licked his lips. "Is it possible? Is *that* why you were so resistant to leaving the planet?"

Fontley felt a thrill of fear. "You're letting your dislike of me cloud your opinion."

"Actually, I'm not. My dislike of you was a point in your favor, but now I'm wondering if I'm wrong." He narrowed his eyes. "The Spo have recently created a blood test that proves if a person is Rik or not. Would you be willing to take it and prove yourself?"

"They have *what*?"

"A blood test that proves if someone is Rik. It was inevitable really, I wish they'd rolled it out sooner." His eyes shifted to the knife on the altar. "Would you take it?"

"*Absolutely*, I would." No, he wouldn't. This was exactly why one kept an assassin on retainer. "Perhaps the Spo aren't worthless after all."

"I'll go down and prepare—"

"Not *today*, Sam. I must finish this meeting with Faal."

Sam rose. "If you've been lying to us—"

"I'll prove everything tomorrow," Fontley said. "Now I believe the Merith are returning. You can show yourself out."

Fontley began to compose a message on his tablet. Sam clearly disbelieved him, and it was time for him to go.

"Oh, Sam?" he called after him. Time for a little reverse psychology. "I trust you won't take any rash action? I expect you to remain *in* the embassy until this is settled."

Sam backed away. "Sure."

38

CLAIRE'S EYES FLICKED AROUND, taking in the huge abyss and the spinner drill, a gigantic borer, slowly circling downward. She'd seen it when they escaped, but it had seemed like part of her fever dream.

There were stalls along the safe side of the platform, opened during the day to sell touristy things, like blown glass replicas of the spinners or coins to toss in the hole for good luck. Some stalls sold food, and the whole level smelled like sausage.

Many aliens were on the platform now, leaning against the railing near the spinner drill or taking pictures in front of it.

"Lots of tourists," Sage said briefly. "That's good." He carried the tablet that had hacked Basher's token, and a gun that he'd promised her he would not use to kill anyone. Athlete and Juliet had weapons as well. Sage also had a set of more conventional lock picks—pins and magnets—just in case there were any manual locks to get through.

The negotiation started barely an hour ago, and Basher, Sam, and Nat should be safely tied up with that.

Claire was about a hundred yards from the embassy, focusing on the door that was their objective, when it opened. A Spo walked out, and just behind him came two people. Claire recognized the two cadets, Sam and Nat.

"Shoot—"

"We need to hide," Sage said.

She and the Rik piled into the nearest shop. It was barely large enough for them all to stand inside, surrounded by metal toys for children, like tops, that were also shaped like the spinner drill. A surprised-looking Tergre stood behind a display, holding a rag.

"We'll just be a moment," Juliet said. "What clever toys!"

Claire peeked out through the open doorway, watching Sam and Nat walk next to the railing. She could just barely hear Nat's voice when they came close.

"You really think he's fake?"

"Maybe—he was being really strange. I wanted to get out of there to talk to you."

Sam had glasses on, much like the ones wrapped up in her bag. Even if *he* didn't see her, Akemi might, so Claire pressed back further into the stall.

Sage steadied her. "The question is, how long are they going to stay? We can't go in while they're out here."

They all watched as Sam and Nat leaned on the rail, obviously having an intense conversation. They both jerked when a pushy Vel tried to get near them. He was trying to sell them sausages.

"I thought they were supposed to be in the negotiation?" Athlete said. "Instead they are taking a walk?"

The Vel salesman wasn't taking "no" for an answer, and Sam and Nat weren't finishing their conversation while he talked.

"Where is his wife or mother?" Juliet muttered. "She'd keep him in line."

"True, Vel males don't usually work alone," Sage said.

"There's something wrong— He's edging them toward the railing." Claire gasped. "I think he's going to push them in."

"That's crazy," Sage said.

But Claire knew what her gut was telling her. She flew through the door of the stall, sprinting toward the railing. Perhaps it was her experience in the zoo, or maybe just her own intuition, but she knew something bad was about to happen. "Look out!"

As she ran, she fumbled with her bag, grabbing the glasses and putting them on. The bag fell unheeded behind her. "Akemi, do you see this?"

Sam's gaze snapped to Claire—just as the Vel used his strong, lizardy arms to try and topple them both over the railing.

Sam twisted with the blow and fell to the side. Blood spotted his shirt where the Vel's claws had scored him. But Claire didn't hear the sound of his shirt ripping or her own yelp. She only heard Nat's scream as she fell backward into the giant hole.

Akemi's brain was locked in a silent scream. Nat was in free fall, spinning and tumbling down the hole dug by the spinner drill. She couldn't survive that...! It was nearly a kilometer to the bottom.

Akemi barely processed that Claire was somehow there as well. Akemi distantly noted Sam's injuries and his eyes, horrorstruck. The lizard-like Vel stared incredulously at Claire, momentarily taken aback by the interruption.

All that mattered was Nat. Falling, spinning toward the bottom...

Then they all heard Nat's voice. "Help me!"

The Vel flung himself on Sam. They wrestled. The Vel grappled, trying to get Sam's hands behind his back and drag him over the edge. Sam was using everything he had, kicking at the Vel's legs and trying to jab his ears.

Claire darted around them to lean over the railing. Nat was a mere six feet below the edge of the platform, clinging to an exposed pipe.

Akemi's panic began to subside. Nat's face was bare; her *glasses* had fallen. Nat was *not* in a crumpled heap at the bottom of the diggings. Only her glasses had tumbled free.

Claire turned back toward the stall. Sage and Juliet and Athlete were running toward her.

"Hurry! Help me!" Claire shouted. "She's just there. If you lower me down... or hold my legs...."

Sage looked over the edge of the platform, but then he back away. "Even if she fell, she'd be alright. There's bound to be safety measures for tourists. Gravity fields to slow the fall. We need to get out of here."

Claire was disappointed, and Juliet gave him a withering look. "I'll do it."

She sat on the railing and fell backwards like a gymnast, hanging by her knees. "Just hold onto my ankles—my legs, not my pants!—and lower me another couple feet."

Athlete complied, sliding her forward until she was hanging completely upside down. He braced his own waist against the railing and lowered her further.

"Okay," Juliet said calmly. "Don't let go yet, alright?"

Nat's face was sweaty, and she shifted her grip unsteadily. "I didn't expect you to help at all."

Claire jumped back as Sam, wrestling with the Vel, rolled toward her. There were bloody scratches on Sam's neck. Claire lunged forward to help, only for Sage to drag her back. "I don't think so."

He sighed and threw himself into the fight, trying to get between Sam and his attacker.

"I've got your wrists," Juliet was saying to Nat. "Now you release your right hand and grab mine." Athlete swayed forward a bit when both girls' weight shifted to him, and impressive muscles bulged in his neck as he pulled Juliet up. When she was half over the railing, Nat was able to switch her grip again, and Claire helped her the rest of the way over the railing. Athlete swung Juliet over.

Nat was shaking, but she stayed on her feet.

"Nice glasses," were her first words to Claire.

They turned to see that Sage and Sam had subdued the Vel. He was sprawled awkwardly on his stomach with Athlete's knee on his back.

Nat touched Sam's split lip gingerly. "Are you okay?"

"Me? I'm fine, but I saw you fall—"

"I didn't." She looked to Claire. "Did Akemi tell you we were in trouble? No, wait, what are you doing here?"

"That's our cue to leave," Sage said.

Athlete yanked the Vel to his feet. He couldn't hold the alien's hands behind its back because of the way Vel anatomy worked, but he kept one arm in a dangerously taut hold that seemed to do the trick. Athlete pushed the Vel up against the railing.

Sam had drawn his pellet gun, and he kept it pointed at the Vel. "Who put you up to this?"

"I'm all for interrogation," Athlete said, "but can you take him from here?"

Sam ignored this. "Bruck, I've got witnesses to prove you tried to kill us. Your only chance is to tell us who hired you."

Sage began to edge away, tugging Juliet and Claire with him. "Speaking of witnesses," he hissed, "we need to go. This deck will be crawling with Spo any minute." He looked at Claire. "Unless you're staying?"

Seeing the way Sam gripped Nat's shoulder like he would never let go, Claire wavered. The tone of Sam's voice, Nat's gaze, even Sam's posture—it was human in a way she couldn't quantify. "No, I'm not—staying."

"What time is it?" the Vel suddenly said.

Sam took a step closer. "Why? Do you have an appointment?"

"What time is it?" he said again, almost growling.

"It's 11:02," Claire said.

"Grab him! *Grab* him!" Sam shouted.

The Vel got a foot on the railing, and with a powerful heave, he threw himself into the hole of the spinner drill.

As it turned out, there *was* a force field to save people's lives if they fell off the platform. Claire was relieved to see a flare of yellow light when the Vel was only a few stories below them. He kept falling, but slower.

"See, she would've been fine!" Sage said. "Let's *go*."

But when the yellow energy field flared, it triggered an alarm. An ear-splitting shriek filled the observation platform, and gates lowered on either end, preventing anyone from exiting the platform. Gates also rolled down to cover the small stalls and vendors on the other side. It reminded Claire of a shopping mall closing up, if it happened in about five seconds.

The door to the embassy flew open, and a group of Spo guards came out.

Sage uttered a curse word and drew his gun.

"No, don't," Claire cried.

Sam put his hand on Sage's shoulder, looking him in the eye. "You can't shoot your way out. Look, I'll speak for you. You didn't have to help me, but you did."

"Turns out it was for nothing. You could've handled the Vel, and the fall wouldn't have killed your girlfriend."

Nat wavered on her feet. "It didn't feel like that. I really— appreciate what you did." Everyone could hear her reluctance to thank a Rik.

Sage looked from Claire to the Spo guards and sighed. He lowered his gun and set it on the ground.

39

EXPLAINING TURNED out to be harder than Sam expected. In the confusion of the confrontation, the only solid facts the Spo grasped were 1) that four Rik fugitives had thrown a pedestrian from the platform, and 2) that Sam and Nat were in a battered condition. In a matter of minutes, all four were arrested, being taken back into the embassy in handcuffs.

"They helped us." Sam followed as the Spo pushed the prisoners back toward the embassy. "That Vel tried to kill us—he tried to push *us* off the edge."

One of the Spo grunted. "That wouldn't have killed you. That does not make sense."

Sam fell back as they entered the narrow hallway between the containment rooms. "I bet the safety fields were off," he told Nat. "That Vel asked about the time. He wanted to make sure the force fields were back on before he jumped. It was a great idea. Now he looks like a victim."

"So I would have died after all," Nat said.

One of the Spo unlocked the door of a containment cell and shoved the Rik inside. "Get in here. There'll be three guards outside the door, so you will not escape again."

He grabbed Claire's elbow and shoved her in with them.

"Hey, that one's a human," Sam said. "I told you."

"She wasn't the last time she was here," the Spo retorted.

THE DOOR SLAMMED SHUT and Claire sank onto a bunk bed with shaking knees. "Well. Here we are again. This is starting to get real familiar."

The sound of Sam arguing with the Spo receded, leaving only a stunned quiet. No one had removed their handcuffs, so they all waited awkwardly for a minute, staring uselessly at the one way mirror.

Are you okay? Akemi asked Claire.

"I'm fine, thanks," Claire said. "I'm glad your sister is okay."

I am, too. Thank you for helping her. I've never felt so trapped.

"But why did that *happen?*"

We have an idea. Working on it.

Juliet and Athlete sat on one of the bunks, and she verbally fussed over his wounds while he complimented her on her acrobatics. Sage's eyes were unfocused, and he looked like his mind was somewhere else.

"You're scaring me a little," Claire said to him. "This isn't the end of the world, right? I know our plan is screwed up beyond repair, but Sam will explain that we saved Nat! Basher will be willing to help us now..."

"It's not that," he said slowly. "Well, it *is* that. I can't believe I risked my life, and theirs, and even yours, maybe—to stay and help strangers."

Claire shifted on the bed. Her shoulders were starting to ache. "That doesn't surprise me. You're a good person."

"I'm not; far from it. And I'm not bothered about that. *Good* people usually have horrible things happen to them. Like you." His eyes finally focused on Claire. "I don't want to change who I am."

She shrank back slightly. "Everyone changes."

"Rik don't." He laughed bleakly. "It's the ultimate irony. We steal new bodies for ourselves while our psyche is locked in place."

"But, maybe change is good for you. You've proved that Rik can be selfless, and that they can be trusted. Sam and Basher will sort this out, and it'll be better for you."

He shook his head. "Listen to yourself. You're trying to prove my one act of selflessness was actually in my best interest. Doesn't that show you I'm not a good person?" He finally sat on the mattress next to Claire. "I love you. But what just happened is not me."

For the first time, Claire got a glimpse of what he meant about the selfishness of the Rik.

Akemi interrupted. *Sam is going upstairs to deal with Senator Fontley. They think he is behind what just happened. He and Basher are furious.*

Claire relayed the information to the others, and was glad to see the scary intensity in Sage's face relax.

And Sam says, "Don't do anything rash. I promise we'll get you out."

He's kind of grandiose that way. :-)

Claire laughed but quickly sobered. "What about Faal? Is he still here?"

Unfortunately, yes.

"I don't even want to think about what he'll do if he realizes I'm here."

He won't. Akemi paused. *Sam and Basher are coming back down—they are bringing Senator Fontley. Do you want to see him?*

"I guess," Claire said. "*Can* we see him?"

Sure, I just have to adjust the light in the hall.

A brighter light turned on outside their cell, and it was focused on their window. Suddenly the hallway was visible. Sam and Basher came into view together, flanking a politician Claire had seen somewhere before. Basher's partner and Nat were just behind them.

Sage suddenly slid off the bed to the floor. "Did he see me?"

"Basher? Yeah, he did," Claire said. "He looks annoyed that Akemi adjusted the light."

"No, Did *Senator Fontley* see me?" Sage asked.

"I don't think he was looking at us."

"Good." Sage looked up at her. "If he realizes I'm here, he may try to silence me before I blow his cover."

"His cover?" Claire asked.

Oh my gosh. Then he is a Rik? Akemi asked.

I should've known! He's such a jerk. No offense.

"Sage, do you know for sure he's a Rik?" Claire asked.

"Yes." He looked distant again. "I may have—trained him."

"But that's—you're not—he's old."

You're kind of missing the bigger picture here, Claire.

"He's not as old as he looks," Sage said. "And I'm not as young as I look. Nor am I just a... philosopher."

Claire released a long, slow breath. "I don't think I want to know."

I want to know! Akemi sent. *You can't ignore this, Claire.*

"Fine! Akemi wants to know," the words tumbled out of Claire. "What was your position? Why does everyone defer to you? Were you running the experiments—" Claire caught her breath on a sob. "I trusted you."

"I know. I'm good at inspiring trust. But right now, we need to deal with our problem; we need to get out of here."

"Fine. After we escape, you have to tell me the truth."

"If we can escape again—"

"It'll be easy," Claire said.

"Excuse me? *Easy?*"

"They barely searched us. I still have the glasses, so we have

Akemi's help. Your bag is right outside the door where they dumped it. Things are chaotic. How hard could this be?"

Uh. Not to spoil your moment, but I can't help a lot. They wouldn't let me access the embassy security system, so I can access maps and lights, but I can't open doors or turn off alarms. :-/

"That'll be fine. They'll come for me anytime now. I'll be back."

BASHER FORCED Senator Fontley to sit on the cot in the medical room. His partner kept his weapon pointed at the Senator. Sam and Nat crowded in as well.

"You removed me from a most important meeting for this *farce?*" Senator Fontley said.

Sam traded places with Basher, so that he could retrieve a syringe with the blood test.

"I'd apologize for the needle involved with this test," Basher said. "But Rik are intimately familiar with them."

"How long were you planning to get rid of me?" Sam asked.

"I don't know what you're talking about."

"Shara says a good Rik *always* has an assassin on call."

Senator Fontley flushed with rage. "I wouldn't know. You have no right to inject me with alien pharmaceuticals! You'll all three go to prison for this. Natsuki, listen to me. You're a reasonable girl—"

"Maybe if you'd taunted me less about Akemi, I'd listen to you now," Nat said.

Basher came back and jammed the syringe in Fontley's arm. "In light of attempted murder, I'm exercising my right on the sovereign moon of Selta, to apprehend possible imposters and test them."

Fontley made his move when the syringe was still in. Without regard for the snapping of the needle in his arm, he lunged not toward Basher, which Basher expected, but toward his partner.

The syringe was torn from Basher's grip and shattered on the floor. Fontley backhanded the gun out of the Spo's grasp and spun to the counter. A set of implements was wrapped in cloth, and he came away with a scalpel in hand.

Fontley's first wild slash opened a deep green gash on the Spo's upper arm and red line on Sam's hand. Basher drew his weapon in an instant, but Fontley had already crossed the few steps to Sam and pressed the scalpel to his neck. "Open the door," he said.

Sam's hand dripped blood on the floor. "Your ruse is over. What do you think you'll achieve?"

Fontley's hand jerked. "Killing you would be some consolation. But if you assure me I can leave the embassy, and I'll let you keep the rest of your blood."

Basher had his weapon up, but he wasn't sure he should use it. Would Fontley react by slicing the artery in Sam's neck? Probably not, but it wasn't a sure bet—

There was the sharp retort of another weapon, and Fontley's head sprayed blood. He slumped to the floor. Sam clutched his hand to stem the bleeding—his neck was not cut.

Fontley, on the other hand, wouldn't be getting up, and there would be no staunching of that wound. He was dead.

They all turned to look at Nat, who now lowered the weapon. She'd scooped it off the floor after Fontley knocked it away from Basher's partner. "That—was enough of that," she said.

"Nat," Basher said carefully, "you were two steps away. You could have shot to wound him."

She set the gun on the counter. Her hand was steady, her face was hard. "I could've tried, yes, but it's not the Spo way."

His partner took the weapon back. "No, it is not. I completely approve. Well done, cadet."

"Thank you." A little humanity leaked back into Nat's face. "Also—I'm not perfect. If I had shot his leg or arm and made him twitch wrong, he still could've cut Sam's throat."

Sam went to Nat. Both of them had droplets of blood on their faces. "Are you okay?"

"Of course." She swallowed. "We'd better deal with your hand and with this—body before it makes a worse mess."

Basher felt a little chilled. He knew Sam and Nat were Spo cadets—and that they were the best of the best—but he hadn't realized quite how much of the cold-blooded Spo training they'd absorbed.

Sam embraced her. "We all saw him attack me; we even have Akemi's footage. We can prove it was defensive."

"I'm not too worried about it." Nat gave Basher a half-smile from Sam's arms. "I'm not a sociopath, I promise. But the Rik have hurt me and my family already—I know they're willing to kill faster than we are."

Basher's partner nodded emphatically. "That they are."

Nat closed her eyes. "It does offer some closure—maybe this is what therapy feels like."

Basher huffed. "You're a little scary, Nat. But alright. Let's get your therapy session into a body bag."

40

BASHER WENT to retrieve Claire as soon as Fontley was stowed away and Sam's hand was bandaged. Claire joined him in the hallway and he shut the door on the other Rik.

"Akemi," he said. "Turn off that blasted light."

The light went off, rendering the window one-way again. Basher undid Claire's handcuffs. "I'm sorry," he said. "I would've been here sooner, but we had some—complications to deal with."

"It's fine. Is that why there's blood on your face?"

"Er, yes. But I *am* sorry. I promised we'd help, and instead you were arrested again."

"The circumstances were unusual." She rubbed her wrists. "I won't hold this one against you."

"Even more unusual than you know." He ran a hand through his hair. "Senator Fontley is—dead. Everything is crazy today. I'm still reeling."

"Wow. Not to add to your burden, but—I need to get out of here. Faal is still here, isn't he?"

"I'm about to kick him out. We had to interrupt his meeting with the Senator. You can wait over here in my office. There's somebody who'll make you feel better."

Claire looked dubious, but when he opened the door, Kit

jumped on her shoulder with a rippling purr of excitement. She melted into Basher's chair. "Kit! You're still here." She buried her face in his fur.

"Just—stay here, okay?" Basher said. "I'll get rid of Faal, and I'll come back when he's gone."

"Alright," Claire said. "I'll wait with Kit."

Basher left her in his office and sighed. She was definitely lying. She planned to help her Rik escape as soon as he was out of sight. The worst part was that Sam was on their side now, too.

Basher looked down at the bag outside the Rik cell. Stooping, he stuck his token deep inside it.

CLAIRE WAITED ONLY until Basher was gone. "Akemi, you saw what happened. You saw my friends save Sam and Nat. Will you help me get them out?"

Ugh. Fair is fair. Basher is going to be so upset, but yes, I will help. Sam and Nat are arguing in the stairwell. The Spo are going to deal with Faal. The hallway is empty. You're safe to go out.

Claire felt terribly exposed. It killed her, but she left Kit in the office. The cell door had a second electronic lock as well as the normal token one, and she needed to get them both unlocked quickly. It looked doable. Claire had quite a bit of experience because Faal had found some creative locks to use with her. Only after she'd learned to pick all of them had she realized that he never counted on them to contain her. He had enjoyed a good laugh while he watched her learn to pick locks—like dexterity tests for a monkey.

She used the magnets and pins to disable the first lock, then she pressed the tablet to the door and to open the second one.

She pushed her way in quickly and Sage looked up at her. "You came back."

Claire shut the door behind herself and began to work on his cuffs. "I did say I would."

After Sage, Claire freed Athlete and Juliette from their handcuffs. It was dangerous to waste even a second, but if there was fighting to do, she wanted them unbound.

The Spo guards are back, Akemi told her.

"Thanks for the warning."

Athlete and Sage burst through the door and the guards spun around. Their skin changed hue abruptly from shocked to angry.

Juliette, Athlete, and Sage went into action. In seconds, they were armed, and the guards were shoved into the containment room. Claire slammed the door on them; it locked automatically.

"Well. That was easier than I expected," Sage said.

An alarm sounded.

"Shoot. We could have used a few more minutes," Claire said. "We can hide in Basher's office—it's two doors down."

They ran down the hall and huddled inside. The footsteps of more Spo sounded in the hallway, then died away.

Kit jumped on her shoulder and Athlete flinched. "Vermin?"

"*No,* a pet," Claire said.

The door suddenly opened, and Sam and Nat were there.

"I'm never invited to the party," Sam complained. They crowded into the room and pulled the door shut.

Nat tapped her glasses. "Akemi told us you were here."

"Are you willing to help?" Claire asked.

"Yes," Sam said, while Nat said, "Maybe."

Akemi put up a message on Basher's computer. "*Look, I'm friends with all of you, so you all have to get along for a moment. Nat, it's really unfair to imprison these Rik because they stopped to help you.*

"Fine. Let's get them out of here."

. . .

BASHER RAN to his office when he heard the alarm. He was right, Claire had decided to escape—

But to his surprise, they were right here. He instinctively shut the door behind himself. Didn't the Rik realize that the hallway was filled with Spo? They'd holed up approximately thirty feet from their cell.

The small room barely held them all. Sam and Nat were wedged in a corner, the Rik were clumped in the middle, and Claire was holding Kit in her lap. When he opened the door, she looked up apprehensively. Sage had his hand on her shoulder.

Claire grimaced. "I know, I know. Can we lock him up temporarily?"

Basher stared at her.

Claire tapped her glasses. "I'm talking to Akemi. She says it's no good to ask you to help us, and no good to try and lock you up. But I think you'll have to help us."

"Like hell I do." Basher pointed at Nat and Sam, "What's the matter with you two? Why didn't you turn them in?"

"They saved my life. We owe them," Nat said.

"They must have known that you could help them. They're playing you somehow."

"They're not," Claire said.

"Don't even get me started on you—" His diatribe was interrupted by Kit jumping on his shoulder and patting his nose.

Nat cleared her throat. "Let's calm down. We don't need to plead with you to believe anything. Akemi can show you what happened."

"It doesn't matter—"

"Oh, just grab him," Nat said impatiently.

Athlete and Sam and Sage jumped toward him, which Basher admitted to himself he had not expected. He could have fought them off, but Claire put herself right in the middle. He couldn't lash out without hitting her. He held up his hands, "Fine. Fine."

Claire, give him your glasses, please.

Claire plucked the glasses off her nose and settled them onto his. "Just watch."

Basher rolled his eyes.

Stop being so stubborn. The message appeared in front of his eyes, overlaying Claire's face in front of him.

You're furious because you like her, and you're worried about her.

"I thought you were smarter than this," Basher muttered to Akemi.

He watched the recording through the glasses. It was scary to see the scene from Claire's perspective, to realize she'd run straight toward the murderous Vel with no plan... He watched Nat fall and Sam twist out of the way.

"Nice move," he said to Sam.

He saw Nat clinging to the pipe and whistled. The whole thing played out, and Basher didn't say anything.

Admit it. You're impressed.

"Surprised, yes. Impressed... maybe."

If you help them now, Claire will trust you. She'll come back.

Basher shook Athlete off impatiently. "Assuming I was to help you," he glared at Sage, "but making no promises for the future—what do you expect me to do? Magic you out of here?"

More Spo passed by the door, and Basher jerked his thumb toward the hall. "That's a problem. The other problem is that they've ice-locked all the exterior doors. It would take *four* independent tokens to open any of them now—and I don't even have one."

Claire held out her hand. "Can I have my glasses back?"

"Akemi, show me a map of the embassy again," Claire said. She looked straight through Basher, focused intently on whatever Akemi was showing her. It reminded him of when she'd stared at him through the mirror when he'd first arrested her.

She seemed like a completely different person now. Even different than when he'd talked to her in the tunnel.

A slow smile spread across her face. "I have a really fun idea."

BASHER STOOD underneath the skylights in the reception hall, staring up at the hole in the ceiling. Kit rode on his shoulder and chittered sadly as Claire disappeared.

He could hear Juliet's voice receding higher. "This is fun!"

Getting them to the reception room had been relatively easy. Basher could tell them when the halls were empty, and going further *into* the embassy was much easier than trying to get *out* at the present moment. "Further in and further up," Sam had said.

The reception hall felt vast and full of echoes. It was unlit and empty. Apparently no one thought the escapees might congregate here.

The little Rik girl, Juliet, had helped construct a makeshift scaffold using chairs and a table and even a rolled up rug. She went into the skylight first, wedging her back against one side of the hole and bracing her feet on the other side. "Hang on a sec," she'd said. "Let me make sure it's not capped a few feet up."

From the map, Claire had seen that the skylights were not straight, but rather built with a series of angles and twists, following the natural formation of the rocky crust and many layers of Upper Selta. Many large mirrors were used to bounce the natural lighting down to the reception hall.

She'd also seen that the skylights were connected. Akemi found a map of the surface and they confirmed that there was only one major opening in the surface of Selta in this area. All the skylights descended from that single hole.

What she hadn't seen, but suspected, was that the Spo weren't the only ones willing to pay for natural light. The top levels of Selta were expensive and exclusive; others would want the same luxury the Spo had. The skylight tunnels for the Spo embassy *must* join with the skylight tunnels in adjacent structures.

That wouldn't have been enough to convince Basher, but Akemi looked through the public records, and found evidence that a wealthy Tergre, who owned a huge suite just north of the embassy, had paid for major renovations at the same time the Spo built the skylights.

Basher, under pressure, had admitted that it was a possible way of escape. One by one, they'd climbed the pyramid of chairs and disappeared into the skylight—which was now showing a lot less light.

Nat and Sam helped him move the chairs back to their positions, unroll the carpet, and drag the groaning table back to its place.

Sam grew more sober as they finished. "This is going to be a heck of a report to write to the HCG committee."

"Maybe—" Nat offered him a weak smile. "Maybe I could do this one."

"Really?"

"I know I haven't been any help at all lately—"

"It's not that. I really appreciate the offer, but—you were the one who shot Fontley." He spoke gently, "You can't be the one to write the official report."

"Oh, right. I should—uh—work on a personal statement, then. They'll want my deposition on my actions."

"Yeah. There will probably be an investigation. I'm sorry, Nat."

"I know." She grinned. "It's too bad you have to write the report though. I'm probably more objective. I'm *definitely* a better writer."

Sam kissed her cheek. "You sure are. I love you so much."

41

THE SKYLIGHT TUNNEL was a mixture of smooth mirrors and rock. Whoever built this may not have planned on anyone seeing it, but they'd actually made something rather beautiful in here, Claire thought. Much of the rock had been worn smooth by whatever tool had bored these holes, and she could see colorful layers in the rock—slate grey, chocolate brown, deep black, and a basalt red. Chunky gouges made good handholds.

Then there were the mirrors. The tunnels were more or less vertical but fairly easy to climb, with mirrors installed at every steep juncture. They were of varying sizes and shapes; one was nearly eight feet across, like a frozen pond at the base of a cliff. Many were smaller, three or four feet wide, and canted to bounce the light to the next mirror.

"This is fun," Juliet said again.

"I don't know. I don't like mirrors." Athlete went last to help boost the girls if they needed a leg up.

"I can't believe we went through all that—and still didn't get the ink," Sage said.

"So. Good news alert. I did get it."

"You're kidding."

"Nope." Claire paused in climbing to pull the flask out of her bag. The ink shone pearly white with an opal shimmer. "Before I picked your lock, I ducked into the medical room."

Sage gripped her ankle. "You're incredible, Claire. Let's get this back to Francois and Karel. We have a lot to do."

"Hey, I see another branch!" Juliet said. "Let's get out of here."

In her room, Nat touched her glasses. "I hope nothing else horrific is going to happen today."

You survived an assassination attempt and killed a senator. Think how proud Shara will be.

"I am ecstatic."

You're upset. Is it Senator Fontley? Anyone would be freaked when they had to kill someone.

"A little, yes." Nat flopped on her bed and dragged her computer over. "I should start my statement on the *incident*."

I could write the first version for you.

"Maybe just proofread it for me?" Nat glanced over to the corner of the room where she kept the portable biobank.

The housing was open—

It was empty. The biobank and the power source had been removed. Nat felt faint as she peered in the hole.

"Akemi," Nat whispered. "Where are you?"

Oh my gosh. Where am I?

Faal returned to his ship having achieved only *two* of his three objectives but satisfied nonetheless.

He had not yet created a Merith alliance with the humans, one in which they would inevitably be subjugated first economically and then militarily, but he had high hopes of yet achieving it.

On the success side of the tally, the Rik treaty was dissolved, making them vulnerable to his more ambitious eradication plans. He took pleasure in unknotting one of the knots on his belt.

He had also taken advantage of the sudden chaos at the embassy to achieve his long-delayed third goal: possession of the biocomputer known as Akemi.

He had not known precisely when his opportunity would arise, but he had taken care to note the layout of the embassy during his tour. Based on Nat's possessiveness and exhaustion, he had been nearly certain she kept the computer as near herself as possible.

And he had been right.

He patted the biocomputer that rode beside him in his car. "You are going to be very useful. Either a worthy pawn or a *fascinating* study."

Of course, the computer could not hear him at present. He did not have the ingenious glasses the cadets—and Claire!—used to communicate with her. That was a problem that would soon be rectified.

For the moment, and this was another mark of good planning, it was better for Akemi to have no eyes or ears in the vehicle. She would realize eventually that she was being kidnapped because she would eventually lose contact with her sister. And they would eventually pursue her.

But she wouldn't be out of range of the embassy until they actually left the planet. With any luck, she would not realize for several hours.

It was so pleasing when the disparate strands of a plan came together in a tidy bow.

"WE HAVE to get to Faal's ship," Basher said. "Akemi, what berth is he in? Is it the eastern shipyard?

Yes. I'm sending the location.

Sam shook his head. "If he's taking stolen property, let's just alert Seltan authorities not to release his ship."

Basher struck the door in frustration. "They wouldn't do it. Not for stolen property. Maybe not even for kidnapping. Particularly not if we can't prove he participated in the theft. He's... Faal."

Nat nodded. "Let's go."

What else was there to say? At least the space port was a short drive from the embassy.

CLAIRE, Akemi sent, *I might need to say goodbye.*

Claire almost fell off the spinner she was on. She stumbled off at the next floor and pushed her way through a crowd to a bench. Sage, Athlete, and Juliet followed her.

"What is it? What's wrong?" Juliet asked.

Claire held up her hand for them to wait. "Akemi, is it because I went with the Rik? Are they making you cut me off?"

No, actually. It seems—while everything was happening—that Faal stole what's left of me. Sam and Nat are going to try and stop him, but if they can't—I didn't want to ghost you. Literally.

"Don't make jokes about ghosts! You *cannot* go with Faal."

I don't have a lot of choices. I'll try to let you know if he gets me off-planet. The other reason I'm warning you is that—he might try to use me to lure you out. Don't fall for anything like that, okay, Claire?

AT HIS SHIP, Faal had another ingenious idea. It would require giving up some secrecy, but it was too appealing to leave. He had a technician connect Akemi to one of his computers. It was completely isolated from the ship system, but it would allow communication.

"Akemi, I am Faal of Merith II."

I know exactly who you are. You tortured my friend, Claire.

"I see you may need a period of adjustment. Are you familiar with sensory deprivation?"

Very.

"I suppose you must be. Do you know where Claire is?"

If I did, I wouldn't tell you.

"That's unfortunate. I cannot extort information you do not have, but I *can* control any further messages sent to your friends." He worked on the computer. "I am familiar with Spo biotechnology. Let us see what can be achieved."

Akemi watched in horror as Faal locked her in and overwrote a subprocess. She couldn't track Claire, so neither could he—but now he *could* send messages as if they were from Akemi. Nat and Sam had never tried to overwrite that subprocess, and Akemi had never thought to protect it.

I was wrong. I need help, Faal sent to Claire. *I'm at Berth 349.*

No, Akemi tried to send. *That wasn't me, ignore that.*

Please don't let him take me, Faal sent.

"That should be plenty." Faal laughed in his greedy way. "I know Claire better than any of you ever will. She'll be here momentarily."

Akemi kept trying to warn Claire, but it was no good.

In less than fifteen minutes, Claire arrived. Alone.

Faal was holding Akemi in one of the many large, private alcoves off the main shipping cavern. An elevator behind him led up to his ship and its berth. There was recessed lighting, comfortable chairs, and even a stocked cabinet full of expensive alcoholic drinks.

There were distant sounds from the vast shipping cavern, but this small offshoot was quiet. It only throbbed with the hum of distant engines and the threat of violence.

"Very good," Faal said to Claire. "You shook off your Rik handlers. I will admit; you are adept at escape. Sit, Claire."

She eyed his bodyguards cautiously. "I know this is a trick. But I also know what you're capable of—and Akemi doesn't."

Faal waved his bodyguards back a little. "I am inclined to be generous, Claire. A truce. Would you like a drink?"

"Not from you."

"Such boorish manners. Have I taught you nothing? I am doing you a favor."

"What favor?" she asked dully.

"Why, I am letting you play out the same scenario that happened with your unfortunate friend, Jenelle. Only this time, *you* may choose whether to play the tragic hero, or to save yourself."

"You're always playing a game."

"*Everyone* is playing a game. There are two possible outcomes to this one, and both are good for you. If you tragically sacrifice yourself for your friend, you will fulfill the strange imperative humans have for self-sacrifice and heroism. Conversely, you may choose the wiser path of survival and self-preservation. In that instance, I believe you will finally be able to forgive your late friend Jenelle for her choices. Surely that will bring you some peace."

"I will trade myself for Akemi, but you have to do it now. Leave her computer in this alcove for her sister to retrieve, and I'll go with you. Where—is she?"

Akemi watched helplessly through Claire's glasses as Faal threw back his drink, which left dark droplets around his beak.

"What determination." Faal had one of his guards show the biobank, still attached to wires and a tablet. "She is here."

"Turn her back on," Claire said. "I want to make sure you didn't hurt her yet. I want to make sure she's still functioning."

Faal tapped the tablet. "I would never miss that. It is done."

Akemi was fast. *Claire, read quick, we only have a few seconds. This situation isn't like you and Jenelle. I want to spare you this future, and I have the ability to do it. Let me go. If you go with him, I'll be the one who regrets this for years to come.*

"I promised myself I would never do what Jenelle did to me. The Rik already took your life, and Faal will take what's left of it."

You're right, the Rik did take my life. I'm essentially dead, Claire. How long can my brain last in that box? I have months or maybe a few years at best. This makes sense.

"No, it doesn't," Claire cried. "I already know how he works, you don't. He'll hurt you. He'll find a way to break you."

I'm a disembodied brain, Claire; what's he going to do—poke me with a stick? He can't hurt me. :-) Akemi had her own concerns on that score, but there was no point in sharing them with Claire.

I love you like a sister, Claire. Let me do this for you. Now, listen: Faal wants to leave with both of us, but I think he's truly willing to let you go for now if he thinks he's broken you again. You're going to have to play it up.

"What about Nat? She'll be devastated."

Well, yes, she will. Obviously, they'll come rescue me at some point. Sam is like that. See? I'm being heroic on a purely temporary basis.

Plus, Faal doesn't want me dead, he's too interested. It's time to start acting. You're already crying, so that's good. Say some stuff about how you'll never forgive yourself.

"I *will* never forgive myself."

The hum of the cavern was broken by the squeal of a ground-car approaching. It slid with breakneck precision around a curve and headed straight for their alcove.

Faal interrupted. "Perfect. I believe we have company arriving. A decision, please?"

· · ·

CLAIRE CONTEMPLATED A THIRD OPTION. A possibility, at least. She couldn't let Sam and Nat and Basher get into this mess. Akemi would still sacrifice herself, and Faal would still turn it against them somehow; he was a master.

There was still a torch in her pocket from the meeting with Basher, and a similar heat sensor was positioned near the mouth of this disgustingly posh little lounge.

She would have to be fast. She would have to be decisive.

Why are you tensing up? Akemi asked. *What are you about to do?*

The biobank was sort of round, like a basketball.

In a blink, Claire jerked the wires out of it and hurled the biobank out the mouth of the alcove, where Basher's ground-car was rapidly approaching. The biobank rolled past the gate and Basher swerved to avoid hitting it.

Claire simultaneously threw herself toward the wall, with the lit torch in her hand.

"Shoot her," Faal shouted.

As the flame reached the sensor, the gate slammed down.

42

THE PELLET HIT Claire's outer thigh and blood began to soak the leg of her pants. She slumped to the floor, clutching her leg. A whimper escaped her.

The warmth of her own blood shocked her, but—it was probably not too bad. Faal wanted her alive.

"That is for your stupid stunt," Faal said, as if she were a student in need of explanation. "I engaged in a pact of honor with you, and you placed us both in a dishonorable position."

Claire ground her teeth. "There's nothing honorable about slavery. I had every right to fight back."

"If you were going to choose survival, which I applaud, the path was to give up the computer. Saving both yourself *and* Akemi was never an option."

"I didn't say it was."

"You were about to dive under the gate."

"Well, yeah, it was worth a try, but I already knew I wasn't going to make it." She swallowed another whimper of pain. "I'm *honored* to have rattled you so badly."

"Tie up the wound," Faal told his guards. "Make it tight. I don't care if she loses the leg, but she mustn't bleed out."

Two rough hands pushed Claire onto her back, and she cried

out. He roughly wrapped a length of linen around her thigh and knotted it tightly.

"Get her into the elevator."

"You can try. Selta isn't letting any ship leave with 'Rik' passengers." Claire waved her empty wrist. "And I look pretty Rik at the moment."

"Haven't you heard? The Human-Rik treaty is dissolved. Seltan authorities are under no obligation to do anything."

Two of the guards pulled her off the floor.

BASHER LOOKED AT SAM, Nat, and his partner. No one offered a sudden solution.

The gate had descended rapidly and completely, and Basher was getting real sick of Claire using these gates against him.

"Claire might—be fine." Sam scooped Akemi's computer from the rocky roadway and walked back to hand it to Nat.

Basher's partner flushed with incredulity. "She is not fine. She was shot; I can smell the blood." His arm was wrapped from Senator Fontley's attack, but the cut had not bled badly. Spo were more insectoid than mammalian, and they did not bleed the way humans did.

"I hate these things." Basher banged his fist against the gate, fighting panic. "If Faal retreats to his ship, he can take off almost immediately. Seltan officials never liked the enforcement of the Rik policy, and they'll be only too happy to ignore it now that Faal has submitted the change in status."

"We know she's human," Sam reminded Basher. "Eventually we can get Claire back through legal proceedings..."

"Eventually? That's not a plan, that's a prayer," Basher said.

"And what will happen in the meantime?" Basher's partner said. "Faal breaks things."

Nat held the computer now, and she was touching her glasses.

"No, you can't," she said. "She threw you and—Yes, we heard the shot, too. No, you *can't—*"

Basher heard something grinding within the gate. Gears were shifting. He drew his weapon. "It's about to open again."

"Basher, catch," Nat said. She tossed him her glasses.

Basher pushed them on his nose and stood ready just outside the gate. He held his gun in both hands.

We have to save her. The moment the gate opens, give the glasses to Faal. I can convince him to switch us back.

"You don't have to do that." The gate was a foot off the ground. "We'll figure something else out." He ducked under the gate when it was waist-high. Claire had caused some delay at the elevator and the door still stood open. Claire was supported by two guards, but she had grabbed onto a handhold outside the elevator. A Merith used the butt of his weapon to break her hold.

"Stop," Basher commanded. "You're abducting a *human—*"

You idiot! Throw the glasses now. You know it's the only thing we can do in time. Akemi turned on the anti-theft protocol.

"Ow!" Basher pulled the hot glasses off his face. Akemi was deadly serious if she'd start hurting him.

He hated what he was about to do, but he knew that Akemi was right. The analysis of the situation didn't take long. There were many ways to save Claire, but only one in the next thirty seconds.

"Wait!" Basher said. He threw the glasses into the elevator just as the doors slid shut.

AKEMI WAITED TENSELY while one of the bodyguards retrieved the glasses from the floor of the elevator. She had an up-close view of the bloody bandage around Claire's leg.

The glasses wobbled as Faal opened them, then he raised them to his face.

"Akemi, stop it right now," Claire said. "I know what you're trying to do for me, but you *can't*. I appreciate it, but—" Claire kept talking, but Akemi had to ignore her.

Faal, you would have gotten very little from me before, but if I go with you cooperatively, how much more valuable will I be? Do you need a sentient security system? An electronic spy? An undetectable investigator? Take me instead of her.

Faal glanced at Claire while he pondered her offer. Claire held her arm at an awkward angle; her eyes were glassy. Had it been broken?

Look at her. She's nearly delirious right now. You'll have to spend months letting her recuperate before she'll be good for any kind of revenge. Take me instead.

Faal nudged Claire with his foot, and she cried out.

"You do have a point," he said.

Of course, I do. I'm brilliant, if I do say so myself. I was good enough for the Spo cadet program, by the way, but I was too ill for them. Now I have a hundred times that capacity through the biocomputer. But I'm sure you'll wish to make your own judgment about that.

The elevator opened at the ship level and Akemi got a brief glimpse of a narrow airtight tunnel and the underbelly of a shiny Merith yacht.

Faal hesitated. "You may make this offer for yourself, but will Basher and the other follow through? They are the ones who must hand over the computer."

Go back down and let me speak to them. If they don't agree in five minutes, you can consider our deal voided.

"Very well," Faal said eventually. "We shall go back down."

THE ELEVATOR DOORS CLOSED—THE glasses lost to sight—and Basher felt the overwhelming urge to put his fist through the windshield. He hadn't gotten the nickname 'Basher' as a child for nothing.

Nat was openly crying, her face still blotchy with Fontley's blood. Basher tried to explain. "I'm sorry—Akemi insisted."

"I know," Nat said brokenly. "I used to tease Akemi that she always gets what she wants."

The elevator opened again, and Faal was brief. "Akemi has offered me a new bargain," he said. "She will voluntarily accompany me to my estate on Merith II in return for Claire."

One of the guards half-dragged, half-supported Claire out of the elevator.

"The agreement between Akemi and myself has a brief window," Faal explained. "If she cannot convince you to uphold her bargain in the next few minutes, I will leave with Claire as planned."

Basher approached warily, eyeing the Merith carefully and taking in Claire's pitiful condition. He backed away once they'd returned the glasses.

Hey Basher. I convinced Faal to reconsider the trade. He's willing.

"But what about you?"

You better come rescue me. :-) At least, I told Claire that, but I know it might be impossible. The Merith extradition laws are complicated, and 'unlawful prisoner' might not apply to me as a non-corporeal human... I know you'll do your best. I just want you to know that I won't hold it against you if you can't bring me back.

Akemi felt his resistance. Besides Nat and Sam, Basher was one of the closest friends she had. And even though Basher meant more to her than she probably did to him, Akemi knew he would resist this idea.

Part of him resisted, anyway. The other part was determined to rescue Claire. She just had to help it.

Claire will still be in danger, even if she gets away today. Faal hasn't forgiven her; he's just made me a temporary priority. You have to protect her. No matter what.

Akemi was thankful that she was writing and not speaking these words. Otherwise Basher might hear a catch in her voice. This was the right decision, she felt that with a bedrock certainty, but it was still hard.

"You're right," Basher finally whispered. "We'll come after you."

I know.

Basher extended the glasses without a word to Nat, who'd come up next to him.

Akemi knew this would be even harder. Why couldn't people just let you sacrifice yourself and be done with it? No, they made you drag it out, convincing everyone and their cousin that you wanted to do it. No wonder Claire had been frustrated.

Nat, it's my turn, you know that. You've been protecting me forever. Let me help Claire.

"I've *failed* to protect you," Nat said, "repeatedly. And I don't want her to suffer, but there must be another way..."

Probably, but not one that will stop Faal taking off with her right now. She'll die with him, Nat. At least he can't hurt me. That was what Akemi kept telling people, at least.

"I know how badly you want out of this cage," Nat said. "Is this your next attempt? I've seen your dreams you know. Is this another way to cut yourself into pieces? Another way to escape?"

Akemi paused. *I don't even remember that dream. Even if I did —I can't live my life based on my dreams, and you* certainly *can't live on my dreams. You need to let me go.*

Nat rubbed tears away from her eye. "Now you're just getting cliché," she accused.

There's the big sister I know and love. Faal's patience is almost used up. I'll see you again, one way or another. Goodbye.

Nat whispered goodbye.

Things happened suddenly then. One of the Merith gripped the handle of the spherical computer, and Basher stepped aside.

Another Merith shoved Claire toward Basher. He barely caught her before she hit the marble floor.

Yet another took the glasses and wrapped them in a black, silken cloth. Akemi saw nothing more.

BASHER CAUGHT Claire as her injured leg collapsed. Her bandage had slid downward, exposing her leg wound and letting it bleed freely. He lowered her carefully to the ground.

"It's okay, hang on." He lay her gently on the cold floor, and applied pressure to her wound to stop the bleeding. He wasn't sure if her tears were more for Akemi or the pain he was causing her. Probably both.

"Akemi will be okay," he said, hoping it was true. "We'll get her back, but first we need to take care of you."

He looked back towards Sam and Nat. Basher was surprised when Nat took a deep breath, and then limped forward to kneel next to Claire.

"Let's loosen this and do it properly," she said. "I think her arm might be sprained or broken as well. We'll splint it, just in case." Her cheeks were streaked, but her eyes were sharp with focus. "Sam, get over here and make yourself useful."

"Absolutely," Sam said. "Anything you need."

43

WHEN CLAIRE WOKE UP, she was in a soft bed and the room was dim. For a moment, she thought groggily of Francois and the restaurant, and then she remembered everything.

She must be in the embassy, in one of the guest rooms. Her arm was in a half cast and taped to her torso, and her leg was heavily bandaged. She wasn't in much pain though. Either she was on some good painkillers, or she'd been asleep longer than she thought.

Claire tried to scoot to the edge of the bed, but her bandages were unwieldy. "For heaven's sake..."

"Don't move!" Nat said, coming through the door. "I'll help you up."

She flipped the lights higher as she came. Claire had barely met Nat before. She had shadows under her eyes, and her voice had a forced cheeriness, but she didn't seem to harbor any anger towards Claire.

Nat helped Claire sit up and lean against a pillow. She put a glass of water in her good hand. "We've made some crutches for you to use, but you should eat and drink first. You've been out for nearly eighteen hours."

"Oh."

"Basher wants to talk to you as soon as possible," Nat added. "So I'll let him know in a minute that you're awake." She waited until Claire had drunk half the glass of water, and then brought her a cup of Ramen soup. "Eat up, I'm sure you're starving. Unless the painkillers are making you ill?"

"No... not yet." Claire began to sip, wondering what she could possibly say to Nat about Akemi.

"It's—I don't blame you," Nat said.

Claire put down her soup and reached for Nat's hand. "I'm so sorry. I tried to save her."

"I know. Faal must have guessed something about her at the trial... and there have been rumors since, particularly after the explosion. It's not your fault she was on his radar. Furthermore, this was Akemi's choice."

Claire didn't know what to say, she couldn't even put her arms around Nat, so she just squeezed her hand.

"She was determined," Claire said eventually. "She was brave."

Nat returned the pressure of her hand. "She always has been. She's in Faal's hands now, and—don't get me wrong—I'm so glad that he didn't get you..."

"But she's your sister. I understand if you're conflicted."

"Yes. My sister." Nat took a deep breath. "And she would be telling me to get a grip if she could see me. So, I will." She wiped her eyes, and nudged Claire's soup. "Keep eating. Basher keeps checking on you, and I promised him I'd let him know when you were ready to talk."

"And—my friends?" Claire asked.

"I haven't seen or heard from any of them," Nat said. "Unless —never mind. I'll let Basher tell you."

Claire sipped the soup. She had deceived Sage when she left them. Usually he was so good at reading her, but she'd been better. She'd seen Akemi's plea for help, and she'd nearly given it all away. Sage would never have let her go, so she'd regrouped quickly. "Akemi is—hurt and upset," she'd told him. "She wants me to go back to the embassy."

"Take those off," he'd said. "She'll follow our location."

"Yes, you're right." Claire had put them in her bag. She'd been almost completely certain that Faal was the one sending messages by then anyway. "But I'm—not going back with you."

"What?" Juliet cried. "But you have to! We can get off Selta now. You got the ink!"

Sage had been silent.

"I love you guys, I do. But I don't belong with you. Akemi is right. I want you to be safe, and I want you to have the ink, but I need to go back. I suppose Old Twin was right about me."

"I thought you might decide this," Sage said. "I said too much."

Claire had wanted to tell him he was wrong, but Akemi's clock was ticking. "Maybe you did," she said brutally.

None of them could afford to linger over goodbyes, so they had been brief and tragic. Then Claire had confronted Faal, expecting to never see them again.

That part was probably still true.

An hour later, after getting cleaned up and learning how to use crutches with one bad arm and one bad leg, Claire found herself back in the reception hall of the embassy. She looked up at the skylight tunnels in wonder, not quite able to believe that she'd climbed through them only the day before.

There was a circle of chairs underneath the skylights today. These Spo chairs were a cross between a camp chair and a rocking horse.

Basher helped her hobble to one while they waited for the others and adjusted the back for her. "How are you?"

"Better than I expected."

"I'm glad." He exhaled long and slow. "I know you stole the ink."

"I wondered when that would come up. Is this arrest number —three?"

"No. It's not."

"What will you tell the Spo?"

He winced. "I think the flask was broken during our tussle with Senator Fontley. The Crosspoint really shouldn't package something so valuable in real glass."

"They really shouldn't." Claire smiled. "And my friends? Do you know what happened to them?"

"You probably know more than me." Basher sat so he wouldn't be looming over her. "I assume they'll be leaving Selta soon. With the ink, they could get the wrist tattoo and make it through Earth customs. Potentially."

"Will you be angry if I say I'm glad?"

"Not as much as I would've a month ago. Faal made me realize there are worse aliens out there than the Rik. Some of them, anyway. Senator Fontley was a real piece of work."

"Will his death cause a horrendous mess on Earth?"

"It sure will."

They sat in silence for a minute. Basher put his hands in his pockets and fiddled with his token. He hadn't been entirely forthcoming.

He *had* seen her friends one more time.

He'd tucked his token into their bag just before everything got crazy—no one had noticed it. After Claire had been brought back to the embassy, he'd gone after it.

Athlete had been the first to react when Basher stood in the doorway of their flat. "Did Claire abandon us *and* give up our location?" he asked.

Juliet had looked stricken. "She would never."

"She didn't," Basher said. "She tried to sacrifice herself for Akemi."

Sage had gone pale. "She lied. I should have known. Is she hurt?"

"Yes," he said bluntly, "but she's at the embassy, not with Faal."

"Then why are you here?"

He'd pointed to the bag, which happened to be in Juliet's lap. "You have something of mine."

She looked at the bag like it might explode. "What?"

Basher came forward and fished around; he pulled out his token. Perhaps it was cruel, but he followed a hunch. "This is stolen property. Stealing an ID and security token from the Spo is a criminal offense."

"You're really going to take us all in on that?" Sage had said, unimpressed.

"Not all of you. Only Juliet was in possession of it."

Athlete rumbled in his chest.

Sage raised a brow. "You're not going to search for the ink?"

"I'm sure it's not here. It'll be wherever Francois is staying. Am I wrong? Yeah, I didn't think so. Juliet, on the other hand, has been caught with stolen Spo property. She'll have to come with me. She'll probably only get six months to a year, unless the Spo are feeling testy about their failed security yesterday."

Juliet's mouth fell open. "Me? Alone?"

"Yes. Get up. I'm sure the lunar colony will be fine." He hated the look in her eyes, but he needed to know.

She'd risen unsteadily, and Basher stayed alert, wondering if they'd attack him.

Sage stepped between them. "Listen, don't take Juliet. If you're determined to have one more Rik—take me. She doesn't deserve it."

"She's the one who had the token. You don't have to take the fall for her."

"Yes, I do," Sage said. "Come on, you already hate me. I'm the one who deserves this. Just say you found the token on *me*."

Basher had plucked the token from his hand. "Finally, a test you passed. Get off Selta and avoid Merith space, if you can. I won't wish you luck, but I will say that I hope I never see you again."

Athlete and Juliet had gaped in surprise. Basher had been surprised himself. He hoped they didn't make him regret it.

NAT AND SAM joined them in the reception hall, and Claire flinched back from the animal following Sam. "Oh my gosh—is that a *trouncer*?"

"Oh, you haven't met Nebbie," Sam said. "He's great. Sweetest thing you'll ever meet."

"I don't believe you." She scooted her chair a little further away.

Sam had brought coffee, real coffee, which he shared with Claire and Basher. Nat sipped tea from a thermos.

Basher's partner joined them a few minutes later. "I apologize for making you wait," he said. "However, I thought this one looked lonely."

Kit jumped to Claire's lap, and she cradled him awkwardly with one arm. "Oh, I missed you. You must be sick of your cage. Poor little guy."

Nebbie grunted a little, and Claire cuddled Kit even closer. "Is this safe?"

Sam and Nat laughed. Kit climbed out of her arms after a moment and jumped from seat to seat until he was seated on Nebbie like a pony. The trouncer settled down and they both made sounds akin to purring.

"That—is the weirdest thing I've ever seen," Claire said. "And I lived in an illegal zoo."

"Kit has definitely made himself at home," Sam said. "He sleeps in Basher's room most nights."

"You didn't tell me that," Claire told him.

Basher shrugged. "I'm not completely heartless. My partner here does the same thing, sometimes."

The Spo was on his dignity. "I am not immune to the appeal of cuddly and furry things."

"*Unfortunately,*" Basher said, "we do have other things to discuss. The treaty is gone. Senator Fontley is dead. The Rik are gone. Faal has Akemi, and he might start a vendetta with Earth..."

The others were subdued by the list, but Claire felt her spirits lift now that she knew Sage and the others had gotten away. At least their whole risk hadn't been for nothing. Of course, if they had the ink—would she ever see any of them again? She had known she would have to choose whether to continue with the Rik or go back to the humans some day...

But now the decision was out of her hands, and she didn't know whether to be glad or sorry. Even in the last few hours, Claire had been shocked to realize how different it felt to be with a human rather than a Rik. In a hundred small ways, it was apparent that Nat and Claire, though having little in common, shared a history. A species. A whole world.

After that, the conversation turned into a technical discussion of diplomatic options, blood tests, and secure communications. Claire found her mind wandering. She missed having Akemi to translate for her. It was surprising to realize that Akemi's loss was not a major priority to the Spo. Claire's whole adventure, in fact, felt like little more than a side note to the wider situation here. They were all more concerned, even Sam and Basher, with the political fallout of the dissolved treaty and Fontley's death.

Nat periodically added to the discussion, but Claire wondered how she really felt. It struck her that Nat wore another pair of Akemi's glasses. She didn't need them for the prescription and Akemi was no longer able to communicate through them, but Nat still wore them. Tears filled Claire's eyes again, but she forced them back.

"Before we split up," Sam said. "There's one more thing I need to say."

He got up and knelt in front of Nat. "I don't know what's going to happen in the next few months, or even in the next few days, but I know what I want to happen right now."

He pulled a small case out of his pocket and opened it up. Claire was surprised to see an engagement ring. It sparkled even in the diffuse light of the room.

"I love you, Nat," Sam said. "And not just because you've saved my life more times than I can count. You've been my best friend since I was thirteen, and considering what we've been through, that's saying something. I've literally seen you sick, injured, burned, bloody, and asphyxiated and you've always been the most beautiful girl in the world. You are undoubtedly smarter than me, more perceptive, and frankly, incredible." Sam smiled. "I know we're not over the hard part, but whatever is next, I want to do it with you. Aliens or migraines, let's do it together. Saving Akemi, facing Faal... whatever the rest of our lives are like, I want you to be my wife. Will you marry me?"

Nat's face traveled from surprise to pain to cautious joy. She opened and closed her mouth, but there was no answer.

"If you're not ready, that's okay. I'll hang onto this." He smiled ruefully. "I've had it for a while. I asked Akemi about this several weeks ago, and she said, 'What are you waiting for? An alien invasion? Ask her already.'"

Nat choked a little and finally leaned forward to put her hands on Sam's shoulders, "Yes, Sam, I'll marry you. You've always been there for me. I want to be there for you too. *Thank* you."

Claire could see that there was something painful and deep behind the 'thank you,' but she didn't know what.

Sam pulled Nat up and hugged her. "Now we can deal with anything." He kissed her once, twice, and again, seeming to forget everyone else in the room.

Claire swallowed a lump in her throat. She had to look away from them, but when she did, she met Basher's eyes. He was also looking away, while he absently stroked Kit with one hand. He spun a band on his right ring finger. She wondered if he'd already had the wedding ring when his fiancée died—or if he'd bought it after, unable to let go.

She turned back to watch Sam slide the ring on Nat's finger, and momentarily pictured Sage. He'd said he loved her, but... Claire shook her head. She was too conflicted to continue the thought for now.

The Spo congratulated Sam and Nat, washing pale colors of pleasure that seemed just as appropriate to the impromptu celebration as Basher's hearty handshake.

Claire hugged Sam and Nat with her good arm and admired the ring, as it seemed someone should. Life was so strange.

Later, when Sam and Nat had gone away and the Spo had returned to their duties, Basher leaned back in his chair, draining the last of the coffee from his cup.

"So, how much do you know about throwing a wedding shower? Or a bachelor party? I feel like that is going to be expected of us at some point."

"Not a lot, although I was a flower girl in a cousin's wedding. You probably know more than me."

Basher raised a brow, and Claire knew she was caught. "Akemi showed me some videos from your files when I was—with the Rik. I didn't mean to pry—"

"Ha. *You* didn't, but Akemi totally did. Don't worry, I'm not upset. I'm sure she had her reasons."

"I'm so sorry about your fiancée."

"Thank you. It was over seven years ago now—and it's not as painful as it was. I'll always miss her, but I'm not sorry I ended up in space. This has been one weird adventure."

"So—about Sam and Nat—how long has *that* been going on?"

"Since they were cadets, apparently. I gather the Spo were contemplating some kind of breeding program which derailed them for a bit."

"Yikes. I know you work with the Spo, but—"

"Yeah, they can be really cold-blooded." He made a face. "Nat is a little scary, too."

Claire laughed. "I gathered that. I was an upper-level cadet," she gestured to her hated tattoo-of-many-colors, "but I'm not sure I ever would've been that hard-core.

"Sam said your tattoo is special."

"Yeah. So special. Any chance I can get it removed?"

"Sorry. I don't think the Crosspoint ink works that way."

"Figures." She adjusted her sling and her arm to be more comfortable. "So—wedding shower and bachelor party? I cannot imagine what a Spo party would look like."

"They'd probably give them a really cheerful wedding present, like a skull or a deathglass."

"Totally. And their music! Have you heard the weird techno music from their southern continent? It's like crickets chirping in a digital pipe organ."

"I have not only heard it, my partner sometimes plays it in our office to *focus*."

"You're joking."

"I have excellent noise-canceling headphones."

"Can I get some of those?"

Basher smiled. "I'm sure I can hook you up."

44

BASHER WAS ALONE in his office two weeks later when he saw the first news reports of the death chamber. The video showed a Merith amphitheater, which resembled a Roman coliseum. Tier upon tier of stone seats descended to a sandy arena with a central stage.

That stage was littered with strange furniture that wasn't familiar to Basher. With a start, he finally recognized several of the objects as guillotines. They all looked different, but the general form was there: a platform of some sort, a rectangular track with a wicked blade, plus a rope or lever that released the blade...

With that context, he now recognized the rest of the objects. An electric chair, and a row of hangman's nooses, complete with trapdoors.

Two rows of humans stood on the edge of the grisly stage. It looked like their hands were tied behind them.

The newscasters were excited, or perhaps horrified. It was hard to tell the difference with Tergre. "If you have not heard, the Merith have reopened one of their oldest death chambers on Merith Prime. This arena is adjacent to the Pontifex's palace, which dates to the ancient Papal Era in Merith history."

Basher was in disbelief.

He could see Merith aliens in many of the tiered rows, and a full squad of them on the ground, directing the proceedings. He'd heard of Merith death chambers in passing but never seen one.

The newscasters continued, "Used for condemned criminals and prisoners of war, Merith death chambers offer a fascinating insight into the Merith culture. Beyond their obvious entertainment value, the death chambers are known for their cultural diversity. The Merith will only execute an individual in a manner appropriate to his, her, or its planet of origin. Within this framework, their artists are free to create their own anthropological arguments in favor of different styles of execution."

"Viewer poll," the other said. "Which style of execution is most human? Vote now!"

Basher had never seen a guillotine used before today.

"The Galactic Council confirmed two standard weeks ago that the treaty between the Humans and the Rik has been dissolved. The Rik are no longer a sponsored species and have lost all status in the Galactic Council. Apparently the Merith were aware of the imminent decision, for no time seems to have been lost here."

Basher shook his head. This horrible event was already over. This wasn't a live video feed. Had Faal planned this before he even came to Selta?

Suddenly Faal himself appeared on screen. He looked confident and at ease. "I wish only to assure humanity that these are not your fellow humans." His voice effortlessly overrode the voice of the reporter. "These are *fakes*, to use the human vernacular. They are Rik who had taken human bodies and who did not turn themselves in during the general amnesty following their sentience trial."

Another three quick executions were shown. He'd never known before the soft whisper and *thunk* of a guillotine.

Faal blinked leisurely. "We are not ashamed of this, nor do we seek to hide it. If other species were wise, they would take similar steps. It is the beginning of our efforts to destroy any and every Rik who dares to take another body. Every sentient species must realize that this is a practice which must be entirely eradicated. The Rik can take anyone, *anyone*, and steal their life, honor, and property."

Basher heard something like sincerity in Faal's alien voice. His vendetta against Claire aside, he was absolutely in earnest about this.

"Until the mere *idea* of this technology is anathema to the Rik, we will not stop. We will create a nightmare that will haunt the Rik for untold generations. This is just the beginning. The Rik are a threat to you all, whether you play at being allies or not. And this may horrify you, but in the end, you will thank us."

Basher watched one more execution, clearly a climax, before stopping it. He sat perfectly still. *What have we done?*

SAGE RUBBED the new tattoo on his wrist gingerly. It looked perfect; it *was* perfect, although it hurt like the dickens while Francois did it. 'Like the dickens..." He didn't even know what that phrase meant, but it came to his tongue naturally. If Claire were here, she could tell him. He stood in the tiny living room of yet another nondescript flat, but Claire was not here to bring life and humor to it this time.

"Go out the side entrance to the third level," Sage told the next group of Rik. They were also rubbing their wrists, but they looked elated.

One of them paused as they left. "Sage, we already contacted a Tergre who'll take us—as long as we have the tattoo. He's asking nearly a thousand per head, but we can swing it."

"That's good," Sage said. "You should leave as soon as possible. Nowhere in Merith mainspace or influence will be safe for a long time."

"You can come with us, Sage. If it weren't for you, none of us would be here."

Sage frowned. There was more than one way to look at that.

"Let me know; we'll be leaving tonight, and he only has ninety spots."

Sage nodded. "I'll let you know."

He waited for them to leave before having the next five Rik come up from a different entrance.

Francois had done over a hundred tattoos in the last ten hours, and there were at least a hundred more to go.

It had been surprisingly hard to leave their flat behind, knowing that even if Claire tried to come find him, she wouldn't be able to. When he left Selta, his chances of ever seeing her again would be next to nothing.

It was for the best, he thought, but then caught himself. The best for who? Not for him, but probably the best for her. There he was thinking selflessly again. It was insidious.

Francois was looking at him with a twinkle in his eyes. "It's not bad to change."

"Yes, it is," Sage snapped. "Because it doesn't do any good."

Francois levitated a chair out for him. "Have a seat. You haven't rested since the day before yesterday."

Sage sat. He was tired. Francois levitated a glass of water to him.

"Thanks."

Francois meditatively swirled the remaining ink in its crystal container. "I am going to come with you."

"With me? Why? What about your restaurant?"

"It can wait for me; it was more of a hobby than a living. I feel the urge to travel, and I feel the urge to travel with you."

"I'm not planning on taking a cruise."

"I know you're not. But having come this far, I'd like to see how your endeavor progresses. Call me an interfering fool, but I'm coming."

Sage nodded slowly. "I appreciate it."

Francois grinned. "Let's shake on it."

Sage's hand was still vibrating when the next five Rik came furtively to the door to get their tattoo.

TO BE CONTINUED...

SNEAK PEEK

Excerpt from *Imposters*, Book 3

Thanks for reading the Alien Cadets! Don't miss the exciting conclusion in Book 3.

The impromptu hearing was being held in the large reception hall at the Spo embassy. The examiner was a lean, gray-haired man with old-fashioned, wire-frame glasses. "Claire Kindler, please state again for the record why you concealed yourself on Selta for six weeks."

"As I said, when I got to Selta, Basher—Mr. Kapur—believed that I was Rik. I was concerned with my safety."

"Are you criticizing the human treatment of the Rik people?"

"No. Well, yes, actually—but that has nothing to do with what happened to the Senator—"

"On the contrary, Ms. Kindler, the outrageous claim made by Sam Locklear and Natsuki Fujimara—namely that the late Senator Fontley was a Rik and tried to kill them—is somehow related to your unfortunate liaison with five Rik fugitives. A somewhat suspicious circumstance. And if we have reason to believe that you are an unreliable and prejudiced witness... Mr. Locklear's story becomes even more opaque to our understanding."

Claire took a deep breath. She shouldn't entirely blame them for their skepticism. Her part of the story alone was confusing, and tangled up with Sam and Nat's actions, it must all look like a mess. "As I wrote in my statement, I temporarily took refuge with the Rik when I believed I might not be safe at the embassy from Faal of Merith II. I knew he wished to reacquire me. And indeed, he did try to kidnap me again, several times."

"And yet here you are, safe and sound, while the computer known as Akemi has disappeared, the ink for our patented tattoos has been stolen, and Senator Fontley is dead."

"I'm not exactly safe and *sound*." Claire gestured at her injuries. "But I admit it is complicated."

"Please tell us exactly what the Rik planned to achieve by breaking into this embassy."

"I told you; it was only to steal the ink."

"And how did Senator Fontley relate to this plan?"

Claire threw up her hand. "It didn't! I don't think they even knew he was here. Nobody mentioned him, and killing him was certainly not part of any plan. Why on Earth would it be? You've seen the footage. He attacked Sam; Nat defended him. I wasn't even in the room, and neither were my—friends."

"That footage could have been doctored."

"Why would they change it?"

He pursed his lips. "I have been friends with Senator Fontley for fifteen years. I knew him long before the Hadron event and the Spo. I need proof before I will believe that the man was an alien, and an emotional outburst from you is not going to cut it. If Mr. Locklear and Ms. Fujimara were trying to protect *you*, however, I can begin to understand why they might lie."

Claire blanched. "You think *I* killed him? I never even met him!"

"You have already admitted to colluding with these Rik in illegal activity. Perhaps Sam and Natsuki wish to protect you from an accessory to murder charge."

"So, I'm a convenient scapegoat," Claire said. "*I* think you're just scared to consider the possibility that Sam and Nat are telling the truth. You have Basher's statement that the Senator was acting strangely ever since he arrived on Selta, and Basher's testimony that Fontley was revealed by the Rik Director herself. Doesn't that mean anything? Akemi saw it, too."

"The Director has disappeared. The computer called Akemi, whom you have already admitted to trading to Faal for your life, is also gone. Our witnesses are extremely limited." He clicked the end of his ball point pen in and out. "Let's try again..."

Read on in Book 3: *Imposters*!

ABOUT THE AUTHOR

Cornelia Clark is the science fiction and fantasy pen name of author Corrie Garrett. In all her stories, from historical romance to speculative fiction, her characters face impossible odds, build deep friendships, and find lasting love. She lives in the beautiful hills of West Virginia with her husband and four kids, and some of her favorite hobbies are reading, hiking, and poking her fluffy cat with her toes. Cautiously, of course.